A
BURNING
OBSESSION

OTHER TITLES BY MIKE OMER

ABBY MULLEN THRILLERS

A Deadly Influence
Damaged Intentions

ZOE BENTLEY MYSTERIES

A Killer's Mind
In the Darkness
Thicker than Blood

GLENMORE PARK MYSTERIES

Spider's Web
Deadly Web
Web of Fear

A
BURNING
OBSESSION

MIKE OMER

Text copyright © 2022 by Michael Omer
All rights reserved.

Published by Thomas & Mercer, Seattle

www.apub.com

Amazon, the Amazon logo, and Thomas & Mercer are trademarks of Amazon.com, Inc., or its affiliates.

ISBN-13: 9781542034326 (paperback)
ISBN-13: 9781542034319 (digital)

Cover design by Faceout Studio, Spencer Fuller
Cover image: © Nattapol_Sritongcom / Shutterstock;
© Denis Torkhov / Shutterstock; © Andy Sacks / Getty Images;
© Milamai / Getty Images

Printed in the United States of America

A
BURNING
OBSESSION

CHAPTER 1

The back of his neck ached after he'd stared up at the night sky for so long. Over the years, he'd crisscrossed the country, had seen the heavens from hundreds of places, but he couldn't remember the night being as clear and raw as it was here in Wyoming. He could almost feel the weight of the heavens crushing him onto the flat plains. Here, it was easy to recall that God had begun creating the world by splitting it in two. No matter which way he gazed, the horizon was as flat and empty as it must have been during the second day of creation.

The only thing marring the perfect horizon was the small farmhouse that stood to the east. An imperfection that Moses Wilcox intended to fix.

He lowered his head, ignoring the urge to massage his own neck. Small clouds of fog swirled as he breathed, the winter's night chill freezing him to the bones, but he ignored that too. His followers were watching in silence and awe, and it was no time to show weakness. He let his gaze slide over their numerous faces, all waiting in anticipation for him to talk. He stretched the silence, knowing from experience exactly how far he could take it. Letting the tension grow until it was almost unbearable, but breaking it before they became restless.

"And God said, 'Let there be a vault between the waters to separate water from water.'" His voice thundering over the wind. "So God made the vault and separated the water under the vault from the water above it. And it was so. God called the vault . . . sky." He raised his head again. The congregation followed his stare, their heads turning upward.

He took a deep breath. "We came here but eighteen days ago. When we arrived, we were hoping for a place we could finally rest at. A place where hardworking men and women would embrace us and would be open to hear the truth." He let his voice slowly drop until it could barely be heard, forcing his parishioners to lean closer, to hold their breath so they could hear him. "But it is not what we found."

Heads shaking sadly. No, it was not what they'd found. Not at all.

"Instead, we met with wickedness and dark hearts. People who had lost their way so completely that they could not be guided. And we tried. Anna Clark spent each day going from door to door, begging people to come to our sermons. Jonathan Hall passed around thousands of flyers." He eyed the people he named, watched them beaming with pride, knowing they would work twice as hard now, and that the others would work harder, too, seeing how he praised those who pleased him. "Not all of us did our very best, but I'm sure they will strive to do better." His eyes landed on Benjamin and hovered there for a few seconds until he was sure the rebuke was clear. Benjamin lowered his head, and people around him shuffled slightly away. Good. In the approaching weeks, no one would talk to Benjamin. No one would even look at him. And in their tight-knit congregation, the shunned man would feel the isolation every second of every day.

"But no matter how much we try, some men and women are nearly beyond saving. They need us to show them the way. For if our message saves even one person from the eternal hellfire, then we have saved them from eternal torment!"

He shook with conviction and saw his intensity mirrored in his flock's faces.

"Some men are sinners, have strayed so far off the path that only fires can cleanse their souls. Be it the flames of hell . . ." He let his eyes linger on the lit torches his people were carrying and raised his voice. "Or the flames of man!"

Six men stepped forward, carrying the cans of gasoline. They marched on the icy gravel road to the house and splashed the liquid on its peeling whitewashed walls. Three of them stepped inside, and he could glimpse them in the darkness, pouring the gasoline on the floor and the few decrepit pieces of furniture.

He strode over to one of the men and held out his hand. "Give it to me, child."

The man, a thickly built farmer named Richard, towered over Moses, but he seemed to shrink in awe at being addressed directly. "It's quite heavy, Father."

Moses said nothing, just kept his hand outstretched, his eyes narrowing. Richard blinked, then handed him the can.

It *was* quite heavy, and its surface was covered in an oily sheen that smeared over his palm and clothes, but Moses didn't care. He splashed the liquid on the wall, inhaling the sharp, heady odor, his heart beating wildly almost as if it were his first time. Over the years, everything became part of a routine. Sermons, food, long rides, prayer. But *this* was the one thing that never lost its edge. The one thing that remained vivid and raw and pure.

He circled the house, feet crunching in the thin snow, pouring the gasoline carefully, until the can was empty. He watched the last few drops dribble on the frosty ground, then stepped back and handed the can back to Richard, who'd followed behind him.

Walking back, he looked at the rest of his congregation, feeling a wave of love washing over him. He would die for each and every one of them. And they would die for him.

Some of them already had.

"Mainstream Christianity has lost its way, misleading their believers," Moses said, watching the torch flames flicker in the wind. "They say that God is love. But they forget. He is many things. God is vengeance."

Excited shouts of assent and fervent amens.

"God wants justice for his people."

Now they were all shouting, leaning forward, arms raised, faces twisted with zeal.

"He is a jealous God!"

Raised fists, screaming calls of faith, their eyes wide. They could hardly contain their need to surge forward. It was time.

Moses raised his finger and roared. "I came to cast fire on the earth, and would that it were already kindled! It is time for a second baptism!"

Their eyes widened, faces awash with elation and joy. Moses smiled back at his flock, knowing what they felt. That holy moment when you were a part of God's will. Those holding the torches stepped forward, the flames flickering in the wind. They reached the house and, almost as one, touched the flames to the structure.

The fire rose, roaring, the flames dancing wildly in the wind, the sudden heat purging the cold from the air. One of the men screamed, jumping back, eliciting shouts of alarm. The man's sleeve was on fire, the consuming flames growing as he flailed in panic. People shot forward, grabbed the man, pulled him away from the fire, and forced him to the ground, rolled him in the snow and the mud, suffocating the flames. He still groaned in pain, but the grimace on his face was intermingled with an elated smile. Being burned by the holy fire of baptism was a mark of honor in their church, and he would wear the scars with pride.

Moses turned his eyes away from the man and back to the fire, the blaze so bright it almost hurt his eyes. The black smoke billowed upward, tumbling as the wind caught it and swept it away. Moses felt his feet carrying him closer and closer to the fire, the air hazy, his skin becoming dry, his eyes watering, the power of the flame mesmerizing him. And then, a scream from inside. The sinner had woken up. Good. It was better to be awake during your baptism, to feel the sins burned away as you once again joined with Christ. Moses listened as the sinner's screams rose, intermingling with desperate cries for help.

Moses stood facing his followers, his back to the flames. Awe filled their eyes as they watched him, the dancing fire coloring the night in a bright-orange glow, smoke enveloping him, flickering embers floating above. He waited expectantly for God to talk to him, and soon he felt it. An urge so powerful, so visceral, it could only come from God, a heavenly sign that again, it was time. His pants grew tight as holy vigor stiffened him.

Anna approached him. "Father, it is time that we leave."

"Not yet," he said. "The names."

"Father, there's no time. The fire department and the police will be here soon—"

"The names!" he roared at her.

Hurriedly, her hand trembling, she handed him a paper with three names. Moses read them and raised his eyes to find the three women in his flock. There. One woman in her thirties, her face plump. The second was younger and thinner, her front teeth protruding in an overbite. The third was . . . ah.

Jennifer was nineteen and had joined the flock not long ago, with her sister. Long hair that reached her hips. A delicate face. A shapely promise under the fabric of her blouse. Feeling the rush in his heart as he watched her, he knew that God had chosen. Tonight it would be her.

He walked over to her and took her hand. Her eyes were full of excitement and dread.

"Come with me," he said, his voice low.

He led her away, into the fields, away from the rest of the flock. Behind them the house burned, the heat scorching his back. The cries for help from within had turned into a wordless scream.

"Are you ready to bear my child?" he asked.

"I . . . yes, of course. But—"

"Take off your clothes."

"But . . . they can still see us."

He waved her concern away. "This is the Lord's wish. Does it matter if we are watched? Do it. Now."

She unbuttoned her shirt, fingers trembling. The orange flames flickered on her bare skin, the smoke swirling around them, the air getting harder to breathe.

Impatient, Moses tore the shirt open. And consumed with lust that could only be God's touch, he lay with the girl on the melting snow.

Behind them, the screams of the sinner finally stopped.

CHAPTER 2

Lieutenant Abby Mullen leaned on the hood of her car, scrutinizing the charred remains of the farmhouse. In the past three weeks, Abby had gone through dozens of documented arsons and had visited the locations of five different burnt-down structures. She'd learned that each scorched house had its own unique appearance. Some would retain their blackened walls, while others kept only their skeletal frame. Piles of debris contained remnants of the lives of those who'd resided there—a half-melted doll, or broken ceramic pots, or a damaged bookcase containing hundreds of charred books. In some houses, it was possible to see through remnants of collapsed walls, straight to the backyard.

Almost nothing remained from this one. A single blackened beam protruded from the ruins. Abby could glimpse in the debris something that might have been a sofa at some point. The metal shape of a fridge lingered in the back. Ash had painted the snow around the structure gray, intermingling with the numerous tire tracks of fire trucks, police cars, and civilian bystanders.

The house was cordoned off by yellow crime scene tape that fluttered in the chilly wind. The black ruins stood out unpleasantly in the thin frosty blanket that covered the surrounding fields. Abby shivered in the cold, the kind of chill that drove her to think of soups, and mugs of hot chocolate, and warm blankets, all of which weren't within sight.

The firefighters and the forensic team had already finished processing the scene the day before, and now the stillness of the area was unnerving. Although there was no one there, Abby couldn't shake the prickling feeling that she was being watched. She glanced sideways across the icy fields at the nearest house, about two hundred yards away. The windows were dark, no visible movement. Maybe a curious neighbor? Or it could be her imagination. She'd taken a red-eye flight to Wyoming, and her nerves were shot from exhaustion.

Adjusting her woolen hat to cover her frozen ears more snugly, she pushed herself off the hood. She walked over to the remains of the house, her feet crunching the icy ground. Crouching, she slid under the tape, then straightened, the sharp smell of the burnt house filling her nostrils. In her mind, she was already comparing this place to the crime scene photos of the other locations she'd investigated.

In the past few weeks she'd been informally investigating a series of arson cases that appeared to be connected to Moses Wilcox. More than thirty years before, Wilcox had been the leader of a religious cult in North Carolina. His cult was, among other things, making heroin and selling it to local dealers. In a subsequent police siege, Wilcox locked his entire congregation in the dining room of the cult's compound and then burned it down. It was publicly known as the Wilcox Cult Massacre. Officially, only three of the cult members survived the fire, all of them children. And one of them had been Abby.

But there had been a fourth survivor. Abby had found out recently that Moses Wilcox had used the chaos of the fire to escape from the police. Presumed dead, so no one had searched for him for three decades.

She carefully stepped inside the house, avoiding the piles of scorched rubble that had accumulated when the house's roof had collapsed during the fire. She accidentally kicked something plastic, and it clattered on the floor. Crouching, she inspected it. It was an evidence marker, left behind. What had it marked? An empty gasoline can? A piece of furniture, miraculously intact? Or the remnants of the home-owner, Jimmie Yates?

While she'd investigated the arson cases, she came upon a parallel investigation by the FBI. She'd talked to the woman in charge of the investigation several times, telling her all she knew about Moses Wilcox. The FBI gave her little information in return. Then, the day before, a certain Special Agent Gray called to ask her a few additional questions. Specifically, he asked about any connections Moses Wilcox might have in Wyoming. Abby didn't know of any such connections, but after the phone call she did a bit of digging and found out that a house had burned very recently, in Douglas, Wyoming, in what the police were treating as an arson case. Jimmie Yates, the owner of the house, had burned to death inside.

Now she looked around her, wondering if this really was related to the case. Had Moses Wilcox been here in Douglas, just a few days ago? Or was she wasting her time and money on a random arson case?

She never would have come here if it wasn't for the threat to her children.

They're my grandchildren, Abihail. They belong with my flock.

Moses had told her that on the phone, three weeks before, after she found out he'd tried to enter her house and talk to her son, Ben, while she was away.

Since then there had been several moments that made the hair rise on the back of her neck. Phone calls to their home number, the caller hanging up as soon as she answered. A stranger contacting Sam on Twitter, writing her, *I can't wait to hear you play.* Ben telling Abby that a woman was standing outside his school, watching him play with his friends, her eyes only on him.

Abby felt as if they were constantly being followed. She found her-self tensing whenever someone looked at her a second too long on the street. A woman took a selfie in the park while Abby and Ben passed by, and Abby followed her discreetly for over twenty minutes, trying to figure out if she'd covertly taken a photo of them. She pounced at Sam whenever her daughter's phone blipped with a new message, asking her who it was, what did it say.

She was going insane. The only way she could know peace was with Moses behind bars. Abby would chase Moses Wilcox to the ends of the earth to protect her children. In this case, she'd chased him to Wyoming.

She glimpsed something in the ashes and knelt to look closer. A piece of red plastic, twisted and warped by heat, its edges blackened by the fire.

"Don't move," a sharp male voice barked behind her.

Reflexively, Abby stood up and started turning.

"I said don't move, or I shoot!" the man shouted. "Put your hands on your head. *Slowly.*"

Very slowly, she did as she was told. "I'm Lieutenant Abby Mullen. I'm a cop." How far behind her was he? The house wasn't large. Was he inside or standing outside? If he shot at her, was there anywhere she could take cover?

The man snorted. "Awesome. Turn around."

She did, shuffling her feet to avoid startling him. Her eyes instantly focused on the gun muzzle that was aimed straight at her. The man holding it was a uniformed police officer. She took in his stance, the tense muscles of his body, his wobbly jaw gritted tightly, his rumpled clothing, his nervous eyes bloodshot and unblinking. Her heart hammered in her chest as she met his eyes.

She should have seen this coming. The police had the crime scene staked out. That house across the field—she'd *felt* that someone was watching. He probably began to approach as soon as she stepped inside the ruins of the house. What time was it? Around eight thirty in the morning. Taking under consideration the appearance of this guy, this wasn't the morning shift. He'd been on the night shift, still waiting to be replaced. It was more than likely that he'd already been seething with anger, wondering where his replacement was. Usually, the younger cops got the night shifts, but this guy seemed about thirty-five, maybe even older. That could mean he'd been assigned the shift because he was a screwup. She hoped that wasn't the case.

"Officer," she said, her voice low and calm. "I'm Lieutenant Abby Mullen from the NYPD. Put your gun down." She ended each sentence in a downward inflection, stating a fact. This man was tired and probably jittery on caffeine. He needed someone else to take charge.

He didn't lower his gun, but she glimpsed an almost imperceptible slacking in his muscles. Even if he didn't believe she was a cop, seeing her face and hearing her soft voice soothed his nerves.

"What are you looking for here, huh?"

Abby heard the engine of a car. Someone approaching. In all probability, this guy's replacement. She didn't want another cop stepping in the house, seeing the gun trained on her. They might get the wrong idea, and the situation would only escalate. She did her best to keep her eyes off the gun as she said, "I'm investigating a case. A serial arsonist. Please put the gun down." She let her tone soften, the voice of a harmless young woman, and fluttered her eyelashes briefly. She wished she wasn't wearing a woolen hat and a bulky coat. The coat, she knew, seemed like it could be hiding anything. And the hat, though warm, was hiding her blonde hair and her protruding ears. Usually, men were less intimidated by a tiny woman with big ears.

"This is Wyoming," he said slowly, as if he suspected she had somehow taken a wrong turn and ended up in the wrong state. "Not New York."

"What's your name?" Abby asked, giving him a bit of a smile.

"I'm Officer Fred Moss."

Why wasn't he lowering the gun? She gave him a quizzical look. "I'm sorry, Fred," she said apologetically. "I should have called and coordinated this with the Douglas Police Department."

"So you're an NYPD cop," he echoed.

As a hostage negotiator, one of Abby's core guides was the 7-38-55 rule. It was a simple equation that stated that when people talked, only 7 percent of what they felt was communicated in their words. Another 38 percent was accounted for in their tone of voice, and 55 percent in their facial expression. The words he'd uttered should have been reassuring. Officer Moss realized she was a cop. But his expression was haunted, frustrated. His tone was hollow. Almost . . . disappointed.

She tried to imagine what he was feeling. A cop in Douglas, Wyoming. His job mostly routine—every day rounding up the same drunks, arresting the same junkies, investigating petty thefts and missing pets. And then, a house was set on fire, a man died. Murder. The police decided to stake out the crime scene in case the murderer came back, and Fred Moss got stuck with the night shift again. Staring at the burnt remains of the Yates residence, trying not to fall asleep, drinking one coffee after another until his heart was hammering and his eyelids felt as if each weighed ten pounds. In the morning, his replacement was late, just like they probably always were. And then, suddenly, a figure showed up. In the distance she could have been anyone. Even a deranged pyromaniac coming to inspect his own handiwork.

Already amped on caffeine and anger, Officer Moss had crossed the distance between his stakeout to the burnt house on foot. What was he thinking as he did so? He'd been scared; she could hear it in his voice when he'd told her not to move. But maybe he'd also imagined himself catching the dangerous pyromaniac who'd killed Jimmie Yates. Handcuffing the deranged murderer and hauling him to the car as the killer begged for mercy. And the entire station, for once, would see what he was worth.

And then he found out he was holding a gun on a tiny woman. *And* she turned out to be a cop. He would be the laughingstock of the station. A man who was already used to being on the bottom of the food chain.

He was standing on a precipice. He knew that as soon as he lowered his gun, that horrible future he was envisioning would catch up with him.

She gave him a mortified smile. "God, I'm such a moron," she said. "I've completely ruined your stakeout. I should have realized you might be watching this place. Oh, shit. I might have spooked whoever did this."

"I . . . yeah." He gave her an annoyed stare, his gun lowering a notch. "What were you thinking?"

"I wasn't, I'm so sorry." Her heart rate settled as the gun shifted away from her. She let out a long breath, masking her fear under a facade of embarrassment. "Are you going to report this?"

"I—" His mouth snapped shut as crunching footsteps approached them. Three more people entered the blackened premises of the burnt house. One was a uniformed cop, probably Fred's replacement. Taller by a few inches and younger by at least five years.

The other two weren't cops. One was a man taller than either of the cops, and wider too. He had a thick mane of black hair and a sort of sloppy smile that was probably supposed to be disarming, but Abby wasn't fooled. His eyes snapped between the lowered gun in Fred's hand, to her face, back to Fred, assessing the situation. This guy was sharp.

His associate was a woman, about Abby's height, her head snug in a gray woolen hat, from which a few stray locks of auburn hair emerged. Her face was delicate and pale, except for her nose, which was quite long and curved. Like her friend, she first looked at Fred, who seemed to wilt under her stare. Then she turned to Abby, gazing at her with a pair of bright-green eyes. It was as if the woman was reading her, like someone might skim the headlines of a newspaper.

"Hey, Moss," the cop who'd shown up to replace Fred said cheerfully. "These are the feds who talked to us yesterday. Who's your friend?"

Abby smiled at the three newcomers. "Hi, I'm Lieutenant Abby Mullen from New York."

The feds both blinked.

"Mullen," the woman said. "What are you doing here?"

The man by her side cleared his throat. "I called her yesterday," he said. Then he turned and smiled at Abby. "I'm Agent Tatum Gray, we talked on the phone. And this—"

"Is obviously Zoe Bentley." Abby smiled back. "It's nice to finally meet you."

"Lieutenant Mullen didn't coordinate with us before showing up," Fred said gruffly. "I almost thought she was the arsonist."

Zoe glanced at the man, looking at him as if he were a gnat. "Only about fifteen percent of arsonists are women, and those are not likely to come back to the crime scene," she said bluntly. "And your forensic team found three empty five-gallon gasoline cans at the scene. I can't imagine a woman like Mullen here carrying them easily, can you?"

Fred stared at the blackened floor sheepishly. Abby briefly wondered what would have happened if Zoe Bentley had arrived first to the burnt house, encountering Officer Fred Moss and his eager gun.

CHAPTER 3

Zoe had no idea what Mullen was thinking, showing up at the crime scene. It wasn't her investigation; it wasn't even her jurisdiction. Best-case scenario, the woman was trying to be helpful, even if her intentions were misplaced. Worst-case scenario, she intended to somehow involve the NYPD, and there were quite enough agencies already involved, thank you very much. Too many cooks, as the saying went, spoiled the soup—and too many law agencies were even worse. They not only spoiled the soup, but they couldn't agree which soup should be cooked in the first place, or even if it should be a soup, and not, say, a cake.

"Lieutenant Mullen," she said. "Did Agent Gray convey that we needed your assistance in this investigation?"

The woman smiled at her, taking off her hat, letting her blonde hair tumble onto her shoulders. She wore a pair of delicate glasses that gave her face a bookish look. Her nose and ears were pink from the cold, and Zoe knew from experience that this meant her own beakish nose was pink too. Ah well.

"I'm sorry," Mullen said, her voice soft. "I should have let you know I was coming." She offered her hand to shake Zoe's.

"Yes. Because if you did, I would have told you there's no need," Zoe said. "If we need any more information from you, we'll call." She frowned at Abby's outstretched hand and, after a moment, shook it impatiently.

"If I'm here anyway, I might as well take a look," Mullen said.

"I would prefer you didn't," Zoe said shortly.

Mullen blinked and eyed Zoe quizzically. "It seems like you're worried I might get in the way of your investigation." She made it sound as if Zoe's request was strange.

"That's right."

Tatum winced at her side. She'd been working with him for several years and knew when he was unhappy with her straightforwardness. But this involvement of Mullen was unnecessary, and she wanted to nip it in the bud.

Abby tilted her head. "I'm sorry. How can I assure you I won't interfere?"

"You can't," Zoe said promptly. "It's my experience that you will." She turned away from the woman and looked around her.

It was the fifth burnt house she'd visited in the past three months, ever since the FBI's Behavioral Analysis Unit had been assigned the case. Though the arsons had occurred in different states, they all shared a similar pattern, what Zoe believed was part of the killer's signature. The victims were always burned alive, their legs bound at the ankles, the hands bound at the wrists.

The MO changed and evolved, as it did with most serial killers. The amount of accelerant increased, and the materials used to bind the victims changed. The locations became more remote.

The span of time between the cases seemed to be getting shorter.

It all spoke of a killer driven by an internal obsession. But the forensics and the efficiency of the crime indicated several arsonists working together. Until recently, Zoe had had difficulty creating a coherent profile for these crimes. The closest she came was that several men with similar fantasies had somehow found each other, probably on a dark web forum, and decided to work together. But commonly, arsonists had an antisocial personality disorder, and pyromania was an impulse-control disorder. A team of coordinated, efficient arsonists was not a likely scenario.

And then, a few weeks ago, Lieutenant Abby Mullen had contacted her, suggesting the crimes were connected to a cult. Everything clicked. A cult wouldn't need several people with similar fantasies. It would need only one charismatic leader whose fantasies guided the actions of his followers.

It was the Manson Family all over again.

From everything Mullen had told her, it seemed likely the woman was right. The serial killer Zoe was searching for was none other than Moses Wilcox, who had been presumed dead. Mullen had been contacted by Wilcox and had even taken a blurry screenshot of him when they'd had a video chat. A woman assumed to be a disciple of Wilcox had set herself on fire in a school in New York in strange circumstances the NYPD were still untangling. Zoe and Tatum had spent the past two weeks talking to witnesses and showing them the images they had of Wilcox—both the blurry recent one and the infamous photo that had been used all those years ago in the news stories about the Wilcox Cult Massacre.

Which was to say, Zoe was glad Mullen had approached her. It had been a very useful tip. But she couldn't see how Mullen could help. Her childhood memories from her life in the cult were nearly useless, and her assumption that she "knew" how Wilcox thought because of their acquaintance was ridiculous.

Frustrated, Zoe pushed Mullen out of her mind. There, she was interfering already. Zoe was supposed to be reconstructing the recent murder, not reviewing Mullen's contribution to the case.

She stepped away from the woman, and from Tatum, and took a deep breath. Then, after taking out the crime scene photos from her bag, she began looking around her. The topmost photo was the charred remains of the victim. The electric cord that had been used to bind the victim was covered in soot and nearly invisible in the photo. But the position of the body was unnatural, hinting at the bindings, although they couldn't be seen. Zoe walked around a pile of debris to the location in which the victim had been found—lying amid the remains of the burnt bed. The forensic team had found traces of gasoline in the floor cracks around the bed but none on the bed or under it. The deepest charring spots in the room were close to the walls. This indicated that those were in all likelihood the points where the gasoline had been poured. They'd set the *room* on fire, not the man. That had to be intentional, and it matched four of the five other crime scenes. This was connected to Wilcox's fantasy somehow. This was part of his signature.

For a brief second the image rose in her mind—the victim, lying on the bed, tied, helpless as the flames rose around him, the heat turning unbearable . . . she pushed the vivid picture away, shutting her eyes. *Later.*

She paced around the structure, matching the photos to the house. The gasoline cans had been discarded inside the structure, each in a different room. But scorch marks indicated the outer walls had been splashed with gasoline as well. In all likelihood, the arsonists had been outside when they'd lit the flame, or there would have been more than one body here.

She shifted the photos, taking a look at the photographs of the exterior of the house. The entire muddy ground was crisscrossed with tire tracks and footprints of the firefighters and police that had shown up.

"What time did the first responders arrive at the scene?" she asked aloud.

"One thirty-two in the morning," one of the cops answered. "The call to the fire department came at seventeen minutes past one. It would have probably been sooner if the Fitzpatricks weren't on vacation."

"The Fitzpatricks?" Tatum asked.

"The people who live across the field." The cop indicated. "They've gone on their yearly vacation to Florida."

"When did they leave?" Abby asked.

The two cops exchanged glances. "I don't know, a week ago maybe?"

"Nah," the younger one answered. "I saw Pippa three days ago during Zumba."

"Zumba? You go to Zumba?"

"What the hell is wrong with Zumba? Anyway, I guess they were still here, so they probably left just before the fire."

Zoe and Tatum exchanged glances. More likely than not, this was not simple bad luck. The arsonists had struck knowing the closest house was empty. If that was intentional, it meant several things. First of all, it meant Wilcox had no interest in burning an empty house. He could have burned the Fitzpatricks' house much more easily and with less risk. *And* it meant planning and patience. Patience didn't come easily to anyone with a compulsive fantasy. Most pyromaniacs had poor impulse control. How did Moses manage his compulsions?

"Any more fires in the area recently?" Zoe asked.

"Nothing like *this*." One of the cops shrugged. "Someone set a signpost on fire. And the abandoned car back near Antelope Creek Drive. You know, teenager pranks."

"Do teenagers usually set things on fire here?"

"I mean . . . not usually, we wouldn't be happy if it was the norm. But you know how kids are."

"What do you think?" Tatum asked. "Stress relief?"

Zoe nodded. "He had to set small fires to keep his compulsions in check. Waiting for the big one."

"Moses Wilcox doesn't have a compulsion to set fires," Abby said. "It's a religious motive. He does it out of a twisted belief that it's a form of cleansing. He wouldn't go setting a signpost on fire."

"Religious beliefs might be his rationalization," Zoe said, "but not the actual reason. He burns people because he has a compulsion to do so. A need. And when that need grows, he postpones it with momentary stress relievers. In his case, setting random stuff on fire."

"That would mean they've been here for a while," Tatum said. "Any strangers arrive in town lately?"

"Not that we've noticed," said Moss. "And it's a small town."

"It would have been a small group," Zoe said. "Five or six people. They could lay low."

"It's more likely that Moses had a larger group," Abby said. "He wouldn't be satisfied with a handful of followers."

Zoe didn't bother arguing. She didn't really care what the woman thought. Perhaps Wilcox had a large following. But like the murders committed by the Manson Family, it was more likely that the actual crime had been enacted by a handful of the most fanatical followers.

She stepped out of the house, crouching under the crime scene tape. She turned around to face the shambling, blackened remains and took a few steps back. Where had they stood, admiring their handiwork? The fire would have been blistering, thick smoke everywhere. But Wilcox, she guessed, would want to stand as close as possible. She took a few more steps back. Here, the fire would have been baking hot but probably just about bearable. And there would be no danger of burning debris hitting anyone.

She could imagine it. Wilcox standing with his group, staring at the fire. Did that satisfy the man's need?

She estimated she was about ten yards away from the house. She flipped through the pages she'd photocopied from the initial forensic report until she found the page listing the items found in the crime scene.

Eleven yards from the eastern wall of the burnt house, the forensic team had found two ivory buttons, 5/8 inches in diameter. Perhaps it wasn't related to the fire.

But perhaps Moses Wilcox needed more than fire to feel satisfied.

CHAPTER 4

The first time Abby had crashed a party was in high school. It had been an awful experience. She kept feeling as if at any moment, someone would point at her, asking loudly what she was doing there. She stayed away from the refreshments, because touching them almost felt like actual theft. She ended up hiding for most of the party behind a large potted plant and only emerged when, to her horror, one of the drunken guests tried to pee in it. She made a solemn oath to never crash a party again.

She broke her oath three years later, at college. Her second attempt had been much more successful than the first. She realized that as soon as she greeted several of the guests enthusiastically, she instantly felt welcome. Sentences like "I didn't realize you were coming too" and "How do *you* know Heather?" went a long way. In fact, the only draw-back of her strategy was that by the end of the party, she found herself actively helping Heather clean up her house. Throughout her college years she'd honed her party-crashing skills to an art form. In fact, she usually enjoyed those parties better than the parties she was invited to.

She was about to crash another party now. And although there was less chance for booze, or exciting romantic encounters, her heart was beating just like it had all those years ago.

The hallways of the Douglas Police Department, and the few uni-formed cops she passed by, made her miss her own familiar surroundings in the New York Police Academy. She ignored the wave of homesickness that assailed her and rapped her knuckle on the door of the meeting room. Without waiting for an answer, she waltzed right in.

The meeting was already in progress, of course. She'd intentionally shown up ten minutes after it had started. If she'd arrived on time to a meeting she wasn't invited to, she would have instantly been requested to leave. Show up late, and chances were that the participants would figure it was less of a hassle to let her sit in.

Zoe and Agent Tatum Gray sat on one side of the table, while Chief Powell, the head of the Douglas Police Department, sat on the other side, alongside two other officers. The meeting room's walls were decorated with framed photographs of past police chiefs, a row of smiling faces who were the only ones unruffled by Abby's brusque entrance.

"Sorry I'm late," Abby apologized with an embarrassed smile. "I was waiting for this meeting to start in the other room. It's lucky someone saw me waiting and pointed me the right way." As she spoke, she made her way to an empty seat next to Tatum.

Powell frowned at her. "I'm sorry . . . who . . . ?"

"Oh! Right, sorry. I'm Lieutenant Abby Mullen from the NYPD. I'm a cult expert and have been researching a string of arson cases that seem to be related to this case. I've been collaborating with Dr. Zoe Bentley and Agent Gray." She sat down and took out a thick folder and two pencils, then carefully placed them on the desk. She took out a notebook as well and flipped through its pages, before grunting in satisfaction as she found an empty one. She took one of the pencils and carefully scribbled the date in the corner.

Zoe gazed down at her with her piercing stare. "Mullen, I made it clear that—"

"Agent Gray invited me to take part in this meeting," Abby interrupted her. "To contribute my expertise in the matter."

Tatum Gray blinked in surprise, probably trying to align this with their conversation. It was true he'd told her this meeting was taking place. And he had told her he appreciated her contribution. Of course, he'd never *actually* invited her, but Abby had chosen to read between the lines.

He turned toward her. Would he point out he'd done no such thing?

But then he grinned. "Right! I'm glad you showed up."

Zoe glared at him. A lesser man would have probably wilted under Zoe's laser eyes, but Tatum settled comfortably in his seat. Working with Zoe, he probably had to get used to her temper.

"Right . . . ," Powell said. "As I was saying before, I'm still not convinced this case is connected to the FBI's case."

Zoe turned her wrath on the chief. "As *I* was saying, the signature of this murder is identical to the other five we investigated. The murder victim was bound in his home, which was subsequently burned. The bindings in all cases are nearly identical—"

"Not according to the material you sent." Powell shuffled a few pages. "You have two victims bound with chains, one with barbed wire, one with an electrical cord, and one wasn't bound at all."

"Forensics indicates the fifth murder victim was bound in the same manner, but the rope used had been burned," Zoe said impatiently. "The MO changed and evolved, but the signature of the murders remained the same. Bound at the wrists and at the ankles."

"Dr. Bentley, that's hardly a unique, uh . . . signature. When you tie someone, you tie their wrists and ankles. You don't tie their pinkies together."

For a second, Zoe looked as if she was about to leap over the desk and strangle the man, but Tatum cleared his throat. "Okay. This case is similar to the murders we're investigating. Let's keep an open mind."

"Fine." Powell raised his hands in mock surrender. "So you think Moses Wilcox killed Jimmie Yates. Why?"

"Wilcox has a compulsive fantasy," Zoe said. "He has a constant urge to satisfy it. When the urge gets too much to handle, he needs to act on it. He can postpone the moment by relieving the stress, and we believe he does that by setting fires. But he can't postpone it indefinitely. At a certain point, he needs to kill."

"Is this like a fetish?"

Zoe considered it. "It's not clear yet. Pyromania is more common than pyrophilia—"

"What's pyrophilia?" Powell asked.

"Pyrophilia is the sexual arousal derived from setting fires."

Powell shuffled in his seat. "I thought all pyromaniacs get off setting fires."

"That's a common misconception. Most pyromaniacs don't experience any form of sexual arousal from fires."

"Come on, Bentley. Maybe they *say* they don't, but why would they do it otherwise?" Powell rolled his eyes.

"This has been researched," Zoe said crisply. "The sexual arousal of twenty-six arsonists and fifteen nonarsonists has been tested by measuring their penile responses to audio logs—"

"Can we please not talk about your psychologist friends measuring forty erections right now?" Powell raised his voice.

"It's actually forty-one," Zoe said sharply. "And as I was about to say, the research noted the *lack* of erections."

Abby found she was getting surprisingly fond of Zoe. It took a special kind of woman to talk in a room full of men about a lack of erections. Powell and his officers seemed distinctly uncomfortable. Tatum, however, looked like all he was missing was a box of popcorn.

"Fine," Powell snapped. "So it's not clear if Wilcox is getting off on his acts yet. He likes to kill. Why kill Yates in particular?"

"Yates was probably an easy target," Zoe said. "Lives alone in a remote house."

"There are houses that are more remote in the area," Powell said. "And we have a lot of people living alone. Yates was a big guy, and it probably wasn't easy to take him down and tie him up. So why pick him?"

Powell was hiding something up his sleeve. He knew something about Yates that they didn't. And he was drawing this out to make a point.

Zoe, however, was completely oblivious. "It's possible Wilcox is attracted to a certain type of house," she said. "Obviously there would be structures he would find more gratifying to burn. Or it's possible Yates reminded him of someone, matched certain physical traits. It can be difficult to assess the reason for the selection of the victim."

Powell was clenching his lips tight, almost as if he was physically holding himself back, letting Zoe keep on missing the mark.

"It could be something to do with who Yates *is*," Abby interjected. "Wilcox, above all else, is the leader of a cult. Everything he does should serve his hold on his cult. Strengthening their belief in him and their belief in what they're doing. If it's murder, he might want them to feel it was needed or justified."

Powell seemed to deflate slightly, and Abby knew she'd struck close to home.

"Jimmie Yates was a convicted pedophile," Powell said. "He was caught trying to seduce an undercover cop online, assuming he was talking to an eight-year-old boy. When we searched his house, we found a stash of kiddie porn. He was released from prison six weeks ago."

"This wasn't in the initial case report," Tatum said.

Powell shrugged. "Everyone here knows who Yates was. We were busy documenting the forensics—there was no need to document in an internal report something we all knew."

"That's why you think this case might be local," Abby said.

"Half the town would come to roast marshmallows on the fire that burned him down, if anyone would have invited them. Since his release I've been getting endless calls about people seeing Yates drive past the local school, Yates ogling a little girl in the supermarket, Yates taking suspicious photos with his phone." Powell leaned back. "You know what? *I* would have roasted marshmallows on that fire."

"Do you have any concrete suspects?" Tatum asked.

Powell retrieved one of the papers from the pile in front of him. "Seventeen-year-old Gretchen Wood was reported missing by her dad yesterday. She left with most of her clothes and approximately four hundred dollars she stole from her parents. Gretchen has a messy history. Drugs, petty theft, expelled from the local school. Her parents sent her to a couple of youth camps that were supposed to help her, but she was a bit of a lost cause. And in Yates's stash, we found a few photos of Gretchen swimming in the pool, back when she was just a kid."

"Your current suspect is a troubled teenage girl?" Tatum asked, raising an eyebrow.

"There's something else. Gretchen's mother said she caught her siphoning gasoline from her car a week ago." Powell had a satisfied smile smeared on his face. "She assumed Gretchen planned to sell off the gasoline to buy drugs."

"What did Gretchen say about this?" Abby asked.

"She didn't say anything. She refused to talk to either of her parents lately."

"Did you interview Gretchen's friends?" Abby asked.

"Yeah. Her friends say she's been acting secretive and excited lately. And apparently, according to her parents, this is not the first time she took off recently. She disappeared twice in the past month. Each time she came back after a few days."

"If she already disappeared a few times before, why did they report her missing only this time around?"

"Because in the previous times she didn't take her stuff with her. And they said that both times, when she came back home, she looked better. Her mom thought she was getting her act together. But this time it feels like she took everything she could. *And* stole money from them."

"Has she been seen lighting fires or buying gasoline?" Tatum asked.

"We haven't had the time to thoroughly investigate this, but so far no one witnessed anything like that."

"Has she been talking about Yates?"

"All the town were talking about Jimmie Yates. So I'd say that's a safe bet."

"What about locating her phone?"

"She left her phone back at her home."

"You think Gretchen burned Yates in his home, and then took off, leaving her phone behind?" Abby asked skeptically.

"Yeah, we think Gretchen had an encounter with Yates a few years ago. Maybe Yates molested her, maybe he just tried to befriend her. Then when Yates was released, Gretchen probably started to think about that. She decided to take care of Yates once and for all. But after burning his house, she got spooked by all the cops, and with the talk about feds getting involved, she decided to make a run for it."

It wasn't impossible, but it seemed unlikely. The murder of Yates had been calculated and complex. A teenager looking for revenge would get a blade or a gun and try to finish Yates off. And even if she did choose to burn his house, the amount of gasoline used, and the fact that Yates was tied inside, seemed like something one teenage girl wouldn't be able to pull off. But Powell was already defensive; he wouldn't be open to hearing all those points. He needed to retain his feeling of control and dominance. After all, despite his reaction to Zoe's description of that research, he obviously wasn't a stranger to dick-measuring contests. Abby tried to find a way to present her thoughts in a delicate manner.

"That's idiotic," Zoe said.

Or they could go that route. Tatum sighed audibly. Powell's face flushed, and he folded his arms.

"*Even* if it was likely that a molestation victim would decide to burn her attacker alive, she wouldn't go through all the trouble of carrying at least three heavy gasoline cans to Yates's house. And she would douse Yates directly, and not go through all this quite elaborate process. Not to mention that from your description, this kid wouldn't be patient enough to wait for the neighbors next door to go on their vacation. And in general, the large majority of arsonists are male, not female."

"Fine," Powell said sharply. "I didn't ask for the FBI's assistance to investigate this. We don't need your help."

"Like I said before," Tatum said in a placating tone, "this case might be related to ours. Maybe Gretchen is responsible, maybe it's Wilcox, maybe someone else entirely. All we want is to get to the bottom of this."

"Well, we'll be sure to let you know if we find out anything," Powell said, tapping his papers on the table. It was obvious this meeting was over, as far as he was concerned.

"Wait," Zoe said firmly. "We need to discuss the next steps. Obviously, the stakeout outside the remains of Yates's house needs to keep going for a few days. And we need to sweep the locations of the other arsons in the area to check for bodily fluids."

Powell stood up. "We'll keep you posted."

Abby distractedly collected her props. While Zoe had been talking, something had occurred to her. Gretchen had left home for a few days twice in the past month. And her mother said that when she returned, she looked better. For a troubled kid like Gretchen, "better" usually simply meant "different." Excited and secretive. And now she was gone, taking clothes with her but leaving her phone behind. A teenager would prefer losing a kidney over her phone. If she left her phone behind, it was likely because someone very persuasive told her to.

Maybe Gretchen had just left home, and the timing was pure coincidence. But maybe Powell was partially right: maybe she had been involved in the fire. After all, a lot could happen in a few days away from home. It was possible that Gretchen Wood had been recruited into Moses's cult.

CHAPTER 5

Delilah Eckert stood in her cramped kitchen and stared at her fingers. Mesmerized, she placed her right hand next to her left hand and examined the difference. Four fingers on her right hand were almost double the size of their equivalents on the other hand. It was like those posts she sometimes saw on Facebook, the before-and-after of a magical diet. That's what her fingers were: a simple example of before and after. Before Brad, and after Brad.

The before-Brad fingers were delicate and elegant, a remnant of the before-Brad Delilah. *She* had once been delicate and elegant. With her rich, smooth blonde hair and her ivory skin, and that fashion taste she'd been so proud of. The after-Brad fingers each sported a large purple bruise. She couldn't bend any of them without a sharp pain that seemed to shoot all the way up to her elbow. Just like the after-Brad Delilah. Bruised and stuck, with every wrong movement ending in pain.

He'd slammed a drawer on her fingers when she was retrieving a spoon for their daughter, Emily. A delayed payment over a mistake she'd made the evening before. Brad was all about delayed payments. He never lost his temper and hit her. Instead, whenever she'd make a mistake, he'd say, "You'll pay for that." In a calm, matter-of-fact voice. Like a barista in a café, quoting the price of a large cappuccino. And she'd feel her gut tighten in a knot. She'd carry the fear minutes, hours, sometimes it could even be *days*. Until she could almost believe that maybe he'd forgotten. And then, when her guard was down, he made sure she'd pay.

Out of toilet paper? "You'll pay for that."

Accidentally raising her voice at him? "You'll pay for that."

Caught talking to their male neighbor? "You'll pay for that." But in a low voice that only she could hear.

Delilah's life was riddled with debts and postponed payments. A mortgage of fear and pain.

"Mommy, I'm thirsty." Emily's voice penetrated her thoughts. Sweet and soft. She turned around and smiled at her daughter. Usually, Emily wore one of the dresses Brad's mother bought her. Ugly corduroy things Delilah hated but never dared to complain about ("You'll pay for that"). But those dresses had buttons and zippers in the back, which Emily needed help with. And right now, buttoning one of those dresses was quite impossible. So Delilah had dressed her in a simple white dress she'd bought her. And in that dress, with her curly blonde hair cascading over her tiny shoulders and her sweet button nose, she looked like an angel. Emily took after Brad in her looks. But to Delilah's relief, she had her mother's eyes, soft and brown. Delilah kept telling herself that the eyes were a window to the soul. That despite Emily's similarity to Brad, she hadn't inherited anything else.

"You know what?" she told Emily. "Today you can have juice."

Her daughter grinned at her happily. Delilah usually tried to be strict about the amount of sugar her daughter consumed. But on difficult days, she could use some happiness. And if happiness for herself was so out of reach, her daughter's happiness was good enough.

She hadn't thought it through. The juice box had a straw, which was wrapped in plastic. So she had to get the juice box out of the cupboard, and get the straw out of the plastic, and manage to stick it in the box, and hand it to her daughter. This was one of those days in which every action was broken into a multitude of smaller actions, and felt like an endless painful task. When Emily finally sat at the table, sipping from her juice box, Delilah was breathing fast, tears of pain clouding her sight.

She shut the cupboard, her eyes shying away from it. She was now afraid of the cupboards and the drawers. She'd found out that in Brad's hands, they could turn against her. Like doors, and walls, and plates, and pens, and a long list of other things in their house. Almost all of their possessions were on Brad's side. This was what Brad excelled in. Teaching her new types of fears. Just like the Inuit had dozens or even hundreds of words for snow, Delilah had found out she could now distinguish between a multitude of fears. That vague fear she felt when she hadn't made a mistake for quite some time and she knew she was about to make one. That sharp fear when he said, "You'll pay for that." The lingering terror of waiting for her payment. The fear that this was her life. The fear that one of the neighbors would say something again. The fear that one day he'd turn on their kids.

Until a few months before, she hadn't been afraid he'd ever hurt their kids. Not because she didn't think it was possible—she had no idea what was beyond Brad's capabilities and morals. But because she thought that if he ever turned on her kids, it would finally be the end. Because she would *never* let him touch the kids. If he touched one of them, she would leave. She even fantasized about it occasionally. It used to be a sliver of hope. He would turn to Emily and say, "You'll pay for that." And then Delilah would pack their bags, get on a bus, and travel to the other side of the country. In some of her fantasies he cried and begged for her to stay. In others, she killed him before leaving, stabbing him with her sharpest kitchen knife. Lovely, cathartic fantasies.

But then, one day, Emily wanted a cookie, and Delilah wouldn't give her one. Emily lost her temper and shrieked. And Brad shot from his chair and strode toward her. And this was it. This was the moment that Delilah would stop him. She would never let him touch any of her children. She stepped in his way. And when he kept striding, veins bulging in his neck . . .

She moved aside. Her panicky brain kept telling her Brad didn't hit the kids, there was no reason for her to anger him. And she stared frozen as he strode over to Emily, crouched in front of her, and roared, "Be quiet!"

He didn't hit Emily. But he could have. And at that moment Delilah realized maybe she would have tried to stop him. But maybe she wouldn't have.

A new fear. The fear that if he turned on the kids, she wouldn't stop him.

A soft cry let her know Ron was awake. She went to their bedroom and leaned over Ron in the crib. He grinned toothlessly and gurgled.

"Hey baby," Delilah whispered. She tried to pick him up clumsily with her left hand, but it was almost impossible. Ron began to cry. Gritting her teeth, she lifted him with both hands, pushing aside the jolt of pain. His diaper was heavy, of course. She'd changed it twice since the drawer incident that morning and was dreading it. She contemplated calling Emily over and suggesting that she change the diaper. She could easily tell her it was a game. They were playing house and Emily was the mother. Or it was Opposite Day, and Delilah and Emily should switch roles. Emily would love it.

But a small voice in Delilah's mind told her Emily would realize the truth. That Mommy wanted her to change her brother's diaper because Daddy had hurt her again.

No. The hell with that. She placed Ron on the changing table and did it all, forcing herself to verify the clean diaper was snug even though it made her whimper in pain.

Finally done, she carried Ron to the kitchen and told Emily, "Come on, let's go for a walk."

She put Ron in his stroller and then paused. Damn it. He wasn't dressed for the outdoors. It was half-impossible to dress him as he squirmed on a normal day, but right now . . . her breath hitched. She nearly gave up there and then. She could turn on the TV for Emily. And then just . . . wait for the day to end. Tomorrow would be easier.

She gritted her teeth and rolled the stroller to his room. She grabbed his blankets from his crib and wedged them around him, tucking him as tightly as she could. Good enough.

Outside in the snow-covered street, she could breathe a little easier. Emily, wrapped in her pink coat, hopped in front of her, her breath steaming. Ron stared curiously at cars driving by. He loved vehicles, and trucks in particular. When a truck would pass by, he would always point at it to draw his mother's attention to this vehicular marvel.

Delilah's mind seemed to be mostly empty. Outside and away from Brad, she didn't have to fear anything immediate. And without fear, it almost seemed like a fuzzy mist clouded her thoughts. She let herself imagine leaving Brad, which felt like a far-off dream. From there she glided to other fantasies, like finding out Brad had been hit by a car. Or that she had a time machine and could go back in time to warn herself. Though she knew it would never work. Imagine her seventeen-year-old self, so sure of herself and the world, meeting this broken twenty-three-year-old wreck. At seventeen, twenty-three was almost the same as eighty—far away, old, and boring. Seventeen-year-old Delilah would tell her she and Brad were soul mates. That he would do anything for her. That twenty-three-year-old Delilah couldn't even remember what love was. And it was true. She couldn't. She gazed at her hands, pushing the stroller down the sidewalk. One swollen, one not. Before and after.

Her feet led her to the church. No surprise there. Lately, she found herself drawn to this place repeatedly. Before-Brad Delilah could hardly be bothered to go to church with her parents on Sunday. But apparently, after-Brad Delilah couldn't get enough of this place. Emily loved it too. Often, on their way home, she'd ask her mom to tell her about Jesus, and God, and about "mirorcles." And Delilah would find herself telling her Bible stories she only half believed herself.

Now after they stepped inside, Emily strolled to the center of the church and whirled around slowly, her hands outstretched. She did it whenever they came there. Delilah rolled the stroller forward and sat down at the edge of one of the pews. She inhaled the stale air, a faint musky smell, intermingling with the scent of burning candles. She used to pray when she came here. Now she only sat there, watching Emily. Ron grumbled in his stroller, and she rocked it slowly back and forth with her left hand, her right hand curled loosely in her lap.

The sound of a door opening echoed in the large empty space, and two men stepped inside. One was Pastor Adams. He was nice enough, but he always made her feel uncomfortable. When he'd meet her, he would look at her with wide, sad eyes. Several times he said if she ever wanted to talk, his door was always open. He once told her that with Brad standing beside her, which was a clear sign that though he had good intentions, he didn't know shit.

She didn't recognize the other man. At first, seeing his white hair and wiry frame, she assumed he was very old. But when he walked down the aisle with Adams, he seemed to be moving with a grace and strength she'd never seen in the older people in her life. He was dressed in a simple white cotton shirt and white pants, which emphasized his suntanned skin.

Both men were smiling as they talked, and it was clear from their body language they knew each other well. They spoke in low tones, the words unintelligible. Adams glanced her way, then leaned closer to the other man and told him something. The other man looked at her. He seemed to pause, eyes widening.

It was time to go.

She stood up. "Emily, we need to go home."

Emily was hopping on one foot down the aisle. "A bit more, Mommy," she piped, her voice too loud. "I'm almost done."

"It's getting late, sweetie."

"Delilah," Pastor Adams said. "This is Father Williams."

Delilah turned to face the two men, who now stood a few feet away. She still couldn't pinpoint the stranger's age. He could be fifty, or seventy, or a hundred and ten. He looked at Emily through delicate gold-rimmed glasses, a smile twisting his lips.

"She's quite a miracle," he said. His voice was low and powerful.

"Yeah," Delilah said, shifting her gaze. "She's very sweet."

"I have some leftover cookies from the charity bake sale we did yesterday," Adams said. "Can I offer some to Emily?"

"We really have to get going—"

"Cookies?" Emily asked, excited.

"It'll only be a minute. I have them right over there. Come on, Emily." Adams led her girl down the aisle. Delilah stared at them, tense. To her relief, Adams didn't attempt to lead her daughter through the door, but instead took her to the far end of the church, where a small table stood with a few boxes of cookies.

"If I could only be a child again," Father Williams said. "To get so excited by the prospect of cookies."

"I don't usually let her have too much sugar this late in the day," Delilah said. "It makes it harder for her to fall asleep."

"Every rule deserves to be broken on occasion. What happened to you there?"

His eyes were fixed on her swollen hand. She clumsily stuck it in her pocket, wincing. "A stupid accident. A heavy box fell on it. I'm a klutz."

"I doubt that it was really your fault. You don't seem like a klutz. You seem quite capable."

She let out a small laugh. "Oh, it was. I just made a mistake."

"Maybe you did. But that mistake happened quite a while ago."

Delilah said nothing. She watched Emily, who was happily nibbling a cookie, as Adams talked to her.

"You know," Father Williams said, "I think there's nothing more difficult than motherhood. Nurturing those tiny souls, protecting them from all the dangers in the world. You've done an amazing job so far."

Delilah glanced at him. "You don't know me, Father."

He smiled at her, his eyes shining. "But I have eyes. I can see your children. They're happy, well dressed, well fed. Was it an easy road?"

She was about to say it was. Easy peasy. And then grab Emily and walk back home. But somehow, instead, she said, "No." Her voice trembled, that one word nearly getting stuck in her throat.

"No, it wasn't," Williams said simply. "It was clearly a difficult road. And you walked it alone. You are quite incredible, Delilah. I hope you know that."

When was the last time anyone had told her something like that? When was the last time *anyone* admired her? The people around her showed her mostly pity, intermingled with condemnation. She knew what they thought. They thought *they* wouldn't have stayed. That *they* wouldn't let that happen to them. They treated her as something broken.

"Thanks." Tears ran down her cheeks. She wiped them hurriedly with her good hand.

He kept talking, telling her how strong she was. How powerful. How smart. It didn't matter anymore that he didn't know her. She *felt* like he did. Maybe he had a gut feeling about her. Maybe, as a man of God, he saw more. She didn't care. She wanted to hear, for once, that she could be proud of herself.

"Why do you come here, Delilah?" he finally asked.

"I don't know, Father."

"Please." He touched her shoulder. "You can call me Moses. Pastor Adams said you've been coming here a lot. Why?"

"To be closer to God?" she mumbled.

"A good reason," he said. "And what do you ask of God, when you pray?"

"I used to pray for help," she said, in a broken voice.

"And you stopped?"

She nodded once.

"Maybe you were praying for the wrong thing," he suggested.

She looked at him, surprised. "Why? What should I have prayed for?"

Moses smiled again, a harder, grim smile. "For justice."

CHAPTER 6

Abby massaged her temple. A throbbing headache threatened to materialize. The light in her garage was too dim, and, in contrast, the glare from her laptop was slowly scarring her retinas.

It had been a week since her visit to Wyoming. But if she had to specify that span of time, she wouldn't call it a week, or seven days. It was more of a blob or a blotch. A thing with no real beginning and end, its texture sticky. And she felt like she was drowning in it.

She'd taken an unpaid vacation from her job at the police academy. On theory, the purpose of the vacation was to spend time with her kids, helping them to recuperate from the trauma of the Christopher Columbus High hostage situation that had taken place the month before. But in practice, she spent the majority of that time investigating Moses Wilcox. She'd combed through the arson cases that might be attributed to Moses Wilcox and searched for anything that stood out. She'd scrolled through web pages or printed them out when her eyes burned. Her desk was a complete mess of reports, photos, and meshing timelines. Her mind was similarly messy, her thoughts about the case leaking into her everyday life. She'd find herself thinking of a burning house, people screaming inside, while her son told her about his day at school. Or she'd go to sleep and dream about piles of endless reports about arsons and fires. Even her sacred time in the bathroom was not safe from accelerants and fire crews' response times.

Luckily, the kids had been with her ex-husband, Steve, since last weekend, giving her freedom from her mommy duties for four whole days. Still, she often worked until the middle of the night, accumulating sleeplessness and compensating with the two Cs—chocolate and coffee. Which meant she was also jittery, amped up on sugar and caffeine. And to top all that, she constantly felt guilty for not spending enough time with Sam and Ben.

Her biggest frustration at the moment was that she had no idea if the Douglas police had made any progress finding Gretchen Wood. Any inclination they'd had to cooperate had gone up in flames after Zoe's god-awful blunder at that meeting.

Luckily, Abby had managed to befriend a woman in the Douglas Police Department named Martha. Although Martha was not directly involved with the murder case, she was happy to share information in the spirit of interdepartmental cooperation—and the woman's own need to gossip.

She dialed Martha now.

"Hello?" Martha's voice, high and chirpy, answered after one ring. "Lieutenant Abby Mullen, how are you?"

"Hey, Martha," Abby said. "How are you?"

"I'm good! You remember the neighbor I told you about? The one with the skirt?"

Abby didn't. "Of course, the neighbor with the skirt."

"Well, we had a long conversation last night, and she agreed to do her best with her washing machine. And I promised to try and keep little Poppy out of her yard. So it's all good—I feel so relieved. You know how a little argument can really weigh on you? I could hardly sleep."

"I'm so glad to hear it. How will you keep Poppy out?"

Abby tuned out the woman's answer as she opened Gretchen Wood's social media accounts. She had Twitter, Facebook, and Instagram, but all three had gone silent ever since she'd disappeared. Abby checked them every day. Nothing new today either.

"So are you calling to ask about Gretchen Wood again?" Martha said, after an elaborate Poppy-related monologue.

"Yeah. Just wondering if there's been any news."

"I don't think they've made any progress. Thompson, the lead investigator? Well, he has some issues with his family, so he's not very focused. There's apparently some tiff about an inheritance. I think it's terrible that people can squabble about possessions after their loved ones die. Isn't it horrible?"

"It's horrible," Abby said dutifully. "So there's been no progress at all?"

"Well, I heard they found out Gretchen Wood bought a five-gallon gasoline can in a local gas station before disappearing, and *that* doesn't look good."

"No, it doesn't," Abby agreed, jotting down, *Wood bought gasoline + siphoned as well. Following instructions, or of her own volition?*

"Poppy, no! Sorry, Abby. I'm feeding my cats, and Poppy scratched Georgette. I don't know what's gotten into him lately. Oh no, the cat food is almost empty. I feel like I buy these things every other week."

Abby smiled. "I know how you feel. I also keep buying food for . . . my . . . um . . . pets." Her gut sank. Her pets. Her damn pets.

Oh, shit.

"Martha, I just remembered something. I'll call you back, okay?"

She hung up and shot from her chair, leaving her room and hurrying to Ben's room. Keebles, noticing her urgency, ran after her, barking.

Abby flung open the door of her son's room, where some very hungry predators awaited.

Throughout the years, her kids had collected a few pets. Keebles, Samantha's dog, was a Pomeranian spitz. Though Keebles was white, Sam had colored Keebles's tail pink and purple so the dog always looked like a sort of unicorn gone wrong. Sam usually took the dog with her to Steve's, but when she didn't, Abby walked and fed her, even though she'd never formally agreed to do that. It just happened. Still, it was easy enough to remember feeding a pet that whined and barked and followed you around.

Ben's pets were a different matter. In what seemed like an attempt to create a one-room house of horrors, Ben had procured a chameleon, a tarantula, and a corn snake. To make things worse, there was a fourth vivarium in the room with dozens of crawling crickets, which were destined to be food for the tarantula and the chameleon.

Although Ben was eight, he was incredibly responsible with his pets. But whenever he went to his dad's home for a long stay, it was Abby's job to feed them. But they didn't eat every day, and Ben's door was always shut when he wasn't there, to keep the crawlies at bay. Out of sight, out of mind. And in her current state, trying to balance her job, her private investigation, and motherhood, they'd slipped her mind.

"Sorry," she blurted, not really knowing who she was talking to. None of the horrifying creatures of hell seemed to be in a forgiving mood. They seemed generally pissed. Even more than usual, and that was saying something.

Damn it, she needed to thaw a mouse. Because thawing a mouse was somehow part of her life. She dashed to the kitchen and yanked the fridge open, taking out a mouse-gone-Popsicle. She put it in the mouse-thawing mug and placed it under running water, hoping Pretzel didn't mind if his food was wet. He would have to deal, because she was not about to put a dead mouse in the microwave.

Then, going back to Ben's room, she picked up the tweezers. She had to hurry. The kids were supposed to be back in a few hours, and if Ben found out she'd let his poor monsters of the abyss go hungry, there would be tears.

She opened the cricket vivarium, which Sam called McCricket, and fished the crickets one by one, dropping them in Tabitha the chameleon's vivarium. Tabitha ate six crickets every three days. Jeepers the spider ate one cricket every twelve days. And Pretzel the corn snake ate one mouse every eight days. Which meant every twenty-four days, like creepy planets aligning, the three ate together. And Abby had missed that auspicious date by two whole days.

Done with the chameleon, she fished out a cricket for Jeepers.

Her phone rang. She considered letting it ring, but as the NYPD's number one expert on hostage negotiation and crisis management, she was always on call. And it would be difficult to explain that a man had jumped off a ledge because she was feeding a spider.

She hurried to her room, the tweezers with the squirming cricket still in her hand. The cricket was getting a very rushed tour of the house. Grabbing the phone, she clumsily answered the call.

"Abby? It's Martha."

"Oh, hey, sorry I had to hang up. You reminded me I forgot to feed my own . . . pets." Abby returned to Ben's room and positioned the phone between her cheek and her shoulder. "You know how hungry they can get."

"You don't have to tell me." Martha laughed. "I just remembered I haven't told you. Gretchen's sister, Maegan, showed up here to talk about Gretchen. They talked to Maegan for twenty minutes, but it led nowhere. She was crying when she left."

"I didn't even know Gretchen had a sister." Abby cautiously dropped the cricket into Jeepers's cage and watched the hairy spider leap out of its hiding spot to grab the thing.

"A younger sister. She's fourteen. She looked heartbroken. I felt really bad because I know her. She has a dance class where I do yoga. This thing has the entire town on edge, you know? Douglas is usually such a quiet place."

"I can imagine." Abby retrieved the soggy mouse from the kitchen and dangled it over the snake's vivarium. Pretzel, unlike his other creepy roommates, liked it when you made an effort presenting his food. If she just plopped the mouse in the vivarium, he wouldn't touch it. "Any idea how I can talk to Maegan?"

"I think she left her phone number. Let me check."

"Thanks, I really appreciate it." Abby suppressed a shiver when Pretzel finally decided the mouse had been satisfactorily dangled and leaped for it, then snatched it and curled around it. She shut the vivarium and left the room, closing the door behind her.

"It's my pleasure," Martha said distractedly. "Hang on. Why doesn't it let me log in? I swear, this new system . . ."

Someone knocked at the front door. Phone still held to her ear, Abby approached the door and peered through the peephole. A smile spread on her face when she saw it was Jonathan Carver, holding a takeout bag. She opened the door and mouthed, *Hi*. Carver smiled and stepped past her to walk to the kitchen. Abby was glad she had gotten the wet mouse out of there.

"There we go," Martha said. "You writing this down?"

"Shoot."

Abby wrote down the number and, after a few more minutes of chatter, ended the call. Stepping into the kitchen, Abby watched Carver as he took two plates and placed them on the table. He then rummaged through the kitchen drawers. They were at that stage where he felt comfortable setting the table but still had difficulty finding stuff.

"On your right," Abby said, leaning on the doorway. "You didn't tell me you were coming."

He flashed her a smile. "Well, I missed you. You canceled our Saturday-night movie date—"

"I'm sorry, it's this case."

"And when I called you yesterday, you were busy."

"I was following a lead."

"And when I sent you a message this morning, you replied with an emoji." He opened the takeout bag, the tantalizing smell of fried cooking and melted cheese spreading throughout the kitchen.

"It was a hearts emoji," Abby said defensively, her mouth salivating.

"Be that as it may, I needed more. Spicy chicken sandwich or nonspicy?"

"Spicy, please." Abby pushed herself from the doorway and hugged him from behind, melting into his body, taking a deep breath of Carver. She wasn't only hungry. She'd missed him. They'd met briefly after she'd returned from Wyoming, and then she'd disappeared into her investigation.

Ever since the crisis in Sam's school, they'd been spending more time together. For the first time since her ex-husband, she might be falling for someone. It felt scary and heady and completely reckless. And so good.

He turned around and tipped his head toward her. She stood on her tiptoes, and their lips met for a long, sweet kiss. Carver slid his fingers through Abby's hair.

"Hey there," he whispered.

Leaning her head against his chest, she listened to his heart pounding. "Hey," she murmured. She held him for several heartbeats, then took a step back. "Thanks. If you hadn't bought this, I would have eaten leftover pizza from yesterday."

"I had a feeling you needed someone to take care of you," Carver said, sitting down. "There are also potato tots with cheese and bacon. See?"

Abby joined him at the table and took a big bite from her spicy chicken sandwich. "Oh yum," she said with her mouth full.

"Ben and Sam coming back home today?"

"Yeah." She glanced at the time. "In a few hours. I forgot to feed Ben's pets and just remembered now."

Carver shuddered. He wasn't a fan of Ben's collection. Then again, neither was Abby, or Sam, or Steve, or almost anyone else. "What do they eat?"

"Human flesh," Abby said, taking another bite.

"Oh? They sell that in the store?"

"No, it's very annoying. I need to hunt them. They make a lot of noise when they go down. And it takes ages to chop them so that they fit in the fridge."

Carver's chewing slowed down, and he looked at his sandwich unhappily.

"Too far?" Abby asked.

"A bit," Carver admitted. "So how *is* your investigation going?"

"I'm looking for this girl from Douglas." She took a big bite from her sandwich, and sauce dripped on her chin. She hurriedly dabbed it away. "Gretchen Wood. She's gone missing. Douglas PD thinks she might have set the place on fire."

"And you don't?"

"It sounds like she was involved, but I think she was recruited to Wilcox's cult. I think he's still recruiting people."

"What does that have to do with the arsons?"

"Maybe nothing." She hesitated. "But it could be a type of initiation. Or a test. I don't know."

"Then you'd have people recruited in the other arson cases. Did you check for missing people?"

"I did. No luck there. I found one person missing in McPherson, in Kansas. Disappeared three days before the arson. But he doesn't fit."

"Why not? You told me anyone can be recruited to a cult."

"Sure, but he's ninety-three and has dementia, so I doubt the cult would be interested. He probably wandered off and couldn't find his way home."

Carver finished his sandwich and leaned forward, running the back of his fingers on Abby's exposed wrist. Heat spread in her stomach. She suddenly wasn't feeling so hungry. At least, not for her sandwich.

"So no missing persons?" he asked.

"Uh . . . no. Um, not exactly. Missing persons is a no-go. But that doesn't mean anything. People recruited to cults don't necessarily disappear, like Gretchen did. They can leave home of their own volition, telling their family. If the police don't link them to the arsons, there's no reason we'd hear about it."

Carver smiled at her. "I can tell you're pleased with yourself. You found something?"

Abby grinned. "Moses targets small towns in different states. He's probably hoping the local police force would be useless in tracking him down. But the upshot is that these are usually tight communities. They notice when people leave. So I just need to find the person who enjoys gossiping about it. I'll show you." She got up and went to her desk to retrieve the printed photos. She returned to the table and set the three printouts between them. "The one on the left is Gretchen Wood. The girl in the middle? Nellie Owens, from Newberry in South Carolina. She left her home quite abruptly, telling her parents and friends she found a job as a project manager in Silicon Valley, which is probably bullshit. Back home she worked as a waitress, didn't even finish high school. She borrowed money from her parents for the move, telling them she'd pay them once she got her first paycheck."

Carver picked up her photo. "And you think she was recruited?"

"Disappeared a day after the fire. Hardly calls home. Completely stopped talking to her friends. Doesn't log in to her social media."

He put the photo back on the table. He'd smeared it with mayonnaise. "And the third one?"

"Frank Berry, from Tennessee. A town called Lewisburg. Left his wife and kid, emptying their savings account. Two days before the arson there."

"Why didn't his wife report him missing?"

"He wasn't missing. He told her he was leaving her. She's filing for divorce, but currently they can't find him. It's the talk of the town. Don't touch the photo. I don't want it smudged."

Carver drew back his hand, bemused. "What about leads from the scene? Forensics, witnesses. Anything there?"

"That woman, Zoe Bentley? She pretty much made sure we'll get zero cooperation from the local police. So all I have to work with are bits and pieces."

"Typical FBI." Carver speared a potato tot with his fork. "Swooping in and pissing everyone off."

"Yup." Abby finished her sandwich and licked her fingers. Then, feeling self-conscious, she stopped and wiped her hands on the napkin instead. "Listen, are you available next Monday evening?"

"You want to go on the movie night you promised me?"

"No." Abby shook her head. She took a sip from her Coke. "Sam has a concert at school. It's something she's been working on, ever since that day."

"That day" was how Abby referred to the day when armed people stormed into Sam's school, took her hostage, and held her for twenty-four hours. It needed no elaboration. There was only one "that day."

"You want me to come to Sam's concert?" Carver asked, surprised.

"I mean . . . yeah. If you don't mind. If you want a date night for the two of us, we can schedule sometime else—"

He took her hand and gave it a squeeze. "That's not what I meant." He smiled. "I'd love to come."

Abby exhaled. "Okay. Good."

"What will you tell Ben and Sam?"

Abby's heart skipped. "I'll tell them we're seeing each other."

"Okay, then." Carver's eyes sparkled. God, she loved his eyes.

Abby stood up, walked over to Carver, and slid her fingers down his shirt collar. "I have something to show you in the bedroom."

"Yeah? What is it?" Carver stood up. "You're not just luring me so you can kill me and feed me to Ben's snake, right?"

"Don't be silly. You have too much muscle. Ben's snake eats only babies."

Carver sighed as Abby led him to the bedroom.

"Too far?" Abby whispered, pulling him to the bed.

"Maybe a bit. But it's part of why I love you."

A tingly sensation swept her body as he kissed her, and she shut her eyes.

CHAPTER 7

The field of forensics has made tremendous progress throughout the years. Virtual autopsy, done with surface scanners and imaging. Rapid DNA analysis. Facial reconstruction technology. The tools Zoe had at the reach of her fingertips were much better than they'd been just five years before. But if she had to name one significant thing that enhanced her work beyond anything else, it would, without a shred of a doubt, be Taylor Swift's album *Lover*.

Taylor got her. And more to the point, Taylor understood exactly what Zoe needed for her work.

Right now, for example, she needed to start afresh, reviewing the arson murder cases from the beginning. And what could be better for that than the quick, light, upbeat "I Forgot That You Existed"?

"Ta, ta, ta, ta, da," Zoe hummed as she cleared her wall of all its photos and notes. "Wrong, wrong, wrong."

She *had* been wrong, like Taylor suggested. She'd focused on the fires. Like a moth, literally drawn to a flame, the brightest thing in the case files. But that wasn't it at all. Moses Wilcox wasn't just a pyromaniac, staring open mouthed at fire trucks. Nor was he a pyrophile, getting sexual pleasure from watching flames.

She should have realized it from the start. When the Son of Sam, David Berkowitz, killed his victims, no one assumed it was because he was obsessed with his gun or with loud explosions. No, he was consumed by the desire to kill.

And so was Wilcox. His ongoing fantasy wasn't about arson. It was about murder.

Taking a step back, she eyed the bare wall in her office with satisfaction. A blank slate. Well, more or less blank. Years of taping photos on the wall had left their mark, with crumbling paint and numerous smudges.

This case was unusual in more than one sense. Usually, when Zoe approached a case, it was her job to figure out the characteristics of the serial killer. This enabled the investigators to narrow down the suspect pool. But ever since Lieutenant Mullen had contacted her, they *knew* who the suspect was. Zoe's job now was to figure out what made the man tick so that she could foresee his next actions. To come up with steps they could take to flush him out of his hideout. To discern where he would strike next so that they could intercept him before it happened.

And there was no shortage of information on him. There was a wealth of books and documentaries and police reports on Moses Wilcox. If she wanted, she could interview hundreds of people who'd met the man a few decades ago. If anything, she had to work to filter out the valuable information from simple noise or misconceptions.

She turned to her cluttered desk. On it, stacked in a precarious tower, were three books about Moses Wilcox and the Wilcox Cult Massacre, one book about cults, two books about Manson, and more than a dozen profiling books that she'd skimmed lately. She stacked them randomly, impatiently, large thick books atop smaller books, none of them quite centered in the pile. By now, the book tower practically defied gravity.

Next to the books were the six photos of the victims. She picked those up. The victims were the real target, not the houses. She taped the victims on the wall from left to right, in chronological order. Four men, two women, The youngest twenty-three, the oldest sixty-seven. Three of them Caucasians, one African American, two Hispanic. No pattern in the demographics.

She taped the crime scene photos under full-body shots of each of the victims and a photo of the burnt-down houses. Then, after a moment of thought, she sifted through the papers on the desk until she found the photos she'd printed of the houses before they'd been burned. She'd found those photos on Google Maps, which still hadn't caught up with the present. She taped each under its twin charred ruins. Those houses were part of what Moses saw when he planned his murders.

After turning to her whiteboard, she drew a line splitting it in the middle. On one side, she wrote *Signature*, and on the other, *MO*. This was one of the core principles in profiling—separating things the killer did as a means to an end, and things that were a crucial part of his plans—his fantasy. The MO changed and evolved all the time as the murderer became more experienced. The signature mostly stayed the same, or changed more slowly, as his fantasies evolved.

Under MO, she wrote, *binding material*. Like Powell had pointed out in that annoying meeting, Wilcox kept changing the things he used. Rope, chains, electrical cord.

Reviewing the photos of the victims, she nodded to herself. She'd been right. The victims were bound the same every time: their ankles bound together and their wrists bound together. But it wasn't, like that frustrating man had said, the way you tied people. The victims' hands were tied in front of their bodies, which was unusual. It was clearly less ideal for the killer—given enough time they might manage to untie themselves with their teeth. But this forced the victims into a certain posture, especially if they curled their bodies to avoid the heat of the flame. It forced them into a posture that was akin to prayer.

Under Signature she wrote, *binding method—prayer posture*.

All houses were burned down using an excessive amount of gasoline. Wilcox could easily burn down the structures with a fraction of the gasoline, and he knew that for sure. Zoe had no doubt the man set fires all the time, even if he wasn't a simple pyromaniac. He was experienced. So why use so much? Maybe he wanted the houses to burn faster?

Or possibly, it was related to the cult. Perhaps he wanted numerous gasoline canisters because it ensured his followers were all involved in the act. Was that possible? Were some of the characteristics of the murder not a result of a fantasy, or a means to an end, but actually related to cult management? This would put those aspects in a third category that was neither a signature nor an MO.

She bit her lip. This was out of her area of expertise. She'd built her knowledge analyzing the biographies, profiles, and interviews of hundreds of serial killers. But these serial killers mostly worked alone, or with one accomplice. What motivated a serial killer to kill repeatedly wasn't the same as what necessarily motivated a cult leader to kill repeatedly. And cases such as Jim Jones or Daniel Perez weren't anything like what they faced now. The only case that seemed somewhat similar was Charles Manson, and she couldn't really make any assumptions off one case. Forensic psychology was about statistics and probabilities, and she needed more data.

She needed a cult expert. Like Lieutenant Abby Mullen.

Annoyed, she reminded herself Mullen wasn't really a cult expert, not any more than Zoe was a Taylor Swift expert. Sure, the woman had an interest in the topic, but she was actually a hostage negotiator in the NYPD, and as far as Zoe knew, Abby hadn't even studied the subject of cults properly.

Surely the FBI had a *real* expert. She would check it out later.

CHAPTER 8

Emily loved Tuesdays because on Tuesday, Daddy always came back from work early, so Mommy would take them to the park because Daddy was very tired from work and needed his quiet. And Emily knew how to be extra quiet because she and Mommy played that game a lot, when Daddy watched TV, and Emily always won because she was even quieter than Mommy, quiet like a mouse. But Ron was still a baby, and he didn't know how to play, which was why they went to the park.

Emily wished it would stop snowing, because when it was warmer, Mommy would let her go on the merry-go-round and go round and round and round. Mommy could spin her really fast and Emily would feel like she could fly and later she would stand and look up to the clouds and the world would keep spinning. Norman from her class told her the world really did spin all the time, but she only felt it after the merry-go-round, which was why she really wanted the snow to stop.

But this Tuesday they didn't even go to the park, they went to church, and Emily told Mommy she wanted to go to the *park*. But Mommy promised her a lollipop later, and that was as good as going to the park, maybe even better, if the lollipop was red.

They met the nice man with the silver hair. They already met him twice before. His name was Moses, but when she told Norman from her class that she met Moses, he said Moses lived a long time ago, and maybe he was even made up, because all the stories in the Bible were made up.

And then Norman pulled her hair, and she cried and told the teacher.

Mommy was happy to meet Moses, and they sat outside the church, on the bench. Mommy talked to Moses, and Ron gurgled in his stroller. Emily played peekaboo with Ron, and he laughed. Then she saw a squirrel dash behind a tree, so she followed it. The squirrel disappeared. Did it climb up the tree? Maybe he had a little house in the tree with lots and lots of nuts. Emily waited but the squirrel didn't come back, so she returned to Ron and played peekaboo with him and he laughed until his pacifier fell from his mouth to the ground. And Ron started to cry. Emily picked up the pacifier and wanted to give it to Ron, but Mommy jumped at her and told her the pacifier was dirty. Now Ron was crying harder because he wanted the pacifier, so Mommy said she would go wash the pacifier and take Ron. She wanted Emily to come with her but Emily wanted to stay outside and wait for the squirrel to show up again, and Moses said he could watch her for two minutes. Mommy wasn't happy about it, but she finally said okay and walked away with Ron.

Emily wanted to go to the squirrel's tree again, but Moses called her.

"Emily," he said. "Come sit next to me."

Emily sat next to him.

"Your mom will be right back," Moses told her.

"I know."

"You look like your mother, you know that?" Moses said.

Emily looked up at Moses. She had to squint because the sun was above him. "Grandma says I look like Daddy."

"No." Moses smiled. "You have your mom's eyes, and you're blonde, like your mom."

"Daddy is blond too."

"Is he?"

"Yes."

"But you're beautiful, like your mother."

Emily felt the words tickle her tummy like words sometimes did, and she stared at the snow.

"You know, I used to know your mother a long time ago. She doesn't remember it, but it's true."

"Really?" Emily scrunched up her face and squinted at Moses again. "Were you friends?"

"Yes. We were best friends. Do you want me and your mom to be friends again?"

Emily thought about it. "Yes. Mommy says friends are important."

"Good. We'll be friends. And you'll have another brother or a sister. Would you like that?"

Emily wasn't sure about that. "Like Ron?" she asked.

"No. They'll be special. They'll be angels."

Emily had a hard time imagining that. "With wings?"

"That's right. Your mom will have another baby. An angel. With wings."

Maybe her new baby brother would take her flying. And it would feel like a merry-go-round. "I'd like that."

"Good."

Emily watched the sky. "When I grow up and be the same age as Mommy, I want baby angels too."

Moses put his hand on her palm and smiled. "If you and Mommy come with me, we could make that happen."

And then Mommy came back with Ron. And Moses told Mommy that Emily said she wants to have an angel as a baby, and Mommy laughed and caressed her hair, and said that Emily had a great imagination, and it was true because Emily could make up all kinds of stories, and Mommy always loved to hear them. And Moses said something about the wisdom of children, and Emily didn't listen to the rest because she saw the squirrel from before.

CHAPTER 9

Back at her desk, Abby checked the time and groaned. Carver's visit, lovely and pleasurable as it had been, had consumed a few hours of her day. The kids were due to be home at any second, and she still had too much to do.

She called Gretchen Wood's sister, hoping the girl would talk to her.

"Hello?" A soft voice, fragile.

"Hi, is this Maegan?"

"Yeah. Who's this?"

"My name is Abby." Abby smiled so that the smile could be heard in her voice. Smiles could go a long way, even if they weren't seen. "A friend of Gretchen's told me I should talk to you."

"Talk to me about what?" Maegan's voice had lost its softness. Abby had a hunch that Maegan had been talking to a lot of people about Gretchen. And that she wasn't happy to do so again.

"About your sister."

"Listen, I don't know who gave you my number. I don't know where Gretchen is, okay? She didn't even talk to me before leaving. And you know what? I don't care if she *did* burn that asshole's house down. Just leave me—"

"I don't think she burned down that house," Abby said before Maegan could hang up on her.

"Yeah? Well, you're pretty much the only one."

"I'm not the only one. You don't think she burned that house down either."

A short silence followed. "That's right, I don't," Maegan said. "But it doesn't really matter. I don't know where she is. And to tell you the truth, I'm not even sure she didn't do it. She sure as hell wanted to."

"She wanted to?" Abby repeated.

"Everyone in Douglas wanted Yates dead."

"It sounds like Gretchen wasn't like everyone. How did *she* feel about Yates?"

"I don't know. I mean, the guy was a pedophile, right?" Maegan's voice trembled.

There was something there. "How did Gretchen know Yates?"

"She didn't . . . look, everybody knew Yates. He was the pervy guy we were told to stay away from, right?"

"To stay *away* from," Abby echoed.

"Yeah, that's right. So that was it."

"That was it?"

"Look, you said you thought Gretchen *didn't* do it."

"I do think Gretchen didn't do it," Abby said. "But I think she knew Yates."

"Who are you again? Are you like . . . a reporter or something?"

"I'm from the New York Police Department," Abby said, hoping she wasn't about to lose Maegan.

"New York?" Maegan sounded baffled. "Then why are you looking for Gretchen?"

"I believe Gretchen is in trouble. She got mixed up with some bad people. And I want to find her before she gets hurt."

"Listen, I'm sorry, I don't know where Gretchen is. If she calls me or something, I'll—"

"Can I make a quick guess?" Abby asked. "And if I'm wrong, Gretchen's probably fine, and you have nothing to worry about."

"Okay." Maegan was tense. She'd doubtless been waiting for the other shoe to drop for quite a while now. Ever since Gretchen left. She needed this resolved.

"Some time ago, Gretchen started to change. She seemed to get excited about something, but she wouldn't tell you what it was. Not at first. She even left for a few days. For a sort of workshop, or camp."

"A seminar," Maegan said, her voice trembling. "She told me not to tell Dad and Mom about it."

"Right. And after that seminar, it was like you didn't know who she was anymore. She wasn't the same."

"Yeah," Maegan said hollowly. "She joined this Christian group. They managed this youth camp that Mom and Dad sent her to. Gretchen even wanted me to go to one of this group's services."

Abby tightened her grip on the phone. "And did you?"

"Yeah. They creeped me out. Their preacher was sorta full of himself. And after the service they tried to get me to go to one of their seminars too. They felt sorta sleazy. But some of the others thought it was great. I mean, Gretchen was totally into it. And a few other people. The preacher had this monthly donation program, and I saw a couple of people talking to him about it. I don't get it, why would anyone pay *this* guy?"

"And you told Gretchen what you felt?"

"Yeah."

"How did she take it?" Abby said, already guessing the answer.

"She totally flipped. Screamed at me for like an hour. And then she stopped talking to me."

"How long ago was this?"

"I don't know. Three weeks ago, something like that."

So two weeks before the arson.

Maegan sniffed. "Listen, I really have to go. I can talk more later, okay?"

"Wait," Abby said. "That preacher. What did he look like?"

"I don't know. Old. He had glasses."

"Can I send you a picture? See if you can recognize him?" Abby said.

"Yeah, sure. I'll call you later, okay?"

"Yes. Thank you, Maegan." Abby hung up and leaned back in her seat.

Maegan was keeping something back. Gretchen Wood *did* know Yates, Abby was almost certain. Were the Douglas police right? Had Yates assaulted Gretchen when she was younger? Or was it something else altogether? She tapped on her phone and found the blurry image of Moses Wilcox. He'd called Abby a few weeks ago to talk. And to say that he was her father. That he wanted to meet his grandchildren. She'd told him to stay the hell away from them.

She sent the photo to Maegan. Then she scratched her leg, something tickling her ankle. Her fingers brushed a thing. A thing that scuttled away.

In her past, Abby had faced down armed terrorists, had escaped a horrific fire, had had her daughter taken hostage. She had nerves of steel, and she knew it. But somehow, despite all that, her reflexive reaction to something crawling on her was not particularly heroic.

"Nyeeaaaah," she blurted, hurriedly brushing the thing away. A dazed, confused cricket toppled to the floor. Its antennae wriggled as it froze, trying to figure out the best way to escape. For a few seconds, they stared at each other in a tense standoff.

She must have dropped it at some point when she'd hurriedly fed Tabitha. That was what happened when—

A second cricket scuttled into the room. The realization of the mistake she'd made sunk in. She'd been in such a hurry. And then the phone call had interrupted her and . . . and . . .

She had forgotten. To shut. The vivarium.

Setting a new high-speed record in the Mullen household, she sprinted to Ben's room and stared aghast at the very open, very empty vivarium. Crickets, delighted with their newly found freedom, scampered to and fro on the floor, the walls, the furniture. How many? Ben had recently bought a new batch; the vivarium had been packed. She looked around at the hall, spotted several more touring the residence.

"Noooooo." She let out a guttural moan. This was a complete disaster. The only meager consolation was that it was the crickets and not the . . .

The . . .

Jeepers was missing. Maybe he was hiding in his little lair?

Abby inspected the vivarium. Jeepers wasn't in his lair. And his vivarium lay open as well.

Somewhere in this house, a large, hairy tarantula was lurking. And even worse, if she didn't find it, Ben would have an epic meltdown.

Sharp barking snapped her out of her shock. Keebles was chasing one of the crickets across the hall, pink-and-purple tail wagging excitedly.

Jeepers. She had to find Jeepers. Abby looked under the bed, the desk, in the bedsheets. She tried to catch a few crickets that scuttled past her, but they were fast, and she had no time. Her number one priority was the eight-legged horror.

Crazed barking led her to the kitchen, where Keebles had abandoned her chase after the crickets, focusing on a new target. Jeepers, pissed off and ready for a fight, was crouched by the fridge. Keebles was barking at him, hopping left and right, nearly insane with excitement.

"Keebles, shoo!" Abby shouted.

Keebles glanced her way, then kept barking at the spider. The spider raised its legs, displaying its fangs to the purple-tailed dog. Keebles floundered back, then resumed barking.

"Get out of here!" Abby screamed at the dog.

Huffing, Keebles tromped off and resumed chasing crickets.

"Okay, Jeepers," Abby said, clutching a coffee mug from the counter. "Let's get into this comfortable, nice mug." She knelt and tried to scoop Jeepers into the mug.

Jeepers scuttled under the fridge.

"Oh, god." Abby groaned. She leaned with her cheek to the floor. The spider glared at her from under the fridge, clearly brimming with evil intent. What now? She couldn't get it out with a broom handle. Jeepers might get hurt.

How did one call a spider? "Here, Jeepers. Psss psss psss."

Nope, that was clearly meant for cats. Jeepers seemed to retreat deeper into his new lair.

"Come on, Jeepers. Ben will freak out. You remember Ben, right?"

Jeepers seemed to consider that. Abby held her breath. She had talked people into surrendering, climbing off ledges, putting down their weapons. Would she be able to talk a spider out from underneath a fridge?

"It seems like you're worried I might harm you," she cooed to the spider. "But why would I do that? It would only upset Ben. How can I help you come out from underneath the fridge? Do you want crickets? We have some yummy, tasty crickets." She shuffled away from the fridge, giving the spider some space. Perhaps she shouldn't have suggested the crickets. She should have let Jeepers think it was his idea to come out for crickets.

But her blunder went unnoticed. Tentatively, Jeepers stepped out from under the fridge. Abby contemplated trying the mug again, but what if the spider retreated? No, there was only one way.

Quickly, she grabbed the spider in her hand, doing her best not to squash it, and placed him quickly in her other open palm. The thing's demonic claws gripped her skin as she stood. Oh god, she might actually die. But she didn't shake him free. Because sometimes, a mother's love was so strong it could even overpower the urge to hysterically hurl a hairy spider at the wall.

She took Jeepers back to Ben's room and dropped him in his vivarium. She carefully made sure it was shut, her heart still beating madly in her chest.

"Mom?" Samantha called from the doorway.

Abby shut her eyes, took a deep breath, then went to meet her children. A high-pitched shriek let her know they'd seen the crickets.

Steve was standing in the doorway with Samantha and Ben. His mouth was agape. Samantha recoiled in disgust, watching a few crickets scuttling across the wall. Keebles crossed the living room barking, chasing another cricket. Ben was staring, his face etched with confusion.

"What the hell happened?" Steve asked.

"The crickets got out," Abby said.

"What about Pretzel and Jeepers and Tabitha?" Ben asked in a high voice.

"They're all fine," Abby said. A cricket strolled up her shoe. She kicked it off, acting as if it was no big deal.

Steve scrutinized the room. "This is . . . this is biblical."

"Thank you, Steve. That's very helpful."

"You'll have to get an exterminator."

"No!" Ben said.

"No need," Abby said pleasantly. "We'll catch them. It'll be a nice afternoon activity, right, kids?"

Sam blinked, then glanced at her father. "I need you to drop me off at Fiona's. I'll be waiting in the car." She turned around and walked away, bag still slung over her shoulder.

Ben bent down and plucked a cricket off the floor. Then, crawling on the floor, he picked up another.

"Did they *all* escape?" Steve asked. "How did it happen?"

There were layers to Steve's tone. Perhaps all Ben heard were the words his father said and the flat concern he exhibited. But Abby was primed to notice things you only saw after you spent years with someone. How he stressed the word *all*, as if her mistake wasn't just a momentary error but a monumental lapse in judgment. And that question "How did it happen?" laced with such incredulous amazement, as if in the world Steve inhabited, such a thing was almost physically impossible.

Steve was the only person on earth who could drive Abby to a homicidal rage. And he could do it by saying something completely innocuous. Like "hello."

"I didn't shut their vivarium properly," Abby said shortly, trying to control her frayed temper. "Thanks for dropping the kids, I really appreciate—"

"Are they in *all* the rooms?" Steve took a step inside.

Abby realized, horrified, that he was about to stroll through the house and inspect it. Among other things, he would step into the bedroom, where the bedsheets were still rumpled, and her underwear and bra were tossed in the corners, and the scents of her time with Carver still lingered . . .

"Yes, Steve, they're everywhere." She stepped in his path, barely managing not to push him back. "I can handle it."

In the background, Keebles dashed after a cricket, knocking down a chair, barking with gusto. Ben ran after her, shouting at her to stop.

"Okaaaaaaaay," Steve said. How could one person stretch a word to such lengths and insert so much meaning into it? Abby suspected this made his day. "I'll be going. Let me know if you need any help."

He finally left, and Abby shut the door, then turned to face her shambles of a house.

Her phone buzzed in her pocket. She took it out and stared at the text. It took her a few seconds to shift her focus and realize what the message meant. It was from Maegan. It said, Yes, that's definitely him.

CHAPTER 10

Moses shuffled in his chair as he listened to Rose going over their finances. As always when she concentrated, her fingers toyed with her cross pendant. A strand of her long red hair had loosened from her ponytail, dangling on her cheek as she went over the report.

Moses was seated on a large padded armchair, unlike his close circle of followers, who all sat on wooden stools. But then again, almost none of them were even half his age. And none of them felt that constant, niggling urge.

Like the prophets of the past, Moses knew God wasn't making things easy for him. No, by now the need to act was like a trail of ants crawling along his spine. His body was constricted in the chair, in this tiny room. He yearned for the release that would come with the flames, and the screams, and the warmth of the woman underneath him.

"The Nelson family down at Washington Loop increased their monthly donation for the youth shelter to a hundred dollars per month, *and* both of them said they would participate in our three-day seminar for the full price, which comes to—"

"Okay," Moses said sharply. "Thanks."

Eyes widened in surprise. It was true: usually he insisted on hearing the details. It was important to maintain control of the group's accounting. But they simply didn't realize the toll it took . . . he clenched his fists, images flashing in his mind. Rose, naked, writhing on the floor, flames surrounding them, a tangle of her red hair clutched in his fist. He shut his eyes, willing the vivid pictures away.

"That reminds me," he said. "Regarding the three-day seminar, I invited another participant. Delilah Eckert. She's my guest. No need for any fee. And she'll probably be coming with two children. A little girl and a baby."

He wanted to tell them the rest. That she was special. She was a gift from God. His past, resurrected. But he didn't have the words for that yet. It was unusual for him to lack words. It could only mean God wanted him to stay silent, for now.

Anna cleared her throat. "I'm not sure we can accommodate for a baby. And the girl might get bored. The seminar is long . . ."

Moses stared at her until the words died on her lips.

"This congregation has done great things," Moses said, speaking slowly, his voice rising. "Are you telling me we can't handle a baby and a little girl?"

"No, Father," Anna said meekly.

"I want *you* to take care of the children throughout the seminar. Make sure the girl is *very* happy. And that the baby doesn't interfere."

Anna's face flushed. She was supposed to be in charge of the seminar's discussions and communal prayers. Moses could see she was trying to figure out how to do that, weighed down by the additional responsibility of handling two children.

"Rose can take over the rest of your responsibilities," he added.

Anna, nodded, lowering her head. "Thanks, Father," she said, her voice full of tears.

"Delilah is a lost soul," he said, his eyes scanning the men and women in the room. "But I glimpsed purity in her. We can open her eyes to the truth. I need you to stay with her at *all* times. I need you to bathe her with love. I want her to feel like the most amazing person in the room. Surround her. Nurture her soul. Make her feel she *belongs*."

He saw the understanding in their eyes. They'd all done this before.

◆　◆　◆

Delilah was just glad to be out of the house. Brad had gone on one of his long work trips, which *should* have felt marvelous. But she was well aware, after numerous similar trips, that he had expectations of her. She should use that time without him to clean the house. Not a quick mop up. When he returned, he'd inspect it. It had to be sparkling clean or . . .

Or, "You'll pay for that."

So there was something almost ominous in her home when he was gone. Every piece of furniture hid dust or a small cobweb. Every crack in the floor hoarded dirt. She intended to spend the weekend cleaning, her right hand still swollen and painful.

But at least this evening, she could go out, meet some people, pretend her life was something else.

Father Williams . . . or as he'd insisted she call him, Moses, had suggested she come over for the whole weekend, for a seminar. She'd politely refused. But she'd agreed to come for one day, to meet people, to talk. As long as she could bring her children.

The seminar was in a farm out of town, which Moses explained they'd converted to a shelter for troubled youths. She was vaguely aware of the place, which had been running for a couple of years. She'd had to take an Uber to get there.

Now, stepping inside, she was surprised to see how nice it seemed. The main room, warmly lit, was crowded with people, all talking in small groups while sipping from plastic cups. Soft music played in the background. Everywhere she looked, Delilah saw people smiling and even laughing. Emily clung to her, hiding behind her leg.

"Delilah, you came!" Moses approached her. Several men and women followed him, all of them in their twenties, like Delilah was. "Everyone, this is Delilah. And these are her children, Emily and Ron."

"Oh, they're adorable!" gushed one of the women and smiled at Delilah. "Little Emily looks like you. So gorgeous."

"She actually takes after her father," Delilah said, blushing.

"Nonsense. She has your eyes and your lovely golden hair. And look at this guy! Can I hold him for a moment?" Without waiting for an answer, the woman held out her hands.

Delilah hesitated, but everyone was smiling happily at her, and she didn't want to appear rude. She carefully handed Ron to the woman, who instantly cradled him and cooed at him. "He's so sweet. Look at that smile! Hey, Ron, hey, little buddy! I'm Anna. Can you say Anna?"

Someone handed Delilah a paper cup with punch. She sipped from it, enjoying the sweet tang.

"Delilah, I love your shirt," another woman said. "Where did you get it?"

Delilah looked at her own shirt, a remnant of days long gone. "I got it online," she said. "But I redid the sleeves, see? I added the lace panels."

"Oh wow, that's brilliant," the woman said, touching the lace gently. "I can't even see the stitches. You're so talented. Do you fix your clothes a lot?"

"I used to," Delilah said. "These days I don't anymore, really."

"Oh, you should. You did an incredible job with it."

By now three women were surrounding her, admiring the work, and someone asked her for advice about fixing her pants. Delilah let herself carry on, feeling herself relaxing for the first time in a while. She hardly even felt the pain in her fingers. When a young man smiled at her, she had a momentary flash of panic, but reminded herself Brad wasn't there.

A woman named Rose called everyone to attention, thanking them all for coming. By that point Delilah's head was buzzing, and she realized Emily was no longer clutching her leg. It took her a few seconds to find the girl, sitting in the corner of the room with that woman, Anna, both of them drawing with crayons on a large page. Delilah smiled at the woman, who smiled back and waved at her. It was so nice to see how this woman loved kids. Ron was now fast asleep in his stroller, and Delilah could focus on the seminar.

Rose talked about a verse from the Bible. "Each one's work will become manifest, for the Day will disclose it, because it will be revealed by fire, and the fire will test what sort of work each one has done." She talked about the test and what it meant. A sort of trial. Delilah was unsure what the woman was going for. Her analysis of the verse seemed to be both too literal and somewhat long winded. But seeing how everyone listened in rapt silence, nodding, she forced herself to listen carefully, trying to be open minded.

Minutes and hours ticked by. Emily had fallen asleep, and Anna carried her to a couch. Delilah wanted to leave; it was getting really late. But every time Rose called for a break, people would surround Delilah, talking to her, asking her what *she* thought about the discussion. And when she answered, stuttering in unease, they all listened to her. Asking her questions. Discussing it with her.

When she finally checked the time, it was two in the morning.

"I really have to go," she told Rose, aghast.

"Why?" Rose frowned, confused.

"It's really late."

"But . . . the seminar continues tomorrow. You can sleep here. We have a bed for you and for the kids."

"I can't! I . . . Emily needs to go to school tomorrow. And . . . and . . ."

Rose touched her arm. "Please stay," she begged. "Tomorrow is a really important day. Father is talking tomorrow—you have to hear him. And then we can drop you back at your place in the afternoon."

Delilah didn't know what to say. She couldn't get an Uber right now, even if she tried.

"Okay, thank you," she finally said, embarrassed.

And Rose seemed so happy at her answer that Delilah felt a strange warm feeling spreading through her body.

◆ ◆ ◆

Moses watched Delilah as he spoke on the second day of the seminar. She kept shuffling in her seat and yawned twice. Once, he caught her checking the time on her phone. He made a mental note to tell Rose to collect the phones from all the participants later so that they were not distracted. At one point, when her baby cried, she got up to hold him, while Rose was talking. Even worse, she wiped the baby's snot with a crumpled Kleenex. She shoved the germ-ridden paper into her pocket and didn't go to wash her hands. Moses could imagine the germs writhing on her hands, crawling everywhere, spreading disease. She would have to learn.

Still, he had no second thoughts or doubts. The moment he'd set eyes on her, he felt as if he'd shed forty years of his life. A true gift from God.

He wanted her in his congregation.

As he talked about God's wrath and jealousy, his eyes kept flickering back to her body, his mind flooded with images. Was she still breastfeeding? Perhaps he should have one of the women find out.

Her eyes were bloodshot, of course. They'd finished late last night, and he'd made sure the participants were woken up at five thirty. They had a lot of content to cover in such a short seminar, and he'd found out long ago that exhaustion made people's minds more open to God's wisdom.

Later, he stepped away and watched as people broke off for lunch. Miriam and that new girl, Gretchen, both walked with Delilah, talking to her animatedly. They escorted her to the buffet, staying with her at all times. It was important, his flock knew, that the seminar's guests would be constantly entertained. Moses didn't want them to get lonely.

And he didn't want them to have time on their own to think.

". . . and like Father said, that verse from the book of Nahum is a direct instruction in the Bible for the second baptism," the woman was saying.

Delilah frowned at her. What was her name again? Miriam? Everything was fuzzy. She'd drunk much more than she was used to the night before, and she'd hardly slept. It had taken all of her will just to stay awake during Moses's speech. She'd understood fragments of it. Things he'd mentioned to her before, when she'd met him alone in the church. Things about God's justice. And vengeance.

She was uncomfortable with this constant talk about God's jealousy and vengeance. It completely contradicted everything she'd known about God's forgiveness and love. But Moses *did* point out God loved everyone. The vengeance and wrath thing was another aspect of this love . . . she tried connecting the lines of thought, but it all scattered, dissipating like smoke in the wind.

"Where's Ron?" she suddenly said, panicking. He'd been in his stroller by her side during Moses's talk, but now—

"He's over there with Anna," Miriam assured her. "See? Anna's really good with kids."

Delilah saw she was right. Ron was in Anna's arms, gurgling happily at Emily, who was singing a song for Anna. For a crazy second, Delilah wanted to dash over, snatch Ron from the woman's hands, grab Emily, and run away. But she was just being unkind. Anna clearly adored her children, and they really did get along well together.

"I had a great time," she said. "After lunch I think we'll go home."

"What? No, you have to stay," Gretchen said.

"Tomorrow we finally talk about the second baptism," Miriam said. "If you don't stay for that, everything else doesn't make sense."

"What *is* the second baptism?" Delilah asked.

"Father explains it best," Miriam said. "You really should stay for tomorrow."

"I can't," Delilah said. "We don't have any clothes, or anything—"

"We can take you back home later to grab a few things," Gretchen said. "It's no big deal."

"I'm really sorry, but—"

"I'll come too," Miriam said. "I can help you pack. I really want you to hear Father's speech about the second baptism."

Delilah kept arguing; she couldn't stay. The kids needed their baths, and their beds and . . . and . . . she had to clean the house . . . Brad would return on Monday . . .

You'll pay for that . . .

But they kept insisting, and now more people were telling her she *had* to stay for one more day. And her arguments fell apart—she was so exhausted already, and they were so persistent and so enthusiastic.

And so happy. She kept seeing how they smiled at each other. How they smiled at her. And they really did care about her. They liked her.

She felt guilty for not taking the lectures and discussions more seriously. After all, these people were all really excited about everything they'd been talking about. She hadn't been paying enough attention. She could stay for a bit more, maybe one more talk, and really *listen*. Back at school, she'd been a good student. She'd been the girl whose notes kids were always asking to copy. She used to have lovely hand-writing. Circular and elegant. And here she hadn't even opened the complimentary notebook they'd given her.

It was like she'd been living in the darkness for so long, and she was getting a glimpse of a faraway light. Maybe if she heard about the second baptism . . . maybe if she stayed with these people longer . . . and she could clean the house tomorrow, she could even work all night before Brad came home . . .

She didn't remember when she'd decided to stay, but at some point, it had happened.

Moses paced the room as he talked. His throat was parched. He wanted to sit down and rest for a bit.

He'd been talking for three and a half hours.

It was the final day of the seminar, the discussion of the second baptism. Two of the seminar's guests had left by now, exhausted by the endless religious discussions. Moses didn't care. They had paid the attendance fee. He didn't really care about the majority of his followers, all listening to him in silence. Sure, he wanted them to hear, to strengthen their resolve, to remind them of what they were doing.

But really, he was mostly talking only to one person. Delilah Eckert.

He knew so much more about her now. He'd gotten extensive reports from his followers. Miriam and Gretchen gave him a long list of topics they'd talked about. Anna told him everything Delilah's daughter told her about her parents. Rose, who'd taken Delilah's phone for the afternoon discussions, gave him a thorough report of Delilah's emails, chats, online search history, call history. He probably knew more about Delilah than she knew about herself.

"'You shall serve the Lord your God, and he will bless your bread and your water,'" Moses said, keeping his voice steady and slow. "'And I will take sickness away from among you. *None* shall miscarry or be barren in your land; I will fulfill the number of your days.'"

Delilah had had a miscarriage two years before, and it weighed on her mind. He added quotes about miscarriage and birth to his sermon, just like he made sure it touched the responsibility mothers had to their children and the wickedness of men who abused their wives.

An endless sermon, woven to lure one woman. It didn't really matter what he said, but the words were there. Miscarriage, abuse, wicked husbands, fear, protect, children, fellowship, care. Things she craved, and things she wanted to leave behind.

Moses never really had any difficulty talking. He had a near photographic memory and could easily recite whole chapters from the Bible by heart. He could also offer his own opinion and interpretation of them easily. From experience he knew an exhausted audience, lulled by a long sermon, was fertile ground. Their hearts were more accessible and open to wisdom.

He crossed the room again, pausing in the middle, turning to his listeners, still quoting Exodus. Delilah's eyes were glazed, the notebook in her lap open, but the pen was lax in her fingers. She hadn't written anything for over twenty minutes. She almost seemed like she was in a trance.

Which was what Moses had waited for.

He raised his voice, shifting from a slow rhythmic steady tone to a forceful, loud proclamation. "And the Bible tells us what we should do about these wicked men. The book of Matthew declares, 'I baptize you with water for repentance, but he who is coming after me is mightier than I, whose sandals I am not worthy to carry. He will baptize you with the Holy Spirit and fire.'"

Delilah sat and viewed the world through a thick haze.

She'd tried to listen, she *really* had. And Moses's sermon had interested her. He'd had so much to say about things she cared about. Things she *wanted*. Things she'd never talked to anyone about. She'd been mesmerized. For the first hour she'd written feverishly in her notebook, filling page after page after page.

But then exhaustion sank in. They'd gone to bed really late last night, too, and woke up at five thirty again. She hoped for a break, but Moses kept talking, and everyone listened in silence and awe. So she forced herself to keep listening, but the words merged together, blending into a strange, soothing blur. Soon, her mind emptied from thoughts about her discomfort, and tiredness, and her worry about Brad's return on the following day.

For the first time in what seemed like years, she was completely relaxed. She was surrounded by people who adored her and her children.

The room was warm, and her swollen fingers didn't hurt even though she'd been writing nonstop. She was almost floating.

Something penetrated her haze. A passionate, vigorous voice. It was Moses.

"'He will baptize you with the Holy Spirit and fire!'" Moses raised his hands, eyes blazing.

People around her were leaning forward, calling, "Amen!"

Delilah's heart beat wildly with excitement. Her breath quickened, her skin tingling.

"'His winnowing fork is in his hand, and he will clear his threshing floor and gather his wheat into the barn, but the chaff he will burn with unquenchable fire!'"

"Amen!" Some of them were standing now, raising their own hands. Delilah stood up without even noticing, as if a powerful force was pulling her upward.

"'Every tree therefore that does not bear good fruit is cut down and thrown into the fire!'"

"Amen!" Delilah was now shouting with the rest of them. Tears were running down her cheeks. Many of the others were weeping as well.

"It is said," Moses shouted, "that God helps those who help themselves. But what if God needs to punish the wicked? Does he only punish those who punish themselves?"

"No!" the crowd roared back.

"Who exacts God's vengeance?"

"Men!"

"Who is it that does his bidding, for a second baptism, a baptism of Holy Spirit and fire?"

"We do!"

And Delilah echoed, "We do," and felt a rush of euphoria and love for all those who surrounded her, and for this beautiful man who'd found her.

CHAPTER 11

"It's strange being here again," Carver said.

Abby nodded. Samantha's school, Christopher Columbus High, still hadn't recovered from the armed siege that had taken place there the month before. They'd managed to clean up the place, replacing the broken doors and slapping a fresh coat of paint here and there. But the library was still being renovated after the fire. And a brand-new metal detector in the entrance, as well as additional security cams, had been installed.

Abby visited the school every morning when she dropped off Sam, but Carver hadn't been back since that terrible day. He had his own share of memories from then and a few scars to show for it too.

They walked down the hallways alongside parents and pupils, toward the auditorium. By the auditorium's door stood a large framed photo of Carlos Ramirez, the teacher who had died during the hostage crisis. A memorial shrine stood underneath—a table covered with flowers, photos, and letters. Abby stopped in front of the table, regretting she hadn't thought of bringing flowers. She'd done what she could to get him out alive, but on some nights, she was still hounded by the what-ifs and the I-should-haves.

Probably guessing what was going through her mind, Carver put an arm around her shoulders. "Come on," he said softly. "Let's go inside and grab good seats."

They stepped into the dimly lit auditorium. Though they'd come twenty minutes early, the three front rows were already full. Abby had wanted to be in the front row for Sam. Now she would—

"Abby!"

It was Steve, waving at her from the first row. Of course. Steve was practically anal when it came to arriving on time. For him, half an hour too early was right on time. Often, when they'd been married, they'd show up to a social engagement with the hosts still in the shower or frantically tidying up before the other guests came.

"I saved a seat for you!" he called over the crowd.

She sighed, approaching him. He was sitting next to Vice Principal Pratchett, an empty seat to his left.

"Hey, Steve," she said.

"Good thing I showed up early," he said, smiling at her. "After all, it's Sam's big night."

"I showed up early too," Abby said. She hadn't meant to say that. She'd meant to thank him for thinking of her. Then again, the road to an argument with Steve was paved with good intentions.

"Sit down." He patted the seat next to him.

"Thanks for thinking of me, but—"

"Hey!" Steve's eyes landed on Carver. "You're Jonathan Carver! The hero of the day."

"Well, I'd say there was a lot of heroism to go around," Carver said, smiling uncomfortably. "If anyone was the real hero of that day, it was Samantha—"

"Aw, you're just being modest." Steve laughed, standing up to shake Carver's hand. "Sam told me you dove into the fire to save her. That takes guts. So you're like the guest of honor or something?"

"No, actually, I'm here with Abby."

"Oh." Steve frowned, confused. Then, his eyes widened. "Oh!"

A year ago, Steve had met a guy Abby had been dating briefly, when he was picking up the kids. And Abby had instantly noted his assessing stare, the automatic comparison. His patronizing smile had indicated his replacement didn't match up to how Steve thought of himself.

Now his face morphed as he probably made the same mathematical comparison, realizing Carver was *dating* his ex-wife. And how did Carver rank on the Steve-o-meter?

Well, he was the guy who, like Steve put it, dove into the fire to save Steve's daughter. While Steve himself was being mostly useless. So there was that.

The expression on her ex-husband's face was so priceless that Abby regretted she didn't have her phone in hand to take a photo. She could have printed it and maybe framed it. But unfortunately, she would have to settle for just remembering this lovely moment.

"Um . . . great! That's great." Steve's smile was frozen on his face, and he kept nodding.

"We need two seats," Abby said, "so I think we'll sit in the back."

"Oh, no need." The vice principal stood up. "You can have my seat."

"No, really, it's no big deal," Abby said.

"Nonsense." The vice principal smiled at her and left.

"Okay, that's nice of her." Steve's grin had lost its distinct shine. "Um . . . oh. I'll move to the left so you two can sit together." The words seemed to cause him physical pain.

For once, Abby felt a tender spot for him. He'd saved her a seat, and now he was stuck feeling like a third wheel next to Abby and her big heroic date. She sat down next to him and put her hand on his arm. "Thanks for saving me a seat, Steve," she said, smiling at him. "That was really thoughtful of you."

He returned her smile. "Sure."

Her phone rang.

"Oh, I should mute it," she said, taking it out of her bag. The number flashed on her screen, and she identified it as one from Wyoming.

"I have to take this," she told Carver. "Be back in a minute."

He stared at her in horror, realizing she was leaving him alone with Steve. Well, both of them would have to deal.

She stepped out of the auditorium. "Hello?"

"Lieutenant Mullen? This is Chief Powell."

The chief of the Douglas police. "Oh, hey. Thanks for getting back to me." She'd left him a message detailing what she'd found out from Gretchen Wood's sister.

"Listen, Lieutenant, I got your message, and like I already told Bentley, we will let you know if there's any progress."

"You are absolutely right," Abby said, checking the time. She didn't have too long to coddle the man's feelings. "But I wanted to make sure you're aware of this lead, because Maegan said—"

"There is no lead." Powell interrupted her. "So Gretchen Wood went to church a few times before setting fire to Yates's house. I fail to see how this has any bearing on the case."

"Well, as I've mentioned in my message, Maegan identified Moses Wilcox as the one who gave the sermon in that religious group—"

"Our detectives talked to Maegan *again*, and she's no longer sure she identified him correctly. They also talked to the local preacher of the Lily Fellowship Church, and he very clearly stated he has never seen a man answering to the description of Moses Wilcox."

"The Lily Fellowship Church?" Abby said, confused.

"That's the church Maegan talked about? The one that Gretchen Wood went to."

"It's not a church, it's a small religious group, probably a cult—"

"The Lily Fellowship Church is definitely not a cult, Lieutenant. It's been here for years. They're also running a youth camp for troubled teens not far from town. They've done an amazing job with some of the kids who go there."

She frowned, confused. There had to be some mistake. Maybe the detectives had misunderstood Maegan. Or perhaps Moses simply used the church as a venue to preach in, or—

"My detectives wasted a whole afternoon on this wild-goose chase," Powell said. "While we need to be interviewing acquaintances of Gretchen Wood, reviewing footage of traffic cameras, searching her favorite hangouts. I'm sure it's different in New York, but here I have two men to do pretty much everything. I won't ask you again. Stop interfering with our investigation."

The line went dead.

For a few seconds Abby just stood outside, staring at the memorial shrine of Carlos Ramirez. Someone had placed a lit candle in the center. Abby stared at the tiny flame and imagined how the candle could easily topple, setting fire to the numerous photos and letters scattered around it. Burning everything to the ground.

Swallowing, she walked over to the shrine and, glancing around her, blew the candle out.

She returned to her seat. Both Carver and Steve were trying desperately to hold some sort of conversation. They were talking, she gathered, about the upholstery of the chairs, which Steve thought had been replaced recently.

"Sorry," she said in a low voice as she sat down between them. "Work." She muted the phone. Then, she quickly opened the browser app on her phone and searched for "Lily Fellowship Church."

The first result led her to a church's website. The Lily Fellowship Church, according to their "About" section, was a religious Christian organization intended to awaken and encourage people all over the country to their role in the kingdom of God. They apparently had various programs focusing on troubled youths, on homeless shelters, and on leadership programs. She skimmed through dozens of gushing testimonials and images of teenagers renovating houses, giving away food and clothing, and playing with little kids in the street.

Did the church in Douglas belong to this organization? Could Moses have hidden within this Christian institution?

The lights around her dimmed, and the crowd murmurs slowly diminished. Abby put her phone back in her bag. She would investigate this more thoroughly later.

Samantha and her friend Fiona stepped onto the stage, and Abby clapped with the rest of the crowd. A few seconds later a third boy joined them—Abby knew his name was Peter, a guitar player. The previous guitarist Sam had played with had never returned to school after that violent day.

Fiona settled behind the drums. Sam took out the violin from her case. But then, to Abby's surprise, instead of playing, she approached the microphone.

"Hi," she said, her voice trembling slightly. "Thank you all for coming. As you all know, a month ago, our school was attacked by an armed group. During the attack, some of us were . . . hurt." Her voice dissipated to silence, and she shut her eyes.

Abby's throat clenched. She wanted to get on that stage, to hug her daughter, to tell everyone the concert was canceled because it was too painful for her little girl. She grabbed the arms of her chair, willing herself to stay put.

After a few seconds, Sam wiped her eyes with the back of her hand. "Sorry. Our teacher, Carlos Ramirez, was killed in the attack. A few of us . . . pupils and teachers, are still having a hard time with the memories. It's sometimes difficult to sleep or to stay in one room for too long. Um . . . if any of you are having a hard time with it, let us know, because we have group meetings where we've been talking about it, and it's been helpful." She let out a shuddering breath. "Anyway, one of the things Fiona and I have been doing was working on some music we wrote. And we wanted to play it for you. The first piece is called 'No Way Out.'"

They began playing.

Abby had heard their new music in fragments, as Sam practiced at home. But she'd never heard them play it together. They started with drumbeats, steady, like a heartbeat. And then Sam joined in with a series of sharp notes on her electric violin. The rhythm quickened, the guitar joining in, everything cascading into an intense, turbulent flurry. Then a sudden pause, stretching for long, too long, Sam's eyes staring ahead, wide and empty, with a single drumbeat every couple of seconds.

No way out.

Abby glimpsed what Sam had felt when she wrote this. The feeling of being trapped, terrified to even move, danger lurking in every corner. She could imagine what her daughter had gone through over the course of that day.

But earlier memories bubbled to the surface.

As a little girl, running down a corridor full of smoke. Hearing the screams of her parents, and of others, her family. An explosion, the searing burn in her neck. Her fingers automatically went up to the old scar.

When it ended, everyone clapped wildly, and Abby joined a few seconds later, almost too dazed to react. She was weeping. Sam's face, on stage, was wet with tears as well, her lips twisted with a hint of a smile.

CHAPTER 12

Saturday, June 11, 2005

The nightmares had woken him up last night, and he'd stayed awake half the night, reading the Gospel of Luke. Now, as he stood outside, watching his group of followers painting the local church's walls, Moses's head began to pound.

He lowered the brim of his baseball cap, the sunlight making his headache even worse. He debated going back to his room in the local motel. But he needed to be seen by the locals. This was all about community ties and—

"Mr. Williams? Can I offer you some water?"

Father Porter joined him in the shade, offering him a paper cup. Moses thanked him and sipped from the tepid water.

"They're doing incredible work," Porter said. "I still can't believe you managed to get all these young people here so early on a weekend. And you didn't even pay them!"

"Charity is its own reward," Moses said softly.

Porter laughed. "That's a nice sentiment, but I can preach about charity all year, and I never get this kind of response."

Moses smiled politely. Of course Porter wouldn't get as much response, with his weak chin, and high-pitched voice, and slow, meandering sermons. The man had no idea how to talk to people. How to make them really *listen*.

"I'm surprised to see you out here in the sun," Porter said. "How is your . . . condition?"

Moses tensed. Did he hear slight skepticism in the man's voice? Did Porter perhaps hint that Moses's skin condition was a lie?

Whenever he went out in public these days, he wore a baseball cap and large sunglasses to hide his face. He did his best to limit his time outside to the evenings, to the dark. All this, justified by his so-called skin condition.

It would take just one person to see the resemblance between him and that famous photo of Moses Wilcox, always shown in documentaries about the Wilcox Cult Massacre. And then, his frequent nightmares would come true. The police would surround him, carry him away. There would be no smoke and flames to camouflage him as he escaped this time.

But Porter's face seemed full of sympathy, and Moses doubted the man had enough intelligence to hide his suspicions if he had them.

He cleared his throat. "Today I feel a bit better. And it's worth the discomfort. I love watching my people as they show kindness."

Porter smiled and nodded emphatically. "If there is anything I can do for your small community, don't hesitate to ask."

You could tell your congregation to come to our seminars. You could ask them to give us a monthly donation. You could contribute to our funds yourself.

There were any number of ways Porter could help their small group, but Moses knew that asking for them would undo all the goodwill he had managed to accumulate these past few months. Not yet.

"We appreciate the sentiment, but there's no need," Moses said.

"Will you come to church tomorrow?"

"Of course." That was the whole point. So that Porter could thank them publicly, and Moses's followers could use the friendly atmosphere to invite some of the parishioners to their next seminar.

"Excuse me," Moses said as he saw Anna approaching. He crossed the street to talk to her in private.

The young woman had joined his group almost a year before. At first, Moses had pursued her because she was the editor of a local paper. He'd figured some positive local press would help convince people to sign up for the seminars. But since then, he'd found that Anna had a phenomenal knack for administration and finance. Under her careful management, they'd managed to reduce their expenses by almost half. She was the one who suggested the communal bank account to which all their working members donated part of their paychecks. *And* she managed to get some of their groups the occasional job. By this point, Moses found her invaluable. She made him think of Abihail. Was his daughter as talented as this girl? As motivated? One day, when Abihail returned to his flock, he would find out.

"How are we doing?" he asked.

"We'll be done by the afternoon," Anna said. "And we'll still have a lot of the paint left, so we can save that for the compound."

"Paint," Moses said bitterly. Once, he had managed a congregation that cycled thousands of dollars. Now, scoring free paint was an achievement.

Anna seemed to sense his frustration. "Tomorrow we'll reap the rewards. I think we can get at least five sign-ups to our seminar. That's a thousand dollars. And some of them will agree to add a monthly donation—"

"It's not enough!" Moses snapped.

He could feel the fury building up inside him. He almost slapped Anna.

If they kept doing this—begging for donations, feeling thankful for every scrap thrown their way—they would never get far. Last month two people had left the group, as easily as if they were quitting a job. And if he couldn't make this work, if people kept leaving, he would be left alone. Just like it had been those few years after the fire. A shepherd without a flock. Spending his time in fear, hiding from the cops.

Anna stared at him in surprise. "We're doing what we can." Her voice was shrill.

She shouldn't talk to him like that. She was forgetting her place. He should punish her. He clenched his fists.

And terror blossomed in his chest. If he did that, she would leave. He would be helpless without her. She would write about him in the paper. With a photo. Someone would recognize him. And the police would show up.

"No," he said, his voice trembling. "You're right. We're doing what we can."

CHAPTER 13

Abby lay in her bed, eyes open wide, Carver's arm over her waist.

He'd come over after Sam's event. Sensing Abby was in a fragile state, he'd been comforting and calm. She'd spent most of the evening in his arms, drawing strength from his presence. It had been lovely, and she hadn't wanted him to go. He'd ended up staying the night.

Now she realized that she was really used to sleeping alone in her bed.

Carver was the best man she could hope for, and she was falling for him. It was a shining beacon of positivity in her life. *But* it also meant she couldn't sleep diagonally. And during the night, she sometimes liked to switch the pillow she was using with the other pillow, getting its fresh fluffiness. Which she couldn't do now, because Carver, apparently, also liked sleeping with a pillow. Also, she had a king-size blanket, which was supposed to be enough for two people, so she wasn't entirely clear on why she had just a tiny piece of it. Did Carver really need to mummify himself when he slept? Was he a descendant of the ancient pharaohs or something? And yeah, he didn't really snore, but he *breathed*, which, while she recognized it was probably necessary, was still yet another thing she had to get used to.

So after that warm, snuggly sleep that followed their lovemaking, she'd woken up at four in the morning and couldn't fall back to sleep.

Finally she decided she might as well make herself useful and gently removed Carver's arm off her, then slid out of bed. She glanced back at him and smiled. His bare shoulder peeked from underneath the blanket, his arm still outstretched to her side of the bed. His face was so peaceful as he slept.

She would definitely get used to sleeping with him in her bed. It was worth it.

After putting on her robe, she padded to his side and gently kissed his cheek. Then she stepped out of her room, went to the kitchen, and put on a pot of coffee. While the coffee slowly trickled into the carafe, she switched on her computer.

She carefully scoured the Lily Fellowship Church website, then searched for other references to the church online. The organization was mentioned a handful of times by people praising it for the work its parishioners did with troubled youths. A mother in Kentucky wrote that her daughter's life and soul had been saved by the church's care. A man shared a local clothing-donation day organized by the Lily Fellowship Church in Frankfort, Indiana. She checked the church's website again, finding a list of people working for the church, their portraits all smiling joyfully from the screen. They all seemed quite young.

She would have to fly back to Wyoming, interview them herself, she realized with a sinking heart. And the local police would make it difficult.

She opened Google Maps and created a new map titled *Lily Fellowship Church Locations*. She went over the online references, adding a pin for each reference that she could link to a location. The mother in Kentucky never mentioned a location, but her Facebook page had several photos she'd posted from her town, in Stanford. And here was another mention of the church on Facebook, in Lewistown, Montana.

Combing the social networks, she managed to identify accounts for the people who were listed as church employees. And from their accounts she managed to pinpoint three additional locations. Then she scoured their friends lists, finding shared friends, checking their own accounts—and here was another one who posted about a local picnic the Lily Fellowship Church was organizing. Another pin. And another. And another.

Finally, she had thirteen locations on her map. She cross-referenced the map with the locations they had for the fires.

Two matches. And two additional arsons were less than ten miles from Lily Fellowship Church locations.

She poured herself a cup of coffee, thinking. Suppose Moses worked for the Lily Fellowship Church in some capacity. In all likelihood, managing a group of people who all volunteered in the church. And they traveled between the branches of the church, all over the country. Except Moses began doing his own thing. Slowly twisting his volunteers' minds to make them his own. And then, once he had amassed a significant following, he'd gotten bolder. Burning houses. Burning people.

Where would he go to next?

His arsons created a pattern of sorts on the map. Indiana, Tennessee, Iowa, Kansas, Wyoming. Moving between states that were relatively close to each other, never more than a day's drive away. And never staying in the same state once he burned someone.

Of the church locations she marked, three were within a reasonable driving distance from Douglas, Wyoming, where Jimmie Yates had been burned to death. One was in Saint George, Utah. A pretty long drive, but within limits. But the city was too big. Moses liked small remote towns. The second, Fort Lupton in Colorado, was much closer and quite small—but maybe too close to Denver. He wouldn't want the Denver PD on his tail.

The third was Rigby, Idaho. Tiny town, quite remote. A woman named Katie Tate mentioned the incredible youth shelter that the Lily Fellowship Church had built there.

Maybe Abby didn't need to fly back to Wyoming. It was better to go to Idaho, where possibly, Moses Wilcox was hiding.

CHAPTER 14

"Let me explain."

Zoe's shoulders tightened as Agent Cesar Griffiths uttered these three words. The man infuriated her. If he was indeed a man. His girth gave his movement a sort of waddle, and he pouted his thick lips in a way that reminded her of a duck's beak. Add to that the fact that his voice had a certain croak. It was the first time Zoe had met the living example of something that looked like a duck, walked like a duck, and sounded like a duck . . . and yet she was pretty sure he was no duck.

She must have let out an impatient snort, because Tatum shot her a warning stare from his seat. She clenched her teeth and forced herself to listen.

"There are several criteria that define a cult. There is something we call 'milieu control.'" Griffiths used air quotes as he said that and spoke those words much more slowly.

Cesar Griffiths was the FBI's cult expert. Or rather, as far as Zoe could figure out, he was an FBI analyst who'd been immersed in the NXIVM cult case and emerged with an impromptu "expert" title. It had taken him three days to find the time to meet with them. She'd been impatient to work with him, because they obviously needed cult expertise to handle this case and create a proper profile for Moses Wilcox.

But instead of sitting down with Tatum and Zoe, he let them sit by the table as he waddled back and forth, lecturing to them about cult mentality. He did seem to know quite a lot about cults, she had to give him that much.

"Agent Griffiths," she interrupted him now. "We should start discussing how this is relevant to the current case."

Griffiths paused for a second and smiled at her. Just half of his thick lips really smiled, the other half remaining flat. "I was hoping to give you a basic understanding of the machinations of a cult before giving you my final conclusions."

"Your final conclusions?" Tatum asked. "What do you mean by that?"

"Well, I've studied your reports, and I outlined the motives driving this cult and its leader."

"The whole point of this meeting was to do this together," Zoe said, her face flushing with annoyance.

"I'll be more than happy to discuss my findings," Griffiths said. "Your knowledge from the field might help."

"Oh, it *might* help?" Zoe asked sharply.

"What are your findings?" Tatum asked. "We can start from there."

"Well." Griffiths sighed. "I was about to explain that cults typically revolve around fear and shame. These are the two core tools at the leader's disposal. And from what I've seen from your reports, it looks like the leader's manner of keeping his followers in control is by demonstrating to them what happens to those who walk astray. In this case, being burned alive. As you've noted, the victims are tied as if they're praying. Praying for what? For forgiveness. Let me explain—"

"You think Moses Wilcox burns people to scare his own followers?" Zoe frowned. "How does that align with anything we've seen?"

"Death by burning is the worst possible punishment. A threat he wields over them to maintain his control."

"One of Moses Wilcox's most ardent followers set herself on fire in New York," Tatum pointed out. "Why would she do that if it's a punishment?"

"She probably convinced herself she deserved this punishment. You wouldn't believe how twisted people's thought process is once they've been sufficiently brainwashed."

"But if fear and shame are how he keeps his cult in check, why would people even join?" Zoe asked.

Griffiths turned to face her. "Well, why do people even join a cult? Let me explain. There are several psychological models. In this case, I favor the 'psychodynamic model.'" Air quotes, talking slowly. "The individual joins because of what they perceive the group does for them. Namely, an answer to death anxiety. In my field, many believe everyone suffers from death anxiety, either consciously or unconsciously."

"It's my field as well. I have a PhD in forensic psychology," Zoe said through gritted teeth. "And I'm familiar with the concept of death anxiety."

"Of course. But Agent Gray isn't." Griffiths half smiled at her again.

"You were looking straight at Zoe when you talked," Tatum pointed out. "And frankly, the concept is pretty self-explanatory."

Griffiths cleared his throat. "Anyway, what I was going to say is that Moses Wilcox provides a simple answer to this death anxiety. Or rather, as we call it, 'thanatophobia.'"

Air quotes yet again. Zoe imagined how it would feel to grab his fingers and bend them back.

"The word comes from the Greek *thanos*, for death. Sigmund Freud, one of the founders in my field—"

"*Our* field," Zoe interjected. "And I believe Agent Gray knows who Freud is too."

"Yes." Griffiths frowned, her interruption cutting his flow. "Um . . . what I was about to conjecture is that it is likely that Moses Wilcox targets two groups of people. Men with average or lower intelligence and women."

"I'm sorry?" Zoe snapped.

He chuckled. "That came out wrong. I was about to say that we're in a male-dominated society, and women have already been conditioned to assume—"

"Are you going to explain to me how being a woman in a male-dominated society feels?" Zoe stared at him in disbelief.

"I was explaining it to Agent Gray."

Zoe turned to face Tatum. "This isn't working for me. I'll end up killing him."

Tatum nodded. "Yeah. This isn't working for me either. Thanks, Griffiths. It's been illuminating."

"But I haven't shared the rest of my conclusions," Griffiths said, annoyed.

"Email them to us." Tatum got up and put a hand on Griffiths's shoulder, propelling him to the door. "Make sure you use small words so we understand."

He slammed the door after the man and sat back down.

"I want points for self-control," Zoe said, still trying to calm her breathing.

"You get all the points." Tatum grinned at her. "I thought you were about to tear his throat out with your teeth."

Zoe took out her phone and opened her mailbox. "It's a new shirt, I didn't want to stain it—Oh!"

"What is it?"

"We got an email from Abby Mullen." Zoe skimmed the email, then, tensing, read it more slowly. "It looks like she might have linked Moses to something called the Lily Fellowship Church."

"How didn't we catch this?" Tatum frowned as he read the email on his own phone.

"Because we were looking in the wrong place." Zoe gritted her teeth. "Listening to Mr. Expert here with his psychodynamic model. She linked it through Gretchen Wood. She joined Moses's cult. Mullen talked to her sister, Maegan."

"She says she's checking out one of the branches," Tatum said. "We should look into the branch in Douglas, figure out what Wilcox was doing there and what his position in the church is."

"And follow up with the church's administration," Zoe said. "If he's working for the church, it shouldn't be difficult to find out his current posting."

Tatum stood up and walked to the door. "I'll go talk to the chief. If we're lucky, we might have Moses Wilcox in custody by the end of the day."

CHAPTER 15

Delilah nestled Ron's head to her breast and leaned back sleepily. She'd been nodding off constantly for the past few days. It was hard to sleep at the farm, where at any given moment people wanted her to come and listen to a certain sermon, or help them figure out how to design a pamphlet, or asked her to fix a pair of pants, or a shirt. Delilah had been used to a completely different pace back home. Hours of staying in the same room, as silent as she could, while Brad sat in the living room, staring at the TV. Or spending the entire afternoon watching the kids outside in the yard because Brad wanted some peace and quiet. Days stretched into an infinity of intermingled boredom and fear.

Not here. Here, everything was exciting, and new, and frantic. She found herself hurrying, trying to do more, to make herself useful. And they were happy to get any help she could give. By now, between sermons and prayers, she was helping with the meals, and cleaning, and sewing. And people kept touching her and smiling at her and telling her how indispensable she was.

It was wonderful.

But now, finally taking a few minutes for herself and for Ron, she suddenly realized she'd hardly had any time with her kids. Most of the time they were with Anna, who seemed to be glad to spend every minute she could with them. Which Delilah really appreciated, but still, she should have been taking care of her children, not letting a stranger do it. Guiltily, she admitted to herself that the only reason she'd taken these precious minutes off was because she'd been bursting with milk.

Like most of the rooms in the shelter, this room sported two double bunk beds with blue-gray diamond-patterned bedsheets. Delilah sat on the bottom bed across from the window, which looked out onto a snow-covered field.

Emily was lying on the floor, drawing on some paper, humming to herself. She now had her crayons. Delilah had brought the box from their home. Along with everything else.

After the seminar had ended, Rose and Anna had taken Delilah home. But instead of cleaning the house for Brad, she'd packed. All of Emily's and Ron's clothes. Some of Emily's favorite books and toys. Things she'd need for Ron—diapers, bottles, pacifiers, ointments . . . the more she packed, the more it seemed impossible. How could she possibly pack up her life in a few bags? If it weren't for Rose and Anna, who helped her through it, she would have given up. And then they went back to the farm to stay there. At first, she was terrified, knowing Brad would be back. He'd be furious, and he'd come looking for her, breaking down the door, and she'd pay for that, she'd seriously pay for that.

But he didn't show up. And now, after hiding for two days, she realized she wasn't as worried. He couldn't find her. And Rose had told her that they would soon leave Rigby. Leave Brad behind forever.

The back of her palms prickled. Her skin was getting dry. They used a very strong soap here in the youth shelter, and the people in the congregation all washed their hands frequently, encouraging her to do the same. It made sense, after all: they lived in tight proximity, and it was important to do what they could to mitigate the chance of catching a cold. Delilah wished they did the same in Emily's school. The amount of times her daughter came home with a cold or a virus, almost instantly transferring it to Delilah and Ron . . .

She shifted Ron to the other nipple, and settled back, letting herself drift sleepily away, just for a few minutes.

"Mommy, look!"

She woke up with a start, wiping her mouth. Ron was still feeding hungrily. How long had she been out? Must have been no more than five minutes, but she'd been fast asleep. She blinked at Emily, who was waving her drawing in front of her.

"What did you draw there, sweetie?"

"It's us!" Emily showed her the drawing, a bunch of stick figures standing on grass. "See? That's you, and Ronnie, and me, and Anna, and Daddy, and Father."

"Daddy . . . and Father?" Delilah's mind was foggy. "You mean Moses?"

"Anna says I should call him Father," Emily said, with a slightly rebuking tone. "She said it's more repsect . . . rescept . . ."

"Respectful?"

"I know the word, Mommy."

"I know you do, sweetie." Delilah stared at the drawing. The figure representing Moses was much bigger than the rest, and Emily had gone to great care coloring his hair and his body. Unlike the rest of them, he wasn't a simple stick figure. "It's very pretty. And is this a bird?"

"No, it's my angel brother."

"I thought this was Ron." Delilah pointed at the little figure she was holding in the drawing.

"Yes. That's Ronnie, and *that's* my angel brother."

"Okay." Delilah yawned. She really was exhausted. "It's a very nice drawing."

"Daddy's sad in the drawing, because he's not with us anymore."

"I can see that." He had a frowny face, while the rest of them had smiley faces. Anna had pretty black hair, while the stick figure representing Delilah barely had two straight yellow lines to signify her own hair. Delilah did her best not to read into that.

"When is Daddy coming to live with us?" Emily asked.

"I don't know if he will, sweetie. I think he prefers to stay at home."

"Why?"

"I don't think he'd like it very much here."

"Yes he will. *I* like it here. And Ron likes it here. And I want him to meet Anna and Father."

Delilah sighed. "Maybe in a few days, we'll see. What's that you drew around yourself?" Yellow and orange curly lines surrounded Emily's own stick figure.

"That's my baptism!"

"Your baptism?" Delilah repeated numbly.

"Yes. Anna said that sometimes we do a baptism for people, and it's very important."

"You were already baptized once, sweetie," Delilah said, tensing. "You don't need another baptism. And they don't do it to kids."

"Anna said they sometimes do. When will Ron grow more teeth?"

"I . . . uh . . . soon. Sweetie, when did Anna say—"

"I have a hundred teeth. Anna showed me how to brush them. Can I teach Ron how to brush his teeth?"

"Yes, of course. When Anna talked about the baptism—"

"Because if you don't brush them, germs can get in your mouth and take all your teeth away." Emily's eyes widened. "What do they do with them, Mommy?"

"Did Anna tell you that as well?"

The door opened, and Rose bustled in. Embarrassed, Delilah tried to cover herself, and Ron cried in frustration.

"There you are," Rose said. "We're about to start cooking dinner. Can you give us a hand?"

"Uh . . . sure, I'll need one more minute."

"No problem." Rose smiled at her.

She wasn't about to leave. Ron was still crying, trying to get to her nipple. Finally giving up, Delilah raised her shirt, and Ron resumed feeding.

"Ron is so big for his age," Rose said.

"He is? I don't know, the doctor said he's in the fortieth percentile."

Rose snorted derisively. "Doctors. What do they even know? I bet they're used to weighing babies that are fed only with fattening formulas."

"I guess so."

"I really admire you for breastfeeding. I had a hard time."

"Oh." Delilah had no idea Rose was a mother. "How old is your kid?"

"She should be five by now." Rose blinked.

Delilah raised her eyebrows. "You've been away from her?"

"For now. But in a few months she'll join us. Once the school year ends." Rose cleared her throat. "Does the breastfeeding interfere with your period? Mine took months until it returned to normal."

Delilah was still getting used to the personal questions she was being asked. The congregation was a tight bunch, and they seemed to know everything about each other. But Delilah was a private person, and the probing question made her tighten up. "It did at first, but by now it's almost back to normal."

"Yeah? When was the last time you had your period?"

"I don't know. A few days ago, I guess."

"Mine was three weeks ago. One of the great things about the congregation is we buy all the feminine products in bulk, so it's much cheaper. When was yours? We need to update the monthly requisition order."

"Uh . . ." Delilah glanced at Emily, who had resumed drawing. "I guess it started last week."

"What, on Monday?"

"Yeah, or Tuesday."

"Cool." Rose gave her a warm smile. "You're lucky it's back to normal."

Delilah exhaled, smiling back. It was so pleasant being smiled at. Finally, Ron pulled back, and Delilah hurriedly adjusted herself. She placed Ron on her shoulder to burp him and followed Rose.

Emily hopped to her feet. "Where are you going, Mommy?"

"To help fix dinner. You want to help us?"

"No. I'll go show Anna my drawing."

"I'd be happy if you helped us, sweetie."

"No, I want to show this to Anna." Emily skipped down the hallway.

Delilah stared at her, feeling anxious. She should talk to Anna. Emily was obviously too young for these religious teachings and was misunderstanding what Anna was telling her. Maybe Delilah should ask Moses if—

"Coming?" Rose asked.

"Yeah." She followed Rose down the stairs. She slowed down as she heard a man raising his voice. It was Richard, a hulking congregation member who seemed to be in charge of general maintenance.

"I told you," Richard said, half shouting. "There's no one like that here. You're in the wrong place."

A chill struck Delilah's heart. This was it. What she'd been terrified of.

Brad had found her. Any minute now he would barge in past Richard, tearing down the hallways, screaming for her. She wouldn't be able to hide. Even if she did, he would find Emily.

Unable to stop herself, she crept closer and peered around the corner at the doorway.

A wave of relief washed over her. It wasn't Brad at all. It was a small blonde woman, her hair pulled back in a ponytail, revealing a pair of cute protruding ears. The woman looked up at the looming Richard, smiling warmly.

"I'm sorry," she said. "It seems like I made you angry. This *is* the youth shelter of the Lily Fellowship Church, right?"

Delilah turned away and walked to the kitchen. Moses stood in the entrance, behind the door, perfectly still. Delilah nodded at him, but he didn't even seem to notice her. His entire focus was on the discussion in the doorway, his jaw clenched tight. Briefly, Delilah wondered who the woman was. But did it matter? She wasn't Brad.

Brad was about to be left behind. Forever.

CHAPTER 16

Abby kept the smile on her face. It was her best one. The straight-from-the-heart, innocent, warm smile she practiced regularly.

The large man in the doorway didn't budge.

She'd had ample opportunity to second-guess herself on the way, flying across the country on what amounted to a hunch. After all, she had no reason to think she'd found all the branches of the Lily Fellowship Church. And even if she had, it was more than possible that Moses occasionally took his followers to locations that had no church representation. Abby had no real idea what the nature of the relationship between Moses and the church was. Was he an employee? A volunteer? Or, what seemed more likely, one of the church's pastors?

It didn't matter. She'd sent an email outlining the connection she'd found between Moses and the church to Zoe Bentley and Tatum Gray. So even if this particular foray resulted in nothing, they would be able to use this lead to do a more thorough search. The FBI had ample resources to locate all of the Lily Fellowship Church branches and find out if Moses worked for them.

But since she was here, the least she could do was talk to the person in charge of this youth shelter and see if they'd ever set eyes on Moses Wilcox.

Except it appeared she couldn't even get through the door.

"I'm sorry," she told the man for the third time. "It seems like we started out on the wrong foot. All I want is to talk to the person in charge for a few minutes."

"They're not available," the man rumbled. He had a voice like an avalanche. "Do you want to leave a phone number? They'll call you once they have time."

"I have a flight to catch tomorrow morning," she said, injecting desperation in her tone. "How can I get in touch with them?" Let him see the problem from her point of view.

He shrugged. "Can't say."

Apparently, he had no desire to see the problem from her point of view. She should have established a better rapport with him before trying that, but she was tired from her trip and feeling impatient. And frankly, sometimes she wanted it to be enough that she was a cute woman with a friendly smile. Not this time, apparently.

Well, she was far from giving up. "It's getting cold, and—"

"What's going on, Richard?" a woman asked behind the burly man—Richard, apparently.

"This lady wants to talk to the person in charge," Richard said.

"I can talk to her, it's all right."

"But—"

"I assure you, it's fine."

Richard turned to look at the woman, who gave him a tiny nod. He moved away from the door. The woman was about forty, her black hair cascading over her shoulders. Her blue eyes crinkled as she smiled at Abby. She stood hand in hand with a little blonde girl who stared at Abby with curiosity. The little girl held a drawing in her free hand.

"My name is Anna," the woman said. "Please, follow me."

She led Abby inside. Down the hall, Abby could hear the clanging of cutlery, some people talking, a cheerful laugh. Anna led her in the opposite direction, still holding the little girl's hand, opening the door to a small office.

"Sorry about Richard," she said. "He gets overzealous. This is a youth shelter, and we have some abused kids here. Their parents sometimes show up, and we've had unpleasant encounters."

"That's okay," Abby said. "I've worked with abused kids myself. I completely understand."

Anna sat behind the desk, gesturing to one of the chairs in front of her. Abby sat down. The little girl stood close to Anna.

"So, how can I help you?" Anna asked.

Abby had considered this thoroughly. Whipping out her badge would get her nowhere. And any approach that included accusing a church employee of any wrongdoing would make Anna defensive and hostile. Abby wanted information, and she wanted them to know that Moses was dangerous. But she had to do it carefully. She gave her an embarrassed laugh. "I really hope you *can* help me—it's kind of a long shot."

Anna automatically returned a smile. "That's okay, no judgment here." She turned to the girl. "Emily, honey, go to the kitchen and join the others, okay? It's dinnertime soon."

"Is there fish?" the girl piped.

"I don't think so, not today."

"Good. I don't like fish."

Anna grinned at the girl, who ran out of the room.

"She's adorable," Abby said. "I have a daughter, but she's a bit older. I still remember how cute she was at this age, though."

"She's wonderful," Anna agreed with a grin. "So you were saying?"

"It's . . . my father," Abby said. "We kind of lost touch, and I wanted to reconnect. And someone told me he might be working in the Lily Fellowship Church."

"Oh?"

Abby gazed mournfully at the wall, letting her eyes glaze. "Last time we talked I was . . . very harsh. We have a complicated relationship, you see? You know what it's like, working with the kids here."

Anna nodded softly.

"And I'm worried about him," Abby said. "I'd really like to see him, to know that he's okay. Maybe apologize." She wiped a single tear from her cheek. Crying at will was a useful talent.

"What's his name?"

Abby let out a long breath. "Moses, but I'm not sure if he goes by that name here. He's changed his name before." She took out her phone and opened the blurry shot she had of Wilcox. She handed it to Anna. "This is what he looks like."

Anna took the phone from her hand and stared at the image, frowning. Abby glanced around her. The desk was meticulously clean, holding only a landline phone, a keyboard, a mouse, and a computer screen facing away from her. The only piece of clutter was the drawing that little Emily had left behind on the desk. A few stick figures standing together, a classic family. Abby could identify a mother holding a baby, and standing next to her, two girls and a boy. The father was much more pronounced in the drawing. Everyone was smiling except for the boy, who seemed unhappy. Emily herself was easy to identify in the drawing. She'd drawn bright yellow and orange lines around herself.

"I'm afraid I've never seen him before," Anna said regretfully, handing her the phone. "But let me check our employee records. Moses, you said?"

"That's right."

Anna fiddled with the mouse and keyboard for a while, then carefully scanned the screen, tongue protruding between her teeth as she concentrated. "We have one Moses working for the church, in our branch in Ohio. But he's twenty-two. Obviously not the man you're looking for."

"Any idea how else I could check?"

Anna thought for a moment. "Send me that image. I'll ask around, maybe send an email. If he works for the church, someone will let me know." She gave Abby her email address.

Abby quickly sent her the email. "Thank you so much."

"Sure. You said you were worried about him. What are you worried about, exactly?"

Abby cleared her throat. "My father used to have some issues. He'd light things on fire and got into trouble a few times. Once he almost burned our house down. I was worried that with the stress of old age, he might relapse. I don't want him to put himself or anyone else in danger."

A flicker in Anna's eyes. Recognition? Worry? It disappeared almost instantly but left Abby with a feeling of unease.

Anna stood up. "Well, I'll look around, and if I find anything, I'll call you."

"That'll be great," Abby said. "Let me write down my number. I'm staying in town until tomorrow morning, so if you find out anything, I'd really appreciate it if you let me know as soon as possible."

"Absolutely."

"Thanks," Abby said, standing up as well. She glanced at the drawing again. "Emily clearly loves her father very much."

"Yeah," Anna said and, with a quick sharp movement, removed the drawing from the desk. "He's the most important person in her life."

The sense that something was off grew inside Abby, like a chilly breeze tickling her spine. "Is there a bathroom I can use on my way out?"

"Absolutely." Anna smiled. "Let me show you."

And before Abby could protest, telling her she could find her own way, that she didn't want to bother her any longer, Anna led her down the hall to the bathroom. A small room, dimly lit, with an overpowering smell of ammonia. Abby stood inside for half a minute, then flushed the toilet and stepped out.

Anna was waiting by the door, smiling, ready to lead her away.

CHAPTER 17

Was he having a heart attack? The erratic thudding in his chest, blood roaring in his ears, trouble breathing. The world spun around him. He was about to topple to the floor. She was here.

He'd received a call from Wyoming earlier. The FBI had shown up at the local church. And the church's attorney had called him as well, saying he got a call from an FBI agent. And now *she* was here.

They were closing in on him.

"Father?" The words were muffled, spoken through a haze. "Father, are you all right?"

He blinked and raised his head, squinting to see through the spots in his vision. Delilah. It was Delilah. Her hand on his arm, concern etched on her face. She'd called him Father, not Moses.

After clearing his throat, he said, "Yes, I was just deep in thought. That woman who came by . . . has she left?"

"Yeah, about ten minutes ago," Delilah said.

Up close, he noticed her smell again. Fresh. Sweet. Already he was feeling much better. He'd been right: this woman was special.

"Where's Anna?" he asked.

"Still in the office, I think."

He strode down the hall, forcing himself to ignore the dizziness and nausea. This was no time to show weakness. He entered the office, where Anna sat, in his chair. He stared at her, and she hurriedly got up and moved aside. He sat down.

"Well?" he asked. "What did she say?"

When he'd seen his daughter, *his own daughter*, at the door, his first instinct had been to tell Richard to send her off. But then he changed his mind and asked Anna to get rid of her. Anna was among the few congregation members he'd told about Abihail and her children.

"She's looking for you," Anna said. "And she told me she's your daughter."

She quickly summarized her discussion with Abihail. His daughter hadn't mentioned she was a cop. She hadn't mentioned their recent conversation.

"But why is she *here*?" Moses asked impatiently when Anna was done. "How did she track me down?"

"She didn't say."

"Why didn't you ask her?" he roared. "How much does she know? Is it the feds? Did they talk to her? Are they working together?"

Anna's eyes widened in fear, and she took a step back. "I don't know! You said she would *join* us. Didn't Deborah sacrifice herself to save Abihail's daughter from those crazy people at that school?"

"Of course she did." He slammed his desk with his fist. "And she *will* join the church, with my grandchildren. Do you doubt me?"

"No, of course not, but—"

"I needed you to get information from her, not to send her off like nothing happened. How dumb can you possibly be?"

A flicker in her eyes. Anger. Moses was surprised. He'd assumed he'd quashed that in Anna long ago.

"How could I know what you wanted me to do?" she whispered. "I've done what I thought would be best. I've made every effort."

"It wasn't enough," he said sharply. "What about tonight? Are we ready?"

"Yes. We already have him. And we've unlocked the house, and—"

"Fine." He waved his hand. Did she really think he needed all those details? "What about the list?"

"I have it here." Anna took out a notebook from her pocket and handed it to him.

He skimmed the short list of names. "What about Delilah?"

"No, I checked with Rose. It's too early. Maybe in four more days."

He clenched his jaw tightly, feeling the anger simmer. It was all wrong. He'd wanted this time to be perfect.

"With the police sniffing around, we probably need to wait a few days for the second baptism," he finally said. "Until we're sure they're not watching us."

"Wait a few days?" Anna said in disbelief. "But . . . we can't."

"Can't?" He frowned.

"Everyone's ready. I told you, we already have him. And if we wait, the police might start getting suspicious. Someone might check up on him, or they might find a witness. And the local crew are starting to get impatient. We promised them we'll leave—"

"Just a few days, damn it! No more than three or four."

"But we . . ." Her eyes widened. "Hang on. This isn't about the police at all. This is about Delilah. You want to wait for Delilah."

He narrowed his eyes. "What did you say? Do you think I even care who it is? I'm following the will of the Lord." He let the word hang in the air. "But obviously, you have lesser thoughts."

She shook her head. "I thought . . . I don't think we should wait. It's too risky. I'm saying this for you. I don't want you to make the wrong decision . . ."

"Do you have your sacred flame with you, Anna?" he asked, his voice low.

Her face turned pale. She nodded fearfully and took it out of her pocket. A bronze lighter.

"Light it," he suggested.

She obeyed. The small flame danced in the still room. He stared at it with fascination. What should she do with it? Perhaps an eyebrow. Or her ear. Or a nipple.

His crotch hardened. But no, not today. It was a busy day, after all. And she was right, even if she accused him with lies. They couldn't wait. Everything had to happen today.

"Your left palm," he said. "Place it above the flame."

She did, the hand inches above the flame, wincing as the heat seared her skin.

"Father, I have sinned against you," she said weakly. "And am not worthy to be called your daughter. Be merciful to me, a sinner."

"How have you sinned?" he asked her.

"I . . . I've doubted you. And blamed you wrongly."

"And you were worthless," he said. "And stupid."

"Y . . . yes."

"Say it."

"And I was worthless and stupid," she mumbled.

"Lower your hand, and say it louder!"

She lowered her hand slightly, the flame almost touching her skin. "Father, I have sinned—"

"Lower!"

The hand touched the flame now, and the smell of burnt flesh filled the air. Tears ran down Anna's cheeks as she cried in pain. "Be merciful to me! I doubted you . . . I was worthless and stupid. I was stupid!"

He raised his hand. "That's enough."

She removed her hand, whimpering in pain.

Moses smiled at her compassionately. "I absolve you of your sins in the name of the Father, and of the Son, and of the Holy Spirit. Amen."

"Amen," Anna mumbled, her hand cradled.

"I've decided we'll perform the second baptism today after all," he told her. "The Lord's work shouldn't wait because of the police."

"Okay," she whispered.

"Go make it happen."

When she left, he was almost certain the anger and doubt he'd glimpsed earlier in her eyes had been burned away.

CHAPTER 18

Emily liked her days at the youth shelter because she slept with Mommy and Ron in the same room and every morning she drank juice, which almost never happened at all, and she didn't need to go to school and sit next to stinky Norman. And Mommy was happy there and she smiled a lot and even laughed, and it was nice. She missed Daddy because Daddy read her bedtime stories and here no one read her bedtime stories, but when he heard how happy Mommy was there, he would want to come too. And she liked Anna because Anna let her watch as many TV shows as she wanted, even *SpongeBob SquarePants*, which Mommy said was too violent, and she gave her sweets and she told her interesting things about God.

But today Anna hurt her hand, and she even cried a bit. Sometimes at home, Mommy hurt herself, and she cried too. And Anna had to do some grown-up stuff, so Rose was looking after Emily and Ron. And Rose thought Emily shouldn't watch too much TV and suggested she draw instead, which wasn't fair, because Emily drew all morning because she planned to watch TV in the afternoon, and now Ron was asleep and she was bored, so she decided to look for Mommy.

Mommy was busy all the time in the youth shelter.

So Emily went to look for her and she looked first in the kitchen, but Mommy wasn't there, only Gretchen, and she was washing pots and looked busy, so Emily didn't want to interrupt. When grown-ups were busy, they sometimes got really angry when Emily interrupted them. So Emily went outside because she heard people talking but it was just a few men and they were carrying heavy-looking cans, and Emily asked what's in the cans but no one answered her and she didn't like the smell and she was cold so she went back inside.

And then she saw Rose talking to Miriam, so Emily walked over to ask where Mommy was but she didn't interrupt their conversation because Mommy told her that's not polite.

". . . don't know," Rose said. "Anna said it's still on, but I can't find her now. And Father is busy."

"What about the list?" Miriam asked. "I heard Gretchen is on it, but I'm on the list, too, and two months ago it didn't take and I wanted another chance."

"That's for God to decide," Rose snapped.

"Yeah," Miriam muttered. "But God tends to choose the younger girls with the perky—"

"Watch it," Rose growled.

"Sorry," Miriam said, looking ashamed. "I was forgetting myself."

"You were," Rose said. "Perhaps you should pray for forgiveness."

They were both silent and Emily thought they were done talking, so she said, "Do you know where my mommy is?"

They both looked startled. Maybe they hadn't seen her. Mommy always said she was really quiet and small, so sometimes people didn't notice she was there.

"I don't know." Rose seemed worried. "I'll help you look in a moment."

Miriam touched Rose's shoulder. "What about the trial?" She glanced at Emily. "Wasn't it supposed to happen tonight too?"

"I don't think we're doing the trial for her. She's too young." Rose stared at Emily as well.

"She's the same age Terry was when he . . . when . . ." Miriam swallowed.

"And look what happened. I don't think Father wants that to happen again. All those people leaving . . ."

"But Father said children—"

"It's not the right time to talk about this," Rose said firmly. "Go pack. We don't have a lot of time left."

Miriam nodded and left.

"Come on," Rose said. "Let's find Mommy, okay?"

She held out her hand, and Emily took it. They walked down the hallway.

"What's the trial?" Emily asked.

"It's a sort of test. You don't have to worry about that."

"Who's Terry?"

"He was a little boy who was with us."

"Did he take the test?"

"He did." Rose paused in the middle of the hallway. "But he failed."

"Why?"

"He was scared and . . . there was an accident . . ."

"You're hurting my hand."

"Oh! Sorry." Rose loosened her grip on Emily's fingers. She knelt and looked Emily right in the eyes. "Did you ever get a shot? Like from a doctor?"

"Yes." Emily frowned. "It hurt."

"But it was important, right?"

"Mommy said we do it so I don't get sick."

"Exactly. So this trial is the same. It hurts a little, but you have to be brave. And you do it so your soul doesn't get sick. It cleanses your sins. And then you get to go to heaven."

"When I got the shot, I cried." Emily's voice warbled. She thought she might start crying right now.

"It's okay to cry. But you have to stay still. Like when you get a shot. You think you can do that?"

"Will it hurt a lot?"

"It burns. It's a small burn. Not too bad."

Emily's throat clenched. "When I got the shot, the doctor gave me a lollipop."

Rose smiled at her. "You know what? If you do the trial, I'll get you a lollipop afterward. What do you say?"

"Okay." Emily let out a small hiccup.

"Good girl. Now let's go find Mommy."

CHAPTER 19

Turquoise. This was what the interior designer of the motel room had gone for. Cheerful turquoise bedsheets to match the lively turquoise drapes and the perky turquoise walls. All of which didn't match Abby's mood one bit. She'd left the church's youth shelter feeling uneasy, trying to pinpoint what was bothering her. It wasn't one glaring thing. It was an atmosphere, a feeling in the back of her neck.

A couple of years before, as an art project for school, Sam had taken a *Where's Waldo?* book, and painstakingly and carefully photoshopped all the Waldos out. And then, being the sadistic daughter that she was, she'd handed the reprinted book to Abby and challenged her to find Waldo. And the more Abby scrutinized the pages, the more she got frustrated, the more she became consumed with the need to find Waldo. Because a *Where's Waldo?* book without Waldo was just plain wrong.

That was a bit like how she felt now, sitting on the turquoise bed in her room. The encounter with Anna had seemed extremely off. What was it? The manner in which Anna hadn't let her roam the halls alone? Abby had felt it even earlier. Perhaps when Anna had searched for Moses on the computer, her eyes sliding too quickly from the screen with her answer, as if she'd already known what she was about to say. Or maybe it was that momentary flicker of emotion when Abby had mentioned Moses's fascination with fire. Or maybe it was something else entirely, something in the room, something she'd glimpsed in the hall, something in the way Richard had blocked her path. Or it was many of these tiny things, tiny details that, combined together, were the telltale signs of a hidden lie.

She'd come to Rigby on the off chance that Moses would be there. And she was becoming convinced she'd been right.

What now? She was out of her jurisdiction, and she'd seen nothing she could use. She contemplated possible actions. Going around town, showing people Moses's photo. Staking out the youth shelter. Breaking inside to search for Moses . . .

The more she thought about it, the more harebrained her ideas became. There really was only one way to go about it. Working with the local law enforcement.

It was a quarter past ten. She googled the phone number for the local police station and dialed.

"Jefferson County Sheriff's Office, how can I help?" a man asked.

"Oh, I thought I called the local police station at Rigby."

"Yes ma'am. But the police office forwards all their calls to us after work hours."

"Right." Abby rubbed her eyes. She'd seen the sheriff's office earlier; it was near her motel. "I'm Lieutenant Abby Mullen, from the NYPD. Is the sheriff available to talk?"

"The sheriff has gone home for the day. I'm Deputy Morin. How can I help, Lieutenant?"

"I'm investigating a case that might be related to the youth shelter in your town."

"The Lily Fellowship shelter?"

"That's the one. I was wondering if you had any issues with individuals in the shelter lately. Perhaps with one of the employees."

"Not that I'm aware of. Can you be more specific?"

"I'm looking for a group of arsonists. They might be hiding in that shelter. So I was wondering if you had any unexplained fires in the area lately or any reports that might be connected—"

"Perhaps it's best that you talk to the sheriff tomorrow morning," Morin suggested. "Or to the local police."

"Yeah." Abby sighed. "Thanks for the help, Deputy."

"My pleasure."

She hung up and rubbed her eyes again. Then she made a second phone call.

Zoe Bentley's voice was sharp and tense. "Mullen?"

"Hi. Did you get my email?"

"Yeah. We're following up on it. We think you're onto something. We have a few eyewitness statements—"

"I think he's in Rigby, in Idaho, right now."

A moment of silence. "You're up there?"

"Yeah." Abby gave Zoe a quick rundown of her guesswork and her visit to the local youth shelter. Was she making a mistake? If Zoe's ego got bruised, it would only make this worse. Perhaps it would have been better to have presented it differently. The last thing Abby needed was another pissing match.

"Okay," Zoe said. "It's not solid, but it's a good lead. We'll make some calls, get a couple of field agents to get to Rigby. We'll tell them to coordinate with you as well as the local police."

"Oh." Abby blinked in surprise. "Okay."

"We might fly over, too, depending on how things pan out. Thanks, Mullen."

"Thank *you*." Abby exhaled.

She ended the call with relief. What she really needed right now was a long shower and then a good night's sleep.

The shower was heavenly, the water steaming hot. Shortly after she'd married Steve, he'd felt romantic one night and had hopped in while Abby was showering. He'd then promptly stumbled out shrieking and later claimed to have first-degree burns. Needless to say, his romantic intentions had vanished for the night. Why would anyone want to shower in water that was less than boiling hot? It was beyond Abby's understanding. She wanted her skin to be pink when she got out.

That led her to thinking about her call to Steve early in the morning. She'd called to ask if the kids could stay at his place until the end of the week. That had kicked off the kind of negotiation between divorced couples in which the past was invariably dredged up. For once, Abby wished he could say, "Sure, and next week, they'll stay at your place—that works." But no, for some reason, her request made Steve bring up that one time he wanted to fly to Paris and Abby refused, which made Abby remind him he'd changed the flight dates, and besides what about the time that Sam had to be driven across the city for a concert and Steve was suddenly sick, which meant he had to bring up her supposed influenza on that big date he had . . .

She let the water run over her back and rigid shoulders, letting the soothing hot touch wash the tension away. Did every divorced couple have an enormous spreadsheet with all their emotional accounting? A spreadsheet in which they both felt like they were on the losing side?

Not to mention she'd had to discuss this with the kids too. Sam gave her the Sam treatment—"Okay Mom, that's fine," with the word *fine* coated with a medium-size glacier. And Ben needed her to coordinate the feeding of his pets, which meant Abby had to call *her* parents and ask for assistance.

And all that for what? It wasn't like she was going on a weeklong vacation to Hawaii. She was trying to stop a madman from burning people alive. And to keep him away from her own children—the same ones who had been complaining to her on the phone.

There should be a special award for cop mothers. And it should be awarded in a public ceremony, in front of their children, their spouses, and their ex-husbands.

As she shampooed the airplane away from her hair, she thought about tomorrow. The FBI would get there, and she would need to brief them. If Moses was really in Rigby as she suspected, it could all be over soon. But what if she'd gotten it wrong? Or if he wasn't staying at the youth shelter, but somewhere else and—

Faraway music intruded on her ruminations. Her ringtone. Damn it!

Hurriedly, she shut the water and got out of the shower, grabbing a towel from the wall. She haphazardly wrapped it around her and raced out of the bathroom, leaving wet footprints in her wake. She grabbed the phone off her bed. It was an unlisted number. She tried to answer several times, her wet fingers leaving droplets of water on the screen, until she finally managed it.

"Hello?" she asked, breathless.

"Abby Mullen?" It was a woman's voice, tense with fear. Abby took a second to peg it—Anna. A vehicle's engine hummed in the background. Anna was in a car.

"Yeah."

"I have some information you need to hear about your father."

"Oh okay, I can come over—"

"I'll come to you. You said you're at the motel, right? Motel 6?"

"Yeah, that's right."

"I'm nearby. I'll wait for you in the parking lot."

"You can come up to my room—"

"I don't have a lot of time. They'll notice I'm gone. They might suspect something. I'll be in the parking lot in a minute."

"Uh . . . okay, I have to dress—"

"Please hurry," Anna pleaded and hung up.

Abby quickly toweled herself to something remotely passable and put on underwear, a T-shirt, and yoga pants. She hated the feeling of the clothes clinging to her still-damp body, but there was no avoiding it. Socks, shoes, coat, and she was out, grabbing the phone and keys.

She hurried down the empty motel hallway, past the front desk, and outside. It was freezing, and she instantly regretted not wearing a sweater underneath her coat. Her damp hair made it even worse. She hunched into her coat's collar, looking around the parking lot at the handful of cars. There, at the edge of the parking lot. A car with its headlights turned on.

Abby waved as she ran to the car. She narrowed her eyes, the headlights blinding her as she approached the vehicle. As she got closer, she could see Anna's silhouette inside.

Time seemed to slow down as her instincts kicked in. Why had Anna parked all the way in the back of the parking lot? And to park this way, headlights facing forward, she'd have to maneuver her car, turning it around, then parking in reverse, which seemed strange in a mostly empty lot.

Except that parked this way, she made sure she would be away from the motel's front lights. Away from the road. Her headlights in Abby's eyes.

Abby swiveled around, spots dancing in her vision. She glimpsed the enormous figure running at her from the shadows. Reflexively her hand went to her side, but her gun was back in her room. She had a fraction of a second to react, his large form looming over her, and she tilted her head slightly and jumped toward him. Her head smashed into his chin, her skull exploding with pain, but she felt a snap, heard a muffled groan. Her glasses flew off, her vision blurring.

Something hit her face, a backhand slap, and she nearly fell down, her ear ringing, tasting blood. Disoriented, she stumbled, squinting around her.

He grabbed her now, his fingers digging into her arms. She heard the revving of an engine, the headlights approaching. She kneed him in the groin as hard as she could. He folded in pain, one hand letting go of her, but the second one still held tight.

"Get her inside," Anna screeched from the car.

The large man yanked Abby, and she lurched forward, feeling dizzy, one step, two steps, a car door opening.

She slammed her hand straight up at his nose, resulting in a crunch. A howl of rage, and the fingers on her arm went lax. She twisted away and firmly kicked down, smashing his ankle. He fell down, and she lunged away. Another blurry figure got out of the car and stepped in her way—Anna.

Abby smashed into her, fingers clawing at the woman's face, probing for her eyes. Anna screamed, stumbling back, and Abby kept running. Someone grabbed her hair, tearing out a clump of it, burning agony flaring on the back of her scalp. She ran.

The big guy was probably Richard, and in a few seconds he would give chase. The two attackers were between Abby and the motel, so she couldn't turn back. Instead she ran forward, her feet slapping on the lot's pavement.

Tires screeched behind her. Anna was probably going after her in the car. Damn it, damn it! Abby was breathing hard, her lungs throbbing. She could hardly see anything. Too dark, too blurry; she needed her glasses.

She pictured the parking lot, trying to recall her surroundings. There was only one entrance from the highway. Her room's window looked out at the back of the motel, and she recalled there was a snow-covered field adjacent to the lot, and beyond it, a branch of Wendy's. Was there a fence between the lot and the field? She didn't know. And it didn't matter—she had only one way to go.

She stumbled as she reached the edge of the lot. No fence, just slippery, icy snow and weeds. Headlights behind her illuminated her surroundings. She ran between two trees as the headlights rushed at her, heard brakes squealing.

She tore through the field, tripped over something, twisted her ankle, fell. Her hands sank into the powdery freezing snow, but she got on her feet, kept running, ankle blazing with pain. She couldn't afford to slow down. The lights of the street beckoned her forward . . . but the Wendy's branch was clearly dark. Closed.

She let out a whimper of despair. All around her were dark buildings. This wasn't a residential area; there was no one here at this time of night. She would have to hide and hope Richard and Anna wouldn't be able to find her, then make her way to the motel, where she could get her gun, and tell the front desk to call the police—

The sheriff's office! It was only a short distance away. As she reached the street, she tried to orient herself. Which way was it? Left or right?

Somewhere behind her, she heard heavy breathing. Richard. And that engine sound in the distance could only be Anna, on her way to cut her off.

Left.

She ran, thankful for the meager illumination the night lights supplied. She ignored the dark useless buildings around her, her lungs freezing as she inhaled the night's chilly air. She'd gotten the direction wrong, she must have gotten it wrong, it was the other way. She could now hear Richard close on her tail, his footsteps loud, his breathing labored, angry.

There! That large structure, and a light. She beelined toward it, running through grass, leaping over a small ledge, and she was at the door, slamming into it—the damn thing was locked.

"Help!" she screeched, slapping the glass door, seeing Richard's silhouette in the reflection behind her getting closer, almost upon her.

A young man appeared inside, dressed in uniform. The deputy. Hurrying for the door.

Unlocking it.

She stumbled inside, breathing hard, heaving.

"What is it?" the deputy asked, voice panicked. "What happened?"

Abby turned around, saw Richard limping away as fast as he could.

"Stop him," she blurted. "Arrest him! He tried to kill me."

The deputy stared at her, then drew his gun.

"Freeze!" he shouted.

A car hurtled into the parking lot and stopped next to Richard. He leaped inside, and they drove away. The deputy ran a few steps after them, then turned to face Abby.

"Are you okay?" he asked in alarm.

Abby sank to the floor, shivering. Her entire body hurt, she was freezing cold, she tasted blood. She wasn't okay, but it could wait.

"I'm Lieutenant Abby Mullen from the NYPD," she croaked. "You should send police officers to the youth shelter. The attackers came from there. And I think they're harboring a serial killer."

CHAPTER 20

"I still think you should have a doctor take a look at you, Lieutenant Mullen."

"I'm fine. It's just a few scrapes," Abby told the sheriff, her voice hoarse.

She wasn't fine. She sat in the sheriff's office, hunched in her muddy coat. The world was still a blur without her glasses, and her face throbbed from Richard's backhand punch. Her mind felt a bit numb. She did her best not to think about the recent events too hard, because there was a risk she'd start crying. And right now, it was the worst thing that could happen.

Sheriff Hunt, a big pink blob in a uniform, sat in front of her. As far as Abby could tell, he had a mustache, because he had some sort of black haze above his mouth. But that was as far as she could see without leaning really close to him and squinting, and she didn't feel like doing that.

Damn it, she needed her glasses.

"Do you want me to drive you back to the motel?" Hunt asked.

"In a bit," she said. "I want to wait for the deputy to return."

Deputy Morin had gone along with a police patrol car to search for Anna and Richard in the youth shelter. Abby was not about to leave before she knew they'd found them. She'd also described Moses to them, explaining he might be there as well and should be detained, because the FBI was looking for him.

Why had they tried to grab her? Had Moses told them to do it? Was he really there? The thought that he might have been across the wall from her when she came to the youth shelter made her nauseous.

"So let's go over the facts again to make sure I have everything right," the sheriff said. "This guy you're looking for, Moses, is working for the Lily Fellowship Church in some capacity—"

"He might be volunteering there," Abby said. "And unknown to the church, he's a leader of a small cult. They're using the church's resources as they travel around the country, burning people alive."

"Right."

Even without her glasses, she could imagine his skeptical expression. "I know it sounds strange, but—"

The door opened, another uniformed blob stepping inside.

"I went by the motel parking lot on the way back," the man said. It was the deputy, Morin. "I found your glasses and your phone."

Abby took them gratefully and put the glasses on. They were bent, sitting on her nose askew. The sheriff and his deputy swam into focus. The sheriff really did have a mustache, a thick broom-like one. He also had bushy eyebrows and generally reminded her of someone, though she couldn't put her finger on it. Someone connected to Ben, her son. A father of one of his friends, perhaps?

Morin was long faced and pimply, his eyebrows arched in a way that gave him a perpetually surprised expression.

"We went to the youth shelter, but the people you described weren't there," Morin said. "Dot told me she'd never heard of Anna *or* Richard. And there was no one there matching the description of that man you told us about, Moses. They let us look through the entire compound, and we didn't find anything—the place is pretty empty."

Abby's gut sank. She fiddled with her glasses, trying to straighten them. "Who's Dot?" she asked.

"The woman who runs the youth shelter," the sheriff said. "She's a sweet lady."

"How long has she been running the shelter?"

"About three years now," Hunt answered. "Since her husband died. I've known her since I was a little boy. Dot wouldn't lie, not in a million years. These people were never there."

Abby nodded, not bothering to argue. Of course Dot would lie. Anyone would lie, under the right circumstances. And, in fact, Dot had lied, because Anna had been there. What did this mean? She wanted to protect Anna and Richard. But why? Was she covering for her friends? Or had Moses gotten to her too?

Abby needed backup as soon as possible. To the police and to the sheriff she was just a woman, covered in mud, far away from her jurisdiction.

"Excuse me for a moment," she said. She unlocked her phone and dialed.

After a few seconds, Zoe's sleepy voice answered the phone. "Mullen? What time is it?"

"It's after midnight," Abby said. "Sorry to wake you up, but I need to fill you in. I think you really should get on the fastest flight here."

CHAPTER 21

It was pitch black outside the car. The only thing Delilah could see was the straight road, illuminated by the vehicle's headlights. Rose sat in the driver's seat, humming to herself. Delilah glanced back at the kids, both of them fast asleep. They'd hardly even woken up when she'd put them in the car. Emily had sleepily asked where they were going, and Delilah had told her they were going on a short drive.

What would she tell her when she woke up? Mommy decided to move you halfway across the country, away from Daddy? We're part of a new family now?

"I hope I packed everything," she finally said.

"You'll be fine," Rose said reassuringly. "If you forgot anything, we'll get it at the new place."

"Is Anna all right?" Delilah asked. The question had been bothering her.

"Why do you ask?"

"I went by the office earlier, and I heard her . . . screaming. I was about to check on her, but then she stepped out of the office. She was crying."

Rose clenched her jaw. "She's fine. She's just under a lot of pressure—don't worry about it."

"Okay," Delilah said hesitantly.

Rose slowed down and parked at the side of the road, behind a large van.

"What is it?" Delilah asked.

Rose pointed at a lone dark house, hardly visible in the night. "We need to make a quick stop."

"What for?"

"You'll see," Rose said, grinning at her. "You need to step outside."

A few figures were approaching their car. Delilah recognized almost all of them. People from the congregation.

"The kids—"

"I'll stay with them. Don't worry about it."

One of the people knocked on Delilah's window. It was that big guy, Richard, his expression blank. "Delilah, you coming?"

His nose was swollen and crooked. Had he hurt it somehow?

"Um, okay." She opened the passenger door. It was freezing outside. "Should I get my coat?"

"Nah," Richard said. "It'll get warmer in a bit. But get the girl too."

"Emily?" Delilah asked, surprised. "She's asleep."

"Wake her up then."

"No need," Rose said. "You can leave Emily here with me."

Richard frowned at Rose. "I thought that Father said—"

"No." Rose was adamant. "There's no need."

He shrugged. "Okay. Delilah, let's go."

Delilah glanced at Emily, unsure, but Rose nodded at her encouragingly. She stepped out of the car and shut the door behind her. Richard stood too close to her. He held a large red plastic can, and despite the wind she could smell the sharp scent of gasoline.

They walked together toward the small house. Richard had a slight limp but waved her off when she asked if he was okay. As they got closer, the smell of gasoline became stronger. A figure stood in the open doorway, arms crossed. Moses. The rest stood in a huddle outside, a group of ten or so, all from the congregation. Two held lit torches, the flames flickering in the chilly wind. Delilah approached them, hugging herself.

"What's going on?" she asked, her teeth chattering in the cold.

The flames lit their excited faces. The mood was jubilant.

"A second baptism," someone said over the wind.

Delilah frowned. She was still hazy on the details of what the second baptism *was*. It was supposedly related to the other facet of God's love and forgiveness. It was about God's justice.

Moses stepped in front of the group. He was dressed in a white robe, and with his long hair and robe fluttering in the wind, he looked almost like his namesake from thousands of years ago.

"As I have observed, those who plow evil and those who sow trouble reap it," Moses said. "And when the Second Coming will transform the world, it would be so. But until then, it is sometimes our responsibility to make sure that happens."

Delilah shivered. Her skin prickled as she listened, her heart thudding fast. Moses's voice carried over the wind as if aided by an unnatural force, each word sharp and powerful in her ears.

"We came to Rigby, hoping to finally find a place free of heretics. A haven we could settle in," Moses said. "But everywhere we looked, we could see darkness and wickedness and evil taking hold. We did our best to change it, to shepherd men and women to the light. Gretchen Wood, for example, went every day from door to door, trying to talk to people's hearts and get them to give more, to try harder."

Delilah glanced at Gretchen, who was beaming with pride. Everyone smiled at her. Delilah found herself smiling as well.

"But no matter our efforts, some men and women are nearly beyond saving. Only fires can cleanse their souls. Be it the flames of hell . . ." He paused, raising his eyes to the torches. "Or the flames of man!" The last words came out in a roar, and Delilah's knees buckled.

The men with the torches stepped forward, but Moses raised a hand, and they paused.

"First, I want our newest member to step inside with me," he said, lowering his voice.

Delilah felt the eyes on her. Silent frowns and murmurs surrounded her. Something was different. This was not what everyone had expected.

"Delilah." Moses motioned with his hand. "Follow me."

He turned to the house and strode toward it. Delilah hurried after him and stepped inside, hardly seeing anything in the dark. The entire place reeked of gasoline.

"Whose house is this?" she whispered.

"No one's," Moses said. "It doesn't matter. What matters is this."

He switched on a tiny flashlight, and Delilah gasped as its beam illuminated a bruised, bleeding face.

It was Brad.

CHAPTER 22

Delilah stumbled back, collided into the wall, her foot splashing in liquid. Her breathing was rapid, panicky. Brad would take her now; Moses wouldn't be able to stop him. He would snatch her and make her pay for leaving with the kids, and for not cleaning the house over the weekend, and for taking all the cash from his hiding spot, and for—

A hand grabbed her wrist, and she let out a weak cry. But it was Moses who held her. Not Brad.

Brad was sitting still on a chair, face twisted in a strange expression, his hands in his lap.

"I'm sorry," Delilah blurted. "I'm so sorry, I—"

"You have nothing to be sorry about," Moses said, his voice echoing in the dark space.

"Delilah," Brad growled. "Tell your new friend to let me go, right now. You tell him that you're my wife and that he's made a mistake."

Delilah blinked. What did Brad mean, let him go?

Then she saw the cord looped around Brad's wrists. His ankles were tied together too. She glanced at the bruises on his face, one of his eyes swollen and half-shut, blood trickling from his nose onto his lips.

"M . . . Moses, you have to untie him."

"No, I don't," Moses said softly.

Didn't he understand it would only make Brad angrier? Even if they left him like this, once he got free, he would hunt her to the ends of the earth. He'd warned her of that countless times, how he knew people who could find her *anywhere*. And when he caught up to her, he'd . . . he'd . . .

The sharp scent of the gasoline in the room was overpowering. And she thought of the torches. Oh Jesus.

"Wait," she told Moses. "What is this?"

"When justice is done," Moses said, "it is a joy to the righteous but terror to evildoers."

"You . . . you want to burn him?"

"What?" Brad blurted. "What the hell are you talking about?"

Moses looked at her. "Me? No. God does. For the Lord your God is a consuming fire, a jealous God."

"I never asked you . . . I don't want this . . ." Didn't she? Intermingled with her horror, she felt something else. Hope?

Moses frowned. "This isn't your call, Delilah, nor is it mine. This is between this sinner and God."

"Wait, listen to me," Brad blurted. "You can't do this. Delilah, tell him he can't do this. I swear, if you don't tell him, you'll pay for it."

Delilah suddenly realized what was so strange about the expression on Brad's face. It was fear and pain. Emotions she was so used to glimpsing in the mirror but which were utterly alien on her husband. She gazed at him in amazement, realizing that though she was afraid as well, it was a fear she wasn't familiar with.

"It's not up to me," she told Brad slowly. "It's your baptism. Your second baptism."

"My second baptism? Listen to me, you bitch. You tell them to untie me right now!" Brad screamed, his voice breaking. He struggled, the cord digging into his wrists, the chair he sat on rocking.

Delilah followed Moses out of the house.

"You should stay back," Moses told her. "You've got gasoline on your shoes."

His voice was matter of fact, as if this was simply an unfortunate accident.

"Wait," she blurted. "We don't need to do this . . ."

"Stay back." His voice was firm. The others glared at her, shifting, standing between her and the house.

Hurriedly, she walked away from the house, toward the car. Rose was leaning on the car, her arms folded. Delilah joined her and turned to stare at the house.

Even from this distance, she could still hear Moses as he turned to the crowd and shouted, "'I came to cast fire on the earth, and would that it were already kindled.' It is time for a second baptism!"

As if in a dream, Delilah watched the two men approach the house, carrying torches. They held out the torches to the wall, and an enormous blaze engulfed the house. She gasped, as did Rose. A flurry of sparks rose to the sky, and Delilah could feel the heat of the flames reach back to where she stood. She no longer needed a coat. Faintly, above the roar of the flames, she could hear a twisting, bloodcurdling scream. Delilah shut her eyes. It wasn't her decision. It was between Brad and God. Between a sinner and the Lord. It wasn't her call.

The screams continued. How long would they last? She opened her eyes.

"Let's leave," she implored Rose.

"Not yet," Rose said, her eyes wide, a faint smile on her lips. "We need to wait for Father."

Delilah turned to look at Moses, who was now speaking in a lower voice. She couldn't hear what he was saying. After a few seconds he stepped forward to the crowd and took the hand of someone—a young girl. It was Gretchen. He led her aside, into the darkness, until they were out of sight.

"Where . . . ," Delilah said. "Where are they going?"

Rose stared into the flames. "To do God's work."

CHAPTER 23

Abby sat in the passenger's side of the sheriff's car, hugging herself, shrinking into her coat. Her motel was barely a couple of minutes' drive away. She stared out the window at the street, where two hours ago, she'd run for her life.

"In the morning you'll need to give a complete statement at the local police station," Hunt said as they pulled into the parking lot of her motel. "And they'll take it from there. And you should probably drop by the local care center, get them to take a look at you."

"Sheriff Hunt, by the morning the people who attacked me might be halfway across the country. Moses, too, if I'm right and he's nearby. We need to go up to the youth shelter and—"

"Lieutenant, like I said before, we will investigate this thoroughly. But we've followed up on your report, and those people weren't there."

The radio crackled. "Sheriff, this is Morin."

Hunt took the mic. "Yeah, go ahead."

"I got a call from the fire department. There's a house fire reported at 343 North. They want our help to contain the scene."

A chill ran down Abby's spine. A house fire. It was Moses, it had to be.

Hunt frowned and glanced at her. He clicked the mic. "Okay, I'm on my way. Alert Chief Richardson. This might be related to Lieutenant Mullen's arsonist. I want a patrol car there as soon as possible."

He put down the mic and turned toward Abby. "Maybe we found your attackers sooner than you expected."

"I'll come with you," she said urgently. "I can identify them—"

He shook his head. "No way. If we need your help, we'll be in touch."

She hesitated, then opened the passenger door. The night's freezing air nearly took her breath away. She got out and shut the door, then watched Hunt's car as he drove away.

Limping as fast as she could, she got to her room. She took off her muddy clothes and put on a fresh shirt and pair of pants. This time, she put on her thick green sweater, as well as a woolen hat. She shrugged back into her muddy coat, then grabbed her bag and her gun. She lurched out of her room and walked back outside to her car.

It was probably only her imagination, but she could detect the familiar scent of smoke.

◆ ◆ ◆

It didn't matter that Delilah had stepped into the car and covered her ears; she could still hear Brad screaming. She sat curled up and sobbing, waiting for it to be finally over. It wasn't her call. It was between God and the sinner. It was justice. But why couldn't she stop hearing the screams? What if Emily woke up and heard them?

Finally, unable to stomach it anymore, she got out of the car and ran toward the raging inferno, ignoring Rose's shouts. She would tell Moses they had to leave. She couldn't be here anymore, she couldn't.

She ran past the congregation members, who were watching the fire, lips moving in prayer. Here, the heat of the flames was almost unbearable. How was Brad even still alive in there? *Was* he alive? She wasn't sure if she was really hearing Brad's tormented shrieks or just the echoes of them in her mind.

Her back to the burning house, she ran in the direction where she'd seen Moses and the other woman disappear. Maybe she could get his permission to take the kids and leave. Surely he would understand that if Emily woke up and heard the screaming, it would be—

She froze, staring into the darkness. In the flickering light of the flames, she saw two figures writhing on the ground, but . . . it was impossible . . . how could they even . . . with the screaming all around them?

She turned away, bile rising in her throat. It was impossible—she must have misunderstood what she was seeing. In the distance she heard sirens, finally drowning out the screaming. Or had the screaming stopped? She didn't know; everything seemed like a strange, impossible nightmare. A fire truck was approaching the house, honking, its siren blaring.

She decided to return to the car and force Rose to drive away. She would tell her Moses gave his permission. She couldn't stay here, not with—

Roaring heat suddenly hit her like a powerful wave, knocking her off her feet. She slammed into the muddy ground with a thud, gasping in shock. The world shook, the night becoming brighter as the flames shot high. Her ears rang, and she gasped with terror. Something heavy landed inches away from her head. She stared at it, a burning piece of wood, as a shower of flaming debris fell from the sky.

The big sound woke Emily up with a start. Mommy always told her she shouldn't be afraid of thunders, because thunders are just the lightning's way of saying hello, but Emily was still afraid. Her chest was beating hard and already she was sobbing, looking around her in the darkness and she wasn't even in her bed, she was in a car.

"Mommy?" she whimpered.

No one answered, and now Ron was crying. He sat next to her in his safety seat, and he was wailing.

"Mommy, Ron is crying!" Emily called.

"Your mom will be right back."

It was Rose. She sat in front, looking outside her window. Emily was relieved to hear the grown-up voice, but she still wanted her mommy, and Ron was still crying. And now another noise, a siren. Sometimes when they walked down the street, they'd see an ambulance or a police car, and Ron would always point at it, because he loved cars, but right now he wasn't interested. Emily glanced outside.

There was a big fire outside.

Emily had never seen anything so scary. All those flames everywhere, and people running in the dark, and the fire truck's red light flickering, its siren hurting Emily's ears. Where was Mommy? They needed to get out of here.

"Mommy!" Emily screeched.

She yanked the door handle, and it opened. It was cold outside but she didn't care, she needed to find Mommy so that they could get out of there. She tried to get out of the car but was yanked back by the seat belt. Crying, she freed herself from the restraint and got out, and stepped on a rock with her bare foot, and it hurt, and now she was crying harder.

"What are you doing?" Rose said. She got out of the car and grabbed Emily. "You can't go there."

"Where's Mommy?"

And then she saw her, Mommy running toward them, covered in mud and dirt, looking scared, and Emily cried harder because she was relieved to see her, but also the look in Mommy's eyes frightened her.

"Let's go!" Mommy shouted. "Emily, get in the car, we're going."

She grabbed Emily's arm and pushed her into the car. And now the three of them were in the back seat, with Mommy's arm around her.

"Rose, drive!" Mommy shouted.

The car's engine started and they drove away. Emily was crying, and so was Ron. Mommy hugged Emily with one hand and whispered in her ear, "Shhhh, Mommy's here now. Everything is going to be all right. Don't worry. Everything is going to be all right."

◆　◆　◆

Abby could glimpse the fire through her windshield in the distance, flickering orange flames and hazy smoke rising to the sky. She floored the gas pedal, as the navigation app gave her instructions in a calm, even voice.

The explosion took her breath away. The flames shot higher, sparks showering everywhere, and a second later, the blast reached her ears, rattling at the car's windows.

"Jesus," she gasped.

Impossibly, the woman's voice in the navigation app seemed unaffected as she told her in a calm, steady tone to turn right.

It took her a few more minutes to reach the burning house. It was pandemonium. Burning debris had fallen everywhere, setting small fires in the surrounding fields. A hundred yards away, a neighboring house had caught fire as well, and people were attempting to extinguish the flames. A patrol car shot past her, sirens screaming, and parked by the house, then two cops jumped out and hurried toward the house.

Heart thudding in her chest, Abby parked her car, got out, and limped toward the inferno, where a few firemen were utilizing a fire hose. The powerful jet of water created a haze, making everything beyond it nearly invisible. A fireman lay on the ground a few yards away, screaming in pain, as a large piece of rubble trapped his leg underneath. A policeman and the sheriff were lifting the rubble to get him out. More sirens were approaching. Abby's ankle twisted, and she gasped and nearly fell, fires everywhere, suffocating smoke burning in her—

—throat. It was getting so hot, and she could hear the screams. Her parents, she needed to get them out. She ran toward the door.

"Abihail, get away from there!"

A hand grabbing—

—her shoulder. She whirled around. It was a firefighter.

"Ma'am, you have to get back!" he shouted at her.

"Did you get the people out?" she shouted back at him.

"No one lives here! Ma'am, please stay away! You'll get hurt." The firefighter turned to extinguish a burning patch in the field.

Stumbling along, Abby looked around her, searching for Anna, for Richard, for Moses. But everywhere she looked, there was nothing but—

—smoke, and distant screaming. She couldn't breathe, could hardly see, the back of her neck burned. Eden and Isaac pulled her with them, half dragging her away while she shrieked, the heat unbearable. Her eyes stung, and she shut them, coughing, trying to get away, and now she could hear people shouting, "I found someone! Over here!"

She fell to the ground, unable to keep going, and opened her—

—eyes. In front of her, on the ground, lay a person, unmoving. They seemed badly burnt.

"Hey." Abby coughed, grabbing the person's arm. "Are you okay? I need help over here!"

She gasped as the burnt skin came apart in her hand. The body lay unmoving, its hands clasped in front of it, as if in a final prayer.

CHAPTER 24

Abby stared at the water pooling on the floor of the shower. Soot and mud turned the water gray as it swirled around the drain. She gingerly touched the point on her scalp where Richard had torn out a clump of her hair. It hurt, and she winced, then probed it again. The pain helped her focus, helped her escape the images of the night and the dark memories from her childhood.

The man she'd found by the burning house was dead. The firefighters thought his body had been flung out by the force of the explosion. No one knew who he was. Like she'd been told on the scene, no one lived in the house. Perhaps it was a squatter? No one had any idea.

Nor was there any sign of the arsonists. The firefighters had reported that when they showed up on the scene, a group of bystanders stood nearby. But they'd been told to get back, and after the explosion and the ensuing chaos, the so-called bystanders had disappeared.

Moses, Abby was now sure, had been in Rigby. And now he was gone.

Dirt had gotten under her fingernails, and she scrubbed them repeatedly. What if it wasn't only dirt? She thought of the burnt body she'd touched. What if . . . what if . . .

She scrubbed harder. It was hard to get it all out. She should have packed her nailbrush. She scraped the soap with her nail, and a bit of dirt smeared over her palm, and now she was scrubbing her hands and unwrapped another soap, forcing it against the back of her hands, her skin getting raw, because that's how you got all the filth out, and the germs, and the burnt skin . . .

The soap tumbled from her hands. She turned off the water, staggered out of the shower, and vomited into the toilet. She let out a sob, then threw up again. Trembling, she stood up and stared at the raw skin of her hands. She let out a shuddering breath and dried them gently. She brushed her teeth to get the bad taste out, then walked out of the bathroom and collapsed into the bed.

Feeling exhausted, she thought she'd fall asleep almost instantly. But she found herself lying awake, moments of fear and pain running through her mind.

Richard's fingers, digging into her arms as he held her tight, Anna shouting at him to get Abby into the car.

Lurching through a field pockmarked with small fires, a towering inferno in front of her, another one she hadn't been able to prevent.

Trying to unlatch the door as a child, hearing her parents screaming on the other side, smoke everywhere.

She curled into a fetal position, hugging one of the bed's pillows, trembling, teeth chattering.

Running in the muddy dark field, Richard behind her, her ankle throbbing.

The burnt body of another victim by her side on the ground, and its smell, oh god, its smell.

The fireman screaming, trapped underneath the rubble.

Her own screaming as her hair was torn from her scalp.

Her parents' screaming.

Heaving, she grabbed her phone. She scrolled to her adoptive mother's number, about to dial. But her finger hovered over the screen. She didn't want to frighten her mom. She wasn't a child anymore, going to her parents' bedroom because she'd had a bad dream.

The images didn't fade, and she needed to hear a voice. A voice she could take refuge in.

She dialed Carver.

The phone rang. A second, two, three, she was about to hang up, already regretting this. It was a momentary bout of panic. She'd get over it soon enough.

"Hello, Abby?" He sounded concerned, groggy, still half-asleep.

"Hey. I'm sorry I woke you up." Her own voice was tiny, shuddering, fragile.

"Yeah. I mean . . . no. Don't worry about it. What is it?"

"I just had . . . I had a really bad night."

"Are you hurt?" Carver immediately asked.

"Yes . . . no. Not really. A few scrapes." She sniffled and wiped a tear. "I'm okay, really. You should go back to sleep."

"No, it's fine. What happened?"

"I . . . I don't want to talk about it. Not tonight. I wanted to hear your voice, you know?" She covered her head with the blanket, lying on her side, phone to her ear.

"Did you see a doctor? Are you bleeding? I can get there on the first flight—"

"I'm really okay." She shut her eyes. "Please. Just . . . talk to me."

"Okay." Carver's voice softened. She could still hear the edge of worry there. "Are you still at Rigby?"

"Yeah, in a motel."

"When are you getting back tomorrow? I can pick you up from the airport."

"I don't think I'll be back tomorrow. There were a few developments. I might stay another day."

"Okay." He sighed, and she heard his bed creak as he moved. She imagined him sitting up, his hair messy from sleep.

"What was your day like?" she asked. Here, in her cocoon underneath the blanket, with Carver's voice in her ear, everything was all right again.

"It was okay. I spent the morning looking at security footage. Five hours of mind-numbing videos from security cams. But I listened to that playlist you sent me."

"What playlist?"

"The one you titled 'actually good music.'"

"Oh yeah." She shut her eyes. Carver didn't typically listen to music. Abby was intent on educating him. "It's good, right?"

"Yeah, I guess, it's okay."

"It's okay," she repeated. "Leonard Cohen. The Pixies. The Doors. David Bowie. Literally the best musicians of the twentieth century. So you guess it's okay?"

"Yeah." She heard his smile, could imagine it, the tiny scar on his chin twisting charmingly. "You know, definitely makes the time go by easier."

She felt sleepy. Maybe she could, eventually, fall asleep. She pictured his arms hugging her from behind. "I should make you a new playlist," she mumbled. "I think I didn't include Nick Cave there. Or the Who."

"Or Britney Spears."

"Did you say Britney Spears?"

"Yeah. Not one single hit by Britney Spears. I was disappointed. I added one to the current list. The one called '. . . Baby One More Time.'"

"You soiled my list with Britney Spears?" She grinned. She was floating away.

"Improved it, you mean?"

"You're an idiot, Jonathan Carver."

"I know."

"But I love you," she whispered.

And she could hear him smile when he answered, "I love you too."

CHAPTER 25

During the night, all the smoke and pain and traumatic memories and regret had condensed into a single lump, which had settled in Abby's throat. Her face still throbbed from the slap Richard had landed on her, and it had also left a mark. More bruises decorated her arms where he'd gripped her. She walked with a limp. The backs of her hands were raw and tender.

A man had burned to death. Moses had slipped through her fingers again.

She'd talked to her kids early in the morning, and it had helped lift her spirits momentarily. But as soon as she'd hung up the phone, her eyes had filled with tears. She really needed a hug from Ben and a sardonic smile from Sam. She didn't want to be so far away from them. The only thing that still kept her half a continent away was the constant threat they faced from Moses and his cult.

She spent a solid ten minutes sitting in her room, feeling sorry for herself. Sometimes, really committing to self-pity was something that needed doing. That task accomplished, she checked her email. She had a new message from Zoe. Both she and Tatum had arrived in Rigby. Zoe asked Abby to join them at the police station. Apparently there was a joint task force now, and Abby was a part of it.

The dismal weather matched Abby's mood. It was raining and windy, turning the raindrops into tiny hostile projectiles that stung

Abby's face as she ran from the motel to her car. On the way to the police station, she flipped through the radio stations, finding nothing, then turned on Spotify on her phone and put on a playlist she called "nostalgia." The playlist was full of songs from the nineties, aimed at reminding her of a simpler time, when she was a teenager, and her biggest problem was her crush on a kid named Mylo.

By the time the playlist reached Sinéad O'Connor's "Nothing Compares 2 U," the lump in her throat had dissipated slightly. What was her high school crush Mylo doing these days? She compared him to Carver, and Mylo came up short. Carver was sweet, and manly, and sexy, and he cared for her. He had that tiny scar on his chin that she loved and an ass to die for. All Mylo had going for him was a slightly torn Iron Maiden T-shirt.

More raindrops as she reached the police station, and she ran hunched inside, the world becoming a speckled blur as her glasses got wet. She was still wiping them as she stepped into the task force room.

The shift in atmosphere was instantaneous. The room thrummed with a hum of multiple people talking to each other or on the phone, intermingled with the static of a police radio adding voices from the field. As Abby put her glasses back on, the murky figures focused. She instantly recognized three of them. Zoe and Tatum sat by the large table in the middle, sifting through papers and printed photos. Tatum's suit was somewhat rumpled, a telltale sign of their rushed flight over. Zoe didn't seem as disheveled, her gray pantsuit immaculate. Sheriff Hunt paced back and forth at the far end of the room, a phone glued to his ear.

Tatum lifted his eyes as she stepped inside, and he smiled, but the smile quickly dissipated, morphing into worry. He'd seen the bruise on her face. She'd done her best to wipe the mud off her long gray coat, but some stains still remained, another testament to last night's events. She walked over, trying to hide her limp.

"Is that from last night?" he asked in a low voice, glancing at her bruise.

"Yeah." Abby sat down and self-consciously touched her sore cheek. "Did you see a doctor?"

"I'm fine. You should see the other guy." She waggled her eyebrows and immediately regretted it, the painful throb in her face intensifying. "Where are we at?"

Tatum leaned back. "We have two field agents here working with the local PD. The sheriff is helping out as well." He glanced at Hunt, who was still talking on the phone. "So far we're focusing on the immediate manhunt. We have officers going door to door in the vicinity of the burnt house and staking out the scene in case anyone shows up."

"Roadblocks?"

"We considered it, but we have too many roads in and out of town, including the highway, which would be difficult to block efficiently. And frankly, if they're gone, they're long gone."

"Yeah," Abby agreed heavily. "Any idea where?"

"They might go to a different church branch. If that's their plan, the closest branch is in Montana. We have agents monitoring it."

It would make sense, and match Moses's previous strategy. Move to a different state. Target someone else. An image of last night's victim flashed through her mind. She pushed it firmly away. "Did you search the youth shelter?"

"We have people stationed nearby, so no one will be coming or going without us knowing it. But they're not as cooperative with us as they were with the local law enforcement officers last night, so we're waiting for the search warrant."

"Our best bet is to figure out Wilcox's next destination," Zoe said, her eyes intent on a few crime scene photos. Abby recognized the crime scene from the night before, the details frozen on paper, without the sensation of chaos, the smell of the acrid air, the feeling of the cold muddy ground. Zoe spread the photos, several of them depicting the burnt body Abby had tripped over the night before, as well as four photos of the torched house. "We're working with the Lily Fellowship

Church's administration, but their records are spotty. It's not clear what Moses's position within the church is. We're not even sure he's a church employee. He might be a volunteer."

"That's what I was wondering about too," Abby said. "I suspect most of his followers are related to that church in some way. Maybe he recruits them as he travels between locations."

"So you think he has a few people in each branch, like small cult cells?" Tatum asked.

Abby shook her head. "No, it wouldn't work. Moses needs to dominate his followers' lives completely. He couldn't retain his control over them otherwise. His followers travel with him."

"Why would the church agree to that?" Zoe asked, frowning.

"I don't know. It really depends on his role in the church. I'm assuming he's a sort of traveling preacher, or maybe a consultant."

A uniformed officer with a boyish face and chubby cheeks approached them. "Um . . . hi. We're ordering breakfast? For the task force?"

"Are you asking us, or telling us?" Tatum asked with a raised eyebrow.

"Asking. I mean, telling. I'm asking what you want. We're ordering from Wendy's." He blinked. "They have sandwiches and biscuits and coffee."

"Just get me some kind of sandwich and coffee," Tatum said.

"I want a maple bacon chicken croissant and a honey-butter biscuit," Zoe said. "I want the bacon extra crispy, that's really important. They can go easy on the maple. And hot chocolate."

The officer stared at her, blinking, his mouth slightly open.

"Do you want me to write it down for you?" Zoe asked impatiently.

"I'm not sure they have—"

"They do. It's Wendy's." She sifted through the photos in front of her again.

"Wh . . . what about you?" The officer looked at Abby.

"Coffee, thanks," Abby said listlessly.

"Get her one of those croissants too," Tatum told the man. He glanced at Abby. "You look like you could use a bite."

Abby didn't think she could physically swallow anything, but she nodded anyway.

Zoe tapped at one of the photos. "Look here." It was a close-up of the body's bound wrists. "Same electrical cord used in the Douglas murder. But the knot he used is completely different. In this case he looped it around the victim's wrists eight times, according to the report. In previous cases it was a shorter cord, and they only looped it twice or three times."

"The knot could be different because the person tying the victim was different," Abby said, trying to control her nausea as she scrutinized the burnt arms in the photo. "Moses would probably let one of his followers do the dirty work."

"That's probably true," Tatum said. "We don't know how many people were involved—" His phone rang, and he answered it, giving them an apologetic look.

"Wouldn't he prefer the same person do it each time?" Zoe asked. "Binding a man isn't easy, especially if he's conscious. I assumed Moses would be clever enough to make sure it's done expertly."

"Everything Moses does revolves around his control over his followers," Abby said. "So for example, he would give this job to someone who needed to feel he's entrusted with an important task. Or he'd give it to someone he wants implicated in the crime, in case that person decides to take off. We can't make any conclusions based on the fact that it's a different knot."

Zoe bit her lip thoughtfully. "It almost sounds like we need to profile each and every one of his followers."

Abby was about to answer when Tatum roared, "A motorcycle? Marvin, you can't ride a motorcycle!"

Zoe rolled her eyes. Abby supposed that this wasn't the first time she'd heard Tatum's family arguments.

"I know that you used to . . . Marvin, I don't care if your damn girlfriend likes it, you're not buying a motorcycle. *What do you mean you already bought it?*"

By this point most of the chatter in the task force room had quieted down, and they all stared at Tatum.

"Marvin, I don't . . . we'll talk about it when I get home. Just feed the damn cat." Tatum hung up the phone.

"Sorry." He cleared his throat.

Abby gave him a rueful smile. "I know how it is. My teenager can drive me insane sometimes. I suppose they all grow out of it eventually. How old is Marvin?"

Tatum pocketed his phone. "He's ninety-one."

Abby blinked. "Oh."

"If he grows out of it, I'll let you know." Tatum grinned.

Realizing the show was over, everyone in the room returned to their business.

Abby looked down at the photos, trying to refocus. "What about an ID on the victim?"

"Not yet," Tatum said. "The victim was male. Unlike the previous cases, the house was unoccupied."

"Up until now, all the victims were burned inside their *own* homes," Zoe said. "I assumed it was part of the killer's signature."

"Maybe the signature is changing," Tatum suggested. "Developing to match Moses's fantasies in some manner."

"Maybe in this case, this house is important," Zoe said. "It could be related to Moses's past. Or it reminds him of something."

"I think it's unlikely," Abby said. "Moses simply chooses locations that are easier. More remote, far from prying neighbors. This house fits the bill."

Zoe shot her a piercing stare. "This house *didn't* fit the bill, because it was empty. If Moses wanted a remote house, he could burn down the one up the street, which *was* occupied."

"Maybe a squatter lived there," Abby suggested. "I'll ask the sheriff if he knows."

She got up and approached Sheriff Hunt. He stood next to a whiteboard, where photos from the crime scenes were taped, alongside a rudimentary timeline of the events. He was busy admonishing his deputy and didn't seem to notice her.

"What's the matter with this photo?" he barked, tapping at the board. The offending photo was a black-and-white security footage printout. Except half of it was pink.

"The printer ran out of cyan," the deputy said apologetically.

"Then change the cartridge!"

"We're all out."

Hunt shut his eyes and exhaled slowly. "Check with people here, maybe they have a working printer. Get this photo reprinted. And why is the timeline in pink too?"

"It's red."

"It looks pink to me!"

"I think the marker is dry."

"Go get some new markers. Black! I want the timeline in black."

The deputy hurried away. Muttering to himself, Hunt pulled off one of the photos and straightened it. He didn't look so hot. Dark pouches adorned his eyes, and a black smudge stained his uniform, probably soot. He didn't seem as if he'd slept at all.

"Sheriff?"

"Mullen." He turned to her, his eyes flickering to her bruised cheek. "Glad to see you're better. See that?" He pointed at the half-pink photo. It was of a parking lot, a car driving away.

"Yes. Security footage?"

"From last night. This is the car your attackers drove off in. We don't have a license plate number, it's too muddy, but it's a black Ford Focus. And this is the guy." He tapped a different printout. Same parking lot, with a man running toward the Ford. His face was only partially visible.

"His name is Richard," Abby said. "He's the one I met in the youth shelter."

"Well, like I told you, he isn't local, and the people at the youth shelter don't know him. They don't know either of them."

Abby had no desire to argue the point. "No good image of the woman?"

"Not from our security cameras. The police are checking out the footage from the motel."

"Any news about the victim ID from the fire?"

"Afraid not." Hunt sighed. "The autopsy is taking place right now, so we might have more to work with around noon."

"We were wondering, do you know if any squatters might have been living in the house that had been burned down?"

"I doubt it, but we could check with the real estate agency that was trying to sell the place." He tilted his head at Tatum and Zoe. "They your fed friends?"

"Yeah."

"The woman was a bit rude earlier."

"She takes getting used to."

"I don't know why anyone would want to get used to that."

Abby shrugged. "Find anything at the crime scene?"

"We know why the house exploded." Hunt slipped his thumbs through his belt. "There was an old-fashioned cooking stove, probably left in the kitchen by the last resident, with one of those cooking cylinders."

"A cooking cylinder," Abby said hollowly.

"Yeah. Once the house was on fire, it blew up."

She could hear the screams. Her parents, she needed to get them out. She ran toward the door.

"Abihail, get away from there!"

An explosion, searing pain on her neck—

"Mullen? Are you okay?"

She was staring, fingers touching her childhood scar on her neck. She blinked. "Um . . . yeah. We should tell the feds about this."

She returned to Zoe and Tatum, Hunt at her side, and introduced them. Then she filled Zoe and Tatum in.

"They must not have noticed it was there," Zoe said. "Maybe they got careless."

"It could be intentional," Abby said softly. "This has happened before."

They all looked at her.

"The Wilcox massacre," Tatum said. "The cooking cylinders exploded, right?"

Abby nodded. Tatum and Zoe exchanged glances but said nothing.

Hunt cleared his throat. "Anyway, like I told Mullen, we'll check with the real estate agency if they had any issue with squatters. But I doubt it. They hadn't made any complaints as far as I know."

"Who lived there before?" Zoe asked. "We think Moses might have had some sort of connection to that house."

Hunt frowned. "A woman named Paula Bridges. No living relatives as far as I know. And she'd lived there alone for more than twenty years. She died six months ago. The bank owns the property now."

Zoe glanced at Abby. "Could she have been related to Moses?"

"Anything is possible," Abby said doubtfully. "But she's not the one Moses targeted. Someone else died. And I doubt Moses would have burned someone random just because he was squatting in the wrong house. How would Moses explain that to his cult? The victim would have to be very specific."

Zoe bit her lip. "Maybe there was no squatter," she said. "I was wrong—it's like Mullen said."

Tatum stared at Zoe as if she'd sprouted chicken wings. "You were *what?*"

"Suppose Moses chose a very specific victim," Zoe said, leaning forward, her eyes flashing with excitement. "But this victim lived in the center of town. Like Mullen said, that wouldn't work—he needs a remote place he can burn before the fire crew shows up. Maybe the victim was important enough for Moses to find an alternative location. Another house to burn. An empty house. In a remote location."

"In *that* case our victim lives in a more central location," Abby said.

"Well, that doesn't narrow it down much," Hunt said. "What would this Moses consider an important victim?"

"Someone whose murder he could rationalize to his followers," Abby answered. "In Douglas, the victim was a convicted pedophile."

"Well, we can check the local sexual offenders," Hunt said skeptically. "It's not a long list."

"That's a good idea, but first, we need your help," Tatum said, looking at his phone. "We just received a federal search warrant for the premises of the church's youth shelter."

CHAPTER 26

Delilah washed her hands, letting the water run over her skin, her mind a whirlpool of fear, and relief, and guilt, and confusion. The events of the past twenty-four hours kept running in her thoughts, short visceral moments, flickering in her mind with no order or rhythm. Brad's terrified face as Father pulled her out of the gasoline-drenched room. Riding in the car with Rose and the kids, passing by fire trucks and police cars, their sirens screaming. Father and that girl, Gretchen, rutting naked in the grass, an inferno roaring behind them. Brad's agonized screeching in her ears. The explosion knocking her to the ground. An endless drive ending next to a large house, a nearby lake barely visible in the inky blackness of the night. Stumbling with the kids into a room with four bunk beds, collapsing exhausted on the nearest bunk. Knowing she was finally free. Knowing what had happened to Brad was her fault.

Emily stood by Delilah in the small bathroom, washing her hands too. She seemed to have recovered from the events of the previous night. She was prattling on about a test she had to take and about a friend she had met, a kid named Terry. Delilah usually loved listening to Emily talk, but right now, she wished her daughter would be silent, let her think in peace. Not that there was any kind of peace to be had in this place. The house they were staying at was much smaller than the farm in Rigby. She could hear people all around her. Footsteps, furniture dragging, beds creaking. In the next room, two of the congregation's women were shouting over the noise of pots clattering, talking about what was for lunch, about the day's schedule, about the evening Bible study.

As if they hadn't just watched a man burn to death. As if they didn't know Father had had sex with Gretchen a few yards away from them, the shrieks of a dying man in the background. Perhaps they really didn't know.

Were Father and Gretchen married? She tried to think back, to remember if at any point she'd seen them together, but she couldn't. And how could they even be married, with their age difference? But surely they were—Father was a pastor after all. If he wasn't celibate, he had to be married.

Even as husband and wife, how could they do it straight after . . . with Brad burning to death a few yards away?

Father was a good man, a man of God, she had no doubt about it. He'd rescued her and her children from a life of violence and had given her meaning. She still remembered the way her heart had thrummed in her chest as she heard him preach. And yet . . . last night. She felt as if she was trying to bring two opposing magnets together. She must have misunderstood what she'd seen. There wasn't any other way to explain it.

She picked up the soap and scrubbed her fingers. The knuckles, the space between the fingers, taking great care to clean under each of her nails. Rinsing the lather away, then scrubbing again. Three times was enough, Anna had told her, to really clean away the germs. And she had to wash the wrists as well, make sure her skin was cleansed before lunch. She was already used to it. She'd heard Father preach about it once, after spotting dirt underneath Richard's fingernails. Germs, a tool of the devil, were impure and brought disease. It was important to get rid of them. Some people cleaned their hands with scouring pads, but that, in her opinion, was probably taking it too far.

It was important to stay clean. She thought back to Father and Gretchen, on the muddy grass, ash fluttering around them. She shuddered, closing her eyes, and scrubbed her hands again. The knuckles. That's where dirt often ended up.

Emily turned away, drying her hands.

"Already done?" Delilah asked.

"I've been washing my hands for hours," Emily said in a whiny voice. "They're clean, Mommy."

One of the women, a twentyish hawkeyed congregation member named Karen, passed by the open bathroom door. She paused in the doorway, looking at them, her lips pursing. She eyed Emily in a manner Delilah didn't like. It was that look parents often got when their kids misbehaved in public, shrieking or throwing a scene. A judgmental stare that spoke of bad parenting and bad genes. Usually, Delilah ignored those looks. But here, she was working hard on making a lasting good impression. The congregation was a tight-knit group. She already felt like she'd somehow messed up last night.

Besides, she saw how people treated that poor guy, Benjamin. She wasn't sure what he'd done, but he always stood alone—nobody would talk to him or even look at him. He kept following congregation members with his pitiful eyes. Delilah felt really bad for him, even though she was sure he deserved it.

No, she had to make a good impression. The last thing she wanted was for them to say she was a bad mother.

"You have to really clean them," Delilah said. "Like Mommy, see? To get all the germs off."

"At home we didn't wash our hands like that," Emily said aloud, a hint of anger in her tone.

"But now we know better, right, sweetie?" Delilah said and exchanged a quick glance with Karen, who was still looking at them. Delilah raised her eyebrows, as if to say, *Kids, right?* Karen's face remained frozen.

"My skin is all scratched from this soap," Emily complained, the anger now clear in her voice. "I'm done."

"No, this is important," Delilah said, raising her voice. "Wash your hands again. And the nails and knuckles like I showed you."

"No!"

Delilah grabbed Emily's hand and scrubbed it forcefully with the soap, while Emily squirmed in her grip.

"Ow, you're hurting me!"

"We. Need. To. Get. The. Germs. Out," Delilah panted.

Karen seemed to lose interest and walked off.

Emily was now sobbing. Delilah rinsed the lather off and saw Emily hadn't been exaggerating. Her hand was covered in red scratches.

"I'm sorry, baby," she whispered in Emily's ear. "We're done now, okay? We're done."

She kept her voice low so Karen wouldn't hear her. Emily went on crying.

CHAPTER 27

Abby watched Tatum as he knocked on the door. He rapped it with his knuckles politely, as if he was a friendly neighbor dropping by to say hello, rather than a federal agent there to execute a search warrant. Sheriff Hunt and Deputy Morin stood behind him, looking uncomfortable.

A gray-haired woman opened the door. "Yes?"

"Good morning, ma'am," Tatum said. "I'm Special Agent Gray, and I have a search warrant for this youth shelter."

She frowned at him and then glanced at the sheriff. "Kenny? What is this?"

"Sorry, Dot," the sheriff said. "We'll have a quick look and be on our way."

They stepped inside, Tatum handing the warrant to Dot. Abby and Zoe followed the three men and looked around. Abby was relieved to be indoors, away from the cold. The rain had thankfully stopped, but the day seemed to get even colder.

The place was distinctly emptier than it had been the day before. Abby could faintly hear music coming from one of the rooms upstairs and a door creaking, some footsteps, a curious teen peering from one of the rooms. Yesterday she could hear talking, laughing, pots and pans rattling. It had felt like there were dozens of people inside.

As she walked from room to room, all she could see was emptiness. Bare bunk beds with nothing but a mattress, empty lockers. She spotted three forgotten socks, a tube of face lotion, and a half-finished pack of cigarettes, all indications of a hasty departure.

She stepped into one of the rooms to talk to a teenage girl, but the young teen only eyed her fearfully, not saying a word. Abby decided to leave her be for now.

Entering a communal bathroom, she glanced at a discarded empty shampoo bottle in one of the shower stalls. The smell of a strong disinfectant lingered everywhere. She stopped by the sinks, staring at them, a light nausea assailing her.

Zoe joined her in the bathroom. "There's a shed in the back with a sharp smell of gasoline, but no gasoline canisters. And I found a metal trash can with some burn marks. I think maybe Moses used it to light small fires for stress relief."

Abby nodded. "What do you think about this?" She pointed at the metal scouring pad on the edge of the sink.

"What about it?"

"Weird thing to find on a bathroom sink, isn't it? I mean, I'd expect a soap dispenser. Perhaps some paper towels. Why this?"

Zoe shrugged. "Maybe they clean the sinks with it."

"Then why keep one on each sink?" Abby pointed at the other two sinks. "They didn't clean the bathroom with those. Or pots and pans. They used these to wash their hands."

Zoe bit her lip. "Wilcox was known to have an obsession with handwashing. You may be right about it."

"I'm right."

"Have you seen this before?"

Abby forced herself to meet Zoe's penetrating gaze. "Yeah. I have."

She stepped past Zoe and out of the bathroom. Then, after taking a deep breath, she went to the office in which Anna had talked to her the day before. Dot stood there, staring angrily at Morin as he placed the office computer in a cardboard box.

"I'll get this back to you as soon as possible," Morin said apologetically. "It's just . . . the feds."

"Get this over with," Dot said.

"This place is huge," Abby said, smiling at the woman. "How many beds do you have here?"

"We have thirty beds in total," Dot answered. "Though we also have a few folding cots we can open if we're packed."

"Does that happen often?"

"Every now and again. We sometimes host volunteers here. We had a group of youths who helped renovate a local playground last year. They slept here."

"They've done an amazing job," Morin said.

Dot shot him a scathing look. Obviously, the compliment wasn't enough to compensate for the fact that he was impounding their computer.

"Thirty volunteers?" Abby asked. "That's incredible."

Dot touched her throat. "No, there were eleven back then. But we had some other kids staying here."

"I'm wondering why you need thirty beds. You could remove two beds from each room and still have enough space for all the teens who stay here, right?"

"It's best to be prepared. We don't want to have to turn anyone away."

"That's very admirable." Abby stepped over to the desk and peered into the trash can. "Do small kids stay here occasionally?"

"Sometimes."

"Did you have any recently?"

Dot hesitated. "No, I don't think so."

Abby bent, prying a bunched-up paper from the trash. She straightened it. "Then who drew this? It looks like a kid who drew a family."

Dot blinked. "I . . . I'm not sure."

"She even signed it," Abby said softly. "Look. Emily. She wrote the *y* backward."

"Oh, now I remember," Dot blurted. "We held a seminar here. A young woman came over with her kids. The girl was named Emily."

The girl had been with Anna when Abby had seen her. "A seminar, huh? What was the seminar about?" Abby glanced at the drawing again. At the tall man with the glasses. Emily had drawn him so much taller than the rest. And she'd colored only his clothing. The rest were stick figures.

"It was about . . . baptism," Dot said.

"The seminar, it was a few days long, right?" Abby asked.

"That's right."

"And some people stayed over from the church? People running the seminar?"

"Y . . . yes."

"But the woman who came with the small girl, with Emily, she just came to the seminar?"

Dot hesitated. "I think she stayed when it was over. For a few days more."

"Do you know her name?"

"No, I'm afraid I didn't catch it."

Abby showed Dot the drawing and tapped on the tall figure of the man. "And the person who led the seminar was this man."

Dot frowned. "I don't—"

"Before you say anything else, remember how many people attended the seminar. How many guests from town. Remember we can ask them too. This man, the man with the long hair and glasses who led the seminar. He's from the church. What's his name?"

Dot hesitated for a few seconds. "He's called Father Williams."

Abby gritted her teeth. "What's his first name?"

"Moses. Moses Williams."

CHAPTER 28

Delilah was cleaning up after the congregation's lunch in the dining room. Anna had taken Ron and Emily for a walk. The kids had grown very attached to the woman, and Delilah was more than thankful for the brief moment to herself.

The door opened, and Gretchen stepped in. She began helping with clearing the dishes. She seemed pale and withdrawn, unlike her usual energetic self.

They worked in silence, Gretchen stacking dishes, Delilah wiping the tables with a damp rag. Then Gretchen accidentally knocked a glass off the table. It crashed onto the floor, breaking in pieces. Delilah, nerves already frayed and trained for years to watch out for sudden noises, jumped in fright.

"Oh, no! I'm such an idiot," Gretchen blurted.

"No harm done," Delilah said quickly, her heart still thrumming in her chest. "I'll get the broom."

She quickly grabbed a broom from the kitchen and swept the floor, the pieces of glass glinting in the afternoon sunlight that shone through the window. Gretchen seemed trapped in indecision, staring at her as she worked.

Finally, the girl said, "It feels good, doesn't it?"

Delilah paused and glanced at her. "What does?"

"The second baptism. Justice. It feels good to see it, right?"

The tone of voice the girl used was a bit strange. It didn't sound as if she was recalling how good it felt. It sounded more . . . desperate. As if she was begging Delilah to agree with her. As if she wanted to be convinced it really did feel good.

"I . . ." Delilah didn't know what to say.

"It's God's will," Gretchen said fervently. "Like Father says. Only fire can clean these souls."

"Cleanse," Delilah blurted.

"Right. Cleanse these souls. He said . . . that man we baptized yesterday. He hurt you, right?"

"Right," Delilah said vacantly.

"Back home . . . there was this man." Gretchen's voice trembled. "He touched children. And a long time ago . . ." The words died on her lips, a tear running down her cheek.

"Did he hurt you?" Delilah asked gently.

"No. My sister. He hurt my sister. And when she told my parents . . . they didn't want to hear. I remember they bought her this big doll, and they acted so cheerful all the time. It was like they were trying to cover up what had happened with fake smiles. You know?"

How many times had Delilah acted cheerfully for Emily's sake? Her own body bruised, she would smile and tell jokes to make her child feel like everything was all right. Yes, she knew all about covering up the truth with fake smiles. She nodded.

"But Maegan . . . that's my sister. She barely ate. And she would come to my bed at night, and just . . . tremble. I'd hold her . . ." Gretchen shook her head.

"I'm sorry," Delilah said softly.

"And after a while this guy went to prison, and Maegan got better. It took years. I remember when I heard her laugh again. I was so relieved. You know?"

"Yeah."

"But he got out." Gretchen gritted her teeth. "And Maegan . . . she started having nightmares. She'd come to my bed again. I didn't know what to do. And then I met Father, and I learned God doesn't want us to pray. He wants us to act."

"And what happened?" Delilah asked, already knowing the answer.

Gretchen stared grimly at the pile of broken glass on the floor. "We baptized him. My sister wouldn't need to be scared of him anymore. And I was glad. It was the right thing to do." Her lips trembled. "Right?"

Delilah wanted to tell her she was right, but the words wouldn't leave her lips. "That man shouldn't have done that to your sister. It was a monstrous thing to do."

"Yeah." Gretchen began cleaning the table again, her breath shuddering. She wiped her cheek with the back of her hand.

Delilah cleared her throat as she swept, desperate to lighten the mood. "So . . . how long have you been married?"

"What?" Gretchen blinked. "I'm . . . I'm not married."

"Oh!" Delilah's gut sank. How was it possible? "I thought . . . last night, I saw, um . . . I must have misunderstood. Forget I said anything." Blood rushed to her face.

"Last night . . . it was you that saw Father and me?" Gretchen whispered. "I thought I saw someone."

"Yeah, um . . . it's none of my business. I mean, if you two are in a relationship . . . I'm sure Father knows what he's doing."

"We're not in a relationship," Gretchen said.

"Oh." Delilah stopped sweeping, staring at the tiny pile of shards intermingled with dust.

"It was God's work," Gretchen said. "That's what we were doing."

"God's work," Delilah echoed. That's what Rose had said as well. "What do you mean?"

"For the war. We need to get our army ready."

Nothing the girl said made any sense. "What army? What does that have to do with . . . what happened last night?"

"I assumed you knew." Gretchen looked at her worriedly. "I shouldn't be the one to tell you."

"Tell me what?" Delilah asked, squeezing the broom handle tightly.

"The great war is coming," Gretchen said. "The end of days."

Delilah eyed Gretchen warily. Up until now she had struck her as a bright girl. Occasionally Delilah could almost glimpse herself in the girl, from all those years ago, when she'd been full of hope, brimming with dreams and ambitions. But the last sentence was so out of character, a phrase Delilah usually associated with drunken homeless men in large cities. Had she misheard? "The end of . . . what?"

"In a few years. We don't have much time. I'm sorry, it must be terrible to hear this from me. Father explains it so much better. Because we will be spared."

Delilah recalled what Father had said about the end of days, but she'd assumed he was talking in parables, or maybe referring to something that would happen in the unknown distant future. She hadn't been paying close attention, assuming he was talking about Judgment Day. Could Gretchen have been taking his words literally? Was the girl a bit slow? "But . . . you mentioned an army?"

"Yes. Father's blood. The blood of the Messiah. Father's offspring will protect us. They will be our guardian angels." Gretchen smiled at her weakly. "So you don't have to worry. And I hope last night I was bestowed with an angel of my own."

"I don't understand . . . you and Father . . . he's been trying to get you pregnant? For this war?"

"The second baptizing is a holy moment. The best moment to conceive an angel."

A chill spread through Delilah's chest. "So every time there's a . . . baptizing, you and Father do *that*?"

"No, of course not." Gretchen frowned. "Not just me."

Delilah's head spun. "There have been others?"

Gretchen touched her arm. "It's a lot to take in. I didn't fully understand it at first either. But give it time. Father explains it so much better than I do."

The door to the dining room opened, and Richard stepped inside. He looked at them both blankly. "Father is about to start the sermon. Are you coming?"

Delilah leaned on the broom, feeling as if her legs wouldn't be able to carry her.

"We'll be there in a minute," Gretchen said.

"Yes," Delilah said hollowly. "There's some broken glass here. We need to clean it up, or someone might get hurt."

CHAPTER 29

Dot had lived for sixty-seven years, and during those years, she'd amassed a large stack of regrets. Her regret about that time she almost ran for mayor but chickened out. Her regret about cheating on her husband twice, even though he'd never found out. Her regret for telling her friend Wanda she couldn't fly with her to Japan, it was too expensive. Her regret that she was late to one of her daughter's ballet shows, missing the solo. All those and more.

And the more time you spent with regrets, the more you got to know them really well. Because a good regret was one you aired every now and again. Replaying it in your mind. Imagining how things would have played out if you'd done things differently. In a way, regrets almost became your friends, ones whom you met during the small hours of the night, or during a weekend sunset, or over a glass of wine.

She now had a new regret. Would it become a friend too? One she'd turn over in her mind again and again?

She shouldn't have lied to Deputy Morin last night.

When he'd shown up, his face distraught, all rush and bustle, with an incoherent story about people from the church attacking a woman from New York, she'd instantly become defensive. She was already a bundle of nerves from the past few weeks, with all those people staying at the youth shelter. And besides, they'd already left, so why stir up trouble? She'd blurted she'd never seen those two he mentioned, Richard and Anna. The way he'd explained things, it almost sounded like a misunderstanding anyway; she was sure there'd be no harm. And then later, when the police called, she'd doubled down on her lie, because that's what you did with lies. That's how lies reproduced, right? You told more to cover for the old ones, because her mother always told her there was nothing worse than being a liar. And Dot understood what she meant—that you had to be careful not to be *caught* lying.

Then the sheriff showed up with those people from the bureau, and she'd had to keep up the show. So a few more lies.

And now this. Those two women, looking at her. One, the little blonde one, actually seemed quite sweet. Her smile was warm, and kind, and understanding. She reminded Dot of her friend Gloria, God rest her soul, the good times they had together. Although this woman . . . Abby, they called her, had much bigger ears than Gloria. And a bruise on her face, the poor dear.

But the other one, whom they called Zoe, she was a witch. The way she glared at Dot with her angry piercing eyes, as if she already knew about all the lies.

Dot sat down behind the desk on the large leather chair. Already she felt better, back in her seat. She folded her arms and looked only at Abby, who still smiled at her.

"So Father Williams," Abby said, sitting down in front of her. "Where is he?"

"I don't know," Dot said truthfully. "They all left last night. They didn't tell me where they were going."

A loud scraping sound made Dot start. She turned her head to see Zoe dragging a chair from the corner of the room, her face impassive. She dragged it to the desk, but instead of placing it next to Abby, she placed it next to Dot, blocking her in. She sat down and took out a notebook and a pen from her small bag, then straightened her gaze at Dot's face.

Uncomfortable, Dot adjusted her chair, distancing herself from the hostile woman.

"To verify," Abby said, placing a phone on the desk. "This is Moses Williams, right?"

Dot glanced at the phone. It wasn't a good picture; it was blurry and didn't do justice to Father Williams's handsome face. "Yes, that's him."

"Okay." Abby reached to grab her phone but accidentally swiped the screen. A different image appeared on screen. It took Dot a second to understand what she was looking at. A dead charred body.

"Oh, dear heavens." She shut her eyes.

"I apologize," Abby said in embarrassment. "I took the photo last night, on the scene. Did you hear about the fire?"

"I heard there was a fire," Dot said, her eyes still shut. "I didn't know anyone died." She was deeply shaken.

"This is why we're here," Abby said. "We want to talk to Father Williams about it. And to Richard. And Anna."

"Father Williams didn't have anything to do with the fire." Dot's eyes snapped open in shock. "And I already told the police I don't know any Richard or Anna."

Abby's face crumpled, and she glanced briefly at Zoe.

"Moses is directly responsible for the fire," Zoe snapped, her eyes blazing. "And this is not the first time. And the man who burned to death was tied up before they burned him. You might think he's innocent, but if you work here, you must have seen things that seemed strange. Like the gasoline they kept in the shed in the back. Or the way Moses kept lighting small fires. You probably heard some strange sermons. Maybe you've noticed other peculiarities—"

"No." Dot was shaking her head violently, her heart thudding. "No, you're wrong, you're wrong . . ."

"Anything you're hiding makes you complicit in the burning of that man." Zoe's eyes were like hot embers, burning Dot's skin. "And he's not the only one. I can show you images of other victims."

"No!" Dot yelled, panicking.

Abby leaned forward, raising her eyebrows. "Zoe, there's no need for this. Let's hear what Dot has to say." Her voice softened when she turned to Dot. "I'm sorry, but as you probably realize, this case is making us all very tense. And the sheriff already told us we can trust you. That you're a wonderful woman who's done so much for this community. You know, I come from New York, and we kind of forget what it's like to live in a community. I wish we had more people like you around."

"Thank you," Dot whispered, a lump in her throat. "I wish I could help more, I . . . I don't know anything about that fire."

"I know you don't. And I'm sure this is all very upsetting. And after hosting such a large group from the church. I get exhausted when I just host a dinner for my extended family. And you had all these people here for . . . what? Two weeks?"

"Something like that."

"And I'm guessing it was a large group, right?"

"Yes, pretty large."

"You know." Abby gave Dot a little smile. "Last Christmas we had my uncle over, with his three kids, and his eldest daughter has *five* kids, because she had triplets, can you imagine?"

"Oh my," Dot said, her body slowly relaxing. When she was a child, her neighbor had had twins. They were a terror. She couldn't imagine what triplets would be like.

"Anyway, I was introducing them to my children, because you know how it is with small kids—they can't really remember who's who—when I suddenly realized I didn't know the kid's name. I mean, I knew it, but it slipped my mind, with all the chaos of the Christmas dinner. Can you imagine how embarrassed I was?"

"It happens," Dot told her.

"Maybe we should continue this talk at the police station," Zoe interjected. "This woman is not cooperating. She's obviously lying about Richard and Anna—"

"No! I'm not!" Dot's head spun. She wanted Zoe to leave. She could talk to Abby, but this vile woman, with her pointed accusations, was driving Dot to tears.

"We could charge you with obstruction."

"Zoe, Dot isn't lying," Abby told her partner sharply. "She got confused. There were a lot of people here, right, Dot?"

"Right," Dot whispered.

"How many exactly?"

Dot watched Abby desperately. She was right—there were so many of them. It was hard to keep track. Anyone would have gotten confused, right? "Twenty-one. Twenty-two, including Father Williams."

"See?" Abby glanced at Zoe. "That's a lot of people to host in such a small place. It's totally understandable that Dot got the names mixed up."

"They'd been here for two weeks," Zoe pointed out.

"I'm sure she remembers them. She was just confused about the names." Abby shook her head and smiled at Dot. "Richard is that big guy. Huge, really. I mean, it's no wonder you'd forget his name, he should be called Goliath."

"Oh, right," Dot said weakly. "I remember him now. Richard. And Anna was that young woman who worked closely with Father Williams. I . . . it's been such a hectic week."

"Completely understandable," Abby said softly. "And I'm sure our visit wasn't helping things, am I right? Working in a shelter for troubled youths, I'm sure this is not the first time the police caused you unnecessary grief. It must get difficult."

Dot nodded, tears running down her cheeks.

Abby smiled at her again, eyes full of sadness. "But Dot, we really need your help to find Father Williams and Anna and Richard. We don't know if they're responsible for the fire, but we need to talk to them. Verify their alibi. Okay?"

"Okay," Dot said, awash with relief. She wouldn't lie to this woman, not anymore. "But I really don't know where they went. They didn't tell me." She let out a shuddering sob.

"That's fine," Abby said. "We just want to know whatever you can tell us. When exactly did they show up?"

"Um . . . two and a half weeks ago. On Tuesday. Father Williams called and said they were coming."

"Does this happen often? Father Williams showing up with a group of people?"

"Not often. About once a year."

"And the church is okay with that?"

Dot frowned. "What do you mean?"

"Is the Lily Fellowship Church fine with Father Williams announcing he's about to show up?"

"Well . . . of course." Dot stared at Abby. "Father Williams is the founder of the church."

CHAPTER 30

Abby stared at the woman in shock. Her expression was frozen, breaking her facade of the supportive investigator. She forced herself to nod in understanding, her mind whirring, processing the information.

Moses Wilcox, according to Dot, was the founder of the Lily Fellowship Church.

Was it even possible? She thought back to the church's website, trying to remember if the website mentioned the date the church had been founded. But it couldn't be—the church had, according to Abby's research, over a dozen branches.

They would have to look into it later. For now, she had this interview to conduct. Zoe's eyes flickered toward her, an unspoken question: *Do you want me to take over?*

Abby cleared her throat. "Okay, so Father Williams would show up every year or so with his group. Are they always the same people?"

"Not all of them," Dot said. "There are a few regulars. Those two I got confused about earlier, Anna and Richard, are usually with him. And I recognized a few other faces. But there are always some new people."

"Do you know Anna's full name?"

"Um . . . I think it's Anna Clark."

"And Richard?" Abby gave her an encouraging smile.

"Richard Turner."

Now that Abby had managed to "jog" Dot's memory, it was coming back pretty accurately. "Was there a teenager with them? A young girl named Gretchen?"

"Yes. Gretchen Wood. She's a very sweet girl."

"And you said in total there were twenty-two?"

"Yes. This is more or less the group size he always shows up with. I think two years ago he had twenty-seven, but that was probably the biggest group."

"And these people, what do they do?"

"Bible studies, cooking, cleaning. They do some volunteer work occasionally. They're good people. And Father Williams is a good man. That's why I know he couldn't possibly have anything to do with that . . . that . . ."

"You may be right," Abby said. "But we have to be sure. You were talking about a seminar earlier. The entire group participated in the seminar?"

"Yes, most of them just listened, but a few of them actively participated."

"Did you participate?"

Dot hesitated. "In some of it . . . I had a few kids here, and I had to take care of them, so I couldn't possibly stay the entire seminar."

Abby smiled understandingly and rephrased the woman's sentence, giving it a positive spin. "You wanted to stay, but the kids you take care of here have precedence, right?"

Dot seemed hesitant. "Yes . . . that's right."

There was something there. It wasn't just the kids. Dot hadn't wanted to participate in the seminar.

"Father Williams's seminar," Abby said. "How did it make you feel?"

"Well . . . Father Williams is a man of convictions."

"But it seems like those convictions might not match your own."

"I . . . he does so many incredible things for the community. This youth shelter, for example, it helps so many lost souls."

"He does a great service to the community," Abby agreed. "So even if some things said in the seminar weren't to your taste, that's not so bad, right? Deeds speak louder than words."

"That's right." Dot exhaled, a trembling smile on her lips.

"But what in the seminar bothered you?"

"He talks a lot about God's justice and vengeance. Father thinks some sins cannot be forgiven and should be punished. Especially cruelty. Abused kids show up here all the time. It's hard to watch it and remain indifferent. And it makes everyone angry. I think Father feels it more than most."

"Father feels it more than most," Abby repeated, nodding. "And he wants to punish the sinners himself?"

"No! Absolutely not. But he thinks we should let God punish the sinners, through us. Let God use us as tools. It's all theoretical, of course. It's his own interpretation of a verse from the Gospel of Matthew."

"'I baptize you with water for repentance,'" Abby quoted. "'But he who is coming after me is mightier than I, whose sandals I am not worthy to carry. He will baptize you with the Holy Spirit and fire.'"

"Yes!" Dot stared at her in surprise. "Exactly. Father calls the baptism with the Holy Spirit and fire the second baptism."

Zoe bit her lips thoughtfully. Abby kept her eyes on Dot, leaning forward. "This is what they talked about in the seminar? The second baptism?"

"Not just that. There was a lot of talk about other things. And like I said, I missed most of it."

They'd return to that later. "Is there anything else you didn't quite agree with?"

"Um . . ." Dot blushed, looking distinctly uncomfortable. "They had weird dynamics in that group."

"What struck you as weird?"

"Like, for example, there was one guy, Benjamin? No one talked to him. It was like in school, when there's a kid who's intentionally left out. You know what I mean?"

"Yeah. So it felt intentional."

"Yes, they wouldn't even look at him. And there was this young woman named Jennifer, and they kept asking her really personal questions I didn't agree with."

"Like what?"

"Like did she get her period, and talked about how she looked . . . like physically. They kept prodding at her—it was very cruel."

"They asked about her period?"

"Yes, they were generally obsessed with the women parishioners', um . . . cycles. They kept talking about it."

This was new. Was this something else Moses was now obsessed with? She could imagine it as an extension of his obsession with germs. Abby filed away this information for later. "Let's talk about yesterday. Did they tell you they were about to leave?"

"Yes, absolutely, they let me know over the weekend that they would leave on Wednesday evening, which was yesterday."

So they'd planned this days in advance, like in Douglas.

"Anything out of the ordinary happen yesterday, before they left?"

"Well . . . they were packing up, of course. I think Father Williams had an argument with Anna Clark about something."

"Why do you think that?"

"There . . . there was yelling from the office."

"Was Father Williams yelling?"

"No. Only Anna." Dot's eyes skittered.

"What did she yell about?"

"I didn't eavesdrop. I just heard her voice."

"But did she sound angry?"

"Not exactly angry. She sounded . . ." Dot took a deep breath. "She sounded in pain. I think she was really upset about something."

Or maybe she'd been in actual pain. "When did this happen?"

"Around noon."

After Abby had shown up. Moses hadn't been happy with her visit and probably took it out on Anna.

"Did you see Anna after that?"

"Briefly. She was busy managing the packing operations. She's usually the one in charge."

"Anything else you noticed?"

"No . . . not really."

"What were the group talking about?"

"I heard some of them wondering where they were going next. And there was talk about a list of names."

"A list of names?"

"Yes. I don't know what it was about, but it seemed to occupy them. They wanted to know who was on a list. I think it had something to do with a sort of extra duty or something."

"Do you know who was on that list?"

"No. I got the impression there were only a few names."

"What time did they leave?"

"I think they left around ten."

"How did they leave, exactly? In cars?"

"Well, they have a van and a few additional vehicles."

"Can you give us license plates of these vehicles? Their brand?"

Dot shook her head. "But I can tell you their colors."

"Okay, we'll write those down later. I want to go back to the day they showed up here . . ."

She kept questioning Dot, while Zoe listened, staying silent. And throughout that time Abby kept thinking about Moses's second baptism. How many people had been baptized like that?

Would there be more?

CHAPTER 31

Thursday, November 17, 2005

"I realize that you are scared. I'm scared too. But this isn't only a setback. It's an opportunity."

Anna stood behind the podium, her voice echoing in the large room. The town hall meeting was being conducted in the local school's gymnasium. It was the only place in the area large enough for the unprecedented turnout.

The local glass factory had been closed just a week before. More than three hundred local residents had lost their jobs.

"In times like these we need to work together," Anna said. "To help each other."

Moses watched her from his seat in the corner, his irritation growing. She was doing it all wrong.

Like the local residents, he was terrified as well. He had just purchased a large farmhouse on the outskirts of town, in which he intended to build a compound for his flock. But this closure was a death knell for the town. Soon, the younger residents would leave. People would stop donating to his group. No one would have money to spare for their seminars or to hire his people.

They would have to leave and start over. But before they did, he was intent on squeezing every last drop from this community. He'd told

Anna earlier. They could use the tensions in town. But Anna was trying to calm people down instead.

"We can send letters to the governor. We can sue for reparations," Anna said. "The Lily group would be happy to organize this."

Some people were already leaving. Others were talking among themselves. Moses clenched his fists.

"We can buy food in bulk for the families who lost their income—"

Moses stood up and marched over to the podium. As he did so, he was vaguely aware that people were staring at him.

"I'll take it from here," he whispered in Anna's ear.

She looked shocked but stepped aside.

He turned to face the crowd.

Suddenly he realized he wasn't wearing his customary baseball cap and sunglasses. He was standing here, the center of attention, hundreds of people looking at him. Any minute now someone would shout "Hang on, I know this guy, it's Moses Wilcox."

They would call the police; he would be arrested. Why had he done this? It had been a stupid impulse. Foolish.

But no one said anything. Everyone watched him in silence. He saw no recognition on anyone's face. Only curiosity. How was this possible?

It was divine intervention. Of course. God was clouding these people's minds. God didn't want them to recognize him.

A wave of relief and joy washed over him. He was, once again, God's messenger, doing his holy work.

"Many of you don't know me very well," he said. "I'm Moses Williams, and I run the Lily group that Anna was talking about."

He watched the faces. He needed their trust, and he needed it fast. He'd been ravenously collecting information about the local residents for years. He was familiar with most of the faces he saw.

"But I know you," he said. "I've been watching this incredible thriving town for a long time. I've seen people do incredible things. Monica Jackson, raising her three children all by herself after her husband died in that tragic accident." He gestured at the woman in the crowd. His eyes scanned the faces, locating others he could name. "Tyler Lewis, winning the state's swimming championship for two consecutive years. Jonathan Hall, who lost his arm in the factory and still managed to open and manage our own wonderful local pizzeria. This is not a community that lets life kick them around. This is a town of fighters."

Some murmurs. People nodding.

"The PUF Corporation closed our factory, thinking we would just lie down and die. But they don't know us. We can rain hell upon them."

He was pacing back and forth, his voice rising, echoing over the crowd. He didn't need the microphone anymore. His voice was being carried by God.

"Do you know who the PUF Corporation are? They aren't Americans. They aren't *Christians*."

He wasn't sure who the PUF Corporation was. Maybe they were Chinese. It didn't matter.

"They are heathens!" he roared.

The crowd roared back.

"When the Amalekites opposed the Israelites, God said, 'Now go and strike Amalek and devote to destruction all that they have. Do not spare them, but kill both man and woman, child and infant, ox and sheep, camel and donkey.'"

People's eyes were wide and intent on him. Some were shouting.

"And I am telling you, when we are done with the PUF Corporation, they will wish they were the Amalekites!"

"Yeah!" someone shouted.

"Yes, we will send a host of lawyers, but we will go to the press and tell them about this, and we will march in protest and shut down their factories all over the country."

Some people were standing now, waving their fists.

"This is a town of good Christians. And Christianity is about love and forgiveness. But it is also about justice!"

He picked up some papers lying on the podium, throwing them in the air with a swift movement.

"There are times to turn the other cheek, and there are times to stand up and fight the heathens! And this is a time to fight!"

He had them, and he knew it. His body thrummed with euphoria. He hadn't felt like this for more than a decade.

"Many of you know that our group, the Lily group, has bought a farm here in town. And I will tell you why." He eyed Father Porter in the crowd. He didn't need the man anymore. "It will be a church. A church that will offer more than prayer and charity to the good Christians in this town. It will offer action! It will offer a welcoming hand to our fellow men. The Lily Fellowship Church. And from there we will fight the heathens until we bring them to their knees!"

Some people had left, and some were whispering among themselves, looking at him worriedly. But many were roaring, and shaking fists, and yelling furiously. He smiled at the crowd and cast a side glance at Anna. Her face was full of awe, and his smile widened.

She saw him as he truly was now. Not just a man of God.

He was God's will.

CHAPTER 32

Abby stepped out of the youth shelter, her mind whirling. Was it possible? Could Moses Wilcox have founded the Lily Fellowship Church? A sudden image popped in her mind. Her as a young child, standing by Moses, watching the field.

"Consider the lilies, Abihail."

He loved lilies. They always had lilies in the compound and in her parents' flower shop. It didn't necessarily mean anything, but it fit.

She leaned against her rental, staring at the youth shelter. According to Gretchen's sister, Gretchen had first met Moses in the church's youth camp near Douglas. If Moses was really the church's founder, he might have intentionally built youth shelters and camps to attract potential recruits. Young troubled teenagers like Gretchen, many of them eager for an authoritative parent figure. She felt ill.

Zoe and Tatum stepped outside and approached her.

"Good work in there," Abby told Zoe.

"Thanks," Zoe answered.

A long pause ensued. Tatum gave Zoe a look and cleared his throat noisily.

"You too," Zoe added.

Abby smiled at her. The truth was, she had enjoyed it back there. For a while, she and Zoe had seemed to be completely in sync, each grasping her role in the interrogation instinctively, without discussing it beforehand. Abby didn't interrogate often in her role as a crisis negotiator. But with Zoe, it had been as easy as riding a bicycle again. Easier, actually, considering that the last time she had tried to ride a bicycle, she'd crashed into a fence within half a minute.

"Can we verify that Moses is the founder of the Lily Fellowship Church?" she asked.

"I think it's more likely he was lying about that," Zoe said. "Giving himself an aura of importance. It's not uncommon with psychopaths. Or men in general."

"It's possible," Abby allowed. "But I think it might be true. The church's name—"

"You think that in addition to being a radical cult leader, he also has enough business savvy to found a chain of churches?" Tatum asked. "What are the chances?"

"He doesn't need business savvy at all," Abby said. "He just needs resourceful loyal followers. Think about it. A cult is a business in which the employees work eighteen hours a day and are paid nothing. In fact, they usually donate all their worldly possessions to the cult. We know the church management is very keen on regular donations. Put a decent administrator in charge of this business, and it would grow very fast."

"Like NXIVM," Zoe said.

"Exactly. Keith Raniere, the founder of NXIVM, created a multibranched organization that cycled hundreds of millions of dollars. Or here's another example—Jim Jones built a town that housed over nine hundred people in the middle of the jungle in Guyana. Bhagwan Shree Rajneesh created an enormous settlement with a fleet of cars and a private plane—"

"Okay, okay, I get it," Tatum said, raising his hands. "If Moses Wilcox recruited a few clever followers, he could use his charisma and influence to create the Lily Fellowship Church organization. We will check it out."

Abby glanced aside at Sheriff Hunt as he joined them from the back of the farm, leaving huge footprints in the powdery snow.

"We also need to follow up on the new recruit," Abby said.

"What recruit?" Zoe's nose was getting red in the cold air.

"The woman Dot mentioned, with the girl. Emily. She came for the seminar but stayed."

"You think she joined Moses's cult?" Zoe asked, biting her lip.

"Dot said she stayed for days afterward. It sounds like she left with them. We need to check if—"

"Hang on." Zoe's eyes glazed. "We had a recruit in Douglas too. Gretchen, right?"

"Right."

"The police there thought Gretchen might have had a past with that pedophile they'd burned alive."

"Yeah," Abby said. Maegan, Gretchen's sister, had talked about it. "Her sister sounded like she thought that might be the case too."

"We thought Moses chose a specific victim in this case," Zoe pointed out. "What if it's the same? What if the victim is related to whoever he recruited?"

She could be right. "It might be a recruitment technique," Abby said, her heart beating faster. If Zoe was right, it was diabolical. Involving the new member with the crime. Instantly implicating them in murder, creating a strong incentive for the new member to keep quiet. And it would make the recruit want to believe in the cult's extreme acts. Was this what Moses had done in each of the previous fires? Was every victim connected to a new cult member?

"So someone from town would have joined the cult?" Hunt asked.

"Yes, we should watch out for any people gone missing," Abby answered. "Maybe they already left. Or they'll leave soon. They might say they're moving away, that they found a job somewhere or—"

"We have a missing person reported," Hunt interrupted her.

"Who?" Abby asked.

"Delilah Eckert disappeared a few days ago with her two children. Her husband was raising hell yesterday morning that we weren't doing enough to find her. And uh . . . they weren't having the best family life. Brad Eckert is a vicious bastard."

"Was Delilah's daughter named Emily?"

"I'm not sure, I'll have to check the missing persons report, but Brad definitely reported a young daughter and a baby son missing along with his wife."

"Where do the Eckerts live?" Tatum asked.

"In West Fremont. Right in the middle of town."

"That would fit," Zoe said. "Like we discussed earlier. They focused on a victim who lived in the center of town, so they had to move him to a distant, empty house they could burn without being caught."

"I have Brad Eckert's phone number somewhere here," Hunt said. He took out his phone and tapped at it. "There we go."

He dialed the number. Abby looked at him as he held the phone to his ear. She could hear the faint dial tone. After a long wait, Hunt hung up. "No answer. I'll swing by the Eckerts' and see if—"

"Hang on," Abby said. "Do you have a photo of Delilah Eckert? Dot might recognize her."

"Oh, yeah, sure. Brad sent me one."

He found it on his phone and handed it to Abby. She glanced at it and instantly realized she didn't need to ask Dot.

It was a photo of the entire family. Brad with his arm over Delilah's shoulder. Delilah's smile was warm and happy, not the smile of a beaten wife. But then, Abby knew how easy it was to fake a smile. Delilah held a small chubby baby with a glazed stare. And between the parents, little

Emily, whom Abby recognized immediately. It was the girl she'd seen with Anna.

"It's her," she said. "I saw the girl. I . . ." The words died on her lips. Something in the photo unnerved her, like a strange feeling of déjà vu. It took her a few seconds to put her finger on it.

Delilah looked almost exactly the same as Abby's biological mother.

CHAPTER 33

"You shouldn't listen to Gretchen," Rose told Delilah. "She's a really sweet, innocent soul. But she's a bit . . . slow."

Delilah cleared her throat. "All those things she said to me—"

"It's hard to follow Father's teachings sometimes," Rose said. "He knows so much, and he wants to convey the knowledge to us as fast as he can. But then people like Gretchen get confused."

"But I saw Father and Gretchen that night—"

"Sometimes the devil makes us see things," Rose said. "Are you absolutely sure you really saw it?" There was something judgmental in her tone.

Delilah had thought she was sure, but was she? The events of that night seemed like a bad dream. It was entirely impossible. She thought of how elated she felt lately when she heard Father preaching. Rose would scoff if she said she was sure. Because it sounded ridiculous. She didn't want to be labeled like Gretchen was, as slow. It did sound like something the devil would make her see. A holy man, rutting in the grass, fire and smoke around them, and the anguished screams of the tormented. It was an image straight from depictions of hell.

"No," she said. "You're right. It was such a crazy night."

"That's right." Rose smiled at her, pleased. "We have ways to battle the thoughts and images that the devil sends us. I can teach you later."

"Thanks," Delilah said, feeling grateful and relieved. Like a large weight had been removed from her heart.

They were sitting in their room at the cabin, surrounded by boxes of pamphlets. Richard had brought the boxes in, and Rose explained Father wanted them to fix the text. The pamphlets were printed on quality paper, an image of a cross in front and a man reading the Bible on the back. The title of the pamphlet was simply *The Lily Fellowship Church*. Inside the pamphlets, there was a quick explanation of the different initiatives that the church was working on and an invitation to take a part in the growing movement, with the church's website.

Delilah and Rose's job was to open each pamphlet and erase three lines, in which one of the church's members was quoted praising their work. Rose had explained this person was no longer a member, and Father refused to distribute the pamphlets with her words on it.

It was mind-numbing work. Delilah would take a pamphlet, open it, carefully delete the three lines with a permanent marker, then fold it again and stack it in another box. Strangely, the more she deleted the lines, the more they were seared into her brain, until she knew them by heart. *Fran Green, church volunteer: "Before I joined the Lily Fellowship Church, I had been lost and alone. Now, I'm part of a family, and every morning I wake up knowing we're doing God's work. The thankful smiles and the gratitude we get from those we help fill me with purpose and happiness."*

It was a strange line to delete. Almost as if they were deleting the faceless Fran's actual purpose and happiness.

They didn't have a desk in the room, so they worked on the floor, and by now the back of her neck hurt. The smell of the permanent markers was making her dizzy and nauseous. The two bunk beds and the boxes took up most of the room's space, making it feel cramped, stifling. She wished she could open a window, but it was too cold.

"Why are we even doing this?" She groaned, straightening and massaging her neck. "Who cares if this person is quoted on the pamphlet?"

Rose glanced at her. "Father is a man of integrity."

"Of course." Delilah shifted, feeling instantly guilty. "But . . . I mean . . . it's not like it's a bad quote."

"This *woman*," Rose said, almost spitting the word, "left us and said bad things about us. She tried to convince others to leave. She doesn't *deserve* to be on this pamphlet. She doesn't even deserve to have us talk about her."

Delilah nodded hurriedly. "Did you know her well?"

"At one time, I mistook her for a dear friend," Rose said with disgust. "We slept in the same room, like you and I are doing now."

"Oh." Delilah took out another pamphlet and deleted the three sentences, the marker squeaking on the glossy page: *Every morning I wake up knowing we're doing God's work.* She thought of her kids. Anna had taken them both on a ride to town to buy some groceries the group needed. Delilah was partially relieved. It's not like she could really give them the attention they deserved right now, and Emily had been excited to go. But she'd been so used to having them with her all the time. And for the past week she'd hardly spent any time with them at all.

"What's your daughter's name?" she asked Rose, taking another pamphlet from the box.

"Lori," Rose said.

"Oh, that's a pretty name."

"Yeah." Rose smiled to herself as she unfolded a pamphlet. "My mom wanted me to name her after my grandma. Gertrude. Like, seriously? You want my little cherub to be called Gertrude?"

"Is Lori with her father?"

"No." Rose pursed her lips. "Lori's dad ran as fast as his legs could take him once he realized I was pregnant. No, Lori's with my parents."

"Oh. Why isn't she staying with you?"

"Well, I was so busy with the congregation these past few years. And I wanted to give Lori some stability and a nurturing environment. And we keep traveling from place to place. And then Father suggested she stay with my parents for a little while. Until we find a place we can really settle in."

"So how long has she been staying with your parents?"

"It'll be two years soon," Rose said in a half whisper.

Delilah had to bite her tongue to avoid shouting, *Two years?* She'd thought Rose was talking about a few weeks. *For a little while*, wasn't that what she'd said?

"But Father told me we'd find a place to settle really soon. He thinks Lori will be back with us by the summer. Maybe when we get to California."

"Oh, good," Delilah said. "When was the last time you visited her?"

"I . . . you know how it can get difficult when you have to say goodbye. And Father said we shouldn't give her mixed signals. In the summer she'll be back with me for good. And it'll be really good for her . . . for us. Because before I had to send . . . before she went to stay with them, my attention was all over the place, and it frustrated everyone. We should be focused on our tasks. For our future."

"Oh."

"I remember this one time." The words were gushing out now, a torrent. "I was trying to read the Gospels, and I couldn't get it done fast enough, and Father said I had to finish by morning, and Lori kept asking me things—just, you know, little things, but it distracted me, and then I eventually shrieked at her and she started crying, and then Father came and wanted to know what was the noise, because he was trying to work. You know, at the time there were other kids at the group, and they kept making a ruckus, you know how kids are, and . . . and . . ." A tear plopped on the pamphlet Rose was holding.

"I'm sorry, I didn't mean to make you upset," Delilah said hurriedly.

"It's okay." Rose sniffed. "I'm glad Father told me to send her to my parents. By the summer she'll be a big girl, and she won't make a lot of noise. She'll let me work, and she won't bother Father. Or anyone."

"I think Father probably changed a lot in the past years," Delilah suggested. "Because he's really nice about Emily and Ron. He always smiles at them, and he never complained."

"Yeah," Rose said. "He's very patient at first. That was how it was with Lori. And with Terry too."

"Terry?" Delilah asked, confused.

"Another child who was with us."

"He also had to leave?"

"I . . . he got hurt. Social services took him."

"Social services?" Delilah asked breathlessly.

"We should really concentrate on the pamphlets, or we'll never be done."

"But what happened to Terry? How did he get hurt?"

"It was a stupid accident. And it won't happen again." Rose shook her head and whispered, "It won't. We don't do that anymore. He said we don't do that anymore."

"What?" Delilah's throat was clenching. "Rose, what are you talking about?"

"I need to focus, Delilah. And you should too. Your box is much emptier than mine."

Delilah stared at Rose in shock. Rose was working fast now, grabbing handfuls of pamphlets and vehemently crossing out the offensive quote. Her lips moved silently in what seemed like a prayer.

Where *were* Anna and the kids? Hadn't they been gone for hours? Delilah had a hard time breathing. The fumes of the permanent markers, probably. She could really use a hug from Emily just about now. And had Anna taken formula for her drive with the kids? What if Ron got hungry?

Why had she been letting Anna spend all this time with her kids, anyway? Thinking back on the past week, she realized there was always something that urgently needed to be done, and the kids would get in the way. And then, there would be Anna, suggesting she and the kids should go for a walk, or play together, or tuck Ron in. Delilah had been so grateful. She loved this community and wanted them to see how useful she could be. But her kids needed her too.

"Maybe we should start a day care for the congregation," she blurted. "Anna and I could manage it, and then Lori could come stay with you. We'd look after her during the day along with the rest of the kids so they wouldn't get in the way. Wouldn't that be nice?"

Rose frowned. "Why do you think Anna would be interested in doing that?"

"She loves kids! I mean, she spends all the time with *my* kids—"

"Because she was told to."

Delilah stared at her.

"I mean . . . someone suggested she could free you so you could get to spend time with the rest of the congregation. Get to know us, and—"

Delilah stood up, her head spinning. How long had she been in this room, fixing pamphlets? How long had she been away from her kids?

She stepped out. Through the window, she saw the car Anna had taken when she rode to town. She was back? Then where were the kids?

"Emily?" Delilah called out. "Emily, are you here?"

Glances in the hallway as she ran past people. "Emily? Anna? Did someone see Anna or Emily and Ron? Emily!"

She was told to.

Running through the rooms in the hostel, opening doors, her heart thudding in her chest, hardly breathing. "Emily! Anna!"

They were nowhere, and now tears of panic were running down Delilah's cheeks. *She was told to.* Terry got hurt, social services took him.

Delilah stepped outside and screeched, "Emily!"

He said we don't do that anymore.

"Emily!" Delilah's screams were hoarse, laden with tears of fear.

A child's sudden wail made her whirl around. Anna was standing by the house pushing the stroller, Emily by her side. She looked at Delilah with wide eyes.

"You woke him up," Anna said. "He just fell asleep."

Delilah dashed to the stroller and whisked Ron out, hugging him as he cried. "Where were you?" she shouted at Anna.

"We returned from town and went around back to build a snowman," Anna said. "Are you all right?"

"Why didn't you tell me you were back?"

"You were busy. I thought you would be glad—"

Delilah crouched and hugged Emily with one hand, the other holding Ron, who was still crying.

"Mommy, I built a snowman outside," Emily said. "Anna says we need a carrot for its nose."

"That's a good idea," Delilah said, her eyes shut. "Let's go look for a carrot. Together."

CHAPTER 34

From what Abby could see, Delilah Eckert's life had come to a screeching halt when she'd gotten married.

One of the cops at the local station had gone to school with Delilah. He'd told Abby she'd always been a good student and quite popular. That she'd seemed happy. Her social media accounts told a similar story. Photos of her and her friends hanging out. Shared posts about things that bothered her, such as animal cruelty and the children in war-torn countries. The occasional empowering meme.

She hadn't posted anything in six years. Her final few posts were all photos with Brad Eckert. Her excited photo of her hand with a large diamond ring. A honeymoon. A happy couple in their new home, Delilah sporting a pregnant belly. And then the posts seemed to trickle to nothing.

Abby sighed and leaned back in her chair, massaging her neck. She had been staring at the laptop screen for the past hour in that Neanderthalian posture humans of the modern era were reacquiring— leaning forward, her neck and back curved like a question mark.

Hunt had gone to the Eckerts' home. It was empty, and the front door was unlocked. In the kitchen, there were signs of a struggle. Brad's and Delilah's phones were still in the house. A bunch of things belonging to the kids were missing—clothing, toys, the baby's stroller, diapers. A lot of Delilah's clothes were missing as well, but it appeared that all of Brad's clothes were still there. It definitely looked like Delilah had decided to leave with the kids.

The neighbors had heard some screaming yesterday morning and the sound of something crashing. But they hadn't bothered to report it. Apparently, screaming from the Eckerts' home was far from unusual, and the neighbors had learned long ago that calling the police didn't help for long.

If there had been any doubt, Brad's dentist helped verify that the latest victim was indeed Brad Eckert.

They were right. Delilah had been recruited to the cult, and Brad had been murdered in some sort of initiation ceremony. Or as Dot had called it, a second baptism.

The task force room had emptied slowly as evening settled. Tatum had gone to the bureau's offices in Jackson, for a law enforcement agencies coordination meeting, which he'd called a "typical pencil-pushing waste of time." Sheriff Hunt had gone to talk to Brad Eckert's mother. Zoe stayed in the task force room, papers strewed around her haphazardly. It seemed like she was in the habit of printing almost anything she wanted to read, which Abby thought was excessive, not to mention bad for the planet. Currently, Zoe was frowning over photos from the crime scene, biting her lip.

Abby had already talked to a few of Delilah's high school friends, and they all said pretty much the same thing. Delilah had drifted off once she and Brad had become a thing. Some of them mentioned Brad was controlling, jealous—that whenever they weren't together, he'd repeatedly call her. One of them mentioned she'd heard that Brad hit Delilah, but she didn't remember where she'd heard it. Not from Delilah, of that she was sure.

Abby needed to talk to someone who'd known Delilah more recently.

She had the phone Delilah had left in her house, and now she opened it. There was no screen lock, and that made Abby think about

Brad again. It was not unusual for jealous, controlling men to demand their spouses remove the screen lock. So that the husbands could check the phone at any time, read through the messages, look through the incoming and outgoing calls. It was one of those small, innocuous signs that spoke of a bigger, darker picture.

She tapped the Facebook app and checked Delilah's profile. Most of Delilah's friends had been added years before. But there was one who'd been added less than a year ago—Paula Cook. And Delilah had Paula's number on her phone. Paula's number came up steadily throughout the list of recent calls from Delilah's phone, every week or two. The last call between them was thirteen days ago.

Abby checked the time. It was just after ten p.m. She called Paula from her own phone.

"Hello?" Paula's voice had a grainy quality.

"Hi, is this Paula Cook?"

"Yeah, who's this?"

"My name is Lieutenant Abby Mullen. I'm investigating the house fire that happened last night. Do you have a few minutes to talk?"

"I was about to go to sleep. I don't know anything about that."

"I won't take a lot of your time," Abby said pleasantly. "I was calling about the victim's wife, Delilah. You know her, right?"

A moment of hesitation. "Yeah. I know her a bit."

"I was hoping I could talk to her, but I haven't been able to reach her."

"Did you try her phone number?"

"Yeah," Abby said, looking at Delilah's phone on the desk. "She's not picking up."

"I don't know where she is. I haven't talked to her in over two weeks. I thought she was at home. She has two kids." A shift in Paula's voice. She was worried. Abby regretted not talking to Paula face to face, seeing her reaction. She briefly contemplated asking if she could come over but decided to keep it short. She could always drop by tomorrow.

"When was the last time you saw Delilah?"

"Probably three weeks ago. We met for coffee."

"How did she seem when you met her? Was she different somehow?"

"Different how?"

"Excited, or worried, or anxious," Abby suggested.

There was a brief silence, and then Paula said, "Worried and anxious wouldn't exactly be different than the usual."

"Because of her husband?"

"You know about Brad?"

"I heard he might have been abusing her."

"You heard right, no might haves there. He was terrorizing her."

"She told you about it?"

Another moment of hesitation. "Yeah."

Abby exhaled. "How do you know Delilah?"

"The local preacher introduced us."

"Why?"

"Just because," Paula said angrily. "Lieutenant, it's really late and—"

"It sounds like he might have introduced you because he thought you had things in common."

For a few seconds, Paula breathed on the other side of the phone. Finally, she said, "Delilah didn't have anything to do with that fire, Lieutenant."

"I know," Abby said. "But we need to find her."

"I don't know where she is."

"If she contacts you, can you ask her to give me a call? It's for her own safety. And her children's."

"Okay," Paula said. "To the number you called from?"

"Yeah. Any time, night or day."

"I'll tell her."

"Thank you," Abby said, but the line was already dead.

A second later, Delilah's phone rang, Paula's name appearing on screen. Abby watched it ringing, debating with herself if she should answer. She let it ring. After a few seconds it stopped.

She removed her glasses, then massaged the bridge of her nose. Even without her glasses, the world a blurry mess of shapes and colors, she could see Zoe's eyes—two small green orbs, staring directly at her.

"What is it?" she asked tiredly.

"I don't understand why you're fixated on Delilah Eckert," Zoe said.

"I'm not fixated on her." Abby put her glasses back on.

She told herself she really wasn't. She was following up on a promising lead. Sure, the woman looked like her biological mother, but that wasn't it. A lot of people were similar to others. Abby had once met her own doppelgänger in a bar in college. It was before the age of selfies, or she would have taken one with her drunken twin for posterity. So Delilah's similarity to Abby's mother didn't really mean anything.

Aside from the fact that Moses must have noticed it as well. And it would have drawn his attention to the woman.

"You've spent the past two hours calling her friends and family and scouring her phone and social media," Zoe pointed out.

"Well, she's a solid lead in this investigation." Abby wasn't keen to point out the similarity to her own biological mother. It would make her own position in this investigation more precarious.

"She's a lead," Zoe allowed. "And so are the vehicles we know Moses and his cult are using. So is the type of electric cord they seem to have settled on. So is the fact that we now know that Moses seems to be the founder of the Lily Fellowship Church—"

"Yes," Abby interrupted. "And you and the bureau are looking into all that. So I'm focusing on Delilah."

"I understand you want to focus on Moses's followers. That makes sense," Zoe said. "In a way, they're the weaker link. But why focus on the person who most recently joined? In all likelihood, she's not calling any shots, she's not making any decisions. I doubt they even trust her enough to tell her anything significant."

"Who would you focus on?" Abby asked, losing her patience.

"Dot gave us a list of names," Zoe said. "So I'd focus on any of the older members—they probably know a lot more. Specifically it sounds like Anna Clark is one of the people in charge. *And* from what we've heard, she's been mistreated recently. If there's anyone who might help us, it's her."

"Anna Clark is probably the last person who would be helpful in any way," Abby said. "You're right, she's high up in the hierarchy, maybe even Moses's right hand. Which means she's been with him long enough to make him the absolute center of her world. He has his clutches so firmly deep in her brain, it's not likely she'll ever turn on him. The only thing she wants is his approval. Yes, he mistreated her, probably punished her. And look what happened straight after. She went after me."

"Just because she did what Moses told her—"

"You don't understand. Moses didn't tell her to grab me. That's not his style. *She* decided to do it because she thought it would please him. Being punished by Moses doesn't push her away from him. It makes her try to regain his favor."

"I don't agree with your analysis." Zoe pursed her lips.

"I've studied dozens of cults, talked to hundreds of cult survivors. I've been in a cult myself—"

"Yes." Zoe cut her off. "And you're quoted in nine scholarly articles that revolve around cult behavior and cult mind control."

"I . . ." Abby was caught off guard. "Yes. Really? Nine?"

"And you cowrote two." Zoe folded her arms. "I read them on the flight. You could have pointed those out to me earlier. I wouldn't have wasted my time on the FBI's so-called cult expert."

Abby gritted her teeth. Zoe managed to be infuriating even when she conceded that Abby knew what she was talking about. "The point is, I know how these people think much better than you . . . don't look at me like that."

"Like what?"

"You're giving me that scary stare of yours."

"What scary stare?" Zoe frowned.

"Your laser-eyes thing."

"I don't have laser eyes."

To Abby's astonishment, Zoe glanced away, looking hurt.

"Okay." Abby raised her palms placidly. "I didn't mean anything by that. Look, the reason I am focused on Delilah is because I think Moses messed up there. He brought her in too fast."

"What do you mean?"

"Recruiting into a cult is a process. People don't become followers overnight. That seminar Dot told us about? That's a typical cult recruitment tactic. Get the person you want to recruit away from everyone they know, monopolize their time, bombard them with the cult's basic agenda and with a feeling of kinship. That's what they did with Gretchen Wood too. Except with Gretchen Wood it wasn't one seminar, it was several—and only after they were certain she was fully swayed, they moved to the more difficult agenda. In this case the murder and burning of what they call an unredeemable sinner. Right?"

"That sounds like a possible chain of events," Zoe allowed.

"But with Delilah, they did one seminar, and a few days later, bam! Burn her husband."

"From what I've been overhearing during your conversations with her friends, she had ample reasons to want her husband dead."

"Yeah, but there's a huge leap between wanting someone dead and burning him alive, right? And then they leave with her and her children. Just a week after she met them." Abby leaned back in her seat. "She's probably feeling uncertain and scared right now. And she has her kids to worry about. It's very likely she'll try to reach out to someone she knows. Both her parents are dead, and she's an only child. It would likely be an old friend."

"And you think when her friend tells her the police are looking for her, she'll call you?" Zoe asked doubtfully. "She's an accomplice to murder."

Abby shook her head. "She's not an accomplice. It's not like that. She was coerced."

"The Manson Family murders were done by Manson's followers. He wasn't even there during most murders. They weren't coerced. They were murderers."

"This isn't the Manson Family. And Delilah wasn't deep enough into Moses's cult to willingly participate in this. She's not an accomplice and not a murderer. At the moment, she's a victim."

"No one forced her to join this group."

"She *didn't* join this group. People don't join cults. They're recruited. And usually they have little control when it happens."

"You make it sound like a disease."

"In a way it is," Abby said. "Moses Wilcox is a sort of cancer, who spreads and corrupts—"

"Moses Wilcox is just a man," Zoe said. "He might be delusional and dangerous, but he isn't a cancer, just like he isn't a . . . I don't know what these people think he is. A messiah or something."

"Okay, but everything he does is intended to strengthen his grip on these people and twist their minds, and he's very good at that."

Zoe frowned. "Not everything he does. If that's all he did, we wouldn't have people burning in their homes."

"I don't know how burning people alive ties into his agenda—"

"I do."

Abby stared at Zoe in surprise. "You know why he burns people?"

"Yes. He has sexual fantasies about it, and when they get too overwhelming, he enacts them."

"I told you, that's not how Moses Wilcox thinks. His entire focus is aimed at his followers and his cult. It has nothing to do with sexual fantasies."

"It has *everything* to do with sexual fantasies!" Zoe said, her jaw clenching. "You told me you know how people in a cult think better than I do. Fine. But I've spent my life studying and profiling people like Moses, and I know much better than you how *his* mind works."

"I know him personally! I grew up in his cult—"

"That doesn't make you a good candidate to profile him. In fact, it probably makes it much worse. You have an emotional bias."

Abby bunched her fists. She was glad she hadn't mentioned Delilah's similarity to her mom. "I can put my emotions aside."

"No," Zoe said simply. "You can't. Look here."

She handed Abby a photo from the crime scene. Footprints in the mud.

"What am I looking at?" Abby asked.

"Two pairs of fresh prints walking away from the house. I initially thought someone was running away from the house, and the other one was chasing them. But I consulted with a forensic podiatrist, and he said they were walking together. The prints probably belong to a man and a woman. And they end up here." She handed her another photo. A patch of grass, clearly squashed.

"What is that?"

"It looks like they lay down here," Zoe said. "Following my request, the forensic team searched and found traces of what looks like bodily fluids in the grass. And look what they just sent me that they found in the vicinity." She held out her phone.

Abby took a look at the screen. It was a photo of a muddy patch in the grass. Covered in mud, almost invisible, was a piece of white cloth. Abby looked at it carefully. It was a pair of women's underwear.

"I'm betting that when the house exploded, they hurriedly got away. She had no time to put on her underwear," Zoe said.

Abby stared at the image for a long time, feeling nauseous. "You think someone was having sex there *while* the house was burning?"

"Not someone. Moses." Zoe paused for a second. "And, well, someone else. I found evidence for this in Douglas as well, but here the crime scene was the most fresh, so the bodily fluids—"

Abby raised her hand. "Okay. I get it."

Could Zoe be right? Abby knew Moses probably had sex with some of his followers. After all, her mom was Moses's follower all those years ago. But could this entire operation of burning sinners be the result of the man's twisted fetishes?

"Back in Douglas, you said it wasn't about sex," Abby said.

"What? No, I didn't." Zoe frowned, clearly annoyed.

"Yes, you did." Abby felt an unexplained need to point out Zoe's mistake. "I would *never* forget that moment. You quoted the article, about . . . about penile response of pyromaniacs."

"I said it was *statistically* less likely for him to be a pyrophile. And I stand by that. I don't think it's pyrophilia. It's about murder and sex. Just fire wouldn't do the trick for him. He'd have to—"

"Let's not," Abby half begged.

"Let's not what?"

"Let's not talk about what turns him on again."

"Okay." Zoe rolled her eyes.

They sat in silence for a few seconds as Abby tried to collect her thoughts.

"But I wasn't wrong," Zoe said.

"Fine."

"I just had incomplete information."

"Sure. Let's go with that."

Abby tried to concentrate on Delilah's social media posts but kept reading the same sentences over and over again. She couldn't focus.

Rummaging in her bag, she found the Twix bar she'd had the forethought to buy earlier. She opened the wrapper when she realized Zoe was watching her.

"You want half?" Abby asked. She didn't feel like sharing *half* of her Twix. But Twix forced her hand, being split into two parts by its very Twix-y nature.

"Hang on," Zoe said. She opened her own bag and produced a Snickers bar. "Trade you half for half?"

"Works for me." Abby grinned.

They traded candy and ate in silence. The chocolaty goodness spread in Abby's body, making her relax. Zoe didn't feel as irritating now as she had before. Then again, she wasn't talking, so that could've been part of the reason.

"You know, I don't do that intentionally," Zoe said. "The thing with my eyes. That's how I look at people. Tatum once said I stare at people like a predator." Her cheeks reddened, and she blinked rapidly, looking surprisingly fragile.

"You have very beautiful eyes," Abby said.

"Really?" Zoe frowned.

"Yeah, sure."

"Oh. Thanks."

Abby swallowed the last bite of her Snickers. "You're right. I'm not the right person to profile Moses. I had no idea."

Zoe nodded.

"But I know how his followers think. And if he's having sex with his followers while burning a person, he'd have to have a really powerful rationale for it. Something that would convince them. Not just the women he's having sex with. *All* of them."

Zoe's lips quirked. "I can't really imagine him explaining it. I mean, what would he say? That it's God's will?"

Abby raised an eyebrow. "That's exactly what he would say."

Zoe snorted. "Why would they believe that?"

"Back in the Wilcox cult, Moses used to say his offspring would be the angels that would protect us during the apocalypse."

"So he's having sex with these women to get them pregnant?" Zoe asked, biting her lip. "That works. It would also make it easier for him."

"Easy how?"

"If Moses believes his own delusions, this would make everything he does part of the greater plan. He might be lying to himself as well."

Abby leaned back in her seat, crumpling the Twix wrapper. "Dot told us Moses's followers were obsessed with the women's menstrual cycles. It might be related. You know, trying to get the dates right, having sex with specific women at the right time to get them pregnant."

"You think he might be keeping a schedule of the women who should be sleeping with him?"

"It wouldn't be a first. Jim Jones did the same thing in his cult." Abby frowned. "Not a schedule. A list. A list of names for the next burning."

"Like the list Dot told us about."

"Everyone wanted to know who's on the list," Abby said. "Everyone wanted to know who would be the woman Moses would have sex with at the night of the burning."

CHAPTER 35

Nighttime was when fear really flourished. Delilah, who was an expert in fear, knew that well.

During the day, there were always distractions. The kids needed attention. There were tasks to be done. Noises and sights to focus on. But as night settled, those distractions dissipated into nothing. With the kids asleep, with the darkness swallowing all colors, leaving behind only shadows and threatening shapes, fear could stretch its many limbs.

Ever since she'd joined Moses's congregation, she'd had a reprieve from nighttime terrors. Being away from Brad, and being too tired to stay awake, she could skip that moment when her head met the pillow, straight to the next morning. Bliss.

But now those hours of lying awake, eyes wide open, came back with a vengeance.

She'd made a terrible mistake.

The moments from the past few days kept spinning in her mind. Moses and Gretchen rutting in the grass with Brad's agonized screams in the background. Gretchen's words, *I hope that last night I was bestowed with an angel of my own*. Rose, talking about her own daughter being sent away. A kid named Terry who got hurt somehow and was taken by social services. The realization that Anna had been spending days with Emily and Ron because she'd been *told* to. To separate Delilah from her children, keep them apart.

She'd leave tomorrow morning. She'd talk to Moses, explain that her kids missed their grandma. That Emily missed her school. That now that Brad was gone, she needed to give them her absolute attention. She tried to imagine how that talk would go, Moses nodding, disappointed but understanding. "If that's what you think is best," he'd say. And she could promise to return to the congregation once the kids were older. He'd like that. He'd been so patient so far . . .

He's very patient at first, Rose had said.

Would he really understand? Would he accept her promise?

He'd been so sweet, and smart, and knowledgeable.

He'd burned her husband alive, had sex with women from his congregation to get them pregnant, told Anna to keep Delilah's kids away from her.

Delilah was no stranger to men talking and acting one way, and then revealing a different, darker side. The first two years with Brad had seemed like a dream. A loving, charming man, constantly showering her with compliments and affection. Sure, later she'd looked back and realized there had been warning signs. The incessant phone calls, fits of jealousy. But at the time she'd thought it all originated from how deeply in love he'd been. And then, a shift. Brad slapping her. Punching her. At first he'd apologize. Later he stopped apologizing, made it clear she deserved it. And even through all that violence he'd still kiss her passionately, whisper that he loved her, surprise her with thoughtful presents. It was like living with two different men.

And now, another man with two faces. Moses, and Father.

Would he expect her to have sex with him so that she could get pregnant? So he could "bestow her with an angel of her own"?

Would he tell her to send her children away because they were distracting her?

Would he hurt her children?

She was hurting her children. She thought of Emily's scratched skin. Of how she'd scrubbed her daughter's hands, trying to . . . what? Get germs out? Or perhaps prove something? That wasn't Moses's doing. That was *her* fault. Somehow, she'd let the people around her push her into doing that. Or had they? She reviewed the past days, trying to figure out why she'd been so frantic about those germs. She couldn't pinpoint the exact moment. This group was changing her. Moses was changing her.

Fear flourished at night. But it didn't necessarily lie. In Delilah's own experience, fear mostly told the truth at night, a truth that during the day she could all but ignore.

Could he really force her to stay, though? It was a congregation, not a prison.

The way he'd looked at her, before burning Brad. *This isn't your call, Delilah.*

Very slowly, she got out of bed. Across the room, on the bottom bunk, Rose was asleep, her breathing steady. Delilah stretched over to the bunk atop hers, where Emily lay asleep, a blonde curl lying across her face. Delilah gently shook her daughter, whose eyes fluttered open.

"Is it morning?" Emily asked sleepily.

"Shhhhh," Delilah whispered. "Almost. We're going for a short walk. Be quiet, okay?"

"Uh-huh," Emily said, rubbing her eyes. "Is Anna coming with us?"

"Maybe later. Come on." Delilah helped Emily climb down the ladder. "Put your coat on."

There had been moments in the past years that Delilah had had to make sure Emily was quiet so Brad wouldn't get mad. Delilah's heart had slowly shattered as she saw that Emily transformed from a boisterous, excited little girl to a silent, meek child. But right now, she was thankful, as Emily put on her socks and shoes and her coat without complaining. Still, Delilah winced at every sound Emily made. Rose, miraculously, kept sleeping.

Delilah had never had time to fully unpack. Most of their belongings were still in her large overnight bag and several plastic bags. There was no way she could take all of it. She grabbed the large bag and the plastic bag with Ron's bottles and formula, already mentally reviewing all the things she was leaving behind. Her cosmetics, Emily's toys and crayons, most of Ron's diapers . . . a long list that almost made her change her mind. But no. Perhaps she'd come back for these things later. Perhaps not.

She plucked Emily's bunny from the top bunk and handed it to her. "Fluffy is coming with us."

Then she crept over to the cot where Ron was asleep. Taking a deep breath, she whisked him out. He let out a tiny wail, but she cradled him, gently rocking him back to sleep. Glancing at Rose, she was relieved to see the woman hadn't woken up.

They tiptoed out of the room and down the hall to the cabin's kitchen. After opening a cupboard, Delilah grabbed a box of crackers and stuffed it into the bag with the formula. She placed Ron in the stroller that sat by the back door. Then she turned the door's dead bolt. Its click was too loud. Soon, someone would come running. She held her breath. No one came.

She opened the door, and a blast of cold air left her breathless. She hadn't realized how chilly it was outside. The kids weren't dressed warmly enough.

Crouching by the stroller, she adjusted the blanket so Ron was tucked well. She rummaged in the bag, found Emily's hat and mittens, and handed them to her. It would have to do for now. They stepped outside, and she shut the door behind them.

She exhaled in relief and looked around her. In the moonlight, the shadowy trees towered around them, the snow-covered ground glowing eerily. The road coiled away from the cabin like a wide flat snake. The town was a couple of miles down the road. They could be there in an hour.

"Mommy, I'm cold," Emily said.

"I know, sweetie," Delilah said, her words expelling clouds of fog. "We'll start walking and we'll get warm, okay?"

"Where are we going? Are we meeting Daddy?"

"We're going to town. I thought we could have some pancakes for breakfast over there. Would you like that?"

"With whipped cream?"

"Do you want whipped cream?" Delilah strode down the road, pushing the stroller.

"Yes, I like whipped cream. And strawberries."

"Then you can have whipped cream *and* strawberries."

"Why are we walking on the road? What if a car comes by and hits us?"

"There are no cars here this late at night," Delilah said, praying it was true.

"Why are we walking at night?"

"I thought it could be an adventure."

"What if there are monsters?"

"There are no monsters here."

"What if—"

"Who's there?" a loud voice shouted in the night.

Delilah's heart sank. Richard stepped out from the shadows, a rifle slung on his shoulder. He glared at them, looking confused.

"It's just us," Delilah said, trying to fake cheerfulness. "Emily and Ron woke up and couldn't go back to sleep, so I figured I'd take them for a nighttime stroll so they don't wake up everyone."

Richard's eyes flickered to the bag on Delilah's shoulder, then to the heavy plastic bag hanging on the stroller's handle.

"I don't think a stroll on the road is a good idea," he finally said.

"Oh, we won't be long." What was he doing there, outside at night? Rose had told her the men had shifts of guard duty, but Delilah never imagined they'd keep at it throughout the night.

"Tell you what," Richard said. "Why don't we all go back and stroll around the cabin? I'll feel better walking with you, knowing you're safe."

"Thank you, but it's really not necessary." Delilah grinned at him and took a step forward.

Richard shifted, blocking her way. With the moon behind him, his shadow stretched in front of him like a giant's.

"Let's go back," he said again. And there was no more room for argument.

CHAPTER 36

Moses stood silently in the rental cabin's dining room. His congregation had pushed the dining table and the chairs to the wall to open up the space. Even so, it was too crowded, and some stayed in the hallway, standing on their tiptoes to peer inside.

Delilah was in the middle of the room, eyes fixed on the floor, her face pale. Her breathing was short, panicky.

Moses wasn't sure he really believed it. Could she have been trying to leave? Richard was certain. He'd caught her walking down the path in the middle of the night with both her kids and most of her possessions. It sounded straightforward enough, but Moses wanted to give her the benefit of the doubt. Surely she wouldn't leave them. Not after all he'd done for her?

"Explain yourself," he said.

"I . . . I couldn't sleep. And the kids woke up. So I thought I could take them for a walk. I didn't think it would be a problem." Her voice was faint, and she wouldn't meet his eyes. Her fingers fidgeted.

Perhaps Richard was right. She definitely felt guilty. Why would she leave?

He knew why. She was afraid. She'd glimpsed the greatness of what they were doing but didn't thoroughly understand it yet. Usually he made sure his newest followers understood the truth before witnessing a baptism. But in her case, he had failed to do that. He had rushed her instead, thinking she would understand it on her own. Perhaps recall their shared past. He would have to mend that now. He would demand from her the same loyalty and fearlessness he demanded of all his followers.

He took out the bronze lighter from his pocket. Holding it high, he said, "We all possess the sacred flame."

The people in the room took out the lighters from their own pockets. Two of them shamefacedly hurried out of the room after realizing they weren't carrying their own sacred flames. Moses made sure to remember their names. He would talk to them later.

He handed the lighter to Delilah, who took it hesitantly.

"From now on this is your sacred flame," he said. "You must carry it at all times."

"Thank you," she said hesitantly.

"Only the wicked need to fear the fire," Moses said softly.

Slowly, the members of his congregation lit their own lighters, dancing flames flickering to life around the room. It was mesmerizing to watch, and the holiness of the moment nearly took Moses's breath away. A few seconds later, following the example of the people around her, Delilah lit her own lighter as well.

"The trial of fire makes us stronger," Moses said. "Our purity is our shield."

"Amen," his followers echoed.

"Do you wish to be forgiven for your sins, Delilah?" he asked.

"Y . . . yes."

"Then let the sacred flame cleanse your sins."

She finally raised her eyes, looking at him, confused. It frustrated him. If she'd listened closely during his preaching, she would have understood what she was supposed to do by now.

"Touch the flame to your wrist," he said.

"Wait . . . ," she said, her eyes widening in fear. "There's no need."

"Only the wicked need to fear the fire," he reminded her again.

"But . . . do you want me to burn myself?"

It was taking too long, and he was getting impatient. Perhaps after she saw how her daughter went through the trial, she would understand. "Where's the little girl?" he snapped at Rose.

"She's outside with Anna," Rose said. "I can get her, but you told me—"

"I think Delilah needs to see how it's done."

"No!" Delilah blurted. "Here, I'll do it. I'll do it!"

She hurriedly lowered her wrist to the flame and let out a cry of pain as the flame scorched her skin. Quickly she pulled it away, tears running down her cheeks.

"You were touched by the sacred flame." He smiled at her. "Like the rest of us."

People were crying with joy. Jennifer and Miriam hugged Delilah, who stared ahead, stunned. Moses licked his lips, regretting that he hadn't told her to hold the flame over her wrist longer. But it was fine, for the first time.

He should call Emily next. The girl needed to pass the trial of flame as well. She was old enough.

He glanced at Rose but hesitated. He remembered what had happened with that boy, Terry. The kid had been so frightened that he'd struggled, and in his panic, his sleeve had caught fire. It had been disastrous. The kid had been taken by social services, the mother had left, and a third of his congregation had quit later, saying it had been too much. And at the time, he'd privately promised Rose that her own daughter wouldn't need to do the trial until she was much older. People weren't always rational when it came to children.

He looked at Delilah as other congregation members went over to congratulate her.

He would postpone Emily's trial of fire. There would be plenty of time for that later.

For now, he would make sure Delilah was kept busy. And he would instruct Anna to keep Delilah away from her children. They only distracted her.

CHAPTER 37

"I really don't know anything else."

Abby estimated that Delilah's friend, Paula, was probably around thirty, though she seemed much older. She was thin, so skinny she looked as if her wrists could snap at any moment. Her eyes constantly skittered to and fro, like those of a trapped animal searching for an escape. Abby spotted the faded bruise on the side of her neck and the way she stood crookedly, as if standing straight was too painful. Even if Abby hadn't spoken to the local pastor and to Sheriff Hunt that morning, she would have instantly spotted the signs. Paula's husband abused her. Hunt said she'd complained about him once but then withdrew her complaint.

Abby sat in Paula's kitchen, large and spacious and meticulously clean. She sipped from the glass of water Paula had handed her—cold water from the fridge with a slice of lemon. Paula sat across the kitchen table, a red vape pen in her hand. She took long drags from it, releasing puffs of vapor that smelled like candy.

When Abby had shown up at the woman's house that morning, Paula had nearly slammed the door in her face. It was only when Abby said she could come back later that Paula had invited her inside. Abby hadn't been surprised. Later, Paula's husband would probably be home. And Abby had a hunch that Paula didn't want her husband to see she was talking to a cop.

"I know you don't," Abby said gently. "But I really need to figure out who Delilah might contact. Aside from you, it seems she's lost touch with her friends. Maybe she has a family member she'd call—"

"Both her parents are dead," Paula said. "She has no brothers or sisters. I think she mentioned a cousin once, in an offhand way—it didn't sound like they were in touch. And as for her in-laws . . ." She took a long drag from her vape pen. "She'd never call those assholes."

Abby nodded sadly. As was often the case, Moses had targeted a woman who had almost no one tethering her to her life. The only solid anchors Delilah had were her children.

"She didn't do it," Paula repeated for the third time since Abby had shown up on her doorstep. "I know it *looks* bad, but Delilah would never—"

"We know who did it," Abby said. "It's not Delilah. But we think Delilah can help us find him. And she might be in danger."

"Oh. Who—"

A phone rang, and Paula jumped. She put down the vape pen and said, "Excuse me for a second."

She got up and walked over to the landline that hung on the wall and picked up. "Hello?"

For a second she stood there, listening. Her eyes widened, and her face became pale. She turned to Abby and mouthed, *It's her.*

Delilah was crouched by the phone, trembling. The door was shut, but she was sure that at any moment someone might open it, step inside, see her on the phone. And then . . .

She wasn't sure what then. She wasn't sure of anything anymore. Any solid grasp she'd had on the people around her had disappeared that morning. Burned away.

Her wrist pulsated in pain. Back home, she'd stocked up on ibuprofen. It had been practically part of her daily routine. But when she'd packed, she'd left most of it behind. Assuming it belonged to her previous life, her life with Brad.

"Paula," she said. "I don't have a lot of time to talk, but I was scared, and I wanted your advice. I . . . I think I'm in trouble."

"Where are you?" Paula asked.

"I don't know exactly. In this large cabin we rented. I think somewhere near Bear Lake. I'm with this Christian group—it's hard to explain." Footsteps by the door. Delilah froze, holding her breath. A loud clatter, someone laughing. *Please don't come in please don't come in please please please please.*

"Delilah? Hello? Are you there? What is this Christian group?"

The footsteps faded away.

"They won't let me see the kids." Delilah whimpered.

"What do you mean?" Paula's voice tightened. "You need to go to the police—"

"No, you don't understand, they could hurt the kids. And we're packing up, we're leaving this place, if I go to the police now, they'll just take the kids with them."

"I don't understand. Where are you all going? How can they take your kids?"

"This morning they took Emily and Ron, and they won't let me see them because I tried to leave and then they made me . . . he made me . . ." She couldn't explain. Not even to this woman, the only one she'd ever told about the things Brad did. She couldn't tell her about—

"Delilah, listen. There's someone here who wants to talk to you, okay? She can help. You've gotta talk to her."

"What? No, Paula, wait!"

And then, a different voice, calm, gentle, strangely familiar. "Hello, Delilah, I'm Abby. It sounds like you're afraid. I can help."

◆ ◆ ◆

Abby could hear the woman's breathing on the phone and knew she was listening. But she hadn't said a word since Abby had taken the phone from Paula's hand. Delilah was probably terrified. At any moment she might hang up. Abby couldn't let that happen. She could trace the location of this phone call. But if Moses's congregation was leaving, Abby needed to know where they were going. Otherwise they'd disappear again, leaving Abby and the feds one step behind.

A good negotiator needed to be a perfect listener above everything else. Prompting their subject with questions, mirroring their own words back to them, to show that they were there, they were listening, they were on the subject's side. But if the subject didn't open their mouth, it was the negotiator's job to do the talking for them. And to make sure that they didn't do anything rash, like in this case, hanging up the phone.

Abby had a few different tones she used when negotiating. She was great at being the friendly, chummy, you-were-just-in-the-wrong-place-at-the-wrong-time girl. Or if needed, the officer who wanted to help, but her dumb superiors wouldn't let her, you know how that is.

Delilah didn't need either of those. She needed the I'm-in-control woman. She needed Abby to tell her she could let go of the steering wheel because she was in safe hands now. Slow, steady voice, deep, each sentence ending with a low note. No questions, no conditions, no hesitation. Every word was a statement.

"It seems like you're worried because the group you're with might hurt Emily and Ron," Abby said. She didn't want to name Moses specifically; she had no idea how Delilah felt about him. For all she knew, Delilah might think that Moses was the Messiah. "It sounds like you're doing everything you can to protect your children. And that's really important, Delilah, because I can help you protect Emily and Ron."

219

She needed Zoe and Tatum right now. As she talked, she took out her own cell phone and found Zoe's contact information. Then she grabbed a pen off the counter and scribbled on a piece of paper that looked like a shopping list, *Talk to this woman, tell her everything that's going on.*

"It seems like you're worried about talking to me, and that's understandable. You don't know me. You don't need to say anything you don't want to. You can just listen." Abby dialed Zoe's number and handed both the note and the cell phone to Paula.

Paula read the note, then stared at the phone. Zoe's voice buzzed from the phone as she answered. "Hello? Mullen, what is it?"

"It seems like you're searching for help," Abby said, keeping her voice steady, her eyes widening as she looked at Paula. The woman seemed paralyzed. "That's why you called Paula. You two helped each other before, when things were rough at home. It's so important to have someone like Paula at your side. Someone who can really understand what you're going through."

Paula took the phone from Abby's hand and stepped out of the room, talking to Zoe in a low voice.

"I really understand what you're going through right now, Delilah," Abby continued. "I know the people you're traveling with. I can help you and Ron and Emily. You don't have to tell me anything you don't want to, but whatever you can say can be a really big—"

"We're in a cabin, near Bear Lake." Delilah's voice was barely a whisper. "Everyone is packing up. I told them I'm going to the bathroom. They'll be looking for me soon. They have my kids."

◆ ◆ ◆

Delilah finally realized why the voice of that woman, Abby, sounded familiar. It was the woman she'd seen before the fire, the one who'd shown up at the youth shelter. Short, blonde, with glasses and a sweet smile. Delilah had no idea who she was, but she sounded like she wanted to help.

And Delilah was desperate.

"Everyone is packing up," Abby said, repeating Delilah's words. "Where are you all going?"

"I don't know," Delilah whispered. "I tried to leave, but there was a man watching outside and he caught me, and then they woke Moses up, and he gathered everyone, and then he asked me where I was going, and then he said only the wicked fear the fire. And then . . ." She let out a sob.

"I'm here, Delilah," Abby said softly. "And then what happened?"

"He gave me a . . . a lighter. And he said I should burn the sin away. I didn't understand, but then he said they would do it to Emily, and I . . . and I . . ."

"It sounds like you were put in an impossible situation," Abby said. She didn't sound shocked or horrified. Just sad. It made the next part easier to say.

"He told me to burn my arm. My wrist. So I did. In front of everyone. No one said anything. And I apologized for trying to leave. And now no one will speak to me. And I don't know where my kids are."

"Okay, I'm glad you're telling me this," Abby said. "Now Delilah, I want you to think really hard. Someone probably said something about where you're going. I know no one will talk to you, but you must have overheard something."

Delilah recalled her conversation with Rose. The woman had said that maybe her daughter would join them when they got to . . .

"California," she blurted. "I think we might be going to California."

"That's great, Delilah. Where in California, do you have any idea? Hello? Delilah?"

Delilah stood frozen, her mouth open in a mute scream.

Moses towered above her, standing in the open doorway.

CHAPTER 38

"I don't understand," Zoe said, her phone pressed tightly to her ear. "Speak slower. When did Delilah call your home?"

"Just now," Paula hissed. "She's on the phone with that cop. She said they took her kids."

Abby's phone call had caught Tatum and Zoe as they were briefing their chief on the latest developments in the case. It had been a long video conference, and when Abby's call interrupted it, Zoe was more relieved than annoyed. But her emotions quickly morphed to confusion when the person on the other side of the phone wasn't Abby but another woman—Paula, Delilah's friend.

"Which cop?" Zoe asked urgently. Tatum stared at her in tense silence, and on the laptop screen, her chief was silent as well, following the events from her own office in Quantico.

"The blonde one, I forgot her name—"

"Mullen?"

"Yes! Abby Mullen. She's talking to her right now on the phone at my house. And Abby told me to call you and tell you. Are you a cop? You have to help her. She's somewhere near Bear Lake, you know where that is? I can give you directions, but I don't know where she is exactly, the lake is big—"

"Hang on," Zoe said, frustrated. "Give me your phone number."

"My phone number?"

"Yes! I need it to trace the call origin."

"Oh! Hang on, I'll check . . ."

Zoe frowned. Didn't the woman know her own phone number?

"There," Paula said, dictating the number to Zoe, who wrote it frantically on a piece of paper and handed it to Tatum.

Zoe cleared her throat. "Okay, Paula, I need your home address—"

"This isn't a local number," Tatum said.

"What?" Zoe gritted her teeth. "Paula, I thought you said Delilah called your home."

"She did. Never mind the phone number. You know where Bear Lake is? You have to get there—"

"What's the number you just gave me?"

"It's the number of the cell phone." Paula sounded exasperated. "Of the blonde cop."

"I don't need Abby Mullen's phone number!" Zoe roared. "I need *your* home number so we can trace the call origin and figure out exactly where Delilah is calling from!"

"Oh."

Oh indeed.

Paula gave her another number. Tatum took it, talking to their chief, asking her to speed things along, to get the call details from the phone company as soon as possible. Zoe focused on Paula.

"What's your home address?" she said. "We're coming over."

If they were lucky, Abby would still be on the phone with Delilah when they arrived.

Betrayal, Moses had learned long ago, tasted like ash. He stared at Delilah, who was crouching at his feet, face frozen in terror, the phone still in her traitorous fingers. And from the phone, a voice buzzed, "Hello? Delilah? Are you there?"

223

He knew the speaker, knew her so very well. How could the same voice fill him with love and dread, all at once? A part of him wanted to take the phone, talk to his daughter again. Instead he plucked the phone from Delilah's lax fingers and placed it in its cradle.

"'When Delilah saw that Samson had told her everything,'" Moses said, "'she sent word to the rulers of the Philistines. "Come back once more, he has told me everything."'"

"Father—"

He grabbed her hair and pulled it viciously upward. She screamed as she staggered to her feet. He shook her hair, Delilah's head wrenching back and forth.

"How much did you tell her?" he roared at the woman as she yelled in agony. "Does she know where we are?"

"N . . . no, I swear," Delilah whimpered.

People bustled into the room, hearing the commotion. Moses pushed Delilah away in fury. How could she? After everything he'd done for her. He had taken care of her violent husband. He'd taken her and her kids under his wing. He had taught her and cared for her. And *this* was how she repaid him?

Whirling, Moses faced Richard. "She was talking to the cops. Even if she didn't tell them where we are, they can trace the call." He wasn't sure how it worked. In his mind, he imagined a room full of screens with maps of the United States. The screen zooming, displaying the lake, a satellite image of the house, a red X, his own face appearing next to it. A young man with an earpiece shouting, *We found him.* "We don't have a lot of time . . ."

He hesitated.

History was repeating itself. They would come, surrounding the house, guns aimed at the windows and the door. He could keep them at bay, tell them they had kids there. A one-year-old baby. And then, he could buy some time.

They had cans of gasoline. By the time the police realized what had happened, the house would be on fire.

"Father?" Richard said. "What should we do?"

And in the chaos, he could escape again. It was what God wanted. God wanted him to spread the word.

"I want you to gather everyone," he started, but his mouth snapped shut.

He'd never manage it. It was daylight. The back door here was easily visible. They'd catch him. He'd have to burn with the rest of his followers. It was God's will. A true trial of faith.

"Get the gasoline." His throat was dry. A tremor in his voice.

Could God really want that? A sudden, powerful chill shot through his gut. A message from God. The divine didn't want him to burn, not today.

"We don't have much time," he said. "We all have to leave as soon as possible. Go get everyone."

"What about her?" Richard asked, glancing at Delilah.

Moses clenched his fists. "There is no redemption for her. She will burn."

◆ ◆ ◆

Zoe's jaw tightened as her foot floored the gas pedal. She was driving them as fast as she could to Paula's address to join Mullen. Somehow, the lieutenant was once again a step ahead of them.

By her side, in the passenger seat, Tatum was yelling at someone on the phone. He hung up in frustration.

"Well?" Zoe asked, impatient.

"The cabin Delilah called from is in the northern part of Bear Lake. It's in Idaho, so the Utah Highway Patrol won't go there," Tatum said, raising his voice over the sound of the car's engine. "Federal forces are on their way, but they're driving from Riverdale, and apparently, watch out—truck. Truck, Zoe, truck! Jesus. What was I saying?"

"Federal forces."

"Right. It'll take them an hour to get there. We're checking if there's a helicopter we can use."

"What about the Idaho police?"

"They sent some people, but they're also too far off. We contacted the Bear Lake sheriff, and he said he'll go there as soon as he's done with a herd of elk that has been blocking the road."

"Elk?" Zoe swerved to overtake a slow-moving car.

"That's what they told me."

"Did you impress upon them the urgency of the matter?"

"I didn't talk to the sheriff directly, but I gather that elk on the road is pretty dangerous."

"So are serial killer cult leaders."

"Yeah. And so is your driving. Are you trying to get us killed?"

Zoe gritted her teeth. "I'm trying to get us to Paula's home while Abby is still on the phone with Delilah."

Just as they pulled up to Paula's address, the front door opened, and Abby stepped out. She noticed them and briskly marched over.

Zoe opened her window. "Delilah called from a cabin at the northern part of Bear Lake," she told Abby. "We sent people over, but it'll take some time. Did she hang up?"

"Yeah." Abby leaned forward, looking worried. "I think someone caught her talking to me. I tried to call back, no answer. Are you going there?"

Tatum cleared his throat. "I don't think it's really—"

"Yes," Zoe said.

"Good." Abby went over to the back of the car and slid inside. "I'll go with you. Delilah said they were packing up. You said it'll take some time for the feds to get there?"

"About forty-five minutes," Tatum said. "The sheriff might get there sooner. It depends. Any idea where they're going?"

"California." Abby put on her seat belt.

"Do you have anything more specific?"

"Nope."

Tatum nodded. "Okay, I think there are only two or three roads going west from Bear Lake. We have the descriptions of their vehicles. I'll coordinate it. It'll be tricky though."

Zoe glanced at her rearview mirror and hit the gas. "On a positive note, maybe one of those roads is already blocked by elk."

❖ ❖ ❖

Most of his congregation was ready. Moses himself had packed up quickly, constantly feeling the time trickling away, imagining the squad cars hurtling toward them, sirens screaming. His heart was about to explode in his chest, his breathing erratic. Was this the end? He still had so much left to do.

He slung his bag on his shoulder, then took a moment to steady himself. It was important that his followers not see the weakness in him. Weakness made people doubt.

Marching outside, he made his way to his car. He slung the backpack into the trunk and slammed it shut. Time to go. The rest would follow when they were ready.

He turned to the driver's seat when Anna and Richard stepped out of the house. Richard was dragging Delilah with him. Her hands were tied in front of her, clasped together in prayer. Good, she *should* pray. Her face was wet and blotchy with tears.

"Father, we're ready to go," Anna said. "What about the kids?"

"Please," Delilah blubbered. "Don't hurt Emily and Ron. They didn't do any—"

Richard shook her, and she whimpered.

227

Moses frowned. He should never have allowed Delilah to bring her kids. After the incident with Terry, he'd decided never to allow children into his congregation again. They twisted their parents' common sense and shifted their priorities. But when he'd seen Delilah, his past resurrected, he'd thought this time it would be different.

He had half a mind to leave the kids in the house, let them stay with their mother in her final moments. He looked at Delilah. Her shirt was disheveled, exposing part of her shoulder. Her eyes brimmed with fear. With her hands clasped in front of her, it seemed as if she was praying for his mercy. Maybe she was. A powerful jolt of desire shot through him. Despite what she'd done, was it possible that God wanted this woman alive?

But how could he ever trust her again? How could he assure her loyalty?

Perhaps it was possible. Perhaps the kids weren't a hindrance, after all. He could use them. After all, the book of Genesis was very clear about how a parent's loyalty could be tested. That was what the binding of Isaac was all about.

He pointed at the large van. "Put the kids there. And put her . . ." He hesitated. "Who's driving the pickup truck?" He needed someone reliable. Someone who wouldn't flinch at the risk.

"Rose and Gretchen," Anna said.

Good. Rose was solid. And Gretchen still had that initial blind passion in her. "Put Delilah in the back of the pickup truck. Tell Rose she should watch her driving. I don't want cops stopping her for speeding and finding the woman in the back, you got that?"

Anna seemed to hesitate, about to say something, but her mouth clamped shut. She'd learned her lesson.

Richard pushed Delilah toward the back of the pickup truck.

"Did you load everything?" Moses asked Anna. "The gasoline, the food, the gear?"

She nodded but then suddenly paused. "Oh! I forgot the boxes of pamphlets in Rose's room."

"The glossy pamphlets?" Moses frowned, annoyed. Those had been expensive to print.

"Yes, we can leave them behind, we should get going—"

"No. I want those packed as well. I don't want them to go to waste."

"They were supposed to go in the pickup truck, but with Delilah in the back, there's no room—"

"Make room!" Moses roared. "Do I have to spell everything out for you?"

Anna paled and hurried off. Moses gritted his teeth and stepped into his car. It was time to go.

CHAPTER 39

Officer Dwayne Crowley stretched and yawned as he stared down the road. He took three steps forward, turned to face the snowy fields. Turned around, took four steps in the opposite direction. Yawned again.

"Looks like it's gonna rain," muttered Gus. Which was classic Gus. That's why they called him Weatherman Gus. Well, to be fair, only Dwayne called him Weatherman Gus, but he was really trying to get it to stick. Gus was always talking about the weather. *It's getting cold, it's getting warm, there's an eastern wind, it's gonna snow, it's snowing, it's gonna stop snowing.* It was like partnering with a human thermometer. Or whatever it was that weather forecasters used.

Dwayne went over to the squad car and retrieved the thermos he'd filled up earlier.

"I bought us caramel apple cider at Fizeez," he said. "Do you want a cup?"

Weatherman Gus stared at him and waggled his mustache, which was something he did when he was offended or displeased. "Why do you always have to get those kids' drinks? Is it too much to ask that you just get us a cup of coffee?"

"I don't like coffee."

"*I* like coffee. You can get a coffee for me and a caramel apple cider for yourself."

Dwayne shrugged. "So what'll it be?"

"Fine." Gus grunted. "Is it warm?"

"That's the whole point of the thermos." Dwayne carefully poured some caramel apple cider in a plastic cup and handed it to Gus. He poured the rest for himself and held the cup close to his face, letting the steam thaw his nose. God, that felt good.

Weatherman Gus slurped noisily from his cup. "So what do you think those guys did?"

"Who?"

"Those people we're here for."

The chief had sent them to block Route 89, going north. They had a list of vehicles to look out for. The owners of the vehicles might be "armed and dangerous," which was a term you didn't hear often, working in the Montpelier Police Department.

"I don't know. Drug dealers?" Dwayne suggested.

Gus waggled his mustache again. A drop spattered on Dwayne's head. Then another.

"Told you it's gonna rain," Gus said. And after a few seconds added, "Gonna rain for a while, now."

"Hey, Gus," Dwayne said, alert. A white Chevy pickup truck was driving toward them. They'd been told to watch out for a white pickup truck, among other vehicles. Dwayne put his drink on the hood of the squad car, and Gus followed suit. Stepping to the middle of the lane, Dwayne signaled for the pickup truck to stop. It slowed down. Putting one hand on his holster, Dwayne stepped forward, feeling tense, the words *armed and dangerous* buzzing in his head.

Two young women sat in the truck, and Dwayne relaxed slightly. He pressed his shoulder mic. "Dispatch, Lima-oh-nine."

The radio crackled. "Go ahead."

"I need a ten-twenty-eight on a license plate number." He dictated the Chevy's plate number.

He watched the women as he waited. They were talking to each other. They seemed tense, but that could mean anything. People were tense when stopped by the police. They immediately wondered if they were driving too fast, or what if the cop found the joint they had in their purse, was it legal in this state, and maybe this was one of those bad cops the media was always talking about.

Both women were kinda attractive, especially the driver, who had long red hair. Dwayne's ex-girlfriend had red hair.

"Lima-oh-nine, Dispatch. All clear."

He exhaled and glanced at Gus. Gus gave him a nod. Dwayne went over to the truck. He glanced at the back, saw that it was covered with a tarp. The rain pattered on the black tarp steadily. He got closer to the driver's window. The driver opened it and smiled at him.

"Hi," she said. She really was pretty. A silver necklace with a cross pendant adorned her neck.

"Morning, ma'am," he said in his official voice. "Can I have your license and proof of insurance?"

"Uh, sure." She rummaged in her bag.

Dwayne glanced at the girl next to her. She seemed younger, a teenager. Her body was rigid with tension. It made Dwayne tense too. What was she worried about? They'd said the license plate was clear, so this probably wasn't one of the vehicles they'd been told to watch out for. He came closer. The truck smelled of gasoline. A gasoline can stood between the driver and the passenger.

"Here you go." The driver handed him her driver's license.

He glanced at it. "Rose Olson?"

"That's me," the driver said.

"What do you have in the back?"

"Pamphlets for our church."

"Can I take a look?"

Her smile was fixed on her face. "Sure. You can even grab a couple for you and your friend."

He gave her a small grin and went over to the back. Unhooking the tarp, he exposed a few boxes and eight more gasoline cans. He eyed the gasoline for a second, then opened one of the boxes. Like she'd said, it was full of pamphlets for something called the Lily Fellowship Church. He shoved his hands deeply into the box to see if there was anything else hiding under the pamphlets, but all he felt was the countless edges of the glossy paper. Beyond the gasoline there was a large burlap sack. He eyed it, stretching over the truck's back to open it—

"Officer? All good?" the woman called pleasantly from the front of the truck.

He grunted, his fingers brushing against the sack. Then he accidentally pushed one of the pamphlet boxes, and it toppled off the back, spilling on the road.

"Aw, shit," he muttered. He hurriedly picked it up, stuffing the pamphlets inside. Some were smeared with dirt, and he guiltily shoved them deep inside the box. Finally, he returned the box to the back of the pickup truck and hooked the tarp back on.

Then, approaching the driver again, he asked, "What do you need all that gasoline for?"

"We're on our way to the West Coast," she said. "Gasoline is cheaper here."

Good thinking. He smiled at her again. "Just one second," he said, taking a few steps back. He clicked his shoulder mic. "Dispatch, Lima-oh-nine. I need a ten-twenty-seven on a Rose Olson."

He gave dispatch the license number.

The answer crackled almost immediately back. "Lima-oh-nine, Dispatch, we have a ten-ninety-nine. It's a ten-ninety-nine."

For a fragment of a second the words scrambled in his mind. A 10-99 was the code for a wanted person. His hand went for his holster as he raised his eyes from the license plate to stare at the two women in the truck.

The truck's engine roared, tires squealing, and it lurched forward, straight at him. He leaped sideways, the truck swerving around their squad car. Dwayne hit the pavement, blocking his fall with his hand, the jarring impact making his jaw snap shut. He rolled and stumbled to his feet. The pickup truck was already dozens of yards away. Gus was facing the truck, gun drawn, aiming. He let out two shots, the blasts echoing in the flat fields around them.

Dwayne dashed for their car, his mind barely registering that his leg hurt like hell. He must have twisted it when he fell. He yanked the driver's door and leaped inside, Gus joining him in the passenger seat. Dwayne switched on the engine and hit the gas, turning the steering wheel as fast as he could, the car swerving north, the two half-finished drinks on the hood tumbling away, leaving brown spatters in their wake. Then he floored it, the engine roaring, Gus flipping on the siren.

The fields outside became a blur as they sped down the road, the rain spattering the windshield. Dwayne gripped the steering wheel hard, teeth gritted, his eyes locked on the faraway pickup truck.

Gus was screaming on the radio by his side. "Dispatch, Lima-oh-nine, we're in pursuit of a white Chevy Silverado going north on eighty-nine. We're about a mile south of thirty-six. Requesting backup, over."

"Lima-oh-nine, Dispatch, copy. All units in the area, please respond."

The staticky voice of their chief crackled, "This is Lima-oh-one. On my way."

More crackling. It was possible that other units were responding, though there weren't a lot of options. Maybe, if there were state police cars in the area, they'd respond. Dwayne pushed the distraction away, focusing on the truck. They were getting closer. As they neared Ovid Creek, the truck disappeared momentarily beyond the bend of the road.

"Damn it, damn it," Dwayne muttered, his foot crushing the gas pedal.

There they were again, a dozen or so yards away. Gus grabbed the speaker and turned it on, his voice amplified with a mechanical screech: "The driver of the white Chevy, stop at the side of the road right now."

The tarp on the back of the Chevy was fluttering, and pamphlets were swirling in the air. One of them plastered itself on the squad car's windshield, and the wipers crumpled it away.

"We're reaching the crossroad," Dwayne said.

"You're clear," Gus said.

They were gaining on the pickup truck fast—was it slowing down? As it neared the crossroad, it swerved, turning left, its tires screeching.

"Jesus!" Dwayne shouted as he hit the brakes.

The truck swerved left and right, its wheels slipping on the icy road. Then, completely losing control, it shot off the road, crashing through the fence and into the snowy field. It rattled forward a few more yards and then stopped, the wheels still whirring.

Dwayne pulled to the side of the road and leaped out of the car, crouched, pulling his gun. Aiming at the truck, he stepped closer. From the corner of his eye, he saw Gus by his side, his gun also drawn.

"Get out of the truck with your hands where we can see them!" Dwayne shouted. They probably couldn't even hear him over the sound of the wind and the rain. He shouted at them to get out a second time. Gus shouted as well. Their voices intermingled, creating an indecipherable mess.

And then, an answer. A woman shouting back at them, the words swallowed by the wind. Dwayne took a few more steps, wondering if the two women were armed like he'd been warned.

The woman shouted again. He could barely piece the words together. "Stay back!"

"Get out of the car!" he roared again.

"Stay back or we . . ." The rest of the words were a jumble.

"Get out with your hands above your heads!" Gus shouted.

They were less than ten yards away now.

"Stay back or we light ourselves on fire!" the woman shouted.

Dwayne froze as he glimpsed something through the truck's window. A small flame, flickering in the younger girl's hand. And the driver was holding the large red plastic can he'd seen earlier, the gasoline pouring from it, spattering them both.

CHAPTER 40

Abby was getting nauseous from Zoe's erratic driving. The woman would floor the gas whenever possible, and when she had to slow down, she would do it too fast, resulting in endless lurches back and forth. According to the navigation app, they were still about forty minutes away from the cabin, though perhaps Zoe's frantic driving could shave it to thirty.

Tatum was constantly on the phone, trying to get reports and coordinating the containment efforts with the bureau, the Idaho State Police, and the Utah Highway Patrol. With him on the phone and Zoe driving, Abby felt useless and forgotten. A single child in a family trip, with Daddy and Mommy in the front seats of the car making all the decisions for her. She regretted not following them in her own vehicle.

Abby couldn't shake the image of this woman, identical to her biological mother, whispering frantically on the phone, face twisted in fear. Was she still there? The local police must have gotten to the scene already, but they'd received no updates.

As he gripped his phone with tension, Tatum's tone rose with sudden excitement. Abby's heart lurched. Were the police there? Had they found Moses? Or Delilah?

"Where are they?" Tatum asked. "Which crossroad?"

Abby leaned forward. A crossroad. Were they talking about a road-block? She clenched her fists, imagining the convoy of vehicles, led by Moses Wilcox, as they encountered the impasse.

He listened and then said, "We just passed Georgetown, we're not far away . . ." He listened some more and then said, "We have Lieutenant Abby Mullen from the NYPD in the car. She's a . . . that's right. Okay, we're on our way." He hung up.

"What happened?" Abby and Zoe asked at the same time.

"The cabin Delilah called from was already empty when the police got there," Tatum answered. "But one of the cult's vehicles broke through a roadblock. The police chased it, and it ended up crashing into a field in Ovid. The police have them surrounded, but they can't get closer. The women in the car are threatening to set themselves on fire. Apparently, they poured gasoline over themselves."

"Is there a negotiator on the scene?" Abby asked.

"No. They want to fly in someone from the bureau," Tatum said. "But I told my chief you're riding with us. She knows who you are. And we're only about ten minutes away. She's talking to the local police chief now, trying to coordinate it. I hope they'll agree to let you take over the negotiation."

Abby exhaled. "Okay. Do we know anything else? The women's names? The car type?"

"Not yet. There's a lot of miscommunication going on. Different law enforcement agencies, and the people here aren't used to these kinds of events."

"How many cops are at the scene? Who's talking to them right now? How long ago did it happen? Is anyone hurt—"

"Abby," Tatum said sharply. "We don't know that. We'll be there soon, and we'll get a clearer picture."

Abby clenched her jaw tightly. She could press Tatum to make a call, try to find things out. But like he said, it would be informa-tion passed between multiple law enforcement agencies. It would be flawed and inaccurate and could potentially hurt more than help. And it wouldn't help her with the fear that was gnawing at her mind. A fear that had its roots in events that had occurred more than three decades ago.

Back in 1987, the police had laid siege to the Wilcox compound. An officer had phoned the compound. He wasn't a negotiator, wasn't trained in crisis management. The girl who'd answered the call had been a seven-year-old named Abihail. He'd been nice, and soothing, and entirely clueless, unable to realize that Abihail's mind had been twisted to do and say whatever Moses Wilcox had told her to. And it had ended in a terrible inferno that claimed fifty-nine lives. Abihail had grown up to be Lieutenant Abby Mullen.

Now she was about to arrive at the scene where two women had had their minds twisted by the same Moses Wilcox. Who were probably determined to die for a man who didn't spare them a second thought. And it was up to Abby to stop it.

CHAPTER 41

The helicopter was the first thing they saw, hovering high above the snowy field. Abby counted the squad cars, their red and blue lights flashing in the rain. Four squad cars and an additional civilian car, all parked at the side of the road.

In the midst of the field, the white pickup truck stood, a zigzagging track in its wake. Abby assumed the reason it had stopped was because the wheels got mired in the muddy snow. Officers stood in the field, keeping their distance from the vehicle. Abby could barely glimpse the silhouettes of figures within the pickup truck through the haze of raindrops.

Tatum parked the car, and Abby leaped outside, the rain drenching her and spattering her glasses. She wished she had put on contact lenses that morning. A man in a yellow raincoat approached them.

"Lieutenant Abby Mullen?" he said, his voice raised above the sound of rain, wind, and the helicopter's rotors above.

"Yeah," she shouted back.

"I'm Chief Naylor. They told me you were coming. We've been trying to talk to these women, but they're not very responsive. But I'll be honest, I don't think they're serious about setting themselves on fire. I'm more worried that girl will drop the lighter by accident."

"Those women are a part of a fanatical cult," Abby said. "We're pretty sure they're serious about this. Who's been talking to them?"

"Officer Dwayne Crowley," Naylor said. "He's a good fellow."

"Okay, do we know their names?"

"The driver's name is Rose Olson. We have her driver's license. I don't know what her friend's name is."

"Are either one of them hurt?"

"Not that we can tell."

"Did they hurt anyone before ending up in that field?"

"Well, they tried running over Dwayne, but he's fine."

That was a bit of good news. "Who is the pickup truck registered to?"

He glanced at the mired truck. "It's registered to Carl Olson. I'm guessing it's this woman's husband. We ran the license plate, it's clean."

So the truck wasn't registered to the church. "Anything else I should know?"

"I evacuated the farm over there." Naylor pointed at the closest farm. "And we have more men coming."

"Okay. I don't want them too close, okay? Keep any additional forces out of sight. I don't want to spook those two any more than they already are." Raindrops trickled down her coat's collar, soaking her sweater. "Can we block this segment of the road?"

"Sure, we can reroute the traffic through Ovid," Naylor said.

"Okay, that would probably be best. And can you pull the helicopter back? It makes talking really hard. I don't want to shout at them."

"Will do."

"Do you have a spare raincoat?" she asked.

"Here, take mine." He shrugged off his coat, handing it to her. "I have another one back in my car."

"Thanks." She put it on top of her already-soaked coat. "Who's Dwayne? I need to talk to him."

"I'll call him over," Naylor said and marched off.

Abby turned to Tatum and Zoe. "I'll need your help. I usually work with a team."

"What do you need?" Zoe asked.

She needed a lot. She wished she had her truck with her. The situation board, the equipment. Her partner Will's experience and reassuring presence. But they couldn't give her that. "Information. You two will have to be my intelligence officers."

"What information do you need?"

"Start with Rose Olson. We have her driver's license, so you should be able to find out who she is. Any immediate family connections. Any good friends she used to have. Ideally we need things from her life before Moses Wilcox."

"I'm on it," Tatum said.

"Zoe, I need you to do some digging about the situation," Abby said. "They apparently drenched themselves in gasoline. I'm worried this entire thing will combust because of the vapors. Can you find an expert who can assess the risk?"

"Sure."

"Once one of you is done, I want a weather forecast." Abby looked around at the rain-spattered snow. "If the rain gets much worse, or if it gets too windy, I won't be able to talk to them, so I want to know it in advance. I also want to know when the sun sets."

Zoe raised an eyebrow. "We probably have hours until that happens."

"Yup. I want to know how many hours. Information is my oxygen—I need to know everything I can."

Naylor returned with a very young officer, who fiddled with his belt nervously. The drops on Abby's glasses made his facial features shimmy and warp.

"Dwayne, right?" Abby said. "Chief Naylor said you're the guy who talked to the women so far. How did that go?"

He looked at her miserably. "I . . . I don't think it went too well, because they're still in there, with that lighter. And they keep quoting the Bible at me, and I . . . I don't know the Bible so well. But I reminded them suicide was a mortal sin. And I kept telling them to calm down, because they were screaming hysterically, you know?"

"Yeah," Abby said. "Did they tell you what they wanted?"

"They wanted me to get them a new car and to let them drive off without following them. The younger woman wanted our car, but I told her we can't do that."

Abby nodded. At least he hadn't promised them anything. "Would you say you established any kind of rapport?"

"Any kind of what?"

"A reasonable relationship."

"Um . . . I don't know. I did the right thing, right? I really tried to be sympathetic."

He'd patronized them, lecturing them about their own religious beliefs. And then he'd told them to calm down, which was the worst thing you could say to anyone who was angry or scared, because it discounted their emotions. "You did great," Abby said. "You don't happen to know the other woman's name, do you?"

"No, I didn't think to ask."

"Okay," Abby said. "I'm going to talk to them now. Chief, in a bit, I'll need you to move all your cops back. They're freaking those women out."

"I'll do it right now."

"No. I want them to feel like it was something I gave them, okay? So wait until I tell you to do it."

Abby turned away from them, approaching the car. The icy ground was slippery, so she took her time, treading carefully. The last thing she needed was to stumble, the jarring movement alarming the women in the truck. As she got closer, she could see the driver—Rose Olson. She'd seen her before, when she'd gone to the youth shelter in Rigby. The passenger by her side was partially hidden from view, but the sudden appearance of a flame in her hand was easily visible.

"Don't come any closer!" Rose shouted at her.

Abby stopped in her place. "Okay," she said, raising her voice. "I'm staying right here."

"If you come any closer, we'll set ourselves on fire," Rose said.

"I understand," Abby said. "I won't come any closer. I don't want anyone to get hurt."

"Then you can tell them to get us a car, like we asked for."

"A car, I'll tell them," Abby said. "My name is Abby."

"I don't care what your name is, just tell them to get us a car." Rose's voice trembled. She was clearly terrified. Was she worried they were going to burn? She'd heard the screams of people burn to death several times before. She knew what she was getting into. But Abby had no doubt that if she felt she had no other choice, she'd do it. They both would. It was up to Abby to convince them there *was* another choice.

"Okay, I'll definitely tell them, but it's not my jurisdiction, so I'll have to coordinate it with the local police. And they will need approval from higher up, and then we'll have to find a car, and a driver, and get it over *here*." Abby looked around her, clearly pointing out they were in the middle of nowhere. "And it will take some time. Is that okay?"

Rose seemed almost surprised. "Yeah. Do it as fast as possible. We want to get out of here."

"I will. In the meanwhile, I don't want anyone to get hurt. And I'm worried that while I'm talking to you, and going back and forth, the gasoline's vapors will catch fire from that lighter. So would you mind putting it out while we talk?"

The other woman leaned across Rose to get closer to the window. "That's not going to happen!" she screamed.

Abby instantly recognized her from the photos she'd seen of the girl on her social media. It was Gretchen Wood, from Douglas.

"It seems like you're worried that if you keep it out, you won't get that car you asked for," Abby said.

"You want us to mess up so those cops over there can storm over and pull us out of the car," Rose said.

Abby acted as if she was considering this. "So you're worried I want to catch you off guard, so that they'll get to you fast enough and you won't have time to react."

"That's right."

"Okay. What can we do to convince you that won't happen?"

Gretchen shook her head. "Nothing. We don't believe a word you say."

But Rose seemed to think it over. "Tell them to pull back," she finally said. "Way back. I don't want any police officers on this field, okay? Just you."

Abby let them see her apparent hesitation, then finally said, "Okay, I'll go talk to them, see if I can convince them to pull back. And I'll talk to them about the car. Meanwhile, make sure you stay safe, okay? Don't drop that lighter." Abby deliberated if she should let Gretchen know she recognized her and decided against it. It would make the girl feel more paranoid. "And you . . . uh . . . what's your name? The one holding the lighter?"

"Gretchen," she answered guardedly.

"Gretchen, you should probably open your window, too, so the vapors don't build up around you. I want to keep you both safe." She gave them a reassuring, tiny smile, then stepped back and hurried over to Captain Naylor.

"Okay," she told him. "We'll talk here for a bit, and then you'll pull your men back to the road."

"No problem."

"If they light themselves on fire, how fast can we act?"

Naylor didn't look happy with the prospect. "According to Dwayne, the back of the truck is stacked with gasoline canisters, not to mention the gasoline in the truck itself. If this thing catches fire, it'll explode. Our firefighters will do what they can, but these women won't survive it, and other people will probably get hurt. I already alerted the hospital, and we have two ambulances on their way here."

Zoe approached them. "What did they say?"

"Nothing useful yet. They want a car. The other girl is Gretchen Wood."

Zoe frowned thoughtfully. "Okay. I talked to the forensic fire expert we've been working with lately. The gasoline's flash point is minus ten Fahrenheit, so even though it's cold, we still have a problem here. The rain makes it less likely that the gasoline will catch fire, but he said we have to do what we can to dissipate those vapors. And we should keep that flame raised high, because the gasoline vapors sink."

Abby hugged herself and suppressed a shiver. She was freezing. "I told them to open the other window, though I doubt they'll do that—it's too cold. But they agreed to keep the lighter out if the police pull back."

"We might want to reconsider that," Zoe said. "According to the guy I talked with, that lighter they have should have enough fuel for an hour at most. If you keep them talking for long enough and it runs out, we can pull them out."

Abby thought about it. "No. I don't want to risk it. If I talk to them too long and the lighter overheats, they might accidentally drop it. And even if it runs out, the lighter's spark can start the fire."

"Okay," Zoe said. "I'll go get that weather forecast now."

"Thanks," Abby said. "And get Gretchen's parents on the phone. I don't know if it's a good idea for them to talk to her, but just in case. In fact, make sure her sister is available as well."

Zoe and Naylor walked off. Abby watched as the officers followed Naylor's instructions and pulled back, out of the field. Leaving her alone with Gretchen, Rose, and a truck drenched in gasoline.

CHAPTER 42

The rain pelted Abby's face, hostile icy drops that ran down her face and neck, soaking into her clothes. Her feet, covered in snow and ice, were freezing. In the car, the two women were whispering to each other. They'd rolled up the window until only a crack remained despite Abby's warning about the gasoline vapors. They'd stopped talking to her entirely a few minutes before, after reiterating yet again that they wanted a car. Every minute or two, Rose tried to call someone, but it seemed like no one answered her calls.

"What happened back there, with the police?" Abby asked, trying to keep her voice steady. "Was there some kind of misunderstanding?"

The air inside the car shimmered with fumes. On top of their fear and desperation, they were probably getting sick, inhaling the gasoline.

"It seems like you're worried the police won't follow up on their promise," Abby prompted them.

She wanted them to talk. Start a conversation. That would buy her time, keep them from killing themselves.

Because that's what they would do, eventually. They would see there was no way out. Their minds were twisted by Moses to believe being captured by the police was worse than death. They would take the only possible route they believed was available to them and light themselves on fire. They probably already guessed they weren't getting that car they'd demanded. Abby didn't intend to try to convince them otherwise. If she cajoled them, trying to reassure them, she would be feeding their fear that the police were lying to them. That would push them away from her.

But she was getting worried. They weren't talking with each other anymore, just staring ahead grimly. She suspected they'd agreed between them to wait a little longer. How much longer? Five minutes? Ten minutes? She had to draw them into a conversation soon.

"Gretchen, I talked to your sister, Maegan."

This got the response Abby had been hoping for. The girl seemed startled. "You . . . what?" she asked, leaning toward the window. "When?"

"A few days ago," Abby said. "She was worried about you."

"How did she sound?"

"She sounded sad," Abby said. "She wanted to know where you were."

Gretchen shook her head mutely.

"It seemed like you two were very close," Abby said.

Gretchen retreated from the window, leaning back. She stared at the lighter in her trembling hand.

"How can I help you talk to her?"

Nothing.

"What can I—"

"Where's our car?" Rose shouted.

"I'm sorry, I don't know," Abby said. "The local police are trying to get it."

"Go check what's going on with it."

Abby made a show of hesitating. She was actually pleased with the demand. She wanted to talk to Tatum and Zoe, her conscripted intel officers. She needed information. Gretchen didn't seem inclined to talk about her sister, and Abby was worried talking about her parents would be even worse. Perhaps Tatum and Zoe could give her something else she could work with. "Okay, give me a few minutes."

She turned away and trudged toward the road, where the police waited, with Zoe and Tatum. Abby was reasonably confident Gretchen and Rose would wait for her to return. They clung to the hope that they *could* get away from all this. And by following their demands, she'd given them the feeling they were in control.

Zoe, Tatum, and the police chief, Naylor, all converged on her as she reached the road.

"How are we doing?" Naylor asked. "Are they going to surrender?"

"Not yet," Abby answered. "I don't have a lot of time. What did you find out?"

"Rose Olson is from Lewistown, Montana," Tatum said. "There's a Lily Fellowship Church center there, focusing on feeding and clothing the homeless throughout Montana. Rose worked there for about a year before leaving on a supposed reassignment from the church three years ago. I talked to Rose's father, Carl, on the phone. Apparently when Rose left, she took her two-year-old girl, Lori, with her."

"Carl Olson? He's the owner of the truck?"

"Yeah. He said he gave it to Rose, but they never registered it to her."

Which meant Rose couldn't give it to the church without Carl's approval. "What about Lori's father?" Abby asked. "Were he and Rose married?"

"No. They were together for a while, and he left town very soon after Rose gave birth. She raised Lori with her parents' help. Carl sounded angry. He'd been opposed to the church from the start. They had a big fight when Rose left, and Rose didn't call for a few months after that. Then she contacted them and asked for money. This became a regular thing—she'd call every few weeks and ask that they transfer some money. Initially, they sent her the money, but finally they refused. She didn't call for a few months. When she contacted them again, she asked if they would take care of Lori for a few weeks. Carl agreed, and a woman from the church drove Lori to her grandparents' place."

"When was this?"

"Two years ago."

"And a different woman from the cult took Lori to her grandparents," Abby said. "Moses didn't want Rose to take her and meet her parents."

"Apparently not. Rose calls every few weeks to talk to Lori. At first she kept telling Lori that it was just for a few weeks, that she would pick her up soon. But after a while, Carl threatened to stop allowing them to talk on the phone, because she kept letting Lori down. She never comes to visit."

"But she keeps calling?" Abby asked. That was important. A thread from the outside world that Moses hadn't managed to sever completely. She could use that.

"Yeah, every few weeks. And Carl sends Rose photos of Lori."

"Okay. Anything else?"

"The rain and wind should get worse," Zoe said.

Abby nodded. More rain and wind hopefully made it less likely that the gasoline would be lit by mistake, but it would make it much harder for her to talk to the women. "Okay. I can work with that. I want Rose's parents to be constantly in contact—we might need their assistance." She gave it some thought. "Tell them not to answer a phone call from Rose's phone under any circumstances. I want this phone call as leverage."

"Got it."

"And get me something useful about Gretchen. She won't engage." Abby turned away and trudged back through the snowy field.

She preferred to avoid mentioning Rose's parents to her. If Rose's father, Carl, had opposed the church from the start, it was likely Rose thought of him as part of the opposition, not very different from the police. Lori, however, was a different story. Clearly, Rose wanted to stay in touch with her daughter. Even better, it sounded like she believed that one day, Lori would return to live with her mother, a fantasy Moses probably fostered as a means to control Rose.

Lori signified a better future, something Abby could use to remind Rose that it didn't have to end here. There were other options.

"Well?" Rose shouted as she came closer.

"They're still working on it," Abby called back. "They're still figuring out how to buy the car. It'll take some time."

"I don't care which car they give us," Rose spit. "You know what? Give me your car—that's good enough for us."

"I'm sorry, I don't have a car. I came here with a couple of law enforcement agents," Abby said apologetically. "But even if I did manage to get you a car, they still need to get the approval not to follow you. They're working on it, we don't want anyone to get hurt."

"It doesn't look that way," Rose said, and there was a shift in her tone. A grim undertone. She was done waiting.

"They told me you have a daughter," Abby said. "Lori, right? I have a daughter too."

"How the hell do they know that?" Rose yelled.

"I think they checked your driver's license," Abby said vaguely. "How old is Lori?"

Rose stared ahead, jaw clenched.

"My daughter is fourteen," Abby said. "I've been away from her for a while now. I really miss her. I call her every evening, and I keep waiting for that phone call, you know? Hear her voice, ask her about her day. I know it's not much, but it's something. I can't wait until I get back home, give her a hug. Fourteen-year-olds don't really like hugging. Is Lori a teenager?"

"No." Rose's voice was so low, Abby could barely hear it over the wind. "She's five."

"She's five? You're lucky. She still likes hugging, right?"

"I . . . yeah. She likes hugging."

"I remember that age so well." Abby smiled. "So many good memories. What's your best memory of Lori?"

Even if she didn't answer, Abby knew the question would prod Rose to think. To remember.

"We . . . uh . . . we liked to cuddle in bed. Sometimes." Rose's eyes glazed. "She would ask me to tickle her. I would tickle her, and she'd laugh."

"She'd laugh," Abby repeated, nodding with a smile. "Does she have a cute laugh?" Of course she did. And even if she didn't, even if she snorted when she laughed, snot coming out, it wouldn't matter. Rose would still think it was the best thing in the world. And Abby wanted her to imagine it, to hear it in her mind.

"It's . . . lovely." Rose wiped a tear away and kept talking, though her voice was so silent, Abby caught only snatches. ". . . like little . . . everyone would smile . . . her eyes . . ."

"What will you do together next time you see her?" Abby asked.

But Rose wasn't listening. She took out her cell phone, fiddling with it. Gretchen was telling her something, her voice too low for Abby to hear.

"It seems like you really love your daughter," Abby said, as Rose put the phone to her ear. "How can I help you get to her safely?"

"You can give us the damn car!" Gretchen shouted.

But Rose didn't say anything, eyes vacant, phone to her ear. She probably knew that even if they got that car, even if they managed to drive away, it wouldn't help her to see her daughter again. Who was she calling? Her parents, to talk to Lori? Or Moses, to get instructions? If she was calling Moses, it could end badly.

Gritting her teeth, Rose tapped on the screen, then seemed to call another number. Good. She'd probably tried her dad, now she was trying her mom. Or their home phone. Abby hoped they would follow Tatum's instructions and not answer the call.

"How can I help you see Lori today?" Abby asked. "It looks like you really miss her."

Rose ignored her, ear to the phone. Abby imagined it ringing, Rose praying for her parents to answer. But it just kept ringing.

Finally she put the phone away, shutting her eyes, her body slumping in her seat.

"What can I do to help you talk to Lori today?" Abby asked.

"You can get us the car," Rose answered, her voice hollow, deflated.

"I am working on that," Abby said. "But it will take some time. And meanwhile I'm worried about your safety. The truck is full of very flammable vapors. We consulted with an expert who told us anything could make them combust. Even something random, like the sun shining through the car's window, or a change in temperature."

Rose's body went rigid. She was scared by the idea. She no longer wanted to die. It was time to take away the false hope these women were fostering.

"I don't know if I can even get them to bring you a car," Abby said. "But once you're safely out of these flammable vapors, we'll do whatever we can to help you talk to your daughter."

"We're not going anywhere," Gretchen said.

"You know what one of the best things about being a mother is?" Abby asked. "You get to see them grow and change. Every day is a miracle. The first day at school. The new friends they meet. That first love. Watching your daughter reading a book in bed. Hearing about her time at summer camp. Celebrating her birth—"

"If we get out of the car, they'll kill us," Rose said hoarsely.

"They won't," Abby said. "Even if they wanted to, they can't. Too many witnesses. Too many cameras. There are already news vans nearby, filming this. And I promise you I'll keep you safe."

Gretchen grabbed Rose's arm. "Rose, Father said—"

But Rose yanked her arm away. "I want to talk to my daughter *today*."

"I promise. We'll get her on the phone the moment you're safe. When you get out of the car, do it slowly, okay? It's icy, and I don't want you to slip and fall."

"Okay."

Abby forced herself to breathe as she watched Rose open the door, put a leg on the snowy ground.

Gretchen lunged and grabbed her shirt. "You're not going anywhere!"

Rose pulled away, slapping at the woman, screaming. Abby's heart skipped a beat as Gretchen dragged Rose back inside. But then Rose hit Gretchen and tumbled outside. She scrambled to her feet and hurried away from the car, toward Abby, heaving, sobbing.

"You're okay," Abby said. "You're doing great. Go toward the road, get away from the car, okay? I'll be with you soon."

"No." Rose gasped. "You come with me. They'll kill me. You said you'll help."

Abby took a deep breath, turning her eyes to Gretchen, who sat dazed in the passenger seat, looking lost. Now that they were separated, it would be easier to convince Gretchen to surrender too. "Okay, hang on."

She took a step toward the car. "Gretchen, how are you doing in there? Are you okay?"

Gretchen turned to her, blinking. And then she raised the lighter in her hand. "I want that car!" she screeched. "If it isn't here in two minutes, I'm doing it! You tell them! Two minutes!" She flicked the lighter.

It sparked but didn't light. She did it again. Another spark, no flame. Like Zoe had said earlier, the lighter had run out of gas.

Abby exhaled. "We don't want to see anyone get hurt," she said. "How can I help—"

But Gretchen wasn't looking at her. She was staring at something behind Abby, her eyes widening.

Abby glanced over her shoulder, and her heart sank. Cops were running toward them. They must have seen the lighter fail to ignite. And they'd figured this was their chance.

"Wait!" she shouted at them. "Don't come closer."

She turned back to Gretchen. The woman held the lighter to her own gasoline-soaked clothes, frantically clicking the lighter.

A flame bloomed.

Abby threw herself at Rose, pushing her to the snow, hearing the sudden whoosh, feeling the dry, searing heat around her. The force of the explosion pushed her away, and she rolled on the icy ground, grasping for Rose, pulling her away from the truck. Scorching pain flared in Abby's back as something sharp bit into her skin. Rose shrieked in pain, and Abby turned to see a large piece of twisted metal lodged deeply in the woman's thigh, blood painting the snow pink.

In the background, the truck had turned into a roaring inferno, flaming pamphlets fluttering in the air, a single burning figure flailing inside.

CHAPTER 43

Abby carefully pulled her shoulder forward, the laceration in her back twinging. When the truck had exploded, a piece of debris had cut a long deep scratch just below her shoulder. The paramedic at the scene had easily cleaned and bandaged it, telling her that he didn't think she needed stitches. She'd gotten off lightly. Unlike Rose, who was evacuated in an ambulance, a large jagged metallic shard still lodged in her leg.

And unlike Gretchen, who was removed from the scene, a black tarp hiding her charred remains.

The past hours were a blur in her mind. Fragmented images and sounds. Tatum grabbing her and dragging her away from the burning truck. People shouting as the firefighters hosed down the flames. Rose, taken to the ambulance, moaning that she wanted to talk to her daughter, that they'd promised her she would talk to her daughter.

The local chief had wanted her to come to the police station. Something about a briefing and reports that had to be written. Abby had been too numb to argue, and it had been Tatum who'd told the chief there would be time for that later, that the three of them needed to talk to the surviving cult member as soon as possible.

And then Tatum and Zoe were guiding her to the car. They drove away, leaving the smoking wreckage behind them.

They were in the emergency room of the Bear Lake Memorial Hospital. She sat on a chair in the waiting area, Zoe by her side. Tatum marched back and forth, talking on the phone. Two nurses walked past them, chatting with each other, one of them laughing. A doctor was called on the PA system. A few chairs away, a middle-aged man sat, his arm around the shoulder of a younger man, their faces etched with worry.

Was it her imagination, or was there a distinct smell of smoke in the air? Smoke and burning flesh. And she could still hear the screeching as Gretchen burned in the car, shrieks of pain that brought back echoes from the past, the screaming of people from behind the door, begging to be let out, her parents calling for help, and she had to open the door, she reached for the latch—

"You're shivering."

Abby blinked. "What?"

Zoe looked at her, frowning. "You're soaking wet. You should change."

"I'm fine." She really was shivering. From the cold? Or the memories?

"You're not fine, Mullen, you need dry clothes. I don't think your bandage should get wet either."

"I don't have any clothes," Abby said impatiently. "My suitcase is back at the motel in Rigby."

"My bag is in the trunk of the car," Zoe said. "Come on. I'll give you something to wear."

"Don't worry about it. It'll dry up."

Zoe stood and held out a hand. "I have pants that are too big for me. They should probably fit you."

Abby let out a snort. "Thanks a lot." Realizing Zoe was not about to let up, she took Zoe's hand and stood up, trying to ignore the flashing pain in her back.

Abby waited in the hospital's main entrance as Zoe ran out in the rain to grab her suitcase from the car. Then they walked together to the bathroom.

Zoe crouched and opened the suitcase carefully on the floor. She took out black skinny pants and a gray blouse with a loose V-neck. She straightened, handing them to Abby. "Here you go."

Abby took the clothes and entered one of the stalls. She struggled with her wet clothes in the cramped space and let out a whimper of pain as she stretched her bandaged back.

"You okay?" Zoe asked through the door.

"I'm fine." Abby gritted her teeth. "It's that scratch."

"Do you need help?"

"I got it." She managed to wrestle her soaked shirt off. "Oh shit."

"What?"

"I think the bandage came off."

"Let me see."

Abby sighed and opened the stall door. She turned with her back to Zoe. "See?"

"Oh yeah, I think I can fix it. Hang on." Zoe's delicate fingers adjusted the bandage. "There. I think it might need stitches after all. It's bleeding again."

"Maybe I shouldn't wear your shirt," Abby said worriedly. "I'll get blood on it."

"It's fine," Zoe said, sounding impatient.

Abby slipped the shirt on. The fabric was soft and warm. "How do you get your clothes to feel so nice?" she asked. "All my blouses feel crinkly after I wash them a few times. And I use vinegar and everything."

"I use a cleaning service," Zoe said shortly.

"Ah." Abby sat on the closed toilet and stared ahead vacantly. "A cleaning service for me and my kids would probably cost a bazillion dollars. Sometimes I feel like my kids change their clothes five times a day."

Zoe gazed at her, eyebrows raised. "Is everything all right?"

"What?" Abby realized tears were running down her cheeks. She wiped them with the back of her hand. "Oh. Yeah. I'm just tired. And I miss my kids. Moses tried to get to them a few times, you know? And I still feel like they might be in danger . . . you don't have kids, right?"

"No. But I know how it feels to leave your family exposed." Zoe's voice grew soft. "A few years ago my sister was stalked by a killer. While I was away on the job, she was attacked."

Abby's voice hitched. "Was she—"

"She's okay. But it was a near thing. When I heard . . ." Zoe shook her head. "It was bad."

Abby swallowed. For a few seconds she just stared ahead, thinking of Sam and Ben, reminding herself that they were all right.

"I wish I could have saved that girl." Her lips trembled.

"It wasn't your fault," Zoe said. "It was that police chief's call to send his people to grab her. If he hadn't done that—"

"We can't know what would have happened." Abby shut her eyes and sniffled. "She was desperate. And I split her from her friend, leaving her alone. Maybe, if I hadn't done that, I could have saved them both."

"Or they both would have died."

"Yeah. Maybe." Abby cleared her throat. "There was this guy, all those years ago, when I was a kid. A cop. He showed up on the scene when our group . . . Wilcox's cult . . . barricaded ourselves. He called us, to talk. And he talked to me."

"He talked to *you*?"

Abby nodded. "A little girl. He wasn't trained. He didn't know what to expect. He tried to be kind and asked to talk to an adult. He didn't know that Moses had told me what to say beforehand. I bought time for Moses to set the place on fire. And I fed that cop lies that enabled Moses to get away. I've read the transcript of that conversation so many times I know it by heart. I always figured a trained negotiator would have managed to prevent what had happened. He would have asked questions. He would have figured out what was going on. Seven-year-old children aren't complicated. I always believed if I ever found myself in that position, things would be different."

"Mullen—"

Every bit of strength in Abby's body had been drained. "Today I tried to help two women whose minds were twisted by Moses Wilcox, and one of them ended up burning herself to death. Maybe there was no way to stop what had happened all those years ago, no matter who would have talked to me. Moses gets into people's heads. He's like this . . . this . . . demon—"

"He's not a demon," Zoe said sharply. "Or a cancerous growth. Or a monster. And he's not a messiah either. He's a man who happens to be very good at making people do what he wants. And his motivations always revolve around sex and control."

"You don't know him."

"*You* don't know him. Trust me. He's a shitty man who gets off on burning people alive. And you didn't fail today—you saved a woman's life, and it's possible you would have saved both their lives if that police chief would have listened to you. But that doesn't matter. It's not why you're upset."

"It isn't? Then why am I upset?"

"Because you haven't slept well for a while," Zoe said matter-of-factly. "And because you haven't eaten anything since breakfast. And because you're wet and cold."

Abby's jaw clenched. There was something maddening knowing in a distant part of her mind that Zoe was mostly right. "Fine," she spit, rolling off her wet, muddy pants. "Let's see if your pants fit me."

They did, though they sat a bit tightly. They were ankle-length pants for Zoe, which meant that for Abby, they were full length. Still, it more or less worked. She examined herself in the bathroom mirror, surprised to see she liked the way she looked in Zoe's clothes.

She strode over to the sink and washed her face. She quickly ran water over her hands, then pointedly shut the water off, ignoring the desire to scrub her hands harder. Exhaling slowly, she collected herself. "Let's go see if Rose can talk to us."

CHAPTER 44

Thursday, May 13, 2008

"What do you mean she's gone?" Moses stared at Anna with mounting fury.

They were in his office in the church's Saint George branch. They had four churches now and were conducting seminars in six different states. Up until that moment, he'd been having a good day, looking into potential real estate deals for their next church. He was considering Montana. And then Anna came to his office with this bombshell.

"Angela said that the Lily Fellowship Church was taking too much of her time," Anna said. "And she missed her parents. She told me to tell you that—"

"I was very clear that if anyone looks like they're about to leave, you send them to talk to me!"

The tension was mounting in his chest again. He was always tense, always stressed. Even now, with his church's success, with his constant traveling. Even now that he knew that no one would ever connect him with Moses Wilcox, that God was protecting him, he still wasn't complete. As if something was missing.

Even the small fires he lit every once in a while weren't enough to calm him down anymore.

He gripped his chair's arms tightly, looking at Anna, who stood across his desk.

"Yes, I know you asked that," Anna said impatiently. "But in this case, I couldn't see the point. You were busy, and it's not like it's a big loss. She was lazy and quite vapid. She has no resources to contribute to our cause—"

"*I* decide if someone is contributing to our cause!" Moses shouted.

Yes, it was true, the girl wasn't particularly useful. She'd originally had some savings, but she had already donated those to their church. But still.

She was just shy of twenty, and whenever Moses talked to her, she seemed very passionate about the church, her large eyes drinking in his every word, her lips parted slightly . . .

"Has she left?"

"She's waiting for her ride outside," Anna said coldly.

Her tone infuriated him. "Tell her to come see me."

"I already told her you were busy. And I won't chase her. She was rude to me. She's gone and that's it."

He moved before he realized it and gripped Anna's hand.

"Hey!" she said, outraged.

He squeezed it tightly, and then, without a thought, he took out his lighter. He'd imagined doing this many times but had never actually considered acting on his impulse. But now he knew that it wasn't a simple impulse. It was too powerful for a simple mortal desire. It was God's will.

He switched on the lighter, the flame dancing and flickering. And then he touched it to Anna's wrist.

She screamed, but he almost couldn't hear it. The rush of euphoria was so all consuming it nearly took his breath away. For a few seconds he completely forgot where he was and what he was doing. Only the flame and the woman's pain existed.

She buckled and twisted, but he didn't let go. She screamed and whimpered and begged.

Finally, he flipped the lighter shut and released her.

He was breathing hard. Anna's face was streaked with tears.

"Anything you want to say to me?" he managed to grunt.

"I . . . I . . ." Emotions flickered on Anna's face.

"Yes?" he growled.

"I'm . . . sorry, Father. Next time I will do as you say."

"Good." He was shaking. He realized his crotch had stiffened. God still had one more task for him. "Angela is still outside, right?"

"Y . . . yes."

"Go outside and send her in here," he said. "Right now."

CHAPTER 45

Abby stepped lightly into the white room, Zoe close behind her. Rose Olson lay on the flat ER bed in the middle of the room, a blood transfusion tube running up her arm. The white fluorescent light harshly revealed the bruises and scratches on her pale skin. Her eyes stared vacantly upward, and she hardly budged as Abby approached her.

"Hey, Rose," Abby said softly. "How are you feeling?"

"They won't let me out," Rose said tightly. "And they won't give me a phone. They won't even let me talk to Gretchen."

Abby sat down on a nearby stool and laid her hand on Rose's. "I'm really sorry. Gretchen didn't make it."

"Oh." Rose swallowed, a tear materializing. After a few seconds she said, "I need a phone. I need to call our church and tell them."

"I'm sure the local police are doing that," Abby said.

"No, *I* need to talk to them. They need to hear it from me. And . . . and I'll need to go there. Talk to our preacher. He needs to know what happened."

Even through all that had happened, Rose still clung to the hope that she could go back to the way things had been. Abby could imagine what she was thinking. If she could only leave this place, she could contact Moses, let him know what had happened. Let him know she'd done everything that she could. And he'd let her come back. The desperation and hope in Rose's eyes were heartbreaking. Her strongest desire was to go back to the group that had completely destroyed her life.

"Your preacher?" Abby asked.

"Yeah. It's important that I talk to him."

"No problem. Is there a phone number we can call?"

Rose blinked and froze. "I'm not sure where he is right now," she finally said. "But I can call our church."

"The Lily Fellowship Church, right?"

"Yeah."

"And what's the name of your preacher?"

"Um." Rose sniffed. "It's um. Father Williams. But if I can only have my phone back—"

"We can't give you your phone back yet," Zoe said from the back of the room.

Rose blinked. "Who are you?" she asked.

"I'm Bentley," Zoe said. "I'm with the FBI."

"The FBI?" Rose whispered. "I . . . why are the FBI involved? It's all a big mistake. We didn't do anything. That cop frightened us, so we tried to get away. We never hurt anyone."

"We're still trying to figure out what happened," Abby said, patting Rose's hand. "I'll check with the cops in a bit, see if you can get your phone back."

Zoe cleared her throat skeptically at that.

"And then I'll be able to talk to Lori," Rose said. "You promised me I could talk to Lori."

"Oh, you can do that right now if you're up to it." Abby smiled at her.

"Really?" Rose's eyes widened. "You'll give me my phone?"

"No, but you can talk on my phone. Hang on." Abby took out her phone from her pocket and unmuted the ongoing call. "Hi, this is Abby. Rose wants to talk to her daughter?"

"Can I talk to her first?" Carl, Rose's father, asked. He sounded tense and angry. Not the voice Abby wanted Rose to hear right now.

"She really just wants a few words with Lori," Abby said, her tone final.

"Okay, hang on," Carl said gruffly. "Here, sweetie, talk to your mommy."

Abby listened as the phone on the other side switched hands.

"Hello?" a sweet childish voice said.

Abby handed the phone to Rose. The woman winced as she put it to her ear.

"Hello?" Rose said. "Baby?"

Abby glanced back at Zoe, who was leaning against the wall by the door, her arms folded. They exchanged quick glances. The tried-and-tested "good cop, bad cop" technique had just been upgraded to "good cop, cute daughter, bad cop." Abby *needed* Rose to talk to Lori. The woman had to remember she had other reasons to live beyond getting back to the cult. Lori was the only thing anchoring Rose to the world, and it was important to establish that, because in a few minutes, Abby intended to destroy Rose's illusions regarding Moses and the Lily Fellowship Church.

"I'm okay, baby, how are *you*?" Rose asked, her voice barely a whisper, tears running down her cheeks. "Yes, I know, I'm sorry. I've been very busy."

Abby half listened, mentally reviewing everything she knew about Rose. Tatum had talked to Dot in Rigby, and she'd told him Rose had managed the last seminar, giving most of the lectures. From what Dot had gathered, that job had been Anna's, but this time, Moses had decided to give it to Rose instead. Rose Olson had been moving up in the cult. Which could only mean she was deeply involved in the cult's other activities. Had she been there when they'd taken Delilah's husband? Had she been involved in the previous baptisms? Burning people alive at Moses's say-so?

She almost surely had been. Moses wouldn't have promoted her otherwise.

If she realized they knew about her involvement in the murders, this interview would probably end quickly. Right now Rose believed she had a chance to return to her previous life.

"I hope I'll see you really soon, baby," Rose said, smiling.

As soon as she figured out that she was facing a long prison sentence, they would lose her. And with her, the chance to catch up to Moses. To save Delilah and her children.

Rose hung up the call and stared at the phone in her hand. Abby leaned forward and took it, then slipped it back into her pocket.

"She sounds like a sweet girl," Abby said, smiling.

"She is." Rose sniffled. "In a month or two, I'll be able to get her from my parents and live with her again." She smiled to herself after she said it, her eyes losing focus.

Abby could imagine Moses feeding her that lie over and over again. *In a month or two she'll come live with us*, he'd say and add a Bible quote. Moses could pull Bible quotes out of his ass for any occasion. And he'd give her his fatherly, loving stare. And then, later, when he'd postpone it, he'd blame Rose, tell her she hadn't worked hard enough. Carefully intertwining her resolve and guilt and frustration and hope together until it was a mental knot Rose couldn't untangle even if she wanted to.

"When did you see her last?" Abby asked with interest.

"It's been a while," Rose mumbled.

"When I worked shifts, sometimes I wouldn't see my kids for three or four days." Abby shook her head. "That was tough."

Rose swallowed, saying nothing.

"When my daughter was Lori's age, I bought her Rollerblades for her birthday," Abby said. "I still remember her falling over and over and over again, until I regretted ever buying the damn things. But she wouldn't give up. And then, next thing I knew, she was whizzing through our house with those things. It was impossible to get them off. She wanted to *sleep* with them."

She watched Rose's face carefully. Saw the moment the woman's eyes widened with realization and horror.

Rose had forgotten her daughter's fifth birthday. Rose's father had told Tatum this when they'd talked twenty minutes before. It wasn't surprising. A week ago she had been running that seminar for Moses. Things must have been hectic; Rose had probably hardly slept.

But still, she'd forgotten. And now she realized it.

Who was the bad cop in this room, really? All Zoe did was fold her arms and look hostile. But it was Abby who punched Rose with a fist of mother's guilt.

"When can I leave?" Rose blurted.

"We still have some questions," Zoe said sharply.

"I told you," Rose said. Her tone had shifted, becoming stressed. "Those officers just scared us. Gretchen . . . she overreacted. But we never intended—"

"We're not concerned about that," Abby reassured her. "We're looking for a woman named Delilah."

Rose blinked. "Delilah?"

"We know that she recently joined your church," Abby said pleasantly. "With her two children. We think she's involved in a case we're investigating. We want to question her."

She watched Rose closely. Delilah was the most recent recruit. Not really a part of their so-called family, not yet. Perhaps Rose would find it easier to give them information about her. Not a real betrayal of her new family. Not a real betrayal of Moses.

"I . . . I don't know where Delilah is."

"But you've met her?"

"Yes," Rose said emphatically. "And maybe I could call and get you that information. Someone in the church might know where she went."

"When was the last time you saw her?" Zoe asked.

"Uh . . . I don't know. A few days ago."

"Really?" Zoe said dryly. "That's strange. Because we know you were staying at the same place near Bear Lake."

"I . . . I don't remember seeing her there. I mean, we were a large group. From the church. And we were very busy."

"That makes sense," Abby said. "Where were you going?"

"W . . . what?"

"You were driving with Gretchen in that pickup truck. It was full of pamphlets from your church. Where were you taking them?"

"We were going to Salt Lake City. To hand them out."

"Oh." Abby frowned, confused. "Then why were you driving north?"

"We must have made a wrong turn. I'm awful with maps—"

"You told that officer who stopped you that you were on your way to the West Coast."

Rose blinked. "Like I said earlier, he kinda scared us. We didn't want him following us."

Abby didn't really care about Rose's answers. They already knew the answers to all these questions. Rose had seen Delilah that morning. Rose and Gretchen were on their way to California to meet with Moses and the rest of the group. But the fact that Rose was so busy fabricating facts meant she was determined not to help them. Not even to see her daughter. Mother's guilt hadn't done the job.

Perhaps anger would work better.

"You know," she said, frowning. "Something is bothering me. You said Lori was about to come and stay with you, right?"

"Yes," Rose said slowly. She seemed wary. Obviously, she realized this wasn't just about Delilah.

"When was that supposed to happen, exactly?"

"Soon," Rose said. "As soon as things at work settled down."

"Oh, things have been particularly busy?"

"Yes," Rose said. "We've been doing so much. The church has new projects all the time, and I need to help manage them. We use the seminars to raise money. I work eighteen, sometimes even twenty hours a day. That's not a good environment for Lori to be in, you know? She needs stability."

"Absolutely," Abby said. "It does sound intense. How long has it been so busy?"

Rose let out a short laugh. "It feels like forever."

"I know how that can be." Abby smiled back. "So how long do you think?"

Rose blinked. "I don't know exactly."

"How long has Lori been staying with your parents?"

"For a while."

Abby waited, nodding, the patient smile still on her face.

"I guess about two years," Rose finally admitted.

Abby widened her eyes. "That's a long time. Deciding to be apart from your daughter for so long must have been difficult. *I* could never have done it."

"I didn't think it would be so long," Rose said defensively. "It should have been a couple of months."

"Why did you think it would be only two months?"

"That's what we estimated at first."

"Who's *we?*"

"Um . . . well, me. And Father Williams."

"But later you saw it was taking longer, so you decided Lori should stay with your parents for two years?"

"No." Rose swallowed. "Time just went by."

"Well, I guess you probably visited Lori frequently during that time. Got a bit of quality time with your daughter?"

Rose nodded hesitantly. Abby smiled at her, reassuring. Rose hadn't been to see Lori once in all this time. And right now she had to be asking herself why, berating herself. She would never blame Moses. That would be Abby's job.

"I assume Father Williams gave you time off to see her every once in a while. It was the *least* he could do."

"He did," Rose blurted. "But I . . . it was always so busy."

"So you didn't see her very often?" Abby asked sadly. "No wonder you both miss each other so much."

"What does this have to do with—"

"But it's all going to end soon, right? Things will settle down, and she'll come live with you."

"Yes." Rose jutted her chin forward.

"Why do you think that?"

"What?"

"Why do you think it's going to get less busy? Is the church out of projects? No more seminars?"

"No . . . ," Rose said slowly. "But Father Williams promised me that we'll get her."

"Oh." Abby frowned. "He's never promised that before?"

Rose didn't answer.

"In fact, someone told me that *you* were in charge of the last seminar for the first time, right?"

"Yes," Rose whispered.

"You must have been even busier than usual. Who told you to run that seminar?"

"Father Williams."

"But didn't he know you were trying to slow things down?"

"Father has a lot on his mind. I can't expect him to—"

"Really? He seemed pretty involved in your decision to keep Lori at your parents."

Rose's eyes flashed. Abby was cutting it close. The woman wouldn't listen to any direct criticism of Moses.

"I was incredibly proud to serve the church like that," Rose said.

"I would be too," Abby said. "Thank god for phone calls, right? At least you could talk to Lori every day."

On and on they went, Abby keeping her tone pleasant but insistent. She was surprised to hear that Rose didn't call very often, then dug in until Father Williams's name came up, then frowned and backed off, shifting to the subject of money. Rose sent her parents money for Lori, right? She didn't? A bit of probing, and Father Williams's name came up again. How had Lori taken it when Rose took her to her grandparents? The farewell must have been difficult. Rose hadn't taken her herself? Why? Father Williams.

In each case Rose would try to explain how it had been *her* fault, *her* decision. But it was easy to sweep away the lies she believed in, to get her to name the one person who really called the shots.

Like Zoe had pointed out earlier, exhaustion and hunger were great to make anyone upset. And Rose was slowly getting exhausted, her answers angrier, impatient. While Abby kept the same tone and pace for an hour, then another.

Lori's birthdays? Father Williams.

Oh, Lori had broken her arm when she was four, and Rose didn't go to see her? Father Williams.

And back to the question of when Lori would finally come to live with Rose . . . Father Williams.

"I'm done," Rose finally snapped. "I need to rest."

"You wanted to leave earlier," Abby said.

"I changed my mind. They said I lost a lot of blood. I should stay here for another day. And I need to sleep. All those questions have *nothing* to do with Delilah or with how we sped away from the cops. They have nothing to do with what happened to Gretchen—"

"They have a lot to do with what happened to Gretchen," Abby said.

"Bullshit. What does Lori have to do with Gretchen?"

Abby decided to gamble. "Rose, did you ever hear about the Wilcox Cult Massacre?"

Rose's confused stare confirmed that Abby's gamble had paid off. She *didn't know*.

"Yeah," she finally said. "I heard about it. I think I saw something on TV about it once. It was that cult who killed themselves all those years ago, right?"

"Not exactly," Abby said. "They barricaded themselves, and Wilcox, their leader, set fire to the compound, killing almost all of them."

"Okay," Rose said guardedly. Her eyes shifted when the word *fire* was mentioned.

"I was one of the only survivors."

"You were in the Wilcox cult?" Rose asked, shocked.

"I was a little girl." Abby sighed. "The police found out later that Wilcox escaped the fire. That he used the chaos to escape unharmed. Nine of those who burned to death had been kids, two of them Lori's age. Kids I knew. Kids I used to play with."

"Why are you telling me this?"

"Did you ever see Wilcox's photo?"

"Probably." Rose shrugged. "On TV or something."

Abby took out her phone and opened the browser. She handed it to Rose. "Search for it," she suggested. "Wilcox photo."

Rose looked at her suspiciously. Finally she tapped on the phone. Abby waited.

It wasn't a connection that anyone would make on their own. But they'd been talking about the so-called Father Williams for the past two hours. Despite herself, by now Rose must have felt a spark of anger toward the man she admired so much. Enough anger, Abby believed, to make her see the man and not just the object of adoration.

Rose's eyes widened. There. Abby let her be as she tapped on the screen, probably switching between photos. Seeing the man she knew so well.

"Wilcox's first name is Moses—maybe you knew that," Abby said. "He founded the Lily Fellowship Church and changed his name from Wilcox to Williams."

"You're wrong," Rose said, putting down the phone.

"Moses Wilcox had a phrase he loved quoting to us," Abby said. "'Consider the lilies of the field, how they grow; they toil not, neither do they spin.'"

The horror in Rose's eyes was palpable.

"You've heard that one?" Abby smiled at her sadly. "I guess he still uses it. Does he make you wash your hands to get rid of the germs? I can see that he does; the backs of your hands are all scratched. I used to wash my hands for hours, until they bled."

Rose stared at her scratched, irritated skin, breathing heavily.

"He didn't particularly like kids back then either," Abby said. "He said we were noisy. We made it hard for him to concentrate."

Rose let out a choking sound.

Abby leaned forward. "We need to find him."

"I . . . you're wrong. It can't be—"

"He's going to hurt more people, Rose. He's getting desperate."

"Father Williams is a good man, he's not a—"

"Tell us where he went before he burns anyone else."

"I don't know!" Rose shrieked. "We were all supposed to meet at a shopping mall in Twin Falls and continue to California from there. He never told us where we were going. And you'll never find them. They left the meeting spot hours ago."

Abby exhaled. "What's the shopping mall's name?"

CHAPTER 46

"I don't think anything unusual happened today," the security officer at Magic Valley Mall said as he led them down the empty echoing space of the shopping mall. "Joe and Grace were on shift, and they would have said something. There was a shoplifter at the cosmetics store. A local sixteen-year-old schoolgirl. Her parents picked her up later. Is that what you're looking for? I have their phone number."

Abby walked briskly to keep pace with Tatum, Zoe, and the security officer, whose name was Kyle. The mall was almost completely dark, and the sound of their footsteps echoed all around them eerily. Ben would invariably yell "Echo!" in a place like this and get excited as his voice bounced back.

"No, that's not what we're interested in," Tatum said.

"Some rowdy teenagers in the video game store," Kyle said hopefully. "Joe told them to leave. And they called him fatso."

"We're looking for a group of adults," Zoe said impatiently. "About twenty-five of them. They would have met here."

"Where did they meet? At the movie theater?"

"We don't know," Zoe said. "That's why—"

"Or maybe at Olive Garden across the street? If they met for lunch, they would meet there, or at Chili's. All we have inside the mall is a pretzel stand."

"Let's see the security footage," Tatum said. "And then we'll be able to tell."

They reached a closed door, the word SECURITY written in large black letters on it. Kyle slid a key in the lock and rattled it.

"The door gets stuck," he said. "We keep asking for them to fix it, but you know how it is." His tongue protruded between his teeth as he rattled the key for a few seconds, until it finally clicked, the door opening instantly. Kyle stumbled inside and then straightened, brushing his shirt with his hands.

The security room was small, a tangible smell of stale coffee in the air. The floor was sticky. Kyle made his way to the security console, where a screen displayed the footage from nine different cameras throughout the mall. Abby's eyes scanned the cameras displaying the vacant stores, the empty wide passages, the dark parking lot. A second later the images shifted, displaying different cameras.

"How many cameras do you have overall?" Abby asked.

"Twenty-two, but the one above the northern passage is busted," Kyle said, fiddling with the controls. "So, what time did you say?"

The cult would have left the cabin soon after Delilah's phone call at half past ten. The drive to the mall from the cabin should have taken about four hours, perhaps less.

"Around two p.m.," Abby said.

"Maybe a bit later," Tatum added.

Kyle's tongue protruded between his teeth again as he typed that in. The screen flickered, people appearing on the screens as the footage from earlier that day appeared. Not too many people. The mall wasn't very busy during the day either.

"That's Joe," Kyle said, pointing to one of the screens at an overweight security officer whose fingers were wedged through his belt. "I don't see Grace, but she's here somewhere."

Abby scanned the footage as they shifted between the different cameras. The video was black and white, grainy, the resolution low. Her eyes hovered over each shopper, trying to find similarities to the people she knew from Moses's group. Was that woman sitting on a bench Anna? Was the large man eating a pretzel Richard? Was the thin man with the glasses entering the clothing shop Moses? She realized she was squinting, her jaw clenched tightly, as she desperately searched for anyone familiar.

After a few seconds, Kyle asked, "Found anything?"

"Can you speed this up?" Zoe asked.

"Sure."

The people on screen dashed through the footage, flickering, too fast to glimpse any details.

"Wait," Abby said. "I can't see them this way—"

"Wouldn't they be together?" Zoe asked. "We're looking for large crowds."

"Not necessarily," Tatum argued. "They might split up while getting necessities. Or eat in different locations. Maybe like Kyle said, they split up and ate outside. I doubt they would all eat pretzels."

"What do you think, Mullen?" Zoe asked.

"I don't know if any of them like pretzels," Abby said distractedly, her eyes following a man with long hair. Or was it a woman?

"Never mind the pretzels," Zoe said, annoyed. "Would they—"

"Wait," Abby said. "What's that?"

Her eyes caught something in the camera overlooking the parking lot. A group of people, huddled together at the corner of the screen. How many were there? Ten, at least.

"Can you show us only the footage from this camera?" she asked. "And slow it down."

Kyle did as she asked. The camera was pointed at the center of the parking lot, and the group stood at the far end. Some of them kept stepping in and out of the frame.

"There's Richard," Abby said, her heart thudding. She pointed at the large man. "See? And I think that's Anna over there. She has her back to the camera, so it's hard to . . . yup, that's her."

She stared at the men and women. Some sat on a bench, talking; others leaned on a car. Two women showed up with a few bags and handed out takeout meals to everyone.

"That must be Emily," Zoe said, pointing at a little girl who stood by Anna. The girl received something that looked like a hot dog and ate it slowly. Abby wished they were standing closer so she could see her face.

"What about Moses?" Tatum asked.

"I can't see him," Abby said. "He's not there."

"How do you know?" Zoe asked.

"Because if he was, he would have been the first to receive his meal. And people would be facing him. He would be the center of attention." She watched as one of the men checked his watch. "No, they're still waiting for him to show up."

"That Audi they're leaning on," Tatum said. "I'm betting that's one of their vehicles. I think we might be able to get the license plate number from it."

Abby waited as the group on screen paced back and forth. Someone took out his phone, made a call, then shook his head and put the phone back in his pocket.

"So who are these guys?" Kyle asked. "Are they like . . . terrorists?"

"No," Tatum said. "Can you fast-forward?"

The footage flickered as Kyle accelerated it.

"Wait!" Zoe and Abby said together. Another vehicle showed up, and someone stepped out.

"Stop," Zoe added. "Rewind and slow it down."

Kyle did as he was told, and Abby watched, her breath held tight. The car parked closer to the mall, and the group all moved toward it. Now, almost all of them were visible. Anna was holding a baby—probably Ron. Did that mean Delilah wasn't there at all?

And then Moses stepped out of the car. There was no way to mistake him. Dressed in white and radiating an authority over the rest of the group, who quickly formed a half circle around him. One of the men approached him first and started talking to him.

"Who's that?" Tatum asked.

Abby looked at him carefully. He was about sixty, bulky, with a wild dark beard. "I don't know—I don't recognize him."

Moses nodded a few times, then turned away from the man, motioning at Anna to come over. She stepped forward, talking to him. He clenched his fists, talking angrily. He faced the camera almost directly.

"Do you think an analyst in the bureau can read his lips?" Abby asked.

"Maybe," Tatum said. "I'll check."

Anna responded. Something in his posture shifted. Anna escorted him to a car parked a few yards away, a white Toyota Corolla. She glanced around her, then opened the trunk and took a step back. It was impossible to see the inside of the trunk from the camera's angle. Moses stood motionless in front of the open trunk. He seemed almost mesmerized. He leaned forward, adjusting something inside, talking to himself.

No. There was something in his motions and posture. This was not a man talking to himself.

"Oh, shit," Abby whispered.

"There's someone in the trunk," Zoe said, voicing Abby's thoughts.

CHAPTER 47

The roar of the car's engine enveloped Delilah, deafening, unbearable, vibrating through her body, through her clenched teeth, rattling through her bones, until she couldn't hear herself think, couldn't hear herself beg for them to stop, couldn't hear herself shriek.

The events of the day flickered through her mind over and over and over, a merry-go-round of violence and fear. That morning, when Moses had forced her to burn her wrist while begging for forgiveness in front of the entire congregation. Her frantic, stupid phone call to Paula, which had ended with her talking to the police. And then, Moses catching her. The fury etched on his face. And she knew *this* time, she would really pay. At first she'd thought they would kill her or even worse, burn her alive, like they'd burned Brad. But instead, they'd tied her up, gagged her, and dumped her in the back of the pickup truck.

She'd lain there, shivering with fear, while they'd argued. They'd needed to put the boxes of pamphlets in the back, but there was no room. For one terrible moment they'd tried stacking the boxes on top of her, and she'd struggled and screamed, the heavy boxes crushing her. Finally, they'd removed her from the back of the pickup and stuffed her in the trunk of one of the cars.

The first few hours in the trunk were horrifying. She was cold and was sure she would suffocate to death. The ropes bit into her ankles and wrists, her jaws aching with the gag stuffed in her mouth. Time stretched endlessly, and she'd thought it was the most terrible experience in her life.

She couldn't have known it was going to get even worse.

They finally stopped somewhere. Exhausted, she lay there, her consciousness ebbing and flowing. And then. Light.

She blinked, the sunlight blinding her. The silhouette of a man towered above her. Moses.

She tried to apologize, sobbing into her gag. She was sorry. She was so sorry.

His expression swam into focus. He gazed at her body, licking his lips.

"I'll remove your gag," he said. "And I want you to remember we have both of your children. If you scream, or call for help, or do anything stupid, they will pay. You got that?"

She nodded fearfully.

He leaned forward to remove the gag, struggling with the knot, but it was too tight. Finally, panting with effort, he managed to slide it out of her mouth and off her chin, letting it hang on her neck.

"Please." She whimpered. "I'm sorry. I didn't—"

"Quiet."

She clamped her mouth shut, shivering in fear.

"When people hear about Abraham and Isaac," Moses told her, "they think it is about obedience. God told Abraham to sacrifice his son, and Abraham obeyed. And I don't disagree. Obedience is an important quality. One you should have tried to acquire."

His voice rose in anger, and she shrank, fearful.

"But it's also a story about sacrifice. And fear," he continued. "And once God saw Abraham truly feared him, he gave him a different choice for a sacrifice. A ram."

"Father—"

"God wants me to test you, Delilah. To see that you are obedient. And that you fear me . . . him. Your child will be sacrificed to show you've learned to fear him."

Aghast, she stared at him. Sacrifice her child? He couldn't mean it. "No, please—"

"But like with Abraham and Isaac, God has provided you with a choice."

"Yes, please, anything," Delilah stammered. "I will sleep with you. I'll let you do anything. Please don't hurt my children."

Moses frowned. "Of course you will do anything. And of course we will have sex. Because you have to be obedient. That is *not* the choice. God has provided a different choice for you."

"What, then?" Delilah whispered.

"You have two children."

She blinked, uncomprehending.

"God only wants one."

Her eyes widened. "What? No, you can't—"

"We will talk again tomorrow. And you will tell me which of them you've chosen."

"Father, wait, no—"

The lid of the trunk slammed shut, leaving her in darkness.

And now, hours later, she lay in the dark trunk, paralyzed with fear, the words still echoing in her mind.

You have two children.

God only wants one.

CHAPTER 48

"Abby?" A soft low voice.

Abby curled into herself, trying to return to that blessed darkness that had wrapped her so—

"Mullen!" Another voice. Sharp, impatient. "We're here. Wake up."

Abby started, blinking in confusion. She'd fallen asleep in the back of the car. It seemed almost impossible. One moment she'd been staring out the passenger window, her mind racing, thinking about Moses, the person in the trunk, the people she'd seen on the security footage. And the next . . .

She wiped her chin. Drool. *Nice one, Abby, way to earn the respect of the feds.* She massaged the back of her sore neck and looked around her. They were back in Rigby. Right.

"We talked to the sheriff," Tatum said, his voice still a bit soft. "He asked if we could drop by the task force room and bring them up to speed. But we can take you to your motel."

"No," Abby said blearily. "I'm coming with you."

She shuffled after Zoe and Tatum. Her entire body hurt. At the back of her throat she felt the beginning of a cold. Standing outside in the rain for more than an hour was probably the culprit. And still, after seeing the footage, she'd considered driving all night to California, in pursuit of the cult.

They stepped into the task force room. Only Sheriff Hunt was there, taping a printed image on the whiteboard. Abby recognized it as a printout from the footage they'd seen at the mall. Zoe and Tatum must have forwarded him the video on the way back.

"Oh good, you're here," he said. "I was almost ready to give up and go home."

Abby walked over to the board and scrutinized the new printouts. Grainy, blurry faces of Moses, Anna, Richard, and little Emily, as well as some other people she couldn't identify. A close-up of the license plate number, almost completely unintelligible.

"I think we can make out a letter or two," Hunt said, following her look. "I think that's a U. And this is either zero or O—"

"It's PFU-1702," Tatum said, looking at his phone. "It's an Ohio license plate."

"Your analysts managed to figure that out?" Abby asked, impressed. It seemed impossible.

Tatum grinned at her. "I know the best analyst in the bureau. The vehicle is registered to the Lily Fellowship Church. Previous owner was Richard Turner."

Abby glanced at the grainy images of Richard on the board. "So he transferred his vehicle to the church."

"Could it be something Wilcox demands of his recruits when they join?"

Abby shook her head. "It's more subtle. He wouldn't want to push away possible followers. They join, and then, a few weeks in, he starts talking to them about their contribution to the church. Mentioning other members who've donated their money, or cars, or homes. And if they don't bend, he applies his classic treatment. Accusing them of not being committed enough. Publicly berating them in front of the other members. Getting everyone to shun them. Eventually, they all give what they own to the church."

"We have an APB on the car," Tatum said. "And we specifically informed the Nevada Highway Patrol."

"Nevada?" Hunt frowned.

"We know they left Twin Falls, heading to California at three," Tatum said. "It's at least a ten-hour drive, and it's not likely they would drive it in one long stretch. We're thinking they'll find a place to stop in Nevada. With any luck, the NHP will spot the car in a motel parking lot."

"I wouldn't count on it," Hunt muttered. "Not if they decide to stop in Vegas. Do we know where in California?"

"We have a firm idea," Tatum said.

They'd discussed this earlier, as they drove out of the mall. According to the ever-growing pile of the church's paperwork the bureau was going through, the church had only one location in California.

"The Lily Fellowship Church is building a shelter for abused women and children in Livingston," Tatum said. "It fits. The town is small . . . not as small as Rigby, but small enough."

"And Moses might want to target abused women as his next recruits, like he did here," Abby said.

"Livingston, huh?" Hunt frowned.

"We have field officers staking out the place already," Tatum said. "If Wilcox and his group decide to make this an all-nighter and drive straight to Livingston, they'll have law enforcement agents waiting for them."

"Okay, that's good news," Hunt said. "So what can I tell people in Rigby?"

"Well . . . nothing, for now," Tatum said.

Hunt raised a bushy eyebrow. "Nothing? I can't work with nothing, Agent Gray. I have half the population of Rigby breathing down my neck."

"They'll have to wait patiently."

Hunt snorted. "I guess you never lived in a small town?"

Tatum folded his arms. "I grew up in one."

"Then you should know what's going on here. Rumors are getting crazier and crazier. I already heard that Delilah burned her husband down with a flamethrower, and another story where she and the kids died in the fire, but their bodies were taken by wolves. Oh! And the third story is that Brad Eckert faked his own death and that the body we found is made of clay. And the phone keeps ringing. My *mother* keeps calling because her friends want to know what's going on, and she's the sheriff's mother, after all. And—"

"I sympathize," Tatum said. "But I don't have anything solid for you yet."

"What about Delilah?" Hunt asked. "I didn't see her in the footage, only her kids. Do we know if she's with them?"

Abby, Tatum, and Zoe exchanged looks.

"We think she's in the trunk of Moses's car," Abby said.

"In the trunk?" Hunt's eyes widened.

"We have no way to be sure," Abby said. "Rose Olson won't corroborate it. In fact, she completely stopped cooperating for now. But we think it's likely."

Hunt shut his eyes. He paced the room a few times. "You know," he finally said, his voice tired. "I should have done more. We knew what was going on. Everyone knew. But whenever I talked to her . . . still, I can't help wondering. If I'd grabbed Brad once. Tossed him in jail for a few days. Talked to her without him breathing down her neck—"

"It probably wouldn't have helped," Abby said automatically. But she knew how he felt. She was still carrying her own very recent guilt over possible mistakes she'd made.

"Yeah." Hunt looked despondent.

"We'll get her out of there," Tatum said. "And the kids."

Hunt nodded, his jaw clenched tight. "Okay," he finally said. "Please call me if anything changes. I'll go grab a few hours of sleep."

"Good night," Abby said.

He eyed her. "You should do the same, Lieutenant."

She watched him step out of the room. Then she turned to face Zoe and Tatum. "Okay, what happens tomorrow?"

"We're taking the first flight from Idaho Falls to Sacramento," Zoe said. "Do you—"

"You're not going without me," Abby said belligerently. "I'm part of this case, and you know that. If it wasn't for me—"

"I was going to say," Zoe said, her sharp tone shredding Abby's angry speech, "do you want me to forward you the flight details?"

"Oh. Um . . . yeah, thanks, that would be nice," Abby said sheepishly. "And you're going to Livingston from there?"

"The stakeout is a federal operation," Tatum said. "They don't want other law enforcement agencies there. Local or other."

"But you can tell them—"

"I'm not on the best of terms with the field office in California," Tatum said apologetically. "They aren't thrilled about me being there either."

"They'll need a crisis negotiator," Abby pointed out. "Delilah and her kids can clearly be used as hostages, and Moses doesn't shy away from using his followers as hostages either."

"You're probably right," Tatum said. "But they have crisis negotiators of their own."

"Fine. But you have to tell them to have one prepared. If this goes to hell—"

"I'll tell them," Tatum said gently. "I know you want to see this through, Abby, and that's fine. But it's nearly over. And it's out of your hands."

CHAPTER 49

Delilah was freezing, shaking like a leaf, trying to curl into a ball, to keep herself as warm as possible. At some point, she'd vomited, and now the trunk smelled rancid. Her body ached from her curled position. Her head pounded. She was thirsty, and her throat was hoarse from screaming.

You have two children.

How long had she been in that trunk? It felt like days. Days of a nightmarish, cramped darkness. Occasionally she would float away, leaving her aching, limp body behind her. She would feel the sweet oblivion of unconsciousness hovering out of reach. And then she would hear him again.

You have two children.

That moment of confusion. Of horror. He couldn't mean . . .

God only wants one.

She kept hoping they would stop, that he would let her out, tell her he'd only said that to teach her a lesson. She was a great learner. She had years of experience. She would make him see she would never cross him again.

But that wouldn't happen. He would force her to choose. No. It was impossible. She told herself over and over. She couldn't choose between her two children, there was no way. He couldn't force her.

And then, as the long drive stretched on, the roar of the engine nearly driving her insane, the sneaky thoughts crept up on her.

If she had to choose, she needed to protect Emily. Her soft, angelic Emily, with her sweet smiles, and her hugs, and kisses, her happy dancing, her curious questions. It was an impossible choice, but if she had to make it, she had to protect Emily.

Except . . . she thought of Ron's giggles when she played peekaboo. His wide, toothless smiles. The way he cradled against her body as he fed. So helpless and pure. She had to keep him safe. She had to, more than anything else.

She couldn't think about it. She refused to think about it. Both her children had to live. She screamed again, the engine swallowing the noise. No, she would insist they sacrifice *her*. Moses would see the truth in her eyes. She wouldn't choose. She refused to choose.

But the exhaustion made her resolve dissipate, and the terrible questions and thoughts crept into her mind again, like mold and rot. What if she *had* to choose?

Then she would have to protect Emily.

But she would have to keep Ron safe.

She was cold, and thirsty, and in pain. The engine's noise was unbearable. But she didn't want the ride to end.

CHAPTER 50

It was just before noon when their flight landed in Sacramento. Abby and Tatum went off to get their rentals, leaving Zoe behind. She stared vacantly at the hundreds of people milling around her.

The more she thought about her profile of Moses Wilcox, the more it bugged her.

A few years before, she'd started jogging and had actually grown to enjoy it. When she ran, her mind was at ease, something that didn't come naturally for her at any other time. Except there were the times she got a pebble in her shoe.

It seemed like a small thing, the kind of event that would cause someone to say, "Oh, damn, I have a pebble in my shoe." Followed by the removal of said pebble.

For Zoe, it was a calamity of epic proportions. She would be in the *zone*, and then suddenly, there would be that irritant. She would try to ignore it, because it wasn't just "getting the pebble out." It was stopping, *and* taking her shoe off, *and* removing the pebble, *and* putting her shoe back on, *and* lacing it, which was five things. And she simply wanted to run. So she would inevitably keep running, hoping that the pebble, embarrassed, would slink away. But it wouldn't. It would stay there and hurt every time she stepped on her right foot (and the pebbles always went for the right shoe, because it was the shoe that pebbles loved).

And finally she would have to stop and take it out, but by that point she would be so infuriated that it would ruin her run and ruin her day.

Moses Wilcox was a pebble in her shoe.

Mostly, his profile was easy to compound. After all, she literally *knew* who he was. There were several books on Moses Wilcox, up until the massacre. So all that was left was to build a solid profile so they could predict his acts and behavior. And she'd *done* that.

Except there were things that didn't sit right with her. Pieces that didn't fit. Behaviors she couldn't explain. Pebbles in her profile.

Abby and Tatum returned, and she followed them outside of the airport. Tatum said something to her, and he had to repeat it three times because she wasn't listening, and by the third time he looked so exasperated that she grumbled, "Yeah, okay." And then he drove off, and she found herself in Abby's car, which was fine by her.

"I'll drop you off at the FBI office?" Abby asked.

Moses was obviously extremely clever and talented, or he wouldn't have managed to build this network of churches. Methodical, too; his pattern of murders used to be predictable, until—

"Zoe?" Abby said again.

"What?"

"I'll drop you off at the—"

"Yeah, okay," Zoe said again.

She peered out the window as they drove down the highway, the flat landscape punctured by rectangular structures and bare leafless trees. Something was niggling her about that footage they'd seen the night before. What was it? Moses had seemed to be lost in his own private maelstrom. Was that what was bothering her? Even now, she couldn't decide if he believed his own bullshit or not. If he did, it would make him more dangerous. More prone to risk and more unpredictable. But that wasn't what bothered her—it was something else.

"You want to grab some lunch before I drop you off?"

Lunch. Now there was an idea.

"Yes." Zoe realized she was starving. "Let's get lunch."

There was a place called Lucille's Smokehouse Bar-B-Que near the FBI office, and Abby said it got nice reviews or something. The smells as they stepped inside made it clear to Zoe they'd chosen correctly. Her stomach grumbled, saliva pooling. She needed to eat *now*.

She ordered the meat combo with ribs and brisket. Abby ordered a chicken salad, which, as far as Zoe was concerned, showed complete lack of judgment. Now that she focused on Abby, she realized the woman was pale and listless. Her eyes were bloodshot, which made sense—they all had hardly slept, and Abby had had it the worst.

"What?" Abby asked.

"You look tired," Zoe answered.

Abby let out a snort. "The understatement of the decade. When this is all over, I'll sleep for a week. And I miss my kids. I talked to them on the phone before we got on the plane, but it's not the same as seeing them and holding them in my arms, you know?"

Zoe didn't really know. "Uh-huh."

"I feel guilty for not being with them more. Sam's still recuperating from that thing at her school, and Ben has always been delicate."

"Well, this is important. They should understand that."

Abby raised an eyebrow. "Sure, because that's what kids are so great at. Seeing things from their parents' perspective."

"Yeah," Zoe agreed distractedly. "Where's Tatum?"

Abby looked at her in surprise. "He went to Livingston to join the stakeout outside the Lily Fellowship Church site. He told you when we landed."

"Oh. Right."

"I thought you were annoyed you were left behind."

Zoe raised an eyebrow. "I'm a civilian consultant. They don't need me in a field operation. But I wasn't paying attention when he said he was leaving."

"You were obviously not entirely there, but I thought . . ." Abby shrugged. "What's distracting you?"

"I'm trying to wrap my head around some loose ends in Wilcox's profile."

"I read your profile this morning on the plane. It seemed pretty spot on."

"It . . . doesn't entirely fit." Zoe frowned. What was it that bothered her? Obviously the acceleration in Moses's behavior in Rigby—

"Do you want to talk about it?"

Zoe blinked. Abby eyed her expectantly.

"Yeah, sure," Zoe finally said. "Let's start with what we know."

"Okay."

Zoe took out a pen and her notebook from her bag. "Back in eighty-seven, Moses Wilcox was leading a cult in North Carolina. Very similar to his cult today—it was mainly young women, with some young men as muscle. But unlike today, he wasn't burning people methodically."

"No, he didn't have that obsession yet," Abby said.

"I think he *definitely* had an ongoing sexual fantasy that revolved around it," Zoe said. "But that's all it was—a fantasy."

"I'm telling you, I never saw a sign that—"

"You were a child. Trust me on this. It was there."

Abby shrugged. "Okay."

"So he had a cult, and a thriving opium-related business going, which already demonstrated his . . . enterprising nature. He's organized, clever, and manipulative. And, of course, preoccupied with power." She wrote it down in the notebook.

"Right."

"Even back then he showed obsessive tendencies. Germs, right?"

"Yeah," Abby said. "And we know he's still on it. We saw it on Rose's hands, and I saw it before on another follower of his back in New York. Those scratches come from aggressive handwashing."

"So we have a deeply obsessive nature, which is a very common tendency in serial killers." She added the word *obsessive* to the list. "He's overly careful, almost paranoid. And he thinks ahead, right? He's a planner."

"I guess . . . ," Abby said. "Why do you assume that?"

"Well, he had a poppy-farming business. That doesn't happen spontaneously. It takes patience and connections and a lot of thought. We can see it today as well. He created a chain of churches catered to funnel money to his cult."

Abby nodded slowly.

Zoe cleared her throat and pushed on. "But there's also a specific moment that's very telling. The fire he escaped in, when all these people died. He'd planned it meticulously *in case the police showed up*—it's obvious. Get them all together in that room with the cooking gas tanks. Make sure there's a dead bolt installed on the *outside* of the door, low enough so a kid could slide it. Then coach a little girl to lock the door and tell the police there are sixty-two and not sixty-three people inside. A girl who no one would think is lying. Slip out the back door that is hidden from sight . . ." She slowed down, as the blood had drained from Abby's face. "I'm sorry. That was insensitive of me."

Abby shook her head. "It's fine. You're right. He plans ahead. Meticulous, deranged plans. And he's paranoid. That's something that's common with cult leaders. They trust no one and always assume everyone wants to betray them."

"Right." Zoe jotted in her notebook. "I don't get it . . . why would he go to Livingston?"

Abby frowned. "You lost me."

"He *knows* the feds are onto him. He probably knows we are going through the records of the church. Would he really escape to yet another branch of the church? Where he assumes the feds would be waiting for him? Being as careful as he is, as paranoid as he is, he would go somewhere else."

"Okay. But he wouldn't just lie low in some motel, right? Because he would have a plan in case the police came for him again. Just like you said."

"Exactly." Zoe slapped the table excitedly. "That explains California."

"You lost me again."

"He was in Rigby. We *know* there was a church branch in Montana, a few hours away. But instead, he aims for California, a day's drive away. Why? Because his plan B, the hideaway he planned beforehand to go to, is in California."

The waiter showed up with their plates. Zoe's meal was everything she dreamed of. She cut a piece of brisket and placed it in her mouth. She shut her eyes, inhaling the flavors of the meat, the smoky tang. And hunger was the greatest spice of all.

"If you're right," Abby said, looking nauseous, "we're back at square one. We have no idea where he is."

"How's your salad?" Zoe asked, chewing. The ribs were fantastic too.

"I don't know. I haven't tasted it."

"You should try the brisket. It's divine."

"Zoe—"

"I don't know if I'm right, but let's keep thinking about it," Zoe said, twirling her fork. "Something else happened, right? For months, Moses and his flock followed the same pattern, as far as we could see. Find a place, settle there for three or four weeks, burn someone alive, and leave."

"But in Rigby they only stayed for two weeks," Abby said, chewing her salad halfheartedly.

"What changed?"

"Delilah," Abby said.

"Why? What makes Delilah special? What would make her—"

"She looks like my birth mother."

Zoe stared at Abby, stunned.

"She's almost identical," Abby said. "I don't know if we're somehow biologically related or if it's a fluke, but they're freakishly similar. My mom was one of Moses's earliest followers. And we know he was involved with her. And there's . . . well. Me."

"So he saw her at Rigby," Zoe said slowly. "And instantly recognized her. What do you think went through his head?"

"You told me I can't really know how Moses thought, right?"

"Never mind what I said. Give it a go."

"I believe he thought of it as some sort of resurrection. I think in his mind, we'll all end up together, with my kids. One big happy family."

"So he feels like he needs to make it happen. And he gets impatient. Usually he would try to make her take two seminars, spend a few weeks with her, before taking her to a burning. But this time it's . . . what? One week, and a seminar."

"Too fast," Abby said.

"Right, and like you predicted, she doesn't react well. She freaks out, calls her best friend, ends up talking to the cops." Zoe chewed a bite of brisket thoughtfully. "Moses catches her and dumps her in the trunk. What is he planning for her?"

"I don't know."

"Is he going to kill her?"

"I don't know."

"But whatever it is . . ." Zoe drank some water. "He'll do it fast."

"Why?"

"Because he knows we're coming for him. Because he's already impatient and stressed."

Abby looked even worse than before. Zoe took Abby's fork from the table and speared a piece of brisket from her own plate. She handed it to Abby.

"Try it," she suggested.

Abby took the fork and ate the brisket. She chewed slowly and swallowed. "Yeah, it's good."

"I'm not giving you any more," Zoe warned. "You can order your own if you want."

Abby smiled weakly at her. "That's fine. I'm not really hungry."

Zoe raised an eyebrow skeptically. "There's something else that struck me as strange. Something about the footage from the parking lot . . . but I'm not sure what. Something doesn't fit the profile we just discussed."

"Well, it's that guy," Abby said immediately.

Zoe frowned. "What guy."

"The old guy Moses was talking to."

Zoe could feel a tingling out of reach. That man on the footage, the one Moses had talked to. Sixtyish, long beard. "What about him?"

"You said it yourself," Abby said. "Moses targets women and young men for his cult. Why this guy? Too old to be extra muscle."

Zoe thought this over, forking mashed potatoes into her mouth. "Maybe he's his right hand or something? Some kind of experienced adviser?"

"Dot said Anna does most of the management," Abby said. "And that he let Rose do the seminar. Besides, like we said, Moses is suspicious. He wouldn't let a man, who he perceives as stronger, have real power within the cult."

"Then what—"

"Money," Abby said. "That's another reason cults recruit. For money. Remember what I told you? Moses recruits members and pressures them to transfer their belongings to the cult. A rich recruit can do wonders for a cult's cash flow."

"Oh, that makes sense." Zoe finished her last rib. She regretted giving Abby a piece of her brisket. "That definitely fits the profile."

"Except . . . ," Abby said slowly. "Why would Moses spend time talking to this guy in the meeting spot? If he's just there to be milked for cash, then why bother with him now at all?"

There. That rush when things fell into place. She saw Abby was getting the same buzz. The scent you got on the hunt.

"Real estate," Zoe blurted.

"Maybe a place in California," Abby suggested.

"We need the guy's name."

Abby took out her phone. "Dot might know him."

Dot did know him. Twenty minutes later they had the guy's name and address. Hank Webber, who owned a ranch in Northern California, in the western part of the Mendocino National Forest.

Zoe called Tatum to inform him about their find. The FBI had to send agents there as soon as possible.

Tatum said he'd let them know, but he also sounded angry. The guys in the field were slow to listen to him and double-checked everything with their own chief. Bureau politics. Tatum and the brass in California had a history and didn't get along too well.

"Well," Abby said, standing up. "It's only a few hours' drive from here. Let's go have a look."

CHAPTER 51

The sun touched the peaks of the woody hills as Zoe and Abby drove down Mendocino Pass Road. Abby hadn't seen a single structure in miles.

"It should be here in a bit," Zoe said, looking closely at the printed satellite photos in her lap. Zoe had originally wanted detailed satellite photos, from the bureau. But apparently that necessitated intricate paperwork, which neither Zoe nor Abby had the patience for.

Google Maps, happily, didn't require any paperwork. And Hank Webber's ranch was easily visible in the online satellite photos—four structures in the midst of a seemingly endless forest. According to the photo, a winding dirt road led up to the structures, and they were now approaching the entrance to that road.

"There." Zoe pointed ahead.

A wire fence ran along the road. A single large metal gate stood in the middle, and as Abby drove closer, she could already see the thick chain holding it shut. She pulled the car aside and parked by the gate. After getting out, she examined the dry dirt road. Traces of tire tracks crisscrossed it, but she wasn't sure if they were fresh. She approached the gate, examining the chain. A large padlock held it shut. But the gate was just a few metal beams in the shape of a large X. There was plenty of space if they wanted to crawl underneath it.

The place reminded her of that viral internet meme—a sign that said, "Trespassers will be shot. Survivors will be shot again." This was that kind of place. Back when it popped up on her Facebook feed, she'd thought it mildly amusing. She didn't feel amused right now.

She returned to the car. "Any news from Tatum?" she asked Zoe.

Zoe checked her phone. "I don't have reception here. I don't have any new messages since the last one."

Tatum had sent his last message about an hour before, updating them that no one had shown up at the branch in Livingston yet, and that the local agents said a couple of field agents would drop by Hank Webber's ranch tomorrow and check it out.

"So, what do you think?" Abby asked Zoe.

"I don't think we should wait until tomorrow," Zoe said grimly. "We should check if they're here, and if they are, inform Tatum."

"That's what I thought too," Abby said. "But I don't want to leave the car here, in case someone shows up after we go in."

She drove around the bend in the road and found a small patch of dirt she could park in so that it was mostly hidden from sight. Then, they walked along the fence back to the gate, and stepped between the beams to the other side.

That done, Abby stopped and listened, her heart thudding in her chest. A few birds. The whistle of the dry wind, a few branches rustling. No car engines, no sounds of people. This was probably a wild-goose chase. More likely than not, they were the only people in the area for miles.

"Let's stick to the trees," Abby said, lowering her voice. "I don't want anyone to see us on the road."

It proved to be more difficult than it had originally seemed. Both sides of the road were thick with bramble bushes, which snagged their shirts and scratched their skin. At one point, Abby pushed past a thorny branch and let it go, accidentally knocking it directly into Zoe's face. After about a hundred yards, the side of the road got steeper and steeper, forcing them to walk in a crouch, one hand grasping at branches and tree stumps to avoid falling.

Still, they managed to follow the track for more than half a mile until it opened up. A steep downward slope stretched directly in front of them, and beyond it, a wide clearing. A large house stood in the middle of it, and across from it, a much smaller cabin. Behind these structures was something that looked like a barn and a shack that was probably used for storage.

Seven vehicles were parked by the main house. Abby's eyes immediately went to the car she recognized as the one with the person in the trunk. And then a movement in the corner of her eye drew her attention. Richard, a rifle slung on his shoulder, paced by the far side of the main house, looking around him. Abby's breathing hitched, and for a second, an image from that night when Richard had grabbed her flashed in her mind.

Very slowly, Abby stepped back, hiding behind a large shrub. Zoe crouched beside her.

"We were right," Abby whispered softly. "We need to call your guys."

Zoe peered through the branches, biting her lip. She took out her phone. "No reception," she whispered. "What about you?"

Abby checked her own phone. "Same."

Zoe tried to dial anyway. Abby watched as she put her phone to her ear, then shook her head and pocketed it.

"We'll go back," Zoe said softly. "We know we had reception a few miles back, right? We need to get there and call."

"Yeah," Abby said, her eyes still on the large house.

Moses stepped out of it, Anna by his side. He pointed at one of the vehicles—a pickup truck—and said something. Anna nodded. Moses walked back inside.

"You go," Abby told Zoe. "I'll watch them."

"Why? They might see you."

"They won't. It's getting dark. And I want to see what they're doing. We only have eyes on three of them. We need to know where the kids are, where Delilah is. If they have more guns. When your fed buddies get here, I want them to have all the information. I don't want this to devolve into another siege. Another hostage situation."

Zoe stared at her. In the growing darkness, with the foliage around them, the profiler's eyes seemed even more predatory than usual. "You'll stay right here? You won't do anything stupid?"

"I'll stay right here. And if Richard gets close, I'll hide."

Zoe considered it for a second. "Okay. I'll do it as fast as I can."

"Don't make any noise. And stay off the road."

Zoe turned around and disappeared into the foliage. Abby was left alone.

CHAPTER 52

For a while, Abby crouched behind the brush, watching the four structures of the ranch as the light dimmed. The last rays of the setting sun painted the sky red, beams of light shining through the tree branches outlining the hilly horizon.

She carefully scrutinized each of the structures, comparing them to the satellite image in her hand, counting windows and doors. Light shone behind most of the windows on the bottom floor of the main house, but the top floor was dark. The smaller cabin was dark too. Every so often she'd glimpse a movement in one of the windows in the larger house. How many people were there? Moses's entire following?

Richard's patrol route circled the four structures, and he walked it slowly, occasionally kicking a rock or raising his head at a bird's cry. The rifle was slung on his back. How fast could he grab it? How well could he shoot?

A door opened. A single figure stepped out.

Moses.

The man who had hounded Abby's memories for the past three decades stepped out of the large house, staring at the red sky. His shoulder-length hair fluttered in the wind as he stood, immobile, head facing upward.

She could get him now. Richard was on the far side of the ranch. She could run down, cross the space between them in less than half a minute, her gun drawn. He was an old man, no matter how strong he looked. He wouldn't be able to fight her. Once she grabbed him, none of his followers would dare get near. No one would shoot at her. She could arrest him, drag him away back to the road, where Zoe would pick her up. And it would all be over.

She stayed perfectly still. She, of all people, knew a hostage wasn't a foolproof plan. It would take only one clever person there to realize they had hostages of their own. To threaten to hurt the kids, or maybe Delilah, if she didn't let Moses go. And they could surround her, prevent her from leaving.

In a couple of hours the FBI would be here in force. And they could do it properly.

She gritted her teeth as Moses lowered his head, then marched toward the parked vehicles. Richard was already getting closer. The chance to grab Moses, if it had ever existed, was gone.

The door opened again. Anna stepped outside, holding Emily's hand. She held something in her other arm, and in the growing darkness it took Abby a second to figure out what it was—the sleeping form of a baby. It had to be Delilah's baby, Ron. Anna led Emily to the cabin. The girl shuffled slowly, her head drooping. She was clearly exhausted.

Moses had stopped walking and watched Anna as she opened the cabin and stepped inside with Emily and Ron. A light switched on behind the cabin's window.

It looked like the kids were housed in a different structure than the rest of the group. It would make it much easier when the feds showed up. It would be best if a quick team entered the cabin first and evacuated the kids. Abby studied the cabin carefully. One entrance. No windows on her side, but there was probably at least one window around the back. She estimated the cabin had two rooms and a small bathroom. Or perhaps it was one large room?

Her eyes returned to Moses. He turned back to the vehicles. He approached one of them and opened the trunk.

From her position, Abby could see the outline of the woman who lay inside.

CHAPTER 53

Delilah shrank as the trunk opened, curling into a tighter ball. She was shivering, her throat dry, her head pounding. Was she sick? Or dying? Perhaps soon her suffering would be—

"Let's get you out."

That voice. Powerful and terrible. Moses. She turned her head, saw his dark silhouette, the glint of his glasses. She let out a whimper.

He leaned above her, grabbing her legs tightly. Then, a sharp tug, and the tight bindings that tied her ankles together loosened.

"I'm going to untie your hands as well, but don't try my patience, you got that?"

She nodded. Or tried to—she was shivering so badly she wasn't sure if her nodding was noticeable. She couldn't do anything even if she wanted to. She was so incredibly weak. He grabbed her arms, and she now realized he was holding a large sharp blade. She froze in fear, her eyes following the knife as Moses lowered it to the rope binding her wrists. A single tug, and the rope broke. Moses carefully loosened the rope from her arms.

"Get out."

She tried to move, fumbled, could hardly raise herself up. He let out an impatient groan and pulled her out.

Leaning against the car, she took a moment to breathe in the fresh air. She was in a forest, and the sky was red. Sunset? Or sunrise? She wasn't sure. Maybe it was neither. Maybe the sky was red because this was its color now. She licked her dry lips and tried to say something, but all she managed was a croak.

"Here," he said, handing her a plastic bottle. "Drink. You're probably thirsty."

She wasn't thirsty; she was way beyond that. She was parched. She drank the water greedily, the bottle emptying much faster than she wished.

"Well?" he said as she lowered the bottle. "Do you have an answer for me?"

She stared at him without comprehension. An answer?

"Which child?" he asked slowly, each word brutally clear.

It hit her now that it hadn't been a nightmare as she'd hoped. He really expected her to . . . no . . . she couldn't . . . not ever . . .

"Please," she croaked. "Please, I'll be good. I'll do anything you want."

He looked at her, disgust etched on his face, and took a step back. It occurred to her that she stank. That she was covered in her own filth.

"Which. Child." His eyes were impenetrable, face etched in stone.

"Please." She whimpered. "Don't make me—"

"We can burn them both."

"Me!" she blurted. "Baptize me. Not them. Burn me. I'm the one who sinned. Burn me."

He stared at her, frowning, not saying anything. She wept.

"Father?" Another voice. Anna.

"Yes. Over here," Moses said loudly. Then, looking at Delilah, he said in a low voice, "Your devotion . . . touches me. It touches God."

A crunch of gravel, and Anna appeared, looking at Delilah with pity and disgust.

"Clean her up. Prepare her for the baptism," Moses instructed Anna.

CHAPTER 54

Abby watched as Anna led the shuffling Delilah to the large house, Moses watching them both. The old man's fists were clenched, his posture rigid. Two women and a man stepped out of the house just as Anna and Delilah reached it. Anna paused to talk to them. Then Anna and the other woman went back inside, while the two men approached Moses. Abby recognized one of them—Hank Webber. The owner of the ranch.

She checked the time. Zoe had been gone for twenty minutes. By now she must have reached their rental and was driving it back the way they'd come, searching for a point where she had reception. How long until the feds showed up? An hour? An hour and a half?

Moses talked to the two men for a few minutes and then walked away toward the far end of the ranch. Webber made his way to one of the cars and opened the trunk. For one crazy minute, Abby thought they'd pull out another person. But no. They hauled out a large plastic canister and what looked like a thick coil of rope.

Webber stepped into the car and fiddled inside. The second man opened the fuel tank of the car and placed one end of the rope inside it. No, not a rope. A hose. A coil of plastic hose. He placed his mouth on the other end. What were they doing?

It took her a few seconds to figure it out. They were siphoning the gasoline from the car. His first attempt ended in failure—he pulled back coughing and retching. Webber stomped over, shaking his head, and snatched the hose from the man's hand. He put it in his own mouth and sucked, then quickly removed the hose from his mouth as gasoline trickled from it. He shoved the tip of the hose into the canister and filled it.

The realization slowly sank in. Rose and Gretchen had been driving a pickup truck full of gasoline canisters. In all likelihood, it was the cult's entire stock of spare gasoline. But that stash had gone up in flames. Now, these two men were siphoning gasoline from the cars to restock. But that could only mean one thing. Someone was about to burn very soon.

A snapping twig drew her attention. Crouching lower in her hiding place, she slowly turned her head.

She'd been so busy looking at the men she hadn't realized that Richard had walked over. He was less than ten yards away, walking in her direction. His eyes shifted; he hadn't seen her yet. But he would, really soon.

Holding her breath, she very slowly drew her gun.

Richard stepped even closer. Eight yards away. Seven.

She shifted, aiming the gun forward. Richard's head snapped in her direction. Had he noticed the movement within the brush?

His arms went for the rifle on his shoulder. Abby's finger tightened on the trigger.

A sound from the ranch made Richard turn away from Abby. She watched the large man, her muscles tight with her effort to remain still.

He took a step away.

She allowed herself to exhale silently. Then looked at what had drawn his attention.

Delilah and Anna stepped outside of the house. Delilah had changed her clothes and now wore a long white tunic. Her wrists were bound in front of her.

CHAPTER 55

Delilah stepped outside into the cold evening wind. Her hair was still wet from the quick shower that Anna had instructed her to take, and the water soaked into the collar of her tunic and chilled her even more. She shivered.

Soon she wouldn't be cold anymore.

She was terrified. Her mind kept conjuring Brad's shrieks of torment as the fire had consumed him. This would happen to her. Perhaps she could convince them to knock her out first. Surely Moses would give her this small mercy.

No, he wouldn't.

But Delilah was no stranger to anticipating pain, and this time would be the last. And she was protecting her children. This, more than anything, kept her placing one foot in front of the other toward Moses.

The rest of the congregation members were behind her, stepping out of the house. She heard their hushed whispers. She didn't look behind. She didn't search for Emily and Ron. Anna had told her they were fast asleep, which was a huge relief. They wouldn't be forced to see their mother burn to death.

They walked over to Moses, who awaited them by the woods, arms folded. Every reflex in Delilah's mind shrieked at her to run, to hide, but she kept walking. And then, just a few paces away from him, they halted.

He looked at her slowly, his eyes running down her white-clad body.

"'She who overcomes will thus be clothed in white garments,'" he said.

"Father," she whispered. "I wanted to ask—"

"And I will not erase her name from the Book of Life."

A glimmer of hope kindled inside her. Was he changing his mind? Would he not burn her after all?

"So? Do you have an answer for me now?" he asked.

"An answer?" she repeated, confused.

"Which child do you choose?"

Her eyes widened, her heart plummeting. No, he couldn't mean . . . "You said it would be me. I told you I wanted to be baptized instead of them. You said—"

"I said God is touched by your devotion. But I agreed to nothing," Moses said, his voice sharp. "You have to choose. You have to prove your loyalty."

"No!" she shrieked. "I can't! Please, you have to burn me. It can't be my children, please, I beg you—"

"Which child?"

She fell to her knees, tears running down her cheeks. "Please don't do this, my children did nothing wrong—"

"Which child?"

"I would do anything. Anything! Just let them go. Anna, tell him. He can't burn my children. Emily is five. Ron is a little baby. Please!"

"Choose! Or they will both be baptized!" he shouted.

She shrieked incoherently. She didn't know what she was shouting anymore. Anything. Anything to protect her children. His eyes were steely, as hard as stone. He would do this. Burn them both. She couldn't let him. She couldn't—

He raised his hand. She stopped talking, still heaving with panic.

"Delilah has made her choice," he said aloud.

She stared at him. Had she? She couldn't remember what she'd said. Was it possible that in her panic she'd named one of her children? No, there was no way.

"Anna," Moses said. "Get the baby out of the cabin."

"No," Delilah breathed.

"The girl will be baptized," Moses said. "A sacrifice and a trial. It is God's wish."

CHAPTER 56

Moses stood above Delilah, feeling the will of God coursing through his body, filling him with strength, with conviction, with desire. He ignored her weeping, his eyes searching the dark wood. Looking. Waiting.

Where was it?

It would show up, of that he was certain.

The congregation all stared at him. Dismay materialized on some of their faces. Disbelief. They didn't understand yet. But they would, really soon.

"Well?" he roared at Anna. "Get the baby out of there!"

"But . . . ," she said hesitantly. "Father . . . I mean . . ."

"Do you doubt me?" he asked, feeling the fury building up in him. Sure, they didn't know. Not yet. But still, they should do as he said.

When he'd opened that trunk and had seen Delilah . . . had smelled Delilah . . . he'd thought she was beyond redemption. And when she'd begged him to let her sacrifice herself instead of her children, he hadn't felt God's will in the matter. God had no more design for the woman. So he figured it was for the best. He would let her go.

But then, as he saw her after she'd been cleaned up, dressed in white, like an angel, like a bride, he'd felt differently. That powerful desire, that will of God, told him she was still meant to bear his children, his soldiers of God. In fact, she would be his wife. Which meant that God needed another sacrifice, as it was before. One of the children.

But then Moses realized it was another test of faith. God wouldn't really need one of the children. He was testing Delilah and the rest of them. Once they demonstrated they were willing to sacrifice a child in his name, he would send another sacrifice in their stead. As he had done with Abraham and Isaac. Perhaps a buck, running through the forest. It all suddenly seemed so clear. It had been God's intent all along. To bring them to this point. His bride dressed in white. A momentous show of loyalty and devotion. No one would doubt him after that.

He just needed them to follow the motions. To show God they deserved his gift.

"Anna," he said again. "Get the baby out of the cabin. We are going to start the baptizing soon."

"Please," Delilah sobbed. "Please don't."

He ignored her. If she didn't want her daughter to be baptized, she shouldn't have named her.

"Father," Hank said. "Perhaps this isn't needed—"

Moses was incensed. All those years, and now, when God was watching, *really* watching, they balked at his commands? He turned to Benjamin, who had been shunned by the congregation for the past month. *This* man would do what he was told. He would do *anything* to get back in Moses's good graces.

"Benjamin," Moses snapped. "Go get the baby from the cabin."

And to his relief and pride, Benjamin didn't even flinch. If anything, he seemed happy to finally get an opportunity to prove himself. He turned and marched toward the cabin.

Moses turned to the rest of them and raised his voice. "'Whoever will not obey the law of your God and the law of the king, let judgment be strictly executed on him.'" His eyes scanned those faces, searching, finding some of them wanting. But in others he spotted the devotion he expected of them all. "Beth, take the canister of gasoline. Michael, Phoebe, I want you two to light the torches."

The three he talked to all nodded, moving to follow his orders.

"This is wrong," someone blurted. "We shouldn't—"

Delilah lunged at Moses, grabbing his pant leg with her bound hands. "Please!" she shrieked.

He kicked her off him, snarling. She hung on. He kicked her again. Shouts. Some of his followers were running away. Where were they going?

Someone moved forward and pried Delilah off Moses. He turned to look at the followers who had run off, three women and a man. Piling into Anna's car.

What were they doing? Was it possible that they were *leaving*?

They doubted his words. God's words. It was intolerable. Sacrilege. "Stop them!" he shouted.

Men and women ran after them. The vehicle rumbled and shot forward, raising a cloud of dirt. Miriam stood in its path, and the vehicle plowed into her. She toppled to the ground, motionless. Moses stared as the vehicle drove away, Karen running for the motionless Miriam, screaming her name.

More shouts. A baby wailing. Moses whirled around. Benjamin walked out of the cabin, holding the baby. Beth was attempting to pour gasoline around the cabin, but another woman grabbed the canister, and they wrestled with it. Michael and Phoebe, the torchbearers, were blocked by Hank, who shouted at them to stop. Moses looked around desperately in the woods. Where was God's alternative sacrifice? If it showed up, he could tell them God had sent it. It would stop this madness.

But the woods were empty. And it was too late to change his mind. If that was what God wanted, Moses would do it. The little girl would be sacrificed in his name.

CHAPTER 57

Abby watched it all, Richard no more than six or seven steps from her, his rifle ready in his arms. She didn't budge, knowing that any movement would draw his attention.

At the ranch, all hell was breaking loose. Moses, it seemed, had lost control. Abby hadn't heard their conversation over the sound of the wind, but whatever it was, it had upset many of them.

Her eyes shifted between the woman who lay in the dirt and Richard. Earlier, she'd contemplated disarming Richard, shooting him if she needed to. But then, as Moses's followers exited the large house, she spotted two more rifles slung over the shoulders of congregation followers. Disarming Richard wouldn't be enough. She needed backup. She needed federal agents.

Another woman fled toward the trees. She ran fast, and at first no one noticed her. Then, a man began chasing her. He was too far behind, she would reach the trees, get out of—

A sharp explosive sound. So close it vibrated through her body. She gasped, her ears ringing.

The running woman dropped to the ground. Abby watched her with alarm, then looked at Richard.

He stood there, the rifle aimed forward. He'd shot the woman.

Below them, people froze. Richard strode down, his gun still pointed ahead. All eyes were on him.

No—one person still moved. The woman with the gasoline can had pried it free from the other woman and was now pouring the liquid around the cabin. The cabin where Emily was.

Now Abby understood what it was all about. Why some of the followers were finally rebelling. Moses had chosen his next victim. A five-year-old girl.

She watched in horror as the torchbearers walked toward the cabin as well. Hank Webber stood in their way. He knocked one of the torches out of the hands of a woman, and it fell to the ground, the flame casting a tiny flickering circle of light on the ground. The other torchbearer swung his own torch at Hank, and now they were struggling over it, and more people were running toward them. Richard turned his rifle at them, but he couldn't shoot without hitting the torchbearer.

Abby moved before she even realized it. Creeping as fast as she could along the tree line, circling the ranch, getting into a better position. She heard a shout of pain but ignored it, kept going. She didn't have a lot of time.

She tripped over a tree branch, stumbled, fell, a rock digging into her side. She got to her feet and kept going, half running, crouched, one hand holding her aching side. She kept going until the cabin stood between her and Moses's followers—hiding her from sight.

Then, her heart in her throat, she beelined toward the cabin, running in the open, sure that at any moment someone would shout in alarm. But all she heard were screams and arguments and confused orders as Moses kept trying to get back control over the situation.

She reached the cabin wall and flattened herself against it. Then, creeping along it, she reached the corner. Spotted a window. But some men and women were standing there, less than ten yards away, shouting at each other. To get to the window, she would have to move in sight of those people.

There was no other option. She shifted, staying as close to the wall as she could until she reached the window. One of the women's eyes seemed to spot her, and Abby froze, but the woman's eyes darted away.

Abby struggled with the window, frantically trying to get it open.

Another explosion. More screams. Abby yanked the window, and it flung open with a bang. Without waiting to see if anyone noticed the sound above the commotion, she leaped through, tumbling into the dark cabin.

CHAPTER 58

Moses stared at the body lying at his feet. Hank lay on the ground, his eyes open, vacant, staring upward at the sky. His shirt was dark with blood.

Richard stood above the dead man, his rifle still aimed at the man's chest. The rest of the flock—or what remained of it—were silent. Moses glanced around him. In the distance the bodies of Miriam and Noelle lay on the ground. Four more had fled. And what was left?

He looked at the faces of the followers. Some seemed angry, some scared. And some . . . expectant. Waiting for him to talk.

One last time he scanned the tree line, searching for a buck. Or a rabbit. Anything. But there was nothing. God had seen their uncertainty and had decided to punish them. It was *their* fault that the girl had to be sacrificed. If only they'd trusted him, God would have provided. Her death would be on them, not on him.

He cleared his throat and inhaled. The scent of gasoline was palpable. He glanced at loyal Beth, who still held the gasoline can. "Is it done?"

She nodded. "Yes, Father."

He usually preferred to use more. But one can of gasoline should be enough. It was a small cabin and made of wood.

"Torches," he said.

Michael and Phoebe, the torchbearers, turned and went to grab the torches from the ground. Michael was limping, a result of his fight with Hank. Moses was disappointed with the old man. He'd been so committed. Never even flinched when Moses had asked him to donate his family's ranch to the church. And now? Dead over a single moment of doubt.

Moses wished they'd finished dealing with the paperwork before tonight. By all rights, the ranch should properly belong to the church.

The torchbearers returned, the flames flickering in the dark. For a second, Moses was lost for words. That had never happened to him before. He *always* knew what to say. He could talk about anything. For hours.

Get it together.

He raised his voice, and it rang loud and clear. "'Blessed is the one who perseveres under trial.'"

CHAPTER 59

Abby got to her feet, her head pounding. When she had leaped through the window, she'd banged her head on something. She gently touched her forehead, wincing at the sharp pain and the sticky sensation of blood. She would have to take care of that.

The room was dark, but she could see the outline of furniture. A stool. A small table with some kitchen utensils. A coatrack. Something lay on the floor, and she crouched to examine it. A small mattress and a blanket. This was where they must have put the little baby to sleep earlier.

She heard a murmur outside. Moses, talking, his voice loud. Even after more than thirty years, she recognized his tone, the inflection of his voice. He was preaching. She couldn't really hear what he was saying, only the occasional word as he raised his voice to emphasize his meaning. "Wicked . . . devotion . . . wrath . . ."

Two doors in the room. One was clearly the front door. She walked over to the other one and turned the doorknob.

Locked.

Damn, damn, damn. She frantically looked around. There! A butter knife on the table. Two quick steps and she had it in her hand. She returned to the door and jammed the knife between the door and the frame, trying to jimmy the door open.

Come on, come on.

Something gave. Her heart leaped in excitement, and then she realized it was the knife. She'd bent the blade.

Moses's voice was rising outside. "Betrayal . . . Abraham . . . sacrifice . . . the flames of man . . ."

She eyed the hinges of the door. Then, carefully, she wedged the bent blade between the hinge pin and the hinge's knuckle. She bent the knife. Nothing. She pulled out her gun and tapped the knife gently, trying to be as quiet as possible, wincing at the noise anyway.

The hinge loosened.

She let out a long breath and pried the pin loose. The door creaked.

Crouching, she worked on the second hinge. At any moment someone would hear the noise and investigate. The pin loosened. She would pull it, then do the third hinge and—

As she pulled out the second pin, the door groaned, and the third hinge snapped free of the rotten doorframe. The door shifted, toppling inward. Hissing in panic, Abby lunged and grabbed it with the tips of her fingers, the knife clattering to the floor. Too much noise. Way too much noise.

She managed to prevent the door from crashing inside. She pushed it, the doorframe groaning as it splintered. She managed to shift it just enough so that she could slide through.

Another dark room. A single bed inside, and a little girl with a tearstained face, watching her with wide eyes.

Abby smiled at her, giving it her best. "Hello," she said, her voice as soft as possible. "You're Emily, right?"

The girl nodded hesitantly.

"My name is Abby. I talked to your mom on the phone yesterday. She wanted me to help you."

Emily sniffled. "I got frightened. There was a loud noise. But the door wouldn't open."

"I know. It must have been very scary."

"Anna told me to stay quiet. But I was scared." Her voice trembled.

"You did great, sweetie."

"Where's Mommy?"

"She's outside. Let's get out of here, okay?"

"Okay." Emily got off the bed.

"But Emily, I need you to be really quiet. Like Anna said. Can you do that for me?"

The girl nodded again.

"And we will leave through the window, okay?"

"Okay. We need to take Ron. He's here too."

"Ron is already outside, sweetie. Come on, let's go. And remember, be really quiet."

Outside, Moses's voice rose to a loud shout. "'I came to cast fire on the earth, and would that it were already kindled!' It is time for a second baptism!"

Oh shit.

Abby held the door as Emily slid through. Then she followed.

And flames erupted all around them with a deafening roar.

CHAPTER 60

The fire roared like an oncoming freight train. The heat was searing, impossible to bear. Abby whirled in the room as it filled with smoke, searching for the window, searching for a way out. She—

—*could hear their screams, the smoke filling the hallway, filling her eyes with tears. They were crying for help. She needed to get them out. She had to get to the—*

—window. She squinted, the air hazy with heat, the smoke everywhere. She gasped in fear, flattening herself against the wall, because she'd been here before, she was—

—*running as fast as she could for the door as their screams got frantic, shrieks of pain. The latch. She had to slide the latch, let them out. A voice behind her. "Abihail, get away from there!" And she—*

—saw herself standing in the smoke, eyes wide with terror, face streaked with tears, wailing for her mother. A little girl, lost in the flames. No, it wasn't her. It was Emily. Abby reached for her, but—

—*someone grabbed her, pulling her back. She screamed in fear and anger, and then an explosion knocked her off her feet, and she felt a searing pain on the back of her neck as the flames—*

—grew, and she now saw the window, and she had to get to it. If she didn't hurry, the fire would consume her. Emily would surely follow her. She took two steps toward the window, heart shuddering in her chest.

Somewhere, a burning beam crashed to the floor, embers shooting up, some singeing her skin. She heard Emily scream in pain.

She whirled around. The girl was surrounded by fire. There was nothing she could do for her, she had to get out, there was no time, she couldn't breathe, it was too late.

Emily curled tighter into herself, hiding her face.

"Emily, get away from there!" Abby shouted. But the girl was paralyzed with fear, and soon the flames would swallow her.

Abby forced herself to move, away from the wall, closer to the flames, to Emily, reaching out.

She snatched at Emily's sleeve and yanked her toward her, grabbed her, held her. Where was that window?

There.

She dragged the girl with her, making her way through the room, the floor already smoking. They had seconds until the entire place went up in flames.

The window, to Abby's relief, was still intact; the flames hadn't touched it or the adjacent wall just yet. But it would be hot to touch, she was sure of it.

She lifted the girl and shouted, "Watch your head!" and then pushed her through. Emily shrieked as she tumbled outside but then instantly became silent. Abby's heart lurched. Had the girl fallen badly? Perhaps breaking her neck as she hit the rocky ground? It was impossible to see anything through the thick smoke.

She was about to climb through the window herself when the windowsill burst into flames. She leaped back and turned around. The front door. That was the only way, but the room was an inferno; there was no way to get across to the front door.

She took another step away from the window.

Then she ran forward and leaped through headfirst, forearms covering her face, eyes shut, a flash of heat striking her face and a jarring impact as she hit the ground outside. She rolled on the ground, eyes still shut, in case her clothes or hair had caught fire. Then she opened her eyes.

The night sky was barely visible through the smoke, but it was a relief to see it. Quickly she rose to her knees, checking herself. She hurt all over, but she wasn't badly burned, and nothing was broken.

Emily lay on the ground a few feet away, by the cabin.

"Emily," Abby hissed, hurrying over to the girl's side. "Are you okay?"

The girl stared at her in shock and pain. She opened and shut her mouth, but no sound came out.

"Can you stand?" Abby asked.

And to her relief, the girl shifted, sitting up.

"Come on," Abby said urgently. "We have to get away."

She helped the girl to her feet. Then she picked her up and ran away from the cabin toward the trees. A second later she heard the crash as the cabin's roof toppled into the raging flames.

CHAPTER 61

Delilah sat on her knees in the dirt, staring at the blazing cabin through a haze of disbelieving tears.

Emily was gone.

She'd heard her girl screaming from inside, and then the screams had stopped, and all that was left was that awful, empty silence. Delilah felt as if her chest were hollow, her own heart burned away by the flames. She kept hearing Moses's voice as he said, *Delilah has made her choice.*

She had done this. She had sent her girl there. Her own angelic, pure, wonderful girl. The girl whose laughter was practically the *only* thing that could make Delilah smile.

It had been fast, unlike Brad, whose screaming had seemed endless. Delilah knew somewhere in the ashes that were left from her soul that this, at least, was a small mercy. It had been fast.

"Come." A voice, above her.

She raised her head and saw that Moses stood above her, holding his hand out for her.

"God has seen your sacrifice. He has seen your devotion, and he forgives you."

Delilah looked down at her hands. She wished she could rip her own throat to shreds and end this life.

"But now it's time for you to do your part. To do God's work."

She heard the words but didn't understand their meaning. If she waited long enough, maybe he would leave her alone.

"Get up. God still has a purpose for you."

A purpose. God's work. Slowly, she understood.

He wanted her to have sex with him. Like Gretchen had told her.

She let out a slow groan, a keening wail. She wasn't about to do anything with this man. With this monster who had forced her to kill her own daughter. *Never.*

"Get up now!"

She shut her eyes, listening to the roar of the fire.

He gripped her arm, tried to pull her up. She snarled and sank her teeth into his wrist—hard. He screamed and slapped her, and she fell to the ground, not caring. Now he knew. She would stay here, and—

"Do I need to remind you that your baby is still alive?" Moses asked. "Would you prefer we sacrificed him too?"

Her eyes snapped open. Ron. Her lone remaining child. He still needed her.

Very slowly, she pushed herself up and got to her feet. Moses took her hand, and she didn't resist. She let herself be led, not caring what happened to her. Not as long as Ron remained alive.

CHAPTER 62

Abby was out of breath by the time she reached the tree line. Her throat still burned from the smoke, and she coughed violently. She put Emily down behind a tree and put her arm over her mouth to silence her coughing. She retched, then spit. Slowly, she managed to get her breathing under control, though her lungs were still gritty, and every breath threatened to start the coughing fit again.

"Are you hurt?" she asked Emily.

The girl blinked, seemingly in shock. Slowly, she nodded.

"Where?"

"M . . . my knee. And my head." Emily's lips trembled.

Abby inspected her. It was hard to see anything in the darkness, but she didn't think the girl was hurt too badly.

"Okay. Here." She wiped the girl's teary cheek with her finger softly. "We got out of there, right? We'll wait here a bit. But we need to be quiet, okay?"

"Where's Mommy?"

"She's okay. I have a friend . . . a few friends who'll show up soon. And they'll find your mommy, and we can all get out of here together." Abby smiled at the girl, a warm reassuring smile.

The girl smiled back. Good. Abby peered behind the tree, her eyes going to the blazing fire. Jesus. The entire cabin was one enormous blaze, the wind buffeting the flames violently. As Abby watched, a nearby dry bush caught fire. Other patches on the ground were burning or smoldering too. Her eyes went to the milling congregation members. Two were creeping toward the vehicles. The others didn't seem to notice, their eyes fixed on the blaze. She spotted the baby in a man's arms. And there was Richard, rifle still in his hand, staring at the fire, face blank.

Where was Moses?

Movement made her turn. There. Two people dressed in white. Moses and Delilah. He was leading her into the trees, about twenty yards away.

Shit. Shit shit shit.

Her hand went for her gun . . . it was gone.

She must have dropped it when she'd jumped out of the cabin.

She crouched by Emily's side. "Sweetie, I'm going to get your mommy over here. Can you wait for me and stay really quiet?"

Emily looked as if she was about to start crying again. "Can I come with you? I'm scared."

Of course she was. It was night, they were in the forest, and she'd just been through a horrific experience. Abby wished Zoe were there to help.

"Tell you what. I want you to close your eyes and think about something really nice. What do you do on your birthday?"

"We go to a restaurant. And I can drink hot chocolate."

"With whipped cream?"

"Yes, with lots and lots of whipped cream."

Abby ran her hand over the child's hair. "Okay. Then I want you to close your eyes and think about your last birthday. About the hot chocolate, okay? And I will run really fast and get your mommy."

Emily shut her eyes, scrunching up her face.

"Good girl," Abby said. And then she turned and ran.

She couldn't see them anymore, so she ran along the tree line in the general direction. She hoped Moses's followers were trained to avoid looking when Moses took one of them. She glanced at the fire, and her gut clenched. A branch of a low-hanging tree had caught fire and was now blazing, the burning leaves crackling and rising in the wind. If this wind kept blowing, the fire might spread to nearby trees. And from there . . .

The movement in the trees drew her attention. A figure in white, a few yards away. She crouched and approached.

Moses stood, towering above Delilah, who lay on the ground, looking dazed.

"Well?" he shouted at her, loosening the knot that held his pants. "Do it!"

Abby didn't wait to figure out what Delilah was supposed to do. She lunged forward, crashing into Moses with all her strength, sinking her fist into his gut. He groaned in surprise, folding in two, toppling to the ground.

She knelt by his side, looking into his face. The face that had hounded her nightmares. That had mocked her, and had threatened her children, and had destroyed her childhood.

He blinked at her, his glasses askew, drool trickling between his lips as he moaned in surprise and pain. His pants were half lowered, revealing faded gray underwear and bony white legs.

This was it? This pathetic old man?

"Don't move," she snarled at him.

She turned to Delilah. "Are you all right?"

The woman stared at her, saying nothing.

"Did he hurt you?" Abby asked.

Delilah shook her head.

"Emily is all right," Abby said. "I got her out of there."

The change in the woman was incredible. It was as if Abby had invigorated her soul.

"Where is she?" she blurted, her eyes shining. She sat up. "I need to see her."

"Yeah, hang on, I'll—"

A sudden crash stole Abby's attention. She whirled and looked toward the ranch.

The fire had spread. A bunch of trees were now burning, and one of them had crashed to the ground, the fiery branches exploding around it, setting small fires everywhere. Moses's followers were running toward them, probably about to warn their preacher of the growing fire.

"Damn," Abby muttered. "We need to—"

"Help!" Moses hollered. "I'm here! Help!"

Abby slammed her fist into the man's face, hearing something crunch under her knuckles. When she pulled her hand away, he was out cold, blood bubbling from his nose. She glanced up. Moses's followers were running fast now, only a few dozen yards away. Abby, Delilah, and Moses were hidden in the trees, but once they got there . . .

"Come on," Abby said. "Let's go."

She grabbed Delilah and pulled her up. They ran into the forest, in the direction where she'd left Emily.

CHAPTER 63

The darkness intermingled with the billowing clouds of smoke, turning the forest into a disorienting maze. Abby resisted the impulse to go for the tree line, worried that Moses's followers would spot them. But the more they stumbled through branches and thorny bushes, the more she became certain they'd missed the spot where she'd left Emily. Or maybe the child had moved. Or maybe one of the men had found her. Or—

She nearly tripped over Emily, who was curled into a ball on the ground.

"Emily!" Delilah blurted. She knelt by her daughter and hugged her, crying.

"Mommy? Where were you? The room I slept in burned! But Anna said I should be quiet. And I tried to, but then I was scared, so I cried . . ."

"I know, baby, I know," Delilah whispered, rocking Emily as she talked.

Abby gave them a moment alone, peering toward the ranch. The smoke was now everywhere, making it nearly impossible to see. She glimpsed movement within the haze, but she was unsure if it was her imagination, the smoke playing tricks on her.

The fire was spreading. More than a dozen trees were now blazing, and numerous smaller fires spotted the ground. The cabin was gone, its ruins still burning, and the large house was now burning. Two of the remaining vehicles were ablaze as well. And the wind was carrying the fire closer to their position.

She returned to Delilah's and Emily's side. The girl was now silent, cradled in her mother's arms.

"We have to move," she said. "They might be looking for us. And the fire is getting closer."

Delilah looked at her, eyes wide. "What about Ron?"

"One of the men took him," Abby said.

"We should look for him—"

"We can't." Abby shook her head. "There are too many of them, and I'm not armed. Law enforcement agents are on their way to help us, and they'll protect Ron. We just have to stay safe until they get here."

"No!" Delilah's eyes widened. "You take Emily. I have to go get Ron."

"You can't," Abby said emphatically. "Delilah, Emily needs you right now. She's in rough shape, and I won't be able to take her alone."

"He's my little boy," Delilah whispered.

"The feds will get him out safely. If you want to protect Emily, we *have* to go. Now."

"Okay," Delilah said hollowly. "Emily, sweetie? We need to go."

Mother and daughter stood up. Abby eyed them worriedly. Emily seemed dazed, and there was something sluggish in Delilah's movements. She'd probably spent the past twenty-four hours in the trunk of a car with no food and no water. She was putting on a brave face, but Abby doubted she could move fast.

"We'll go that way." She pointed into the forest.

"But . . ." Delilah squinted at the fire. "That's where the fire is spreading to. The wind—"

"There's a river in that direction, not far from here," Abby said, taking out the crumpled satellite photo from her pocket. She examined it briefly with her phone's flashlight. "I think it should be pretty shallow, and once we cross it, we should be safe from the fire." She prayed she was right, that the river was really shallow. The way back to the road was blocked by the flames, and moving the opposite way would send them back to Moses and his followers. It was the only way to go.

She began moving, glancing back to see that Delilah and Emily were following her. They shuffled forward carefully, hand in hand. Every few seconds, Abby would glance back and pause to wait for them. She tried to move slowly, but even at the snail's pace she maintained, she still had to wait.

The fire was getting closer, the smoke getting thicker. Embers floated around them.

Abby turned to Delilah and Emily. "Emily, I'll carry you for a bit now, okay?"

"Okay," the girl mumbled.

Abby picked her up and caught Delilah's eyes. "We have to move faster."

The woman nodded.

Abby quickened her pace, now stumbling noisily through the brush. It was hard to move through the thick foliage with the girl in one arm. At one point she stumbled on a root and nearly crashed to the ground. She started coughing again, her breath heavy. She hoped none of Moses's followers were close.

And then they emerged from the trees, and she spotted the running water. Her heart instantly sank. She'd hoped the river would be shallow, but she now saw that it was, in fact, not a river but a stream. Too shallow and too narrow at points. She wasn't sure it would hold the fire back.

"Here we are," she forced herself to say cheerfully. "Let's cross."

"Should we take our shoes off?" Delilah asked.

"Probably better not to," Abby said after a second. "It's dark, and we can't see what we're stepping on."

She moved gingerly into the water, Emily still in her arms. The water was freezing, and she gritted her teeth as she shuffled to the other side, the water barely reaching her knees. She crossed it within seconds and carefully placed Emily on the rocky bank. Delilah crossed next. She slipped halfway across and splashed into the water, drenching her white tunic. Abby rose in alarm, but Delilah was already back on her feet and on the other side, shivering.

"What now?" she asked, teeth chattering.

Abby eyed the forest, the trees' outlines dark against the orange glow of the raging flames. "Now we wait for backup."

CHAPTER 64

"Father?"

"Oh god, is he—"

"Shut up, he's fine. Father? You need to wake up. The fire—"

"Maybe we should carry him."

"That's a good idea. Richard, can you—"

Moses opened his eyes, a sharp pain shooting through his skull. One of his eyes wouldn't open properly. "I'm fine," he whispered. "Give me a minute."

He looked up, the air thick with smoke. What had happened? Did he fall, or . . .

Oh. Abihail. It was Abihail. Somehow, impossibly, she was here.

"Where's Delilah?" he whispered.

"She's gone." It was Anna's voice, anxious. "We think we saw her running into the forest. Did she do this to you?"

"No." He groaned, sitting up. His head pounded. "It was my daughter." He squinted at them. Benjamin, incredibly, still held the baby in his arms. But aside from him . . . there weren't many left. Only eight of them. How was it possible? Where were the rest?

"Your . . . your daughter? That cop?" Anna asked, her eyes widening.

"Yes." Moses stood up and glanced around "What . . ."

His voice died as he took in his surroundings.

The raging fire. Enormous. Glorious. Spreading across the horizon, a billowing pillar of smoke rising to the heavens. It lit the night, turning it to day.

"'And the Lord went before them by day in a pillar of cloud to lead them along the way,'" he whispered. "'And by night in a pillar of fire to give them light, that they might travel by day and by night.'" He was smiling, joy filling his soul.

"It's enormous," Anna agreed. "But we have to leave. It's spreading this way too. Luckily, the wind is mostly carrying it away from us, so we have time. We can cross through the ranch to the road, see? That part has already burned, so we'll be able to walk there. Once we get to the main road—"

"We're not leaving," he told her. "This is God's way of helping us find our way. Find Delilah. And my daughter."

"Father, we can't do that," Anna said, sounding impatient. "We saw her running that way. See? *Toward* the fire. We can't—"

"The fire is our guide." He gazed at them. "Thousands of years ago, Moses led the Israelites out of their captivity in Egypt, a pillar of fire showing the way. And now, at the end of times, Moses comes again, leading you chosen few to our redemption." He examined their faces. Saw the conviction in some . . . the hesitation in others.

"How long ago did you see her?" he asked.

"A while," Anna emphasized. "It's likely that the fire already consumed her. A second baptism, like God intended. We can't—"

"Again you tell me what I can and can't do?" he asked softly.

Anna's mouth snapped shut.

"We'll go after them," he said again.

"I'm not going," Clint blurted. "I'm getting out of here. We should *all* get out of here."

"You're coming with us!" Moses roared.

"The hell I am," Clint snarled and raised his rifle. "Get away from me."

Richard lifted his rifle, too, aiming it at Clint. For a second they both stood frozen, neither man moving an inch.

"Enough," Moses said in disgust. "If you want to leave *now*, when we're so close, do it. Richard, let him go."

Richard lowered his gun. Clint seemed to hesitate, but then he walked backward, eyes still on them. After a few more yards he turned and jogged away, glancing over his shoulder. A few seconds later Trudy bolted after him, calling for him to wait for her.

"Okay," Moses said. "Let's go."

"What should I do with him?" Benjamin asked, holding up the baby.

"Leave him here. He'll slow us down. God shall protect him."

Benjamin hesitated. Moses clenched his jaw. Would he disappoint him as well?

"I can take him to safety," Anna blurted. "To make sure he isn't hurt."

"Fine," Moses spit. "You're useless to me anyway."

She flinched as if he'd slapped her. A second later she took the baby and turned away.

Moses looked at the rest of them. "And now we're six." He scrabbled for meaning. "On the sixth day God created man." His voice died away. He couldn't remember the quote from Genesis. If only they'd been twelve, it would have been perfect. He would have had so many great things to say about twelve.

"Let's go," he finally said. "Richard, you lead the way."

They stepped into the forest, the fire's light showing the way.

CHAPTER 65

Abby watched the treetops as the fire came closer. A terrible orange glow spread across the sky, exposing the immense clouds of smoke. It gave the forest a surreal, nightmarish appearance. Something small fluttered slowly by her side, then another, and another. Snow? She held out her hand, and a tiny thin gray flake fluttered into it. Ash.

Delilah sat by her side, shivering miserably, her clothes still drenched. Between them, curled on the ground, Emily lay, sleeping.

Abby glanced at Delilah. Now, up close, she could clearly see what she'd glimpsed before. No wonder Moses was obsessed with the woman. Delilah could have been Abby's biological mother's twin, if she'd been born thirty years ago. It brought back memories Abby had barely remembered. *Good* memories, of her time in Moses's cult. Mainly trailing after her mom in the field, but also going to the flower shop and making bouquets and curling up in her mother's lap. She wiped a quick tear.

A tree, thirty yards away, crashed to the ground noisily, showering sparks. Emily woke up in a start.

"Shhhh," Delilah said, caressing her hair. "It's all right."

The girl fell back to sleep.

Abby smiled at Delilah. "She's exhausted."

"Yeah," Delilah whispered, still caressing the girl's head.

"My name is Abby, by the way."

"I know. You're the one who talked to me on the phone. I saw you when you came to look for Moses, back at . . . Rigby."

"You did?"

"It feels like years ago."

Abby nodded.

"Do you think Ron is all right?"

"When I saw him, he was being carried to safety by one of the men. He should be fine." Abby prayed she was right.

"When will they come? The . . . backup?"

"Very soon," Abby said. "My friend went to call them more than an hour ago. And the fire probably won't last for long. It's February, after all."

Delilah cleared her throat. "I saw on the news that it's the driest winter California ever had. I think it hasn't rained for weeks. Everything is dry everywhere."

Abby swallowed. "I see. Well, like I said, they should be here pretty soon, and they'll show up with firefighters. Hang in there. We're almost done."

Delilah looked at Abby, tears in her eyes. "I made a choice. They forced me, but I made a choice."

"A choice?" Abby repeated automatically.

"Moses, he said . . . Emily or Ron. He forced me to choose. I begged him to take me, but he wouldn't. And I was begging him, I don't even know what I was saying, but I guess I said Emily's name. And if you hadn't saved her . . . and now, how can I go on? How can I look her in the eyes every day, knowing that I . . . that I . . ."

"You didn't," Abby said. "I was there when it happened. I heard everything. You didn't tell them to take her. You begged them *not* to take her or Ron. And Moses must have misheard."

The lie came easily. Abby hadn't heard anything. She'd only seen it happen. And it was possible, even likely, that Moses had pushed Delilah

342

to the brink, *forcing* her to make the choice. But what good would it do for Delilah to know that?

"Really?" Delilah whispered, looking at her with wide eyes.

Abby gave her the sincere smile she'd long ago perfected. The smile of someone who couldn't lie, even if they wanted to. "Absolutely. You never told them to take her."

"Oh, thank god," Delilah breathed.

Abby wasn't paying attention to her. A tree on the bank upstream was blazing wildly, and a sudden gust of wind blew through the flames, carrying them across, igniting another tree. On their side of the stream.

She shot to her feet. "We have to move."

Delilah shook Emily awake while Abby examined the satellite photo. She did her best to estimate where they were. About two miles to the south, there was a large forest clearing. A place where maybe, just maybe, they would be safe from the flames.

Aside from that patch, there was only a thick forest, dry after years of drought, fuel for the fire to consume.

CHAPTER 66

Zoe saw the fire miles before she reached the ranch's gate.

She did her best to keep her eyes on the road, while stealing glances at the vast orange horizon. Perhaps it wasn't what it looked like. Though she could think of nothing else it could possibly be. The forest was on fire.

And as she reached the ranch gate, the flames were easy to see through the trees.

Abby. She had to find Abby and get out of there. She'd already informed Tatum about Moses, and he was coming with the finest of California's federal agents. They could sort out this mess later on.

She parked the car by the gate and crouched under the fence as she'd done with Abby earlier. But this time, she didn't move through the trees. Instead, she jogged along the dirt path. The wind was blowing away from her, but she could still smell the thick smoke that billowed everywhere. She hoped Abby had the sense to wait where they'd separated. She'd get her, and they could retreat to safety.

Abby wasn't there.

All four structures of the ranch were in cinders. The vehicles the cult had come in were in pieces, the tires gone, aluminum puddles surrounding the wreckage. The trees around the ranch were either gone or still burning. Less than twenty yards from her, a clump of trees was blazing, the fire crackling, embers shooting through the air, the flames burning the dry vegetation on the ground. Given enough time, the fire would reach her too.

"Abby!" she shouted.

And then, impossibly, a baby's wail.

Zoe whirled, saw the woman standing in the burnt clearing, a baby on her shoulder. Zoe squinted through the hazy air. It was Anna Clark.

"Don't come any closer!" the woman shouted at her. She took a step toward the burning trees.

Zoe raised her hands in what she hoped was a reassuring manner. "I won't. Don't do it."

Tears streaked Anna's cheeks. "You're with Abihail?"

Zoe hesitated. "Yes," she finally said.

"Did she tell you that she's Moses's daughter?"

"She said that might be the case."

Anna let out a short, bitter laugh. "She ruined everything. From the moment she showed up . . . we were doing good, you know?"

This woman wanted to talk. She didn't want to die. She *wanted* to be persuaded to come over to Zoe. To surrender. All Zoe had to do was convince her.

What would Abby do? Zoe tried to think of Abby's methods, the little she had explained. Information was key. And she had to look like she was listening. Most people just wanted to be heard.

"Doing good?" Zoe repeated.

Anna frowned at her. Perhaps her tone was wrong. Tatum always said she sounded hostile. Perhaps she sounded as if she was dismissing Anna's claims. Damn it. She was the wrong person to do this. Where was Abby?

"Father wanted us to go into the forest, after Abihail and Delilah."

Zoe's heart leaped. Abby was alive.

Anna raised her voice. "I thought it was a bad idea, and he cast me out, just like that." She made a dismissive motion with her hand. She stared at the flames. "I'm a devout believer!" she screamed.

345

"Okay," Zoe said. "I hear you. Please, let's calm down and talk about this."

The woman glared at her, then took a step toward the flames. "It's all over. But I can still show him. I can still prove that I am worthy."

Zoe looked at her desperately and realized the awful truth. This woman really did want to be saved. She wanted to hear the right words, feel like she was understood. That there was hope. And then she would step away from the flames, with the baby, and they would both be safe.

And Zoe wouldn't be able to give her that.

Abby could, Zoe had almost no doubt. She would listen, and she would make the right expressions and use the right tone and say *just* the right words, and she could save them both.

But Zoe couldn't. And that meant she needed to change her strategy. She needed to focus on saving the baby.

What had Abby told her about Anna? Moses was the absolute center of her world. It wasn't likely she would ever turn on him. The only thing she wanted was his approval. It didn't mean Anna would do everything Moses said, but she would do anything she thought Moses expected of her.

"A second baptism, that's what you call it, right?" Zoe called.

Anna hesitated. "That's right." She glanced at the flames, looking fascinated by the bright glow.

"And that's what you want to do now?"

Anna eyed her resolutely. "That's what I'm *going* to do."

"But would Moses want you to baptize the baby?"

Anna hesitated. "He doesn't care what happens to the baby."

"Doesn't he? Isn't he a good man?"

"He is! He's a great man."

"Would he really want the baby baptized as well? Right now? Are you sure that's what he would have wanted?"

Anna shrugged. "The child's soul would be saved. Isn't that the most important thing?"

"It won't be," Zoe said sharply. "And yours won't be either. I'm a special agent. If you run toward that fire *with* the baby, I'll shoot. To save the baby. And neither of you will reach the fire."

She prayed the woman wouldn't realize she didn't have a gun. Or demand to see her badge.

Anna tensed. She seemed about to bolt toward the flames.

"But," Zoe hurriedly said, "if you give me the baby, I'll let you go to the flames."

Anna looked at her. "Why should I trust you?"

"I wouldn't risk the baby," Zoe said simply. "Once he's in my hands, I wouldn't be able to shoot you or chase you. You'll be free to do it."

Anna considered this. Finally she nodded and raised the baby, holding him away from her body. "Move slowly," she warned. "If you draw your gun or try to grab me, I'll run for the fire. And if I can't make it, I'll bash his head on the ground."

"Okay."

Zoe took a deep breath and slowly walked toward Anna. A large burning branch fell from one of the blazing trees, and at the loud crash, Anna tensed, and Zoe thought she would bolt. But she didn't. She waited, her eyes never leaving Zoe's.

Finally, they were a few feet from each other. Anna held the baby out for Zoe to grab. "Take him slowly with *both* hands."

Zoe reached and gently took the wailing baby.

Anna turned and sprinted toward the flames, never looking back. Zoe stared at her as she plunged into the fire. And the screams began.

Zoe turned away, carrying the baby back to the car. She tried to tune out the shrieks of pain, listening only to the baby's cries.

CHAPTER 67

"Please," Delilah called behind Abby. "I have to stop for a second."

Abby wanted to tell her they couldn't. That they had to run a little bit longer. That the fire was getting closer.

But she couldn't. Because she had to stop too. Emily, whom she carried in her arms, felt like she weighed a hundred pounds. Her lungs were burning, and she kept hacking and coughing. They'd been wandering through the trees for what felt like hours. And though she didn't say it out loud, they were lost.

She stopped, gently laid Emily on the ground, and sat down beside her. The girl stared around her sleepily. How much smoke had Emily inhaled in the cabin? She needed a hospital.

Abby glanced back. In the distance, she could see that malevolent orange glow, could hear the oncoming roar. The stream had bought them some time, for the most part holding the fire back for a while. But now the blaze was past it and coming for them fast.

She licked her dry lips, thankful that she'd had the foresight to drink from the stream before they'd left it. She'd told Delilah and Emily to drink too. Otherwise, they probably wouldn't have made it this far.

Once the fire began catching up, the smoke had become a problem. Even before, navigating in the dark wood had been difficult, but the smoke had turned the forest into a cloudy, suffocating labyrinth. And by now, Abby suspected they'd gone past the clearing she'd been aiming for. Her only direction was *away*. Away from the fire.

She counted to ten and got back up. "Come on."

"Just one more minute."

"We don't have a minute." Abby lifted Emily in her arms and climbed up the woody hill again. She heard Delilah staggering after her.

She kept going, each step a momentous task she had to overcome. Every time she glanced back, the fire seemed closer. The distant, hungry roaring was relentless. She was so exhausted that she didn't feel terrified anymore. But the hopelessness crept in.

They reached the top of the hill. Abby allowed Delilah and herself another rest as she looked around. Up here she could see the blaze. It was horrible to behold. A wall of flames, moving, taking everything in its path.

"I hope Ron is all right," Delilah said listlessly, her voice gritty with smoke.

"By now he's probably in the hands of the feds," Abby said. She had no idea if that was true, but the baby had a much better chance of surviving this night than they did.

"What's that hum?" Delilah asked.

"It's the fire," Abby said tiredly.

"No. Listen."

Abby listened. Delilah was right. That wasn't a fire. It was a—

"Plane!" Abby shouted, pointing at the blinking lights in the distance. "It's probably a firefighting plane!"

She took out her phone and activated the flashlight app. Then she waved her hands, gripping the flashlight.

"Over here!" she shouted desperately, even though she knew there was no way she'd be heard.

It flew closer, then swerved above the fire and released a torrent of water. Wherever the water hit, the flames instantly died. But it was a small patch, and the rest of the blaze continued. The plane turned and, to Abby's crushing disappointment, flew away.

She tried to find some hope. The plane would show up again. Firefighters were here. It was just a matter of surviving until they overcame the fire. She surveyed the forest desperately.

"There's the clearing!" she suddenly said. They *had* missed it, but not by as much as she'd thought. It was about two hundred yards away.

"We have to get there," she told Delilah. "We'll be safe there."

Delilah got up. "How?" she asked slowly.

The fire was moving fast, and it would soon block their path. Sure, they could try to go around it, but Abby was sure if they did that, they would only get lost.

There was no negotiating with fire. There was only one way to do this.

"Fast," she said, already picking Emily up.

And now they were running, beelining through the forest in the direction of the clearing. It was a downhill run, which was easier but riskier. Abby stumbled twice, her heart lurching each time. Her knees felt as if they were about to disintegrate. Her breathing had metamorphosed into one long coughing fit.

And now the flames were around them. Bushes and trees burning, the heat unbearable, roasting her face, her hands. Delilah was shouting something behind her, it was impossible to hear, the roaring noise of the fire and, and . . .

That hum again, much closer than before. She raised her head. Oh shit.

"Duck!" she screamed, diving to the ground, covering Emily with her body.

The torrent of water from the plane hit her, driving her down, knocking her breath away. The flames hissed all around her, the smoke and the watery mist intermingling into a thick cloying cloud.

And then the plane was gone. Abby could breathe again. The fire raged on in the forest around them, but right here, where they stood, in a patch of mud and ash, it was silent.

She raised her eyes. The clearing was a few steps away. They were safe.

CHAPTER 68

When the Israelites fled Egypt and reached the Red Sea, Moses stretched his hands, and God parted the sea, allowing them to pass through.

And now, it was the same. They walked through a sea of flame, but Moses had wished for a way through. And God parted the fire, sending a plane to pave a road for them. Moses stepped ahead of his followers, on this blackened earth. Fire blazed all around them, but they were safe.

And the road led them in the general direction where he'd earlier glimpsed a flashlight waving. The direction from which he'd heard a woman shout.

He thought about that plane. God might have guided the pilot's hands, but God hadn't sent it there. God hadn't called the fire department and told them there was a fire. Someone else had. And there were additional firefighters there. And if Abihail had found her way to him, she must have contacted all those who hounded him. The police, the FBI, the CIA. They were all here, looking for him. The fire kept him safe for now, but the end was near.

But he'd felt that way before, and then God showed him a way. And it would be like that again.

A sound. A woman's voice, talking in the distance. He paused, listening intently.

There.

He turned toward the voice and made his way on the blackened mud, his devoted followers in his wake.

When the forest opened and he saw Delilah and Abihail, he wasn't surprised.

They were sitting on a large rock in the middle of the clearing, and their faces were turned his way. They'd heard him approaching. But there was nowhere to hide.

"Hello, Abihail," he said, stepping into the clearing.

They looked poised to run, and he quickly said, "If any of you try to leave, Richard will shoot you."

Delilah seemed terrified. She hugged her daughter—the girl who should have been gone by now. And her daughter hid her face in her mother's lap. His breath hitched. Three decades ago, he must have seen Abihail's mother hug Abihail in just the same manner. And now they were all here.

Abihail, unlike Delilah, didn't seem afraid. Wary, but calm.

"So," she said. "Here we are."

For a few seconds neither of them said anything. Richard moved forward, and Abihail tightened in response. But Moses grabbed Richard's arm, holding him back. This had to end eventually. But he wanted Abihail to understand.

He cleared his throat. "'Train up a child in the way she should go. And when she is old, she will not depart from it.'"

"What book is that from?" Abihail asked him.

"Proverbs." He smiled at her.

"Was it really using the female pronoun? *She* will not depart?"

"Well, no," Moses admitted. "I made a small adjustment."

Abihail returned his smile, looking almost bemused. "Fair enough. I don't know if it applies in our case. I don't think this is the way you wanted me to go."

"It wasn't about what *I* wanted," Moses said. "It was about what God wanted. If I had *my* way, I would have been gone long ago, with the rest of our Family."

Abihail frowned. "I thought it was *your* plan. You told everyone to gather in the dining room. And then you told me to tell the police we were sixty-two. So they would assume you died."

"No!" Moses said fervently. "That was never my plan. I planned for all of us to go together. But on that day, I heard a powerful voice inside me. And he said I needed to survive."

He recalled that day so vividly. How he had planned the fire, and then that sudden, terrible wrenching fear. A fear so strong it had to come from God.

"He told you you needed to survive?"

"Yes. And that's when I had that message in my mind. A revelation. I could keep doing God's work, like he wanted, if the police assumed I was dead."

"If the police assumed you were dead?"

"I left, and hid, and waited," Moses said sadly. "Can you guess how long?"

Abihail looked at him intently, and then she said, "Three days."

He smiled at her lovingly. "That's right. 'And that he was buried, and that he rose again the third day according to the scriptures.'"

As he said that, the wind grew stronger, shrieking in his ear. The fire roared in response.

It was coming.

CHAPTER 69

As he stood in front of Abby, his tunic billowing in the wind, the fire behind him rising as if it heard his words, she had to do everything she could to keep her terror deep inside. She wore an expression of curiosity and interest. A bit of admiration, too—that went a long way with Moses. But if he saw fear, it would be over.

She needed to keep him talking.

The feds or the firefighters would be here soon. As long as Moses talked and she listened, no one would be shot. No one would be burned.

It shouldn't have been difficult. After all, if there was anything Moses loved, it was talking. She'd heard him preach for hours before dinner as her stomach rumbled. She had to keep doing what she did best. Ask questions, repeat his words, ask him to explain. And keep her fear in check. Why did her heart race so fast? Why was it that when he quoted the Bible, she felt as if she needed to bolt?

"How did you start the Lily Fellowship Church?" she asked.

He smiled again and began talking about how he had started raising money. How people were happy to follow him. Abby kept plying him with questions. How? Why? Questions that had no short answers, that kept him going. She eyed the fire, which was slowly surrounding the clearing. Even the area that had been drenched by the plane was slowly catching fire again. Soon the flames would be all around them. Would this clearing be large enough to keep them safe? She glanced at the dry weed and bushes that grew within the clearing. Fuel for the flames.

The hum of the plane. Her eyes darted up, seeing the flashing lights as it flew above the forest. Moses paused and followed her eyes, frowning.

"I remember that quote from the Bible about the lilies," she quickly said. "Is that where you got the idea for the church's name? How did it go? 'Consider the lilies of the field, how they grow. . .' uh . . ." She paused, waiting for him to pick the quote up.

But he didn't. Instead he glanced around at the growing fire. And then back at her. "We can talk about that later," he said. "We need to go."

"Go?" She stared at him. "Go where?"

He pointed at the forest behind her. "I want us to keep moving. All of us."

"But . . . the fire will spread. This is the safest place."

He looked at her pityingly. "We are not waiting here for your friends. We go into the forest. And we end as God wants."

"You want us to burn to death?"

"Weren't you listening? It's not about what I want. It's about what God wants."

She gazed at him, at his merciless eyes, and saw that look of fierce conviction she remembered from her childhood. This man was a true fanatic. He would rather die in the flames than get caught. And he would take them with him. She had to buy more time.

"But . . . why take Delilah and little Emily? Why not leave them here?" She got up and stepped toward him. "I'll go with you. But they can stay here."

The fire reached the clearing's edge, the air thick with smoke. Already small patches of flames dotted the clearing. Sparks flew around Moses as he shook his head.

"We all go together."

"They'll slow us down," Abby pointed out.

"Father, she's right," one of the men said. "We don't need to drag the kid along—she'll slow us down."

What was this really about? Moses did nothing purely for spite. Everything had a reason. Even if he preferred to die rather than get caught, there was no reason to . . .

Did he really prefer that?

Zoe had told her, *He's a man who happens to be very good at making people do what he wants. And his motivations always revolve around sex and control.*

He was the man who had towered above her when she was a child, pointing at the sky, speaking for God.

Close as he was, she could see his swollen nose. Remembered how he'd looked, lying on the floor, moaning, his pants pulled down.

Was he really the extreme religious fanatic she kept imagining? A man who would do anything for his faith?

He'd raised numerous churches. Built a devout following. Left a trail of destruction behind him.

But he was also a creep who simply got off on power.

She couldn't fully untangle the two men in her mind. But she suspected that right now Moses did not prefer to die. He wanted to live, and to escape incarceration, so he could keep doing what he did. Controlling people's lives and using them for sex.

He was planning to do the same thing he'd done before. Let them burn in the fire, as he fled to safety. Their bodies would be ashes by the time they were found. He was hoping the police would presume him dead again. And it would only work if everyone there died. If no one was left to tell the police how many of them had been there. That was why he wanted everyone to leave the safety of the clearing, even Emily.

Now that she realized this, could see it from Zoe's perspective, Moses seemed different. His eyes weren't wide with religious fervor. They were wide with dread. His fists weren't clenched in conviction. They were clenched in terror.

He was consumed with fear.

She could use that.

"Let's go," Moses said again, impatiently, and walked toward them.

Abby glanced at Delilah and mouthed, *Stay there.* Then she stepped forward, approaching Moses. As she got closer, she swerved, beelining to a burning bush, and took out the satellite photo from her pocket.

"Stop!" she shouted.

He did, and Richard aimed his rifle at her.

"This is a satellite photo of the entire area," she said. "We're surrounded by miles of forest. A forest that's going to burn to the ground. But there's a pond not far from here. The photo shows its location." She wore an expression of sincerity, masking the blunt lie.

The words sunk in. Moses could calculate the risk. His chances were much better with the photo in his hand.

"Give it to me," he commanded.

"I will. I want us all to get out of this safely. But first I need Richard there to give me his rifle."

"He can shoot you and take it," Moses pointed out.

"Maybe." Abby leaned toward the burning shrub, the photo dangerously close to the flames. "But I think I'll have time to drop it."

Moses smiled at her. "If that's what God wants," he said.

"Is it what he wants?" Abby asked.

She saw the struggle on his face. For a few seconds no one moved. In the distance, the hum of the plane grew louder. The fire was now almost all around them. Time was running out.

"How do I know you won't burn it anyway?" Moses said.

"Why would I? It wouldn't serve any purpose."

Another long pause.

"Fine," Moses spit. "Richard will give you the rifle, but without the clip. I don't want you using that thing on us."

"Okay." After an agreement, it was important to set out the details. Leave nothing to chance. "I want him to remove the clip and put the gun down. And then I want you *all* to walk back a few yards. I'll go get the rifle, and then I'll give you the printout."

"No," Moses said. "Richard will lower his weapon. Then you put down the photo and place a small rock on it. *Then* we take a few steps back."

Abby nodded.

Richard frowned at Moses. "Father, are you sure?"

Moses looked at him, and Richard blanched. He removed the clip and unshouldered the rifle, then placed it on the ground.

Abby didn't take her eyes off the man as she slowly knelt and placed the printout on the ground. Then she reached for a small rock and put it on top of the photo. If Richard reached for his gun, she could easily still burn the printout.

"Now step back," she said.

Moses stepped back, as did most of them. Richard stayed where he was.

"You too," Abby said.

"Do it," Moses said angrily.

Richard stepped back.

Abby exhaled and edged over to the rifle, never taking her eyes off the small group. She picked up the rifle and stepped back, then returned to the rock where Delilah and Emily waited.

Moses hurried forward and snatched the photo from the ground. He examined it. "Where's the damn pond?" he shouted.

"There's no pond," Abby said. "I'm sorry."

Moses stared at her furiously. "Then I guess we do it my way. We all go into the forest together. And God will decide what happens to us. Richard, go get them."

"I don't think so." Abby raised the rifle. "There's still a bullet in the chamber of the rifle."

Moses blinked in shock. He glared at Richard. "You didn't remove the bullet in the chamber?" he roared.

"You didn't tell me to," Richard said fearfully.

Moses's eyes bulged with fury. He whirled at Abby. "You can't shoot all of us."

"I'll start with you," Abby suggested.

For a few seconds, there was only the wind and the roar of the flames. The hum of the plane was getting closer.

"You were supposed to be an angel in my army," Moses said.

The humming was getting louder. It sounded different.

"Sorry to disappoint," Abby said. She could see the lights approaching above from the corner of her eye. It wasn't a plane.

It was a helicopter.

"Nobody move," Tatum's voice hollered through a megaphone. "Everyone stay right where they are."

A bright spotlight shone at the clearing, momentarily blinding Abby.

Richard began running. Was he running at her? She tensed, but no, he was running toward the flames. Following Moses's orders. Never to get caught. To set himself on fire before that happened.

But as he got closer to the fire, reflexes took over. He tried to stop, stumbled, and fell, his hand in the flames. His shirt caught fire, and he got up, shrieking in pain, running, the wind fanning the flames. He fell down again, rolled on the ground, all the while screaming. It seemed to go on forever, but finally the flames died. Richard groaned, barely moving.

Abby let out a shuddering breath, relieved to see that Emily's face was hidden in her mom's chest.

"Everyone get down on their knees and raise your hands," Tatum shouted.

The rest of Moses's followers did as they were told. Only Moses was left standing. He'd shuffled toward the burning tree line and was now only a few yards away.

"Moses Wilcox, get down on your knees and put your hands up!"

Moses stared at the flames, then at the chopper. And then, slowly, he dropped to his knees and raised his hands.

As the chopper lowered, Abby approached Moses, rifle still aimed at him. "You could have run to the flames," she said. "Let the fire purify your sins, like you preach to your congregation."

He looked at her impassively. "I wanted to. But it wasn't God's will."

"God's will?" she shouted over the noise of the chopper rotors. Her finger trembled on the rifle's trigger, itching to squeeze. "Is that your elegant way of admitting that you're a coward?"

His jaw clenched. "You turned your back on me, Abihail. You would never understand."

She let out a short barking laugh. "I actually think I understand, Moses. I finally understand."

CHAPTER 70

The chopper's engine made it impossible to talk. Abby sat back, watching the paramedic taking care of Emily. As soon as they got on board, Abby had told the agents to help the girl. Emily seemed sleepy, sluggish, and Abby had no idea if it was mostly due to shock, exhaustion, or smoke inhalation. Now, as the paramedic placed an oxygen mask on Emily's face, Abby allowed herself to relax. This, like pretty much everything else, was out of her hands.

Tatum handed her a helmet with headphones. She placed it on her head as the chopper rose in the air.

"Glad to see you're still alive," Tatum said, his voice buzzing in her headphones. "You were lucky. The pilot of the firefighting plane spotted you."

"Yeah," Abby echoed. "Lucky."

She was relieved that Moses and his followers were on board the second helicopter. She felt like if she had to be in the same space as them, she would fall apart.

"The baby," she said. "Ron, is he—"

"He's fine. Zoe has him." Tatum grinned. "I've seen some weird shit during my time in the FBI, but Zoe holding a baby in her arms is way up there. Top five for sure."

Abby automatically returned his smile. She glanced outside.

"Jesus," she muttered.

The fire stretched across the forest. Walls of flames raged as they consumed everything in their path. And behind them, all that was left was black, scorched earth. Could Moses see this? Did he feel satisfaction at this horror?

"Yeah, it's pretty bad," Tatum said. "Firefighters say there has been no rain for weeks."

"But they're containing it?"

"It'll take time," Tatum said, his voice sounding grim. "It might be days."

Days. Days of *this*. Looking at the blaze ravaging the forest, Abby realized how lucky they really were. Surviving this seemed almost impossible. She glanced at Delilah, who was kneeling by the paramedic, looking anxiously at her daughter.

"They need to get to a hospital," Abby said.

"You all do," Tatum said. "He's flying us to rendezvous with an air ambulance that will take all of you to a hospital."

Abby nodded. After a minute she asked, "What about the rest of Moses's followers?"

"We arrested three who were trying to leave the premises. And we found four burnt bodies at the ranch. We're still looking for the rest."

"A few left in a white Toyota Corolla."

"Okay, I'll alert our people. We have roadblocks along the roads leading out of the Mendocino National Forest. They can't go anywhere." Tatum switched to a different channel, his voice gone from Abby's ears. She was relieved. She needed a moment alone.

She was drained. The past few hours had been hectic and terrifying, and now that they had ended, she felt like a marionette whose strings had been severed. *It's finally over*, she tried to tell herself, thinking of Moses and his trail of death. *I'm safe. Delilah and her children are safe. Ben and Sam are safe.* But whatever relief she wanted to feel wasn't there. Only emptiness.

The helicopter landed, and Abby took off her helmet and hopped down. She was about to offer Delilah and Emily help, but Tatum, the paramedic, and another man were already assisting them. They weren't her responsibility anymore.

Everywhere she looked, there were flashing lights from fire trucks and police cars. People shouted over the sound of the helicopter's rotors, and the air smelled of smoke. Even here, miles away, she could still see the orange glow of the flames.

She spotted Zoe walking over to her. To Abby's surprise, Zoe held Delilah's son, Ron, in her arms, his head resting on her shoulder as he slept. Abby met her halfway.

"I told you to wait for me," Zoe said, a tiny smile twisting her lips.

"Yeah, I got distracted." Abby glanced at the baby. "How—"

"Anna Clark had him," Zoe said. "I, uh . . . convinced her to hand him over."

"Good," Abby said, looking at the peaceful expression on the sleeping baby's face. "Where's Anna?"

"Dead."

Abby's eyes met Zoe's. Something was different in the woman's penetrating gaze.

"She killed herself," Zoe said. "Ran into the flames."

"Oh. There was nothing you could do."

Zoe bit her lip. "There wasn't. You know, whenever I help put a killer behind bars, I save lives. Sometimes, I stop killers just before they kill again. But when I realized that the lives of this woman and the baby were hanging by a thread, depending on what I said . . . on my ability to figure out what that woman with her twisted logic wanted to hear . . ." She shook her head. "I don't envy you, Mullen. I wouldn't want that job, not in a million years."

"It grows on you." Abby smiled weakly.

"Ron!"

Abby turned to see Delilah running toward them, tears in her eyes. "Oh, thank god!" She wept.

"Here." Zoe handed her the baby. "I think his diaper is wet or something. But he's fine."

"Thank you!" Delilah blurted, cradling the kid.

"You're welcome." Zoe brushed the soggy spot on her shirt with apparent discomfort.

"Lieutenant Mullen?" A man approached them. "The airlift to the hospital is about to land. Would you mind coming with me?"

"I'll be there in a minute," Abby said.

The man escorted Delilah and Ron away. Abby turned to Zoe, who held out her hand.

"It's been good working with you, Mullen."

Abby took Zoe's hand, which was surprisingly delicate. "You too, Dr. Bentley."

Zoe frowned. "I am about to do some research about cults. There's a clear link between the control the cult leader has over the lives of his followers and his disregard for human life in general. And when it intersects with violent fetishes, it can easily lead to a case such as this." Her eyes widened in excitement as she talked. "We need to establish protocols to handle that kind of dynamic—"

"Okay, but I have to go to the hospital."

Zoe blinked. "Well, I didn't mean right now. Is it okay if I give you a call?"

Abby grinned at her. "Sure, I'll be waiting."

Zoe's expression had become distant. Abby suspected she was already composing protocols in her mind.

Abby turned away and walked over to Delilah, who stood cradling Ron while looking at Emily, who lay on a field gurney. A dozen yards away, a white helicopter, its lights blinking in the darkness, was landing. Its wind buffeted Abby's face as she joined Delilah.

"They said Emily should be fine!" Delilah shouted over the helicopter's noise. "She's exhausted, and she inhaled some smoke, but she'll be fine."

"Good!" Abby shouted back, relieved.

"Thank you so much." Delilah's face filled with gratitude.

Abby squeezed the woman's arm and smiled. Delilah turned to her daughter, caressing her face and talking to her.

Watching Delilah, Abby was filled with a deep longing for her own little boy and girl. She was ready to go home.

CHAPTER 71

The sky turned blue that Saturday morning, after a weeklong stretch of depressing gray. Abby figured she could go somewhere with Ben. To her astonishment, Sam said she'd tag along. A fourteen-year-old teenager wanting to spend time with her mother and her younger brother? It was like reading about the birth of a two-headed calf.

They took Keebles with them and went to MacNeil Park. Carver called on the way and asked if he could join them. Abby hesitated, but Sam, hearing only one side of the conversation, said with a smile, "Tell him to meet us in the park."

The park was blanketed with a thick layer of powdery snow. The sunlight, shining through the bare trees, sparkled on the white ground. Keebles, who had a complex relationship with snow, ran back and forth, barking excitedly, her pink-and-purple tail wagging.

Abby strolled slowly, hands in her coat pockets, a tiny contented smile fixed on her face. Carver walked by her side, patiently listening as Ben regaled him with facts about tarantulas.

". . . it's not *poison*, it's *venom*," Ben said impatiently. "They have venom glands in their chelicerae."

"Their cheli-cerae?" Carver asked slowly.

"That's those things they have below their eyes." Ben placed his own fingers under his eyes and wiggled them to demonstrate. "That's where they have their fangs. They can retract the fangs like a pocketknife. Bam." Ben's imaginary fangs stung an imaginary prey.

"How delightful," Carver said queasily. "So the cheli-cerae are the parts in the front of the spider?"

"Some of them. They also have the pedipalps that they use to crush their food with. And the male spiders—"

"Maybe enough about spiders?" Sam interjected. "Carver doesn't want to hear about that."

"I'm all right." Carver smiled at Sam.

"Oh, really?" Sam asked sweetly. "Do you want to hear about spider semen? Because that's what the male spiders do with the pedipalps. Do you know where they insert their pedipalps?"

"Um." Carver looked mortified. "I . . . uh . . ."

Abby snorted in amusement. "Kids, go run ahead with Keebles. Her barking is driving me insane."

Sam flashed a quick look at Abby, then at Carver. She grinned and told Ben, "Race you to that tree!"

They both ran with their unicorn-Pomeranian in tow.

"Be careful!" Abby shouted after them.

Carver sidled next to her and slipped his arm around her waist, drawing her to him.

"This is nice," Abby murmured.

"It is," Carver said. "I could get used to this."

Abby took a deep breath, her eyes turning to the water, the waves lapping at the shore below the park with a steady relaxing rhythm. She really *could* get used to this.

The shiver of fear came with no warning, as it sometimes did lately. The feeling that something lurked somewhere in the shadows. That something this good couldn't last.

She'd thought that once Moses was behind bars, she could forget about him. Leave that part of her life forever behind. But of course, nothing was ever so simple. They needed her to testify. They needed her to convince Delilah to testify. Zoe told her that people from the Lily Fellowship Church were demonstrating daily in front of the prison where Moses was being held. Abby could imagine them visiting him every day, trying to smuggle something to him. A box of matches. A small container with alcohol or gasoline. Moses didn't need a lot to create havoc.

Maybe he didn't even need his followers. She could imagine him impressing the prison staff with his religious rhetoric. He could slither his way to kitchen duty, where he had access to fire and flammable gas. The day before, she'd called Zoe in a panic, telling her to make sure that he was kept away from the prison's kitchen.

And Moses wasn't the only thing that loomed. Concerns about the coronavirus were increasing. Delilah had told Abby that Moses mentioned the virus in his sermons, pointing out that the end was near. When she watched the news, his doom portents seemed almost real. And—

Carver squeezed her waist and pulled her closer.

"Stop that," he said. "I can feel you tensing up. Everything is okay."

Abby exhaled slowly. He was right. Everything was okay. She looked at the kids. Sam had thrown a snowball at Ben, and now both of them were locked in a frenzied snowball fight, shrieking and laughing. Keebles barked, running around them, tangling both of them with her leash.

Abby sneaked her own hand under Carver's coat, seeking his warm body. She leaned her head against his chest and smiled. The fear dissipated into nothing.

"You know what I want?" she said dreamily. "Hot chocolate."

"We can do that," he answered. "I know a place nearby."

"With marshmallows."

"Marshmallows? What are you, eight?"

"I know what I want. Don't try to marshmallow-shame me."

"Okay, we'll get you your hot chocolate with marshmallows. You know why?"

"Because you want me to be happy?"

"Because I love you."

She purred happily and burrowed deeper into him. Ahead of them, Sam was pointing out something in the water, and Ben was jumping up and down excitedly.

Abby shut her eyes, listening to the waves, to the kids, to Carver's breathing.

Yeah, she could get used to this.

ACKNOWLEDGMENTS

Of all the books I have ever written, this one, for whatever reason, was the hardest. There's a certain feeling of dread that only authors with a looming deadline and an empty page are familiar with, and that dread was an almost constant companion this time around. Thankfully, a bunch of people had my back and helped me get through it. Liora, my wife, is my ever-present coach, mentor, and accomplice. I lost count of the amount of brainstorm sessions I had with her. Here's what I do remember—I was completely stumped when trying to figure out the climax of the book. I had a half-written draft that looked like a road trip comedy written by Thomas Harris, and it was going nowhere. I wanted the climax to be about the final showdown between Abby and Moses but couldn't make it work. And Liora told me that I was missing a crucial character there. When I asked who, she said, "The fire." She was the one who thought of the out-of-control forest fire that made the end of the book so exciting.

My editor, Jessica Tribble Wells, wrote me an email immediately after reading the draft of the previous book, *Damaged Intentions*. She told me we needed to talk. When we got on the phone, she asked me point-blank what my plans were for Zoe and Abby. I told her that I figured they could work together in the third book, and to my relief, she said it sounded fantastic. We discussed their dynamic together, and that brainstorm session was the foundation of the duo's interactions throughout the book. Jessica's notes, as always, pinpointed with laser-sight accuracy the areas where my draft needed work to make it shine, and this book is incredibly better thanks to her work.

I taxed Christine Mancuso's fear of fire to its absolute limit in this book. She beta read my draft, which came back with notes like "Why are you doing this to me" and "I should have skipped this chapter." Despite that, she gave me crucial notes regarding the pacing of the book, which made it even more gripping.

My parents, Rina and Haim Omer, both read my early draft. My mom had a bunch of notes, which she delivered on a phone call that left me a bit dazed. My dad had one note, which we argued about because he thought he was right, whereas *I* also thought he was right, but it annoyed me. Eventually I fixed all their notes, which is why my readers won't have to read through several really flat, emotionless scenes.

Abby's negotiation techniques and dialogue were written with the incredible help of O. Shahar. He was (and still is) ever so patient in helping me through every hurdle in the negotiation scenes. The tense negotiation with Rose and Gretchen would never have worked without his assistance.

My developmental editor, Kevin Smith, is always a pleasure to work with, and this time was no exception. He helped me through some gnarly issues with the book, and together we figured out the flashbacks that fleshed out Moses's background. He was also the one who insisted that Marvin should show himself in this book as well, a small bonus that all of us deserved.

Stephanie Chou's sharp eyes caught endless mistakes throughout the draft. I am also lucky that she has personal experience with tarantulas as pets, which helped me fix some glaring spider-related errors.

My agent, Sarah Hershman, is always there to cheer me on. She is always a pleasure to work with, and this book would probably never have been published without her belief in my writing.

When it comes to social media, I'm a bit of a mess, and Stacy Mann came to my rescue. She was a huge help throughout this series, and I'm really lucky to have met her.

And of course, this book would *never* have come to be without my amazing readers, who fell in love with Abby, grew to hate Moses, and wrote me countless emails, comments, and reviews, telling me and the world how much they enjoyed my books. Thanks so much to all of you.

ABOUT THE AUTHOR

Mike Omer has been a journalist, a game developer, and the CEO of Loadingames, but he can currently be found penning his next thriller. Omer loves to write about two things: real people who could be the perpetrators or victims of crimes—and funny stuff. He mixes these two loves quite passionately in his suspenseful and often macabre mysteries. Omer is married to a woman who diligently forces him to live his dream, and he is father to an angel, a pixie, and a gremlin. He has a voracious hound that wags his tail quite menacingly at anyone who dares approach his home. Learn more by emailing him at mike@strangerealm.com.